BLAMED

The Dragon's Game
BOOK V

H. N. Henry

Presse Dragon Libre

Free Dragon's Press

Trois-Rivières, QC, Canada

FREE DRAGON'S PRESS
Huard, Norman Henry
220 B Farmer
Trois-Rivières, Québec, Canada, G9A 3E6
www.hnhenry.com

Publisher's Note: This is a work of fiction. Names, characters, places, and incidents are a product of the author's imagination, except for his use of the Cree language in Roman orthography to number and title chapters and as one of the languages spoken by certain characters; and also for his use of certain Tai Chi exercise names. Locales and public names are sometimes used for atmospheric purposes. Any resemblance to actual people, living or dead, or to businesses, companies, events, institutions, or locales is completely coincidental.

Book Layout © 2014 BookDesignTemplates.com

BLAMED The Dragon's Game BOOK V by H. N. Henry—1st edition.

ISBN 978-0-9958419-6-3

Dedication

To my nephew, Francis.

Uneasy lies the head that wears a crown.
—WILLIAM SHAKESPEARE

CHAPTERS

In the Maze *Âpihtâwâyihk*   1
Return to the Land of Skulls
Kiwetotam Mistikwânikan Askîy   13
A Place to Rest *Ayiwepowin*   77
Mysteries of the Maze *Mâmaskâc Kîkway Âpihtâwâyihk*
                                                                      79
Going Home *Kîwewin*   101
My Son *Nikosis*   105
Taken Away *Sipwehtahaw*   111
Her Letters *Omasinahikaniw*   123
The Invitation *Wihkomitowin*   133
Return to the Land of the Danu
Kîwêw Askîy Paskwaskisiw   155
Visiting Three Places *Kîhokewin Nistwayak*   163
Old Friends *Kayâsi Otôtêmimâw*   175
To Moreena *Natawi Moreena*   199
To the Center for the Dragon Arts
Mêtawêwikamik Paskwaskisiw Naspasinahikewin   219
To the Castle *Kihci-Okimâwikamik*   223
To the Cave *Yâwâtakan*   257
The Amulet *Kanawisimowin*   273
The Hunt Begins *Mâcîwin Mâcipayin*   295
Denial *Ânwehtamowin*   305
The Hunt Ends *Mâcîwin Kisipayin*   317
The Concert *Miyometawestamâkewin*   333
One For Another *Meskociwepinikewin*   341
The Switch *Mîskotinam*   357
Confrontation *Nôtinikewin*   381
Daughter *Mitânisimâw*   397
Wedding Day *Wîkihtahiwewin Kîsikâw*   405
To the Maze *Âpihtâwâyihk*   441

— † —

FROM BANISHED
THE DRAGON'S GAME
BOOK I

Legend tells us dragons fly so high they can see the future.
Reason tells us that to know the future is a curse.
Our hearts tell us the seeds of hope are sown in the reality of
the present.

— † —

FROM BRANDED
THE DRAGON'S GAME
BOOK II

Reality tells us that to lose hope is to welcome death.

— † —

FROM BETRAYED
THE DRAGON'S GAME
BOOK III

Hope tells us light lives even in the darkest places.

— † —

FROM BRED
THE DRAGON'S GAME
BOOK IV

Darkness tells us it will change us if we venture there.

— † —

In the
LAND of SKULLS

— † —

In the Maze
Âpihtâwâyihk

— † —

Light tells us darkness wraps the gift of fate
in the fear of the unknown.

— † —

† NOW: *in the fifteenth year of*
rebuilding the maze in the Land of Skulls

Only one dragon flies above this land. What is Danuka hunting?

"Moooother!" It was Alizarine. Fear and panic accompanied her distant scream.

"Mooother!" Louder this time. Alizarine's getting nearer. I better wait here. She'll find me. No sense in trying to run to her in the maze. What's frightened her this time? For the past year it's been nightmares since the Little People left. But this is daylight.

"Mooother!"

Alizarine's choking on her screams. I'm right here. Come. I'm waiting for you. I know you'll find me. You always do.

Alizarine's footfalls were getting closer. She's stumbling. She's in a panic. What's wrong, Alizarine? I'm right here by the well. I'm not moving. Just like I've always promised you. That way you can find me. Have you ever not found me in all these years building the maze?

"Mo ... Mo ... Mo ... " The word was no longer coming out, only the out-of-breath first syllable.

You're almost here. Come to me. Alizarine stumbled through the inner maze gateway. A hundred paces from Nagora, she cradled her basket in one arm as she ran with her other arm outstretched in case she fell. Alizarine did fall in a panic as she looked over her shoulder up into the sky. Lucky for that dragon egg. How had it survived all of Alizarine's bumps and falls over the years?

"Mooother!"

See. I'm here. Don't worry. Come. Nagora bent to one knee and reached out with both her arms.

Alizarine's tiny outstretched hand was grasping in Nagora's direction. Her head was twisting and turning every which way as her big, frantic eyes scanned the sky. When Alizarine reached the first stone pillar of the outer circle, she stopped and leaned her small back against it while she continued to search the sky and catch her breath. She glanced over at Nagora only once.

You see me now Alizarine. Are you reassured?

Now both her arms cradled the heavy basket to her as she scooted over to the next stone pillar to survey the sky from there. Alizarine must feel secure beneath the huge stone lintel the pillars support. Maybe she thinks she's out of sight. Alizarine's breathing slowed. Now she was looking at Nagora as she swallowed, licked her lips, and mouthed the word "Mother."

No, I won't call out to you, Alizarine. Waiting was always the best way with Alizarine. There was more to the six-year-old's body she had been living in these past years. Almost fifteen years now, by Nagora's count. The six-year-old's mind focused on the one thing that mattered most to her, her beautiful dragon egg. The only times she ever let go of it was when she was alone with Nagora, deep down in the well-hole cave.

Nagora waited and watched.

Alizarine peeked out at the sky from each side of the pillar and then she looked at Nagora. Alizarine's gauging her next move. Come on. Run to the inner circle of pillars. I'm right here. Come.

With a final glance skyward, Alizarine grasped the handle of her basket with one hand and ran with her other hand, reaching out to Nagora. Again, as Alizarine looked over her shoulder she fell, and this time the big egg and the sheepskin she had wrapped it in spilled from the basket. The dragon egg rolled free on the ground ahead of Alizarine, displaying an intricate network of red and gold veins on its blue surface. Sunlight glinted off the recessed gold veins. Alizarine rushed forward in tears on hands and knees, crying, "My egg! Oh! My egg! My beautiful egg!"

I could almost feel sorry for you. You're right, Alizarine. It is beautiful. And precious.

When Alizarine reached it, she let herself fall on her side, cradling the egg in her lap to protect it with her arms and legs. Once she had secured it, she looked skyward again, then to the sheepskin and basket, and then to Nagora. Get up. You can make it.

Alizarine got on her knees, and bent over her egg. She held it in one arm as she used her other hand to help herself crawl over to the sheepskin. It's a wonder you can carry that egg. I need both hands to hold it, and when I do, there's at least another hand span from the tips of my fingers of one hand to the other.

Alizarine rolled the dragon egg onto the sheepskin, covered it, and then reached over to the basket handle as she looked up to the sky. As soon as her hand found the basket handle, she pulled it over to her and nested the egg inside it as fast as she could. Alizarine stood, stumbled forward, and paused to look all around the sky before running to the nearest stone pillar of the inner circle.

Nagora pursed her lips so as not to smile. Alizarine didn't like to be laughed at, not in the slightest. There you go. Now come to me. You're safe here.

Alizarine stared at Nagora as she tried to control her tears and her breathing. She reached out with one hand to Nagora and silently mouthed the word "Mother" over and over.

Nagora waited.

Alizarine pursed her lips hard and breathed deeply through her nose as she grasped the handle of her basket with both hands. She walked with a determined step, not letting her eyes stray from Nagora, until she was in her arms.

Nagora held Alizarine to her. She cradled Alizarine's sobbing head with one hand and placed her other hand over the child's hands that held the basket handle. Alizarine's frightened eyes scanned the sky through a never-ending flood of tears.

When Nagora's son, Dannor, was young and in a similar situation, she would talk to him, console him, and ask him questions to get to the cause of his predicament. Not so with Alizarine. To do so was to invite anger, screams, and tantrums that would last until nightfall. In fifteen years, Alizarine hadn't changed.

Now Dannor was fourteen and had gone hunting for several days with his father, Lars. Dannor was a young warrior-in-training, just as Nagora had been when she was his age. Nagora and Lars were training their son.

There was nothing much to be done with this ageless, crying child she held. Wait for her to speak was all Nagora could do. Nagora couldn't even ask a single question. Dannor could because he had a way of talking to Alizarine. It was more like Dannor was talking to himself and answering his own questions when in her presence. For some reason, Alizarine would slip into his unusual conversations and thus he could question her indirectly. Dannor had a way of doing so that seemed so natural. Why haven't I been able to learn to do the same thing? I'll just have to wait. Hopefully as soon as her sobbing settles.

"Mo … Mo … Mother. I, I, I saw it. In the sky. I saw it. It was b … b … big."

I could ask what you saw, but I know better not to. I'll wait.

"Mother." More sniffles. If only you would let me help you blow your nose. It would make it easier for you to breathe and speak. Dannor never shied away from helpful contact and the comfort it provided. Alizarine hated it unless she initiated it.

"Mother, it was big. It was in the sky. It was a big shadow. It was in the sky, but close to me. It went fast. It came by two times. It looked at me, Mother. I'm scared."

Nagora patted Alizarine's hands and waited for a question from her. This might take awhile. I might as well get comfortable while I wait. Nagora sat on the ground, placed Alizarine in her lap, and began to rock her in her arms. Could it be? Has the time come? Sarah is fifteen now. Is she ready?

Nagora swallowed and tried to hold back the tears that filled her eyes. The last time she had held Sarah was on the fourth day after her birth, just before handing her over to her dear friend, Paruline. Nagora always called her Pare. It was the agreement Nagora had struck with her dragon, Danuka. She was to give her baby daughter, Sarah, in exchange for one of Danuka's eggs that contained a baby dragon.

Now the memory of those four days with Sarah and Paruline shook Nagora's insides. She had to bite her lip to keep from sobbing. That duty-bound decision she made had left a deep wound in her heart, and now once again, the regret of abandoning her child tore at the wound. The memory of those four days with her sweet infant, Sarah, suckling at her breast, was still vivid in her mind, but it did not fill the void of wondering what almost fifteen years with Sarah might have been like.

Paruline had delivered Sarah to Sagora, Nagora's twin, as part of the deal with Danuka. In a letter to Sagora, Nagora had requested that if neither she nor Lars returned, Sarah was to be placed in Paruline's care so she could raise Sarah as her own and with Paruline's father, Geirador, to train her in warrior skills.

Oh! Pare! How I miss you. As much as I miss my Sarah. Our infrequent letters only make it worse. I hope somehow you and Geirador have continued to have a hand in training her. Sarah will have to be strong. She knows not the destiny that awaits her. That I'll be the one to announce it to her fills me with foreboding.

Nagora swallowed. The thought of how similar her own past was to Sarah's eased the pain she felt in her heart. Sarah, when my mum was in exile here in the Land of Skulls, she too had to abandon me. She had my sister, Sagora, to help console her. Thank the stars now I have a son. Dannor has been my consolation. I don't know if I would have found the strength to hold to the path I know will reunite us. My mother, Tagnyoriva, held to it by throwing herself into her work in this land as a healer. I, in turn, have devoted my time to re-building this maze. Mum and I worked for the same cause. I only learned days before coming to the Land of Skulls that my mum was alive and living here with a sister I didn't know I had. I was close to my eighteenth birthday. Sarah, I don't know what you know of me, that I am your mother or even that I exist. Believe me. Not a day goes by that I don't think of you.

Sagora, my twin, we reunited only briefly. You were my mirror image I did not know existed. On the same day of our reunion, your hand broke that mirror by pressing the red-hot brand to my forehead to mark me, the returning twin to this land, as different from you. But now, since you have remained in the Land of the Danu away from Gabe, the man you love, this land is now my home and no longer yours.

We're still a family separated from each other. The four of us were together only once, for part of a morning in King Raynhard's presence in Windhaven. It was the day after the battle on the plain opposite the Isle of Smoke to free Da and Danuka, the last dragon in the Land of the Danu. Even in Windhaven, there was chaos, so much to do, so little time to savor victory. Immediately the role of apprentice Dragon Talker and protector of Danuka's eggs fell to me and took me away from you. I could not shirk that duty.

It was the only time we ever held each other and looked into our eyes as a complete family. It was a moment that held so much hope for the future, for our king, for our family, for the Land of the Danu and its people, and for the future of the dragons. That hope for our family was not destined to last. Will we ever reunite? What do the stars hold for us?

We were all busy. Planning to be together again always seemed to fall through for one reason or other. We came close once, Sagora, when you, Mum, and I got together at Geirador's with Pare. But Da wasn't there. From what I heard from Geirador that time, Da was planning to return to sea on his beloved Sea Wolf. Can you blame him? He was Raganora's prisoner all those years in a cave with Danuka, in that vent hole on the Isle of Smoke.

Da was supposed to have trained Sarah. She's worn the dragon's blood tear amulet since I put it around her neck. I sealed Sarah's fate when I did that, like Mum sealed mine when she gave it to me. What will the amulet hold for my Sarah, other than what I know it holds?

Oh! My sweet Sarah! If only I could let this pass and spare you from what it will do to you.

Damn you, Alizarine! If it weren't for the curse, I might have risked going to see my Sarah. Fear of what you might do to her is what has kept me away, as well as the fear of what I know she'll have to do to you.

Nagora wiped away the tears and placed her hand on her right thigh. Even through her leather legging, the tips of her fingers could feel the scars beneath as she looked around her at the mass of ancient stone walls. Nagora had resurrected them to rebuild this primal hatching place, long ago used by dragons.

Will it ever be used again? Will dragons ever find life here again, in peace, in safety, without fear of men? Will dragons fill this inner circle with gold-veined eggs containing baby dragons that will hatch in clouds of steam? Will the hatchlings then feed on the red and blue veined eggs in the outer circle?

For a moment, the weight of all the stones she had lifted over the years now seemed to rest on her, weighing her down so she would never move again. Yet she must move again and carry on the fight, for there was still a sliver of hope in what awaited her.

In the Land of the Danu, again Mum has lost herself in her work, like she had done here, to help heal a sick people so they can rebuild a land that was once strong. Tagnya has dedicated her life to do what she does best, heal. Mum did you try to help Da heal?

You, Sagora, according to your last letter, are a mother of twin boys, by your man, Prince Gabe of the Land of the Skulls, whose people still live in fear of twins. Not all, but many. Gabe's infrequent visits to his boys make him a passing presence in their lives. You've decided to let them choose whether they wish to return to their da's land when they're of age. If they choose to return, one will have to brand the other. How will they ever come to that decision? Sagora, you must find the situation so ironic. What does the future hold for your twin sons?

What does it hold for my Dannor? Sagora, how I wish I could travel to you to introduce my son to your boys so they would know they have a cousin and an uncle, Lars. And their Aunt Nagora could smother them in hugs and kisses. But no, I can't. I remain shackled to this witch child until it is time to fulfill the curse. When that will be, I know not. Lovable as she appears to be in her six-year-old body, inside it hides an ancient witch with powers unfathomable. It's best I keep her from you and my Sarah.

Alizarine's breathing had slowed. Has she fallen asleep? Nagora leaned over to look at her face. When Nagora touched the little witch's chin, Alizarine's eyes opened wide. The fear was still there. She reached out a trembling finger to touch the Tiwaz brand on Nagora's forehead.

Then Alizarine looked to the sky and slowly turned her head in all directions. Nagora did too. After, Alizarine pulled Nagora's arms tighter around her and leaned the side of her face against Nagora's upper arm. Her eyes were open and stared at the only inner maze exit that led out.

Anyone taking any of the three other exits would be lost in the maze until Nagora went looking for them. Only Alizarine and Nagora knew their way in and out of the maze. Although, Nagora suspected that Dannor had figured it, but he was not letting on for some reason. From the day baby Dannor began to walk, he took to falling asleep holding Nagora's thigh. The little fingers of his right hand would roam over her scars. In the beginning Lars had asked, "What's he doing there?"

Nagora had shrugged and answered, "When I try to put him in his bed, he cries until I bring him back and let his fingers finish exploring. Only then can I put him back in his own bed."

"If it allows my little man a full night's sleep, so be it," said Lars. The nightly traveling of Dannor's fingers had lasted for a year.

Lars would only enter and leave the maze with Nagora at his side. Early on, he had gotten lost many times as Nagora and the Little People built up the stone passage walls of the maze. He must've realized how much time he wasted trying to find his way through it, so he gave up trying. It wasn't like him to give up, but her man valued his time. Still, he vowed someday he would devise a plan to take him in and out without help.

Remains to be seen, my Lars.

Nagora rocked Alizarine and let her mind travel back to a day, almost fifteen years ago. She and Lars were on their return journey to the Land of Skulls, preparing to enter Skull Bay with Alizarine on Hope, her unicorn.

Return to the Land of Skulls
Kiwetotam Mistikwânikan Askîy

† THEN: *in the days before the rebuilding of the maze in the Land of Skulls*

Nagora, Lars, and Alizarine stopped before crossing the bridge King Godomor had named after Nagora, as Edana, in honor of her victory with the help of his Hundred Best warriors. Godomor had proclaimed it Edana's Victory Bridge. Lars's wolfhounds, Aydan and Lyam, waited on the bridge. "Nagora, we can still turn back," said Lars.

"No. This is where I must go. My path has been drawn for me. I've been shown the way," said Nagora.

Lars pointed to the tops of the center posts of the side trusses of the timber bridge. A skull rested on top of each. The skulls faced each other, their empty eye sockets staring across the space of the bridge. The one to Nagora's right was split close to the center line of the forehead into the nose cavity and down, taking out one top and one bottom front tooth just to the left of center.

"Vorpinger." Just saying his name gave Nagora a sour taste in her mouth. The one to her left was Rhysonnger, Vorpinger's younger brother.

"They paid for their treason, Nagora, and you won the support of Godomor's Hundred Best," said Lars.

Nagora's eyes found Lars's. I hope you see my admiration for you. "If it weren't for you, one of those skulls up there could have been mine. You gave me hope when I no longer had any."

Lars's grand smile grew on his face. How I love that grin. He made light of her compliment by reaching over his left shoulder to touch the crossguard of his great sword. "I was itching to get this wet. What better way than at the service of the lady I love."

Nagora felt her face redden. She had ordered him to do her bidding without question that day. Despite the wounds it had earned him, he had forgiven her, and now she swam with desire into the blue of his eyes.

"Mother, do we put Hope's horn on now?" Alizarine's question interrupted Nagora. Once again, I have to win Godomor's trust.

"Yes, Alizarine, we'll do that now."

They dismounted. Lars brought the white leather helm Geirador had designed to hold the narwhal tusk on the mare's head. Nagora pulled the tusk from its sheath. "Hold Hope's bridle, Alizarine. That's right. Stand facing her. Good girl." Within moments the helm was on and the tusk strapped in place. "Now Hope is ready to make a grand entrance at Skull Bay."

"Mother, Hope is beautiful."

Nagora patted the white mare's neck. "Hope is indeed beautiful, Alizarine. Just like you."

"I know."

Your beauty is only in the newly cursed body you inhabit, little witch. Deep inside hides the witch, Hag, responsible for so much ugliness in the Land of the Danu. I stopped your evil plan just in time. Someday I'll put an end to you too.

Lars helped Alizarine climb onto Hope and then Nagora up onto Storm. "Don't worry. Godomor has you in his heart. He trusts you." Trust, it was the glue that bonded Nagora to Godomor. As their horses clomped across the timber floor of the bridge, that thought made Nagora look forward to seeing him again.

As they approached the skull-covered gates of Skull Bay, more than the usual number of guards took position at the top of the stone wall. Many were waving.

"The sentinels must've recognized you, Lars," said Nagora.

"They recognized Edana's unicorn and they recognized you on Storm," said Lars.

"It's not the same reception as when I rode up to these gates the first time. And I'm not wearing a safe-passage talisman."

The huge, skull-covered timber doors of the gate swung open before them. Warriors waved and called out, "Edana! Lars! Welcome home!" in the language of the people of the Land of Skulls.

"Am I hearing that right, Lars?"

"Welcome home, Nagora. You hear well."

Nagora and Lars waved back. How does Alizarine feel? Nagora had no way of guessing other than looking at her as they passed through the open gate. Alizarine seemed proud as any six-year old riding a horse, even though the welcome calls did not name her.

As they wound their way past the stone-fenced fields and corrals which separated the stone huts and lodges of the residents of Skull Bay, memories of the ritual signing to ward off evil from the returning twin flashed in her mind. The signers, in rapid sequence, covered their eyes, lips, and ears, slapped their hands twice in front of them, and then covered the tops of their heads with their hands. Banished from our eyes—not to be seen. Banished from our lips—not to be spoken of. Banished from our ears—not to be heard nor heard spoken of. Banished from our hands—not to be touched. And the most difficult, banished from our minds—to be forgotten.

Today, no one signed. Many just looked up and continued with their work in the fields. Some waved and called to others and pointed back at the riders and called out, "Nagnuska tykommi iyammani," in their language.

After hearing this repeated several times, Nagora looked over at Lars. "I know 'nuska' means 'healer,' but I don't understand what they're saying."

"Nagora, bringer of medicine and truth. They're acknowledging what you did."

Nagora nodded. Like Mum and Sagora, I've earned a healer's recognition. Tagnuska, Sagnuska, and now me, Nagnuska. Okay, I'll tell all to Godomor and hope for the best. "Lars, do we go to Godomor's Grand Hall?"

"No, we'll go to his new lodge, next to Gabe's."

"Godomor has taken Mum's advice?"

"Aye! He has. He's truly grateful for being healed. He wants to stay well. Plenty of sunlight and fresh air now. No more dark dampness in the cave at the back of the Grand Hall."

Godomor and Gabe themselves greeted the three riders as they dismounted.

Right away, Nagora made a point of introducing Alizarine. "Alizarine, meet King Godomor and his son, Prince Gabyndor."

Godomor's son smiled at Alizarine. "You can call me Prince Gabe."

"Welcome to the Land of Skulls, Alizarine. Did all those skulls frighten you?" asked Godomor. Lars translated Godomor's first words.

"Oh no, King Godomor. When I'm with Mother and riding Hope, I'm never afraid."

Godomor smiled. "Hope is your unicorn. She is the first unicorn I have ever seen. I heard about them. She is beautiful."

"Thank you. Do you want to see my beautiful egg?" asked Alizarine.

"Yes, Alizarine. Please show it to us," said Godomor.

Alizarine set the basket at her feet and pulled aside the sheepskin.

"Oh! My! Alizarine! It is a most beautiful egg," said Gabe.

Nagora touched Gabe's arm. "I have much to discuss with your da. Do you think you and Lars could go introduce Alizarine to Umma's children? I'm sure they would love to see Alizarine's egg too."

"Sure, we could do that." Gabe put one knee to the ground. "Alizarine, would you like to show your beautiful egg to some of our friends? You would make them happy if you did."

"Will you stay with me if I do, Prince Gabe?"

"As prince of this land, it will be my pleasure and my duty to stay with you while we visit our friends. Lars and I will stay with you until your … ," Gabe hesitated, "mother comes for you."

"Okay." Alizarine looked pleased with the attention. Her hand adjusted the sheepskin over her egg.

As Gabe stood, Nagora reached out and squeezed his arm in thanks. "We'll talk later. Lars has letters for you. I think one is from Sagora."

Gabe winked and bowed toward Alizarine. "Lady Alizarine, may I hold your hand and lead you to our friends? Lars will follow with Hope. I'm sure they will be happy to see your unicorn too."

Alizarine smiled and took Gabe's hand.

Godomor put an arm around Nagora's shoulders as they watched Alizarine leave with her escort. "Come, *Ka Peyakot Mahihkan*, you have much to tell me."

Nagora smiled at Godomor. She loved being called "Lone Wolf" by him when he spoke to her in the language of *The People*, the first people of *The Land*. It was the language her dragon, Danuka, spoke and the same language the Little People, the *Mêmêkwêsiw*, spoke. Thanks to the dragon-tear amulet she had once worn since birth, the language became part of her, as if she had always spoken it.

When he did not call her Lone Wolf, he called her *Mitanisimaw*, Daughter, and she called him *Ohtawimaw*, Father.

"Welcome home, my daughter. The walls of my new lodge are strong and much sunlight comes in from the windows, just as your Tagnuska wished. My fireplace holds a good fire in winter. Come, we will sit there and I will make a small fire so I can hear your story. To see you again warms my heart, *Mitanisimaw*."

"My heart too is warmed in your presence, *Ohtawimaw*. I have thought of you often. I am pleased to see how well you look. You even look younger." His shoulder length hair was combed and tied at the back with a black leather lace. Like the black hair on his head, his trimmed beard and mustache were evenly streaked with white. His complexion was as polished and fine as the tanned leather on her horse's saddle.

"I am not the sick old man you met the first time our paths crossed. Now I am strong again, Nagnuska—tykommi iyammani." Godomor reached out and took both of Nagora's hands in his and held her gaze. Nagora accepted the sincere compliment—bringer of medicine and truth. Godomor had spoken it from his heart and it made her eyes tear.

Godomor guided Nagora to a chair opposite his, near the fireplace. He gathered pieces of kindling and a few small logs from the neat pile that rested next to the fireplace. He set them next to the grate. He pulled milkweed silk from a bag on the mantle and made a small bed of it on the iron grate. Godomor crisscrossed the small kindling pieces on top of the silk fire starter and then stacked the small birch logs on top. With a strike of a flint on his knife blade beneath the grate, the milk-weed blazed and the kindling caught fire.

Godomor sat back in his chair and watched the fire grow. Nagora kept her eyes on the fire as she waited for him to speak. It was the way.

"*Ka Peyakot Mahihkan*, you have come a long way to visit me. You must have a story to tell. Is it about the path Lone Wolf finds herself on now?"

Nagora did not rush her reply. Godomor would give her all the time she needed. She took a deep breath. "Yes, *Ohtawimaw*. It is. I will tell you all that happened before so you will know all I know about how I have found myself on this path. I do this today, Father, because I believe you will have a story connected to my path that may help me."

Godomor listened, looked from her to his fire, and stared into the flames. When he nodded, she began from the day she left Skull Bay with his Hundred Best warriors. Godomor listened, nodding now and then. At several points in her story, he curled a finger of his right hand. He only interrupted her telling when he added logs to the fire. When Nagora cried as she told of abandoning her baby, Sarah, in exchange for a dragon egg containing a hatchling, he held her in his arms.

Nagora hadn't been able to control the flood of her tears as they spilled. "Tagnyoriva too cried when she handed you over to your uncle, Dangor, and many times afterward. So will you, my daughter. It is necessary," said Godomor as he held her close to his heart.

When Nagora finished telling the events, Godomor closed his eyes and took a deep breath. When he opened his eyes, he looked over at her. "*Ka Peyakot Mahihkan*, you carry a heavy burden on this path. By telling me your story, I now share the load with you. Your story is safe with me in my heart. You are right, *Mitanisimaw*, I have a story to guide you."

Godomor's words gave her comfort. Nagora was glad she had not held anything back. That he had a story to help her was a reward, and she welcomed anything to give her guidance.

Godomor uncurled the first finger of his right hand and held it in his left. "Your dragon led you here because it could not express the ancient memory in another way.

"First, your dragon flew you here in the light of the moon. You carried your baby in your womb on that ride. Danuka took you over the rock-strewn coastal plain near the cove where Sagora had taken you, Tagnuska, and Dangor. Danuka showed you the cave opening on the seaside cliff there. That is the place your path is taking you. The legend you heard about that place is only that. Later, I will tell you the true story of that ancient hill of stones and the plain it rests upon.

"Second," Godomor uncurled his second finger to place it next to the first one in his left hand, "your dragon has given you a map and a plan."

Nagora stared at Godomor. He must read the bewilderment on my face. A map and a plan of what?

"You do not know it as that, but I do. Come over to the window with me. I will show you."

Godomor stood and bent to reach for the unburnt end of a piece of kindling that had slipped from the grate in the fireplace. Holding it in one hand, with the other he led Nagora over to the window, knelt on one knee, and set the stick on the stone floor. "Stand here before me." He pointed to Nagora's right leg. "Show me the skin on your leg. Spread your legs more."

Nagora unfastened the leather legging at her right hip and pulled it down below her knee to show her scars. They resulted from the ritual cuts she'd made with the gold-handled hunting dagger King Raynhard had given her as a reminder of her duty to him.

Godomor knelt on both knees next to her and ran the fingers of his left hand over all the scars, taking his time. Then he touched his right thumb to the scar at the top of her inner thigh near where her legs met. Godomor ran his thumb in an arc over the scars until it met the thumb of his left hand. He had placed it just below her right buttock, almost at the back of her thigh. Then he ran the thumb back to where it had started its run at the front of her thigh. "You see the arc?"

"Yes."

Then Godomor pulled his two thumbs down Nagora's thigh until they met at the side of her knee. "You see the shape my thumbs have traced? Where have you seen this shape before?"

Nagora took a breath. Where? It must be an obvious place.

"You've seen this shape inside of a circle alongside others like it."

Of course! "The shape made by two spokes of a wagon wheel, running from the wheel down to the hub."

Godomor sat back on his heels, nodded, and traced them again. "Good. The arc is part of the wheel. Your knee is the hub of the wheel. The lines from the arc down to your knee are two spokes of the wheel.

"Now listen with care. Have your Lars draw this shape and all the scars exactly as you cut them. Have him draw them on a piece of vellum that fits your thigh."

Nagora nodded as Godomor's hands made motions to accompany his explanations.

"When he finishes drawing the first side, he must draw its mirror image on the other side of the vellum. Since he cannot see through it, have him make pin holes through the drawing from the beginning to the end of each cut. The pinholes will mark the cut line on the mirror side to align them with the first side."

Godomor turned the imaginary first side over with a slow motion of his hands. "You will have one piece of vellum with drawings on its two sides. With that piece Lars will use the pinholes to mark on a larger piece of vellum where he will draw the aligned cut lines. First, he marks the first side, and then he marks the mirror side next to it. He repeats marking the two sides until he has a circle with eight parts. Lars will have marked four pairs of the first and mirror sides next to each other. All the marked cut lines, from where they begin to where they end, will be aligned and ready for Lars to draw."

As Nagora followed Godomor's gestures of flipping over the imaginary piece of velum and using pins to mark the cut lines to be drawn, she imagined the circle in her mind. What is it? It can't be a wheel, but with the arcs joined and the spoke lines coming down, it will end up being round like one. A map and a plan? Of what?

Godomor picked up the stick and with its charred end drew on a slate stone of the floor—one half of a wheel with five spokes, half a hub, and half a wheel rim. Adding three more spokes, Godomor completed his drawing of the wheel on the stone. He pointed the stick at it. "Like a wagon wheel with eight spokes. Remove the eight spoke lines. The final drawn marks of your cuts that remain will create the path into and out of the circle maze."

"A maze!"

"Yes. What you will get is a map and a plan to rebuild the ancient maze. It protected access to the well at its center and to the inner and outer circle perches around the well. Dragons used those perches long, long ago when they came to the maze to hatch their eggs."

Godomor's words confirmed what was now taking shape in her mind. *How does he know this? He will tell me when he's ready.*

Godomor placed his left thumb on the scars at the side of Nagora's knee. "Once you see the final circle plan of the maze, the well will be here, at the center." He touched the middle of her knee.

From her knee, Godomor moved his thumb up her thigh half a finger's length to the scars there. "This will be the inner circle."

Godomor's thumb went up another half finger's length. "This will be the outer circle.

"Here," his thumb moved up another half finger's length, "will be the inner wall of the maze with its four gates. Only one will lead out. The other gates will lose those that venture past them.

"When you see the plan, you will know the way and you will be able to rebuild it."

I can't wait to ask. "Why was the maze destroyed?"

"Come. We will sit by the fire again."

...

Godomor placed another log on the fire, uncurled a third finger, and placed it in his left hand. "*Mitanisimaw*, do you remember the first story you asked me to tell you, the one about what caused Winter to leave *The Land*?"

"Yes, *Ohtawimaw*. I keep that story in my heart."

"You remember that a long, long time ago, Winter had come to stay in *The Land*, not just for several months, but for many, many years?"

"Yes, Father. My favorite part of that story is how eagle and crow got their colors."

Godomor smiled back at her. "It was my favorite part too when I was young and my great, grandmother told me that story. She told me many stories her elders had told her, the same stories their elders had told them. This is how I know of what Winter did to the maze that protected the ancient dragon nesting rings."

Godomor made storytelling motions with his left hand and its fingers. They allowed Nagora to see the events.

"All those years during Winter's stay, it brought heavy blankets of snowfall with it. The snow kept piling up deeper and deeper, pressing down on the snow beneath to turn it into ice. All that weight changed the surface landscape of *The Land*."

Nagora saw the maze imprisoned by the ice.

"The descendants of *The People*, who followed Winter to its land, now had a new land to discover. The descendants who stayed behind because they were too old, too weak, too sick, or too young to make the journey also had a new land to discover.

"As the snow and ice of Winter melted and moved away from *The Land*, it left a changed and scarred landscape. Many of the old landmarks from the stories of the elders were no longer visible to guide them."

Nagora imagined the moving masses of white ice melt and slide over the landscape, leaving it scarred, like the big blocks of winter ice in the bay of her childhood. They often changed the shape of her beach and sometimes the surrounding cliff faces.

"So Father, when Winter left, the maze which protected the ancient dragon nesting rings no longer stood."

"Nor did the inner and outer rings. Winter left a wasteland of rock and stones spread over the hill and the surrounding plain."

I remember looking out over that plain with Sagora. Now the immensity of the task that lay before her was taking shape. "Father, you know that place. You have seen it. You know how distant those rocks and stones are strewn. Have I been chosen to rebuild that ancient place? How can that be? That is an impossible task."

Godomor held Nagora's gaze as he uncurled the last finger in his right hand and placed it with the others in his left. "*Mitanisimaw,* a legend of *The First People* of *The Land* foretells the coming of a woman warrior bearing a piece of a magic map on her body—a map of a place from before the time when Winter came to stay for many years, an ancient place. Rebuilding it is possible. *Ka Peyakot Mahihkan* will have to ask for help."

Nagora looked from Godomor to the flames of the fire and back to Godomor. Her hands shook in front of her, trying to control the desperation that had invaded her. "Ask for help?

Who would help me with that? I have nothing to pay for help. Even if I had, who would want to labor on such a task? I would need many hands with as many strong backs. Not to mention tools, Father."

"Think, my daughter. You have already paid the *Mêmêkwêsiw* and they were grateful. They said you gave them something even they could not pay for—hope. They even gave you what you need to call on them again. I see it there." Godomor pointed at Nagora. "It hangs from your neck."

Nagora reached for the pierced gold dragon coin hanging on the fine leather lace around her neck. "The *Mêmêkwêsiw*? I called on the Little People for help once with this coin. They returned it. They said it could bring me luck."

Godomor smiled. "Thanks to the *Mêmêkwêsiw,* I have been able to tell you how to make the map. But first, you have to find the well to be able to call the Little People."

Nagora's hands fell to her lap and her shoulders slumped. "Father, one impossible task to complete before I undertake another impossible task."

Godomor was smiling again. "*Ohtawimaw* can help *Ka Peyakot Mahihkan* with this task."

Nagora sat up straight. "Father, you can? How?"

"How does a well get its water?" asked Godomor.

"From the rain?"

"Would the rain that falls into a well be enough to keep it filled with water?"

"Probably not. There must be water in the ground, some-how," said Nagora.

Godomor held his hands out palms up and then pushed back his sleeves. He waited for Nagora to do like him. "Imagine you are the ground. Imagine the blood in you is water. Where does it flow?"

Nagora pointed to the veins on her wrist. "In these."

"Some are big enough to see and some you cannot see. Just like the water veins in the ground. Now if several water veins flow to the well to fill it, that means they all meet at the well."

Nagora held up a finger. "So how do I find those water veins and the well where they meet? Do I dig in the ground?"

"Without digging. I will tell you how to find the water veins by walking over the ground with willow branches."

Nagora's brow furrowed with a question. "I don't understand. How?"

"Daughter, remember when Sagora led you to the cove near the stone field? On your way down the narrow valley to the cove, you passed a stand of willow trees."

Nagora nodded. I remember.

"Here is what you will do: Cut two willow branches, no bigger than the thickness of your thumb, from a spot on a bigger branch or the trunk. Next cut the two branches to the same length, no longer than one of your arrows.

"At the thickest ends, cut through the bark about a hand's span from the end." Godomor spread the fingers of one hand and showed the distance between the tip of his thumb and the tip of his little finger.

Then he brought his palms together. "Roll that section of the bark in your hands until you can pull it free of the branch. When it comes off, keep it. Do the same for the other branch and then do the same for the bark on the thinner ends of the branches."

Nagora was repeating the motions with her hands as if she were rolling the branches. At the same time, she repeated the instructions in her mind.

Godomor waited until she finished before continuing. "When you are out on the rock field on the plain, bring the branches and the bark tubes with you. Also, cut and bring many other willow branches with you. And bring a skin with water so you can wet the insides of the bark tubes."

Nagora logged the instructions in her mind and nodded.

"Choose a spot where you want to start your search. Let your heart guide you as you take in the terrain around you and imagine where water might flow underground to the well. Keep in mind that the well and its water are most likely deep in the ground somewhere under the hill. Don't be fooled if the branches lead you up the hill."

Nagora shook her head. What does he mean? "How will they lead me, Father?"

"Pick the spot where you will start your search. Face the top of the hill as you see it from that spot. Make a quarter turn to the right so that the top of the hill is now off your left shoulder. Wet the insides of the bigger bark tubes. Place the smaller bare ends of the branches inside the tubes. Hold the tubes straight up and down in your hands with the tips of your thumbs just touching. Do not squeeze the bark tubes. The weight of the big ends of the branches should bend them forward." Godomor pretended he was holding them. Nagora did the same.

"With the branches bent over ahead of you and the same distance one from the other," Godomor held both arms out straight, pointing at Nagora, "walk forward slowly. You will not have a choice in the rocky field. Keep walking until the branches move away from each other to your left and your right." Godomor opened his arms so they pointed in opposite directions.

"What does that mean?"

"It means you have come close to a water vein. The spread branches indicate there is a water vein nearby in the ground below. Stop there. Build up a cairn of stones to mark the spot. If there is soil amongst the rocks, stick one of the extra willow branches you brought with you into the soil.

"Continue walking a dozen paces past the spot you marked. Then turn around to face your marked spot. Adjust your willow branches and walk slowly toward your spot until the branches spread again. Mark that spot with a stone cairn, or a willow branch, as you did the first one. You should be a pace or two from the first marker.

"The water vein flows underground in the middle, between the spots you marked." Godomor used his left palm to illustrate as he explained. With his right hand, he pointed to the bent up first and last fingers. "Your marked spots." Then he ran his finger along the length of his palm and on between his two middle fingers. "Where the water vein flows below ground."

Nagora nodded and smiled.

"Now walk all the way back to the place you began walking with the willow branches. When you are there, walk about fifty paces toward the top of the hill. Stop there and repeat what you did the first time to find the vein. You will find it again. When you do, mark the spot with two stone cairns or two willow branches like the first time.

"Then continue on. Every fifty paces mark those spots where you find the vein. Keep doing this until you no longer find the vein. When you look back at all your markers, you should see the path the water follows beneath the ground."

Nagora began to speak.

Godomor held up a finger and answered Nagora's unspoken question. "Then it will be time to move on to look for a new vein. Two more would be best. If they all come together at the same spot and do not continue on beyond there, chances are you have found where the well could be."

"So I will have to prepare many branches. It could take more than one day to find the well."

"Yes, my daughter. Begin each day's search with fresh cut branches from which you will make new bark tubes."

"Could Lars help me with this? Could he also search for water veins but in a different spot from me?"

Godomor took a deep breath, pausing before answering. "*Ka Peyakot Mahihkan*, not everyone has the gift to find the path water walks. You are a chosen one and I know you have that gift." Godomor pointed to his own forehead and then to Nagora's. "*Kîya ostesimâw mahihkan* will try the search for water. Only then will your brother wolf know if he has the gift."

How I hope *kîya ostesimâw mahihkan*, Lars, has the gift and that together we will find the well.

"*Ohtawimaw*, thank you for listening to my story. Thank you for your story and for your help. You have brought light to my path."

"*Mitanisimaw*, focus on each step of the journey. The destination will take care of itself."

"Your words give food for my thoughts. I will remember them and think long on them."

Godomor stood and reached for Nagora's hands to help her from her chair. Then he held her in his arms before walking her to the door of his lodge.

Godomor spoke an order to one of the guards who left at a jog.

Before letting go of Nagora's hand, Godomor said, "*Ka Peyakot Mahihkan, kitimakeyimiso.*"

"I will, Father. I will be kind to myself."

Nagora's reunion with Umma was a tearful one, especially when she returned Umma's scarf to her. Umma had given it to her uncle, Dangor, the night of the feast at Godomor's Grand Hall to celebrate the departure of the Hundred Best. "Dangor wore it every day until his death. Not a day went by without him mentioning your name."

Umma bowed her head as she turned the scarf over in her hands. "Dangor's the second man I've cared for in my life, Nagora. That makes two too many to lose."

It was a difficult moment for Nagora also as the witch, who in great part was responsible for Dangor's death, was in the house with them now, though in a different body. Nagora had tried to kill Alizarine right after her transformation, but was unable to. That's when she realized the only way would be as Heqet had stated in her curse.

Alizarine, someday you will pay. Until then I am stuck with you.

"Umma has insisted that we stay with her until we decide what our next move is," said Lars.

Umma reached for Nagora's hand. "You can't stay at Lars's place. It's barely a roof over his head. It's a wonder he still has a head on his shoulders. It's small and he's not equipped to do any serious cooking. Stay with me. My children will keep Alizarine company so you two can go about with whatever planning you have to do here."

Nagora hugged her. "You're so generous, Umma."

"Nagora, this was your home for a few days, and Tagnya's and Sagora's for many years. You know your way around here. Please, make yourself at home for as long as you need."

"Thank you, Umma."

With having to trundle Alizarine around with them on the rock-strewn hill and plain, it had taken seven days to find what, in the end, turned out to be the well's location. Lars had the gift to find water, though the first vein he found led past and perpendicular to where Nagora's first vein ended. The next two veins they found both converged where Nagora's first vein ended and did not continue on.

Is this where the well is? Wouldn't it be nearer to the top of the hill, if not at the top?

"Now what?" Nagora asked.

Lars crossed his arms over his chest. "Nagora, I'm not lifting another stone in this enterprise until I have the map and we have a plan about how we're to go on about this. We can't keep doing this from our temporary shelter. We have to build a lodge with easy access to water. We need food. We can't always rely on the kindness of others.

"I have earnings to pay for help to build a lodge. Most of the raw materials are at hand." Lars waved his hand around at all the rocks. "What lumber we need, I can buy. And we will need tools. I have a few, but we'll need more. And don't forget, I work for Gabe. My wages will buy us food. How much

34· H. N. HENRY

time I'll be able to give to your project will have to be calculated and negotiated with Gabe."

Lars was right. In her excitement, she had rushed on hoping all would fall into place. They had only begun and there still was no sure sign this spot was the well's actual location. Only when she found it could she call on the Little People for help.

The next time they would return to the cairn-marked well location, it would be with the map made based on the scars of the cuts she had made on her on her thigh with the gold-handled hunting dagger.

For days, when Lars returned to Umma's from his work with Gabe, he and Nagora would stare at the map and try to understand the why of its plan. The maze was to protect access to the central hatching area, with the well in the middle.

Nagora found the pathway through the maze. Lars could see it when she traced it with her finger, but as soon as she lifted her finger, he lost it. What he could keep, and that he marked on the plan, was which exterior opening of the maze led to its interior gateway. There were four gateways, but only one allowed access in or out of the hatching area.

Then one day in Umma's infirmary, Lars pounded on the map, shaking the table beneath it. "Damn it! What's missing is a scale to this plan. If we had an idea of its scale, we might have a better understanding of the possible location we found for the well. And we would have a distance from the well to the perimeter of the maze. We could mark that off and see if it made sense." Lars leaned over the table and rested his hands on the map spread out before him.

"Where would the actual entrance to the maze be? On the inland side or the seaside of the rocky plain?"

My man's impatience is mounting. "Lars," Nagora pulled herself to one of his arms, "there's no rush in solving this. We have time to think on it. Let's build our lodge first. While we're working on that, ideas will come, perhaps even a solution. Anyway that long-ago Dragon Talker, whoever she or he was, knew what they were doing for the dragons. We may never know that."

Lars straightened up. His eyes were as wide open as his mouth. He placed a hand over Nagora's. He was blinking and looking around the infirmary room they were in. Then he looked at Nagora, closed his mouth before letting it turn into a grin. "Bring me vellum, a writing brush, and ink. You've just given me a clue for the scale!" Lars kissed Nagora's forehead.

The next morning Nagora found Lars asleep, slumped over the table where she had left him the night before. One of the three candle lanterns still burned. Sheets of vellum littered the floor around his chair. In one hand, he held a single sheet of vellum with a list of symbols and numbers.

Have you figured it out?

Nagora did not disturb him. Instead, she went back to the kitchen to help Umma with the cooking of the day's meals.

"When do we eat, Mother?"

"In a while, Alizarine. Let's take time to look around first. Why don't you look out to sea? You might spot a boat's sail."

"I'll sit on this rock then."

"Good, Alizarine. Tell us if you see a sail."

"Or a whale," said Lars.

Nagora stood next to Lars on top of the hill on the rocky plain. They had spent the previous three days staking out the perimeter of the maze based on the calculations Lars had made. Thankfully, they had the help of the six builders who would help Lars build their lodge. Otherwise, they still would have been at it for days to come.

Alizarine had stayed with Nagora, nearest to the well spot. That way, she was out of the way of the others and had less ground to cover while Nagora maneuvered the rope that hung down from the tall post Lars had planted at the well spot.

The rope's length was the radius of the maze. As Nagora and three builders moved the rope around the center well spot, Lars, with the help of the three others, drove stakes or piled rocks to mark the perimeter's location. When they finished, they knew the size of the maze.

"It's huge, Lars," said Nagora.

His eyes scanned the marked perimeter as he slowly turned on the spot where he stood. "If my guesses are right, aye, it's huge. I figured if many people entered the maze, they would have to go in single file. So I set the width of the maze paths on the ground to a man's shoulder width.

"And I set the base of the maze walls to the span of a man's arms. I have no way of estimating how high the walls are—at least higher than the tallest of men. Using the path shoulder-width measure plus the base of the wall arm-span measure gives the perimeter we've staked out.

"And the inner and outer rings are a guess based on my es- timate of Danuka's size being that of a full grown, mature dragon. I'm guessing thirty-six dragons in all. The outer ring would hold twenty-four. The inner ring would hold a dozen. That's what I worked with. I could be off the mark."

"Well, you could be close to it too."

Lars shrugged and pointed. "That's a lot of rocks to move. And if we're to believe that the inner and outer circle perches are made like you saw on the Stone Stander drawings years ago, I have no idea how we'll rebuild those if they were torn down. The perch pillars would be so big and tall, not to mention the lintels that rested upon them."

"One day at a time, Lars. We'll see as we go."

"If you were the one who planned this originally, Nagora, where would you put the entrance to the maze? Looking out to sea? The perimeter marks are about a hundred paces from the cliffs there. Or on the inland side where the sun is highest at midday? Or on the side where the sun rises? Or the side where it sets?"

Why can I see the way into the center of the maze, but Lars can't? Should I even speak this thought out loud?

"Lars, when I show you the way in through the maze on the map, you can see it. However when you try to find it on your own, you can't. What if there truly is no way in through the maze?"

Lars looked from Nagora to Alizarine and back to Nagora.

What's he thinking?

Lars folded his arms across his chest. "I've asked myself that question over and over again. The only answer I can come up with is that the way is only visible to those it is meant for. Just the same, I feel there is another way in and out."

Nagora frowned. "Like some lodges that have two ways in and out?"

"Yes."

"It's damn big enough to merit that." Nagora nodded as she bit her upper lip.

"Perhaps there are three ways in and out." Lars pointed up. "The obvious one, from the sky, on the back of a dragon."

Nagora laughed. "Now that would make sense for a Dragon Talker."

Lars pointed at her. "Dragon Talker, I want you to make sense of where you would put the entrance. Sleep on it. It'll come to you."

Nagora hugged her man. "Time to eat. Alizarine must be starved."

While Nagora and Lars waited for Alizarine to finish eating, they looked off toward where Lars had decided to build the lodge. He pointed across the valley. "We had three possible locations for our home. I think I like the one at that big stone bluff. It's the highest up and the one with a direct water source we could access from inside the lodge. There's a patch of reed grass right next to the stone's flattest wall. That means there's water in the ground there year round. In that mostly stony soil, I'm guessing from a spring. We would have to dig and test. If the water level replenishes to its initial level, we could have our well there. The stone bluff's wall would make up one side of our lodge, like Geirador's. If the ground around the well is stone laden, it could support walls of stone. If not, we would have to build with timber. And that side of the bluff is exposed to the sun's travel all day, so we would have good light."

It's good to hear the excitement in your voice. You've already sold me on the merits of the location of our future home. How convinced are you? Let's see.

"I don't know." Nagora took hold of his arm and leaned against it.

Lars pointed. "You see the notch just facing us?"

"The one near the top of the stone?"

"Yes. That would be a spot for a small third floor room where we could have a view seaward and a clear view over to here."

Nagora poked his shoulder. "But look at the distance I'll have to go to wash in the stream."

"It'll be your stop on the way home. I'll make you a shelter over the stream, like the one at Geirador's. Anyway, if we chose either one of the other two possible lodge locations, we would have to haul water and we would most likely be snowed in because they're lower down in the valley."

Nagora leaned against his shoulder. "I agree with your choice, Lars. Having water and those views will be good. Farther away from these rocks and more hospitable after a day's work here. It'll be good to rest my eyes on green grasses and be able to smell the sea air. And watch your child play in the sun."

Nagora's last words must have taken a moment to register in Lars's mind. When they did, they brought him to his feet. He shot a quick glance over at Alizarine on her rock in the distance and then he bent to lift Nagora into his arms. "Say that again. Say it's true." His eyes were wide open and focused on hers, unblinking and waiting for her to answer.

She smiled up at him, nodded, and said, "From what I know, it is. The next time I see Umma, I'll have her confirm it, but yes, Lars, I carry your child in me, our child."

Lars swept her up in his arms so quickly she had to grab onto his neck. "Nagora, I can't wait to carry you across the threshold of our new home. Today you make me a happy man. I'm going to be a father. I love you." He kissed her and then gently set her down before placing a hand on her belly.

Nagora put a hand over his. "Still too small to feel, but when he or she is big enough, you'll marvel at the kicks." And today I marvel that you still love me. That to me is a mystery. When I told you about my night in the cave with Raynhard when Sarah was conceived, the control Danuka's essence had over me, and her words: "He is our king. We will not deny our king," you could have left me right then. Are we truly destined for each other? Have our brands truly bonded us? If I can bring this child to term and offer him or her to you, Lars, I will feel I've earned your forgiveness and your love.

Godomor was pleased with the plans of their lodge Lars had shown him, and he offered to send ten extra men to help construct it. Nagora guessed Godomor had another reason for sending more workers, but she was not going to complain. Instead, she took it as an opportunity to get involved in the construction, learning techniques that would help with re-building the maze.

The builders had erected two stout tripod apparatuses with long levers set atop each tripod. Once in position, with varia-ble counter weights, a lever could be pivoted and rotated to lift heavy loads. One tripod can even move the other with the help of the lever. Now that is clever. These tools will be in-dispensable to move rocks as we dig for the well.

Surprise visitors arrived mid-morning of the last day of summer, almost three months to the day since they had started their project. Godomor, Gabe, and Umma with her two daughters, Ronja the eldest and Noora the youngest, came to celebrate the completion of Nagora's and Lars's lodge and small barn. Their visit turned out to be more than that.

"*Ohtawimaw*, your visit warms my heart today. It is a joy to see you. Welcome to our home," said Nagora as Godomor held her in his embrace.

"*Mitanisimaw*, we arrive unannounced, bearing gifts to make your new lodge comfortable." Godomor released her, but kept an arm around her as he reached out to Lars to bring him closer. "Please accept these blankets." Godomor pointed to the hide-wrapped bundle on the pack saddle of the mule Gabe had been leading. "They will help keep you warm as the nights become colder. In winter you will not have to get up to feed your fire as often."

Gabe had a hand on one of the ropes that held the bundle. "Lars, I'll need your help to bring this in."

"Thank you, Godomor. How thoughtful of you and Gabe," said Lars.

Godomor smiled and pointed Nagora in Umma's direction. "Umma will need your help."

Umma stood smiling next to her mule. The bundle it carried was smaller. "Food for our feast today and surprises for you."

Umma's girls waved to Nagora as they joined Alizarine who had been sorting and stacking stone chips left over from building the walls of their lodge.

"Umma, you shouldn't have. I know how busy you can be." Nagora took her in her arms and whispered. "I need to speak to you in private. Soon."

Umma smiled at Nagora, nodded, and winked. "As soon as we bring these in. Let me take care of it." You must have heard from Lars already.

Lars and Gabe had already untied the bundle which they set on the table. The smell of lanolin was invading the kitchen space as Lars spread the woven woolen blankets over the backs of the chairs. "Look at these blankets Nagora. Aren't they magnificent?"

Godomor is so generous. He truly treats me as a daughter. "The embroidered vines and flowers on their borders are beautiful. Lars, Godomor and Gabe have spoiled us. And the patchwork on those sheepskin blankets. So much work! I didn't know there were black sheep in Skull Bay. Thank you, Gabe. Thank you, Godomor." Nagora hugged them.

Umma unwrapped one of her parcels. On one of the cupboard counters, she set aside crates of earthenware jars of various sizes. Nagora shook her head as she scanned all the jars. "Umma, I can't believe you found time to do all this! What's in the jars? I'm guessing preserves."

Umma pointed. "Honey in these big ones. Jams in these wax-sealed ones. Pickled herring in these with the cork stoppers."

Nagora's hands went to her face. "Lars, can you believe this? Oh! Umma! You are precious!" Nagora took Umma in her arms.

When Nagora let go of her, Umma pointed to her other parcel. "Lars, a leg of lamb and a goat's hindquarters. I think you know how to prepare them on a spit. Onions, potatoes, carrots, and garlic in the smaller bag. After you've shown

Godomor around, get those ready to go into a pot. While you do that, I have something to discuss with Nagora in private."

Nagora touched Umma's arm. "I have one thing to take care of before we talk." Nagora turned to Alizarine. "Ronja will help me bring the blankets up to your bed. Did you say thank you to Prince Gabe and King Godomor?"

Alizarine had one arm through the handle of her basket and her other hand was petting the checkered sheepskin blanket that hung over the back of the chair she stood next to. Alizarine looked to Gabe and then to Godomor. "Thank you for the blankets."

Gabe winked at her and Godomor gave her a big smile.

Godomor, I wish I could thank you aloud for the attention you show to this ageless witch child. I know you have your reasons for allowing me to bring her to your land, knowing full well the damage she did in the Land of the Danu. My hope is that while she is here, she causes no harm to you or your people. Deep down, this witch seeks the death of the last dragon in the Land of the Danu. It is my duty to prevent that.

Nagora picked up two woven blankets and Ronja took the sheepskin one. "Alizarine, you're a lucky girl. These will fit your bed perfectly. Lead the way. When we come back down, you can continue playing with Noora and Ronja outside."

Nagora led Umma outside, up and around the side of their lodge to the spot overlooking the sea where she did her daily ritual exercises. "Umma, you must have heard from Lars. I'm with child. I've missed two of my bleedings. And I have other signs I'll tell you about. I'm so excited that you've come today! I'm sure you'll confirm it for me!"

Umma smiled and nodded as she took Nagora's hands in hers, and Nagora described the other signs she had, telling Umma they were almost the same as with Sarah.

"All you say tells me you are. I am happy for you, Nagora, and for Lars."

"By the stars! Umma, I knew it! And now you confirm it. It makes me so happy." Her happiness overrode the question that lingered in the back of her mind—how will Alizarine consider my child, as a sister or a brother?

"You are strong, Nagora. Your baby will be strong. Tell me about Sarah's birth."

After Nagora told of her water breaking sooner than expected, and how Paruline had helped with the delivery, Umma said, "I see no reason carrying this child will be different than it was for Sarah. Though, if the child is a boy, you may notice that you will carry it higher. You must keep a calendar, like you did for Sarah. Send Lars for me, or come to me before your water breaks, even if you have to stay for a week or two." Umma squeezed Nagora's hands. "I think you should share this news with those you love today. It will make our feast even happier."

Back inside the lodge, Umma stood at Nagora's side and cleared her throat. "The lady of this house has an announcement to make." Umma stepped away from Nagora.

The children were still outside. Nagora looked from Gabe to Godomor and then to Lars. "Not only do I have an announcement to make, so does my man. Come join me." She waved Lars to her.

Lars's mouth grew into a huge grin as he looked from Gabe to Godomor and to Umma, who smiled back at him and nodded. You know Umma confirmed it. Godomor and Gabe smiled. These two are getting confirmation too. Nagora held out her arms to Lars who rushed toward her with an onion in one hand and a knife in the other. He stopped midway to deposit them on the table before picking Nagora up and swinging her around. Lars set her down and held her eyes with his before turning to Gabe and Godomor. "Nagora is with child."

Nagora smiled at him. "Aye! Umma has confirmed it!"

Lars held up a finger next to his face and moved it back and forth as he looked about the room, obviously thinking of what he wanted to say or perhaps do. "I ... I must ... will ... Godomor! Will you marry us? Now? Errr ... Today? Please. Please, Godomor, it would be a great honor if you would marry us today. Will you?"

Godomor smiled and pointed at Nagora. "Did you ask her?"

Nagora had to suppress giggles that rose inside her as she watched Lars's unusual, fumbling behavior. She wrung her hands and pursed her smiling lips to help control her own excitement.

Lars's mouth dropped open again as he blinked and wagged his finger again. He turned to Nagora, bent to one knee, and took her hand in his. "Will you marry me?"

Nagora pulled him up. "Aye! I will marry you."

"Today?"

"If that is your wish."

"It is my only wish today." Lars looked to Godomor. "My Lord Godomor, will you marry us today? Nagora said yes."

Of course I said yes. Oh, Lars, you know I love you so. I'd never say no to my protector.

Godomor smiled. "Yes, I will marry you, this evening. Those of us here today will gather before the stars so we and they will be witness to your union."

After they had feasted and toasted the new lodge, the coming child, and the couple to be wed, the visitors all assembled on the bluff with a view to the sea under a starry sky.

"Today, before me, Godomor, King of the Land of Skulls, before all assembled here and before our star ancestors above, let it be known we are here to witness with these rings, Lars and Nagora choose to be wed."

Nagora looked to the stars. I'll never forget this day.

Umma stepped forward with the three children. Each held a candle. Umma placed a ring in Nagora's palm. It was woven mariner-style from the fine tip of a willow branch stripped of its bark. So that's why Lars disappeared shortly after proposing. Made by his hands for the two of us. I'll treasure this ring more than one of gold.

Then Gabe stepped forward, with the children lighting his way, and he gave a similar ring to Lars.

Lars reached for Nagora's hand. "With this ring, I, Lars, choose you, Nagora, to be my wife." Lars slipped the woven band on Nagora's finger.

Her heart beat faster as she reached for the hand of the man she loved so dearly. "With this ring, I, Nagora, choose you, Lars, to be my husband."

Godomor took the arms of their ring hands and lifted them as high as he could. "We assembled here and our star ancestors above witness you, Lars and Nagora, are wed today. You have chosen to live together as husband and wife. May the stars look with favor on your decision."

Nagora and Lars kissed.

My happy day! We are now a family. You, the father, and I, the mother with child. May the stars look favorably upon us.

The next morning before leaving, Gabe took their hands in his. "Nagora, Lars, I'm truly happy for you. Soon I'll be leaving to visit Sagora. It'll be my proud duty to bring news of your wedding and your child-to-be to your family and friends.

"In her last missive, Sagora informed me she would be spending the coming winters working with Tagnya because there was still so much work to do to help the people of the Land of the Danu. Sagora said she would only return if she were pregnant. I plan to visit her as often as it takes to get her with child and bring her back to marry me." Could it be she hasn't told you about Sarah? Could that be her reason for not returning?

Nagora leaned her head against Lars's chest as they watched their visitors disappear in the distance. Lars's decision, to ask Godomor to marry us was made in the moment. Often they're the best kind. It's only now I think of Mum, Da, and Sagora, and Pare and Geirador not being present to share in our joy. Even if we had wanted them to be, Sarah's existence wouldn't allow it. Or it would have made arranging it so difficult. I have no regrets.

While building their lodge, Lars had befriended Jari, whom, along with his new wife Jenni, he had hired to cook the meals for the builders. When not cooking in the kitchen tent they had set up, Jari also lent a hand to the builders.

Now that Nagora was with child, Lars hired the young couple to continue to help Nagora with the chores. Jari and Jenni would also help Nagora learn the language of the Land of Skulls.

One time Nagora had said, "The more I hear it, the more I realize it has elements of the language of *The People* and the *Trader's Tongue*. Speaking it every day helps." Lars had picked that as the excuse for hiring the couple. Ah, my man, you are just trying to make my work lighter because I'm pregnant. You are taking care of me and the baby I carry.

Jari and Jenni prepared a garden plot for the following year. They cut up and turned the sod, cleared away the stones in the ground, and set them at the garden's perimeter. They even spread and worked into the soil all kitchen scraps and animal manure.

When Lars was away, Jari and Nagora worked at clearing rocks from the well spot. Alizarine accompanied them to the work site with Aydan.

Visiting the big cave, located on the seaward cliff wall below the edge of the maze perimeter, was something Nagora and Lars had discussed often but had kept putting off. With Lars's announcement, it was finally going to happen. "Gabe will be gone for almost a month. I'll be taking over his duties in Skull Bay while he's in the Land of the Danu. Before Gabe leaves and with Jari and Jenni here, I think now would be a good time to climb down to the cave on the sea cliff face."

Nagora stepped over to him. "I'm going with you, Lars. Don't give me that look. I can still climb. I want to see that place too. Besides, we don't know what's down there. I don't want you walking into danger on your own."

"What about Alizarine?" asked Lars.

"What about her? Alizarine has shown interest in making dolls with Jenni. I'll have Jenni prepare everything so Alizarine will want to stay with her."

Lars nodded. "Good. Let's prepare what we need for our day of exploration."

Lars and Jari set a rope over the cliff's edge and then Lars did a first exploratory climb to scout for the cave entrance. "We have to move the rope about fifty paces that way if I'm not mistaken. So much for the cave being aligned with where we think the well is."

"That's just the entrance. We won't know which way it goes until we're down there. Is the rope long enough?" asked Nagora.

"Yes, and I want it to be long enough to reach the water below and then some."

"Are you planning on going for a swim?"

"Only if I have to." Lars grinned at her.

Lars wore a smile as he climbed back up over the cliff's edge a second time. "It's the cave entrance, all right."

He slipped the strap of his big sword's scabbard over his head and set it to rest on his left shoulder. He handed Nagora his blades. "Here, you wear these."

"But they're yours. Do you think we'll need our weapons?"

Lars looked at Nagora, and right away she regretted her question. Nagora had said she didn't want him to walk into danger on his own. Dangor had trained her to always be prepared to expect the unexpected when on the trail. Her uncle's words came back to her: "When on the move anywhere, Nagora, I've learned to be prepared for trouble. It's being unprepared that often let's one walk into it."

Nagora slipped the straps of the sheath of the big skystone blade over her shoulders and adjusted the two small knife holsters on each strap so they were comfortable beneath her arms and at her sides. She flipped the brass latch which held the big blade in its sheath on her back before pulling the blade free. For a moment, she held it before her face. The Tiwaz symbol etched on the blade near its handle mirrored the brand on her forehead.

For a higher cause. A cause yet to be won.

"What's mine is yours. Besides, Sarah has your set, and you gave your uncle's away to pay a debt," said Lars.

Lars's words gave Nagora a chill as she returned the blade to its sheath. Once the side of the blade's tip struck the brass plate above the sheath's opening, it slid home with an easy push. Nagora flipped the latch over the up-curved crossguard. This is the first time you mention Sarah since I told you all about my stay in the cave with Danuka and Raynhard. I try not to think of what is coming, but when I hear Sarah's name, I can't help it.

"You still practice your ritual warrior exercises every morning. The blades become you. Geirador didn't give you the first set he made for no reason," said Lars.

Once a warrior, always a warrior. Aye, she still focused on those daily exercises near the cliff's edge, looking out to sea behind the big stone outcrop which protected their lodge. Years ago, Dangor had taught her the ritual exercises: ward off, rollback, press, push, pull, elbow strike, shoulder strike, advance, retreat, look left, gaze right, center balance. Nagora repeated them a hundred times each morning session. She did them with a different weapon in hand, no matter the weather, one day slow, the next day fast.

At times like this one, the repeated exercises gave her the strength to focus on the present moment of each day's task without worrying about what will come.

"When there's slack in the rope again, Jari, send down the bundle." Lars had tied all the items together in a net, then he tied the net to a lighter rope than the one they would climb down. The bundle contained their lunch rations, waterskins, lanterns, tapers, a pry bar, a bow, and a quiver of arrows. He looked at Jari. "Once we pull the bundle into the cave with us, and I give two tugs on the rope, untie this end."

Jari was nodding.

"You can go back to the lodge, Jari. Don't wait for us here."

"No, I would just as soon work at the well spot. I'll move more rocks."

"Be careful with that big lever. Don't make any foolish moves on your own. We'll tell you all about the cave when we get back."

Nagora scratched the heads of Lyam and Aydan. "Look at these two. They want to come."

Lars smiled and pointed to Jari. "Lyam, Aydan. Stay with Jari. Obey Jari."

The hounds slunk over to sit at his side.

"Don't look so sad, you two. We'll be back well before nightfall," said Nagora.

"Don't worry about me," said Jari. "These two will keep an eye on me. Be careful down there."

...

Lars pulled Nagora into the mouth of the cave. Her eyes took it in. "It's so big! Almost ten men high and as wide. A dragon can fly in here, no problem." There was a trickle of water at her boots, which spilled out of the cave entrance at her feet. Nagora bent down to touch a finger to it to taste it. "Fresh water."

"It'll be interesting to find its source," said Lars, as he reached out to the netted bundle of supplies and pulled it into the cave. With Nagora's help, they set the bundle on a dry spot of the cave floor. He gave two tugs on the rope.

As soon as it loosened, he pulled it in, coiling the lighter rope before slipping it over his head onto his shoulder. "What do you say we come back here to eat? We'll only take one waterskin and a handful of rations for our scrips."

Nagora pointed out to sea. "I like the view. That's a plan! Less to carry.

"I'm surprised no birds nest here. Though they do stop by." She pointed to the droppings at the edge of the cave mouth.

"Easy pickings for those that prey on them," said Lars. "They stand a better chance defending their nests on a small ledge with their backs against a cliff wall. And it's easier for them to kick their young out as soon as they can fly."

The day I handed Sarah over to Pare, she was four days old. So far from being able to fly on your own. Now you're going on four months. Why do I feel like I've kicked you out? Will you ever forgive me, Sarah? I had no choice.

Nagora swallowed as Lars handed her the bow and quiver. No time for crying now. Save it for the night when he sleeps.

She slung the weapons in place on her shoulder, along with the two lanterns Lars had set at her feet. He carried four of them and the pry bar on slings he had improvised. Lars handed her an unlit taper. He lit one and carried three others under his left arm. "Give me one of those, Lars."

Lars didn't argue. He held his taper high as they walked toward the darkness ahead. "I'll light yours over there."

As soon as Nagora's taper caught fire, she pointed at the ceiling. "Look." It was a picture of a dragon with wings spread, as seen from below. The image was almost life-sized.

"Who could have drawn that?" Lars asked what Nagora was thinking.

"I saw drawings like this one, but smaller, in the cave in the vent shaft hole on the Isle of Smoke." Nagora's mind went back to the Little People she had called to help her in Raynhard's secret cave. From what she had seen of the Little People as tiny points of light, they had no problem at all traveling along the cave ceiling there. If they can walk on the ceiling of a cave and make a dragon's shed skin seem to come alive, they can surely draw on a ceiling too by rigging whatever support they need. "Perhaps the Little People drew this."

About a hundred paces in, they found another drawing on the ceiling. This time, the dragon's wings were bent as when Danuka entered Raynhard's smaller cave. "Look, the cave gets smaller here," said Lars.

The next drawings they found were not far, fifty paces away. Dragons, drawn in profile with their wings folded and walking on their hind legs, seemed to eye them from each side of the cave wall. "The cave is even smaller here. Do you think these drawings are to guide the dragons as they fly in here?" asked Lars.

"Makes sense. I've seen no places where tapers could be set to light the way enough. I know Danuka can see in the dark so much better than we can. These drawings just might be to guide them in, to let them know when they have to stop gliding and fold their wings in to land safely."

"Maybe you're right. Without the drawings, they might not have enough references other than experience to guide them in. A first-time flight in here could get them hurt."

Not far from there, to their left, was an opening. The main cave seemed to continue on. Nagora pointed to the drawing above the opening. "It's a much smaller drawing of a dragon. I can't read the symbols under it. Can you, Lars?"

Lars stared with his mouth open and shook his head. "No, I can't. Could it be a name?"

"I have no idea. Shall we go inside?"

Lars nodded.

Nagora led. "Danuka could fit through here. It's about the size of Raynhard's cave entrance."

Lars held his taper higher as they moved into a vaulted chamber. "Wow! Look at all those drawings! The dragons are beautiful. No two are the same. Their wings are spread in every imaginable flight shape, all of them in flight and drawn in different shades of grey. If I'm not mistaken," he pointed to a section at the edge of the chamber ceiling, "down there are the hatching circles. In that drawing no dragons have landed on the lintels. And there are no eggs of either kind in the rings."

"The dragons are just like the ones in the cave where Danuka lived with Da. He said there were other caves in the vent hole. Da said he would fly to them with Danuka to make her use her wings to keep them strong."

"Do you think there are other dens like this one?" asked Lars.

"That's what we're here for, to find out about this place. Let's go see."

Further on, they came to two other dens, as Lars had called them. The next one was to their right and then another to their left.

Past those two dens, the cave opened onto a huge, high-vaulted chamber with a small lake in its middle. On the shore of one side of the lake, stood two tall columns, reaching to the ceiling. On the shore behind the columns was a space Nagora judged to be big enough for six or seven dragons the size of Danuka. "Wow! I know what these are used for," said Nagora.

"What for?"

"The shedding time. When dragons shed their skin, like Danuka did when I was with her in the cave. To have access to water like this makes it easier. The dragons would have those columns to rub against to help make the old skin separate from the new beneath. The water helps too by getting into the space between the two skins."

Lars walked on ahead along the shore of the lake until he was standing opposite the two pillars. "I think you're right. Look." He held up his taper to point with it. The drawings on the high ceiling were just visible. Some depicted dragons in the lake, while others showed dragons winding their way in and out of the lake and around the pillars. One showed a dragon breathing fire. "Looks like the lake is fed by a stream that empties into it at the other end. What'll we discover next?"

"Lars, do you have any idea if the way we've come so far has been in a straight line, or have we been moving on a curve?"

"Good question. I haven't been thinking about that with all we've seen. Tell you what. I'll stand at the other end of the lake where the stream runs into the chamber. You head back the way we came. Try to stay near the middle way. If you hear me whistle, that means I've lost sight of your taper. Otherwise, keep going until you see daylight."

Just before she arrived at the first den they had come upon, Lars whistled. Nagora turned around and headed back to him.

"When I lost sight of your taper proper, the glow coming from it was strongest from my right as I watched in that direction. I whistled as soon as there was no glow to see," said Lars.

"I was almost at the first den when you whistled. That means if we were on a straight line from the entrance to that den, then our path curved left from there. We might be headed toward the well we're looking for."

Lars nodded. "That could be. Let's continue on."

They passed three more dens, one to the right, the next to the left, and the third to the right again. Each had an image of a dragon drawn above its entrance with different symbols beneath. They moved on. Lars spoke up. "I think the cave has gotten smaller here too. My taper seems to light up more of the ceiling."

"I think you're right, Lars."

They moved on for almost a count based on the marks Lars had made on the tapers. With no daylight as a reference, these markers helped keep track of time, as did the marks on the lantern candles. A day's work was twenty-four counts, and a day was three times that. Counting to keep track of time had become almost second nature to Nagora, with the sun to help, but not so in the dark. They took in the floor, the walls, and the ceiling as they went until Lars stopped. Calmly, he whispered, "Come stand next to me. Hold your taper up next to mine. Be quiet. Just watch and listen."

Nagora did as Lars had asked.

What am I listening and watching for?

Nagora began a count in her head as she looked up at the flames of the tapers.

"There," he whispered.

"There where? My arm is getting tired."

"Shh. Quiet." Lars was whispering again. "Give me your taper." He held them both in his left hand and put his right arm around Nagora.

Nagora listened with her eyes on the tapers.

"There," he whispered again.

The flames of the tapers flickered.

"See that?"

It was her turn to whisper. "Yes."

"Listen."

Standing still, her eyes on the flames and her jaw slack, she waited.

"Hear that?"

"No, but the flames flickered again. What do you hear?"

His voice was back to normal. "The sound was almost like a bell at sea, in the fog and at a great distance. When I worked on a Moroes Island whaler, sometimes the fog would set in before we got to port. We would pick our way through the fog by listening for the fog bells onshore. It sounded almost like that, but it didn't come at regular intervals like a fog bell."

"If we move on, maybe you'll hear it again. I didn't hear it. However, I believe you. What caused the flames to flicker?"

"There's a small draft in here. It may be the pressure of the wind rushing past the cave entrance. Although, if it was that, I would expect the flames to move toward the entrance. Instead, they moved in the direction we are going."

Lars handed a taper back to Nagora and they moved on.

Half a count later, Lars stopped again and reached back for Nagora's hand. She took it, stepped next to him, and held up her taper. "Nagora, this isn't natural. What I mean is, from the first steps we took inside this cave, I've had this feeling, and now this confirms it. Look at the way the cave is shaped now. It's almost like a tube, as if we were looking inside of one of the willow branch bark tubes, but not as smooth.

"Whatever Dragon Talker dug this out of solid rock has all my admiration. This whole cave is not some natural occurrence, like Raynhard's cave. Someone planned this cave, designed it for a purpose, and carved it out of solid rock. How? I have no idea. My eye cannot see the mark of the tool or tools that did this."

Nagora pointed. "Look there, ahead. See the drawings that spiral up from the bottom, around, and down again? Could they be guides? If so, leading us to what?"

"I guess we'll find out soon enough."

"What do you make of these drawings ahead, Lars?"

"Chains or knotted ropes strung one peg to another? At least that's what they remind me of."

"Hmm. Have you ever, in your life, seen a tube with ropes or chains strung in it like this?"

"No. I've only ever seen ropes or chains hanging down the inside of a—well."

They both stopped moving and looked at each other.

"Are we thinking the same thing?" asked Nagora.

"I think we are."

As they moved on, their boots no longer splashed through the trickle of water. Instead they sunk into the sandy, silty muck from which the water oozed.

Further on, the wet sediment turned into stones and rock debris that gradually rose to the cave ceiling, blocking any further progress. Near where they stood in the tube, three new drawings appeared, equidistant from each other. The ones on the walls were opposite each other. "What can they be?" asked Nagora.

"I'm not sure, but I am guessing a fourth one is on the floor under the debris here, opposite the one on the ceiling." Lars kicked at the debris pile on the floor.

"Let's find out." Nagora planted her taper further ahead on the debris slope. Lars did likewise and lit a third taper which he also planted. He loosened the debris run with the pry bar and then went to his knees next to Nagora. Together, they dug with their hands until they were pushing away the wet sediment covering the cave floor at the spot directly below the drawing overhead.

Nagora reached into her quiver for an arrow. She used its feathers to sweep away the last of the wet sand particles, revealing the drawing on the stone floor. "Get a taper."

Lars held the taper above the sweeping arrow.

"You guessed right. There it is. The fourth one." Nagora sat back on her heels before the drawing. Lars stood opposite her. They were both quiet.

"Well," said Lars, "what do you think it is?"

Nagora ran her fingers over the symmetrical lines and then sat for almost a quarter count in that position, looking at the drawing. "It's like the maze map. We don't see the actual maze, only its plan. I think I know what this represents. It's the mouth of a big spout, seen from head on."

Lars pointed to each of the drawings. "So four spouts pour what into what? Water into a well?"

"Perhaps. Water is valuable. It could be something precious, something of greater value." Nagora was piecing together all the information she had learned from the stories Sagora and her father had told her about the dragons. "From what we are seeing now in this cave, we can say the maze aboveground must have existed. Long ago in its middle, there was a hatching circle for baby dragons."

Nagora held up a finger. "If that is so and the dragon eggs heated up enough to melt the gold veins of the eggs before the young burst forth in clouds of steam, the melted gold must've seeped into the ground.

"Anyone who went to the trouble designing this did so to collect that gold. It would make sense the well is in the center of the hatching circle. The molten gold from the eggshells would flow to the well, to be collected there. But how?"

Lars seemed puzzled by what Nagora said. "If that's the case, that the eggs heat up enough to melt the gold veins, there must be something inside the eggs that protects the dragon young before they, like you say, burst forth. Perhaps a magical liquid that clings to the inside of the shell and evaporates as the gold melts, allowing the young to survive. That would account for the steam when the young break out of the shell— a mystery we'll probably never understand."

Nagora was nodding. "But we're not if that's how it happens. Perhaps the young break the shells and squeeze out between the gold veins, bending them enough to get out. And only then is the gold melted. In time we might find the answer." She pointed behind Lars.

Lars turned from her and held his taper toward the debris slide, examining it before speaking. "This pile of rubble could be from long ago when Winter's ice and snow left. When it did, it destroyed the maze and the hatching circles and in the process, rocks and stones from those structures got pushed or fell into the well."

Nagora was nodding. "If that's so and we dig past this pile, we would come to the well shaft. I don't think I would want to dig upward, if that is where the shaft is. There are more rocks and muck waiting to fall."

Lars rubbed his chin with one hand as he looked at the rubble mound that rose from his feet to the cave ceiling. "Let's clear away as much as we can from one side to see how close we can get to the well shaft. Perhaps the shaft continues downward over there. I'm curious to find where the water comes from."

Nagora nodded and held up a finger. "Godomor said I have to have access to the well to call the Little People. Lars, in your calculations, did you figure out the size of the well, what its measure should be from one side to another?"

"If I'm right, it should be about three times the span of my arms."

Nagora let her jaw drop. "Wait! What if it's as deep or deeper than the distance of our climb to get down here? And it's filled with rocks and stones of all sizes? Can you imagine the work involved to dig and hoist all that out?"

"Not a task you'd envy, is it?" asked Lars

Nagora slapped her hands on her thighs before standing. "Okay. One day at a time. Maybe we'll discover it's not so bad after all. Shall we get to work for a while and then take a break to eat?"

Lars grabbed the pry bar. "We should've brought a shovel. I wasn't expecting to be digging. On the next trip down here." He jabbed the bar into the pile ahead of him. "Left side or right side?"

"Left."

"Left it is."

After three counts, they had just stopped and were about to head for the cave entrance to eat. In the moment of silence when Nagora stretched her back and Lars examined his hands, they both heard it. They looked at each other. Nagora was wide-eyed and nodding as she pointed to her ear and mouthed the words: "I hear it." It was as Lars had described it, a distant bell ringing at irregular intervals.

"That's closer, Nagora," Lars whispered. "I think I know what it is." He pulled his big sword free of its scabbard, grabbed the pry bar with his other hand, and climbed up the mound to the ceiling's edge. He laid his sword down and jabbed the pry bar into the space where the rubble met the ceiling. Then he picked up his sword and moved back.

Lars counted, "One, two, three," as he struck the pry bar each time with the broad side of his sword. He paused for a count of three and then struck the metal bar three times again. Lars repeated this a third time, stopped, and held a finger to his lips.

The answer came. The distant bell repeated the pattern Lars had struck out.

The smile on Lars's face grew wider and wider as he struck the pry bar again, but this time on three counts of two.

Again, the answer came back, repeating Lars's pattern.

Lars pointed to Nagora. "You should see the grin on your face!" He pulled the pry bar free and returned to Nagora's side. "You know who that is?"

Nagora nodded. "Jari! Lars, we found the well spot!" She threw her arms around Lars.

Lars hugged her. When he let her go, he found the waterskin and took a big swig from it. "Let's go to the mouth of the cave. I'm hungry for more than the rations in my scrip. We'll bring another waterskin when we come back."

As Nagora finished her portion dried venison, she looked out to sea and wondered aloud, "If Godomor knows the existence of this cave, others must too, other descendants of the *First People* who lived in this land, or others who might have discovered it from the sea."

Lars shrugged. "What Sagora told you about it is the same as I was told, the legend of the thirsty giant crawling out of the sea, wanting a drink of fresh water from a witch's well.

When not getting it, he destroys her abode and all the land about it. Many perhaps know that version.

"As for discovering it from the sea, a mariner would need the right conditions to come close enough to get a good look at the cliff face. What's seen from a distance at sea doesn't always appear to be what it actually is. In good weather, they would have the sun in their eyes until they got close enough. In cloudy weather, the sea conditions would most likely be rougher. Either way, they would have many rocky shoals to sail through. I would not risk it.

"And that beach in the little cove nearby, I doubt that it would tempt the most desperate Outlander raiding party to come ashore. They would have the same shoals to navigate. Besides, fishers in these parts know Skull Bay is the closest safe harbor. To my knowledge, none of them venture along this coast to fish. Soon as the weather turns for the worse, this coast gets hit first. No fun trying to run from a storm. Even less fun trying to run into one."

Nagora spit out a piece of nut shell. "Well, if ever we rebuild the maze, people will surely come to see it. Then perhaps the true legend of this point of land will surface. Let's get back to work."

Their tapers had all burnt out and they were down to their candle lanterns. Lars worked closest to the well hole, prying loose the occasional bigger rock and maneuvering it back to Nagora where, together with a rope tied around it, they hauled it over to the pile of other big stones.

After digging some more, Lars called to Nagora. "Bring your lantern."

Nagora was standing behind him. Lars had bent down on one knee. When she held the lantern over his shoulder, he turned and threw water at her with cupped hands. "Let me get out of the way. Take a look."

When Lars stepped behind her, she held the lantern and knelt down in the space Lars had occupied. "Is that an iron grid?"

"Iron? I think not. It's not rusted at all. It's a metal of some kind."

Nagora counted a dozen interwoven metal bars that criss-crossed each other, leaving square spaces through which she could stick her hands to touch the water. To her right was a heavier piece of metal that rested on the edge of the well hole, and it crossed over the grid of metal bars beneath it.

Lars had cleared away the muck and soil beyond the heavy piece. Nagora reached over. What she touched felt like metal as well. As she ran her finger over it, an image came to mind. It was hammered metal, like she had seen on the metal strapping sometimes used on shields. She rinsed off her fingers. They came away rust free.

Nagora stood. "What do you make of it?"

"There's a metal grid over the well at this level. I think a metal bridge spans the grid. We'll know once we've cleared all this away. This is as far as we'll go today," said Lars.

"You're right. To go any further will be dangerous. Now we're sure we've found the well. Best we work our way down from the top."

"So we're done here. Time we head back. Do you think you can climb the rope?" asked Lars.

Nagora nodded. "After a short rest and a few bites from the leftover rations, I'll make it up."

...

Jari and the dogs were waiting for them when they reached the top of the cliff. "So we're in the right spot? You heard me digging? The dogs heard you before I did."

"Aye, we heard you! You returned Lars's message. We were so happy you answered! We knew we were in the right spot."

As Jari helped Lars coil and haul up the rope, he listened to Lars describe what they had seen in the cave. Lars placed a hand on Jari's shoulder. "You must see it someday."

"I would like to. Come and see what I uncovered. I'm sure it's part of the rim of stones around the lip of the well."

Aydan and Lyam led the way to the well. "Wow! Look at those stones! You didn't waste any time today," said Nagora.

Jari pointed at the pile of big stones. "I was getting two and three per load in the rope net. Once they were in, hoisting them and moving them there with the lever wasn't a problem. Then I tied in the cowhide and shoveled in all that dirt and pebbles. I figure once we get the whole rim cleared, we'll be surrounded by mounds of what we've dug through."

Nagora was standing on part of the well rim. It was arc-shaped, almost three paces in length. From the inner arc to the outer arc edge, it was three times the length of her foot. She stepped one foot off the rim into the hole Jari had dug on its outer side. It was knee deep.

Jari pointed near the outer rim. "If you sit on the rim and bring your foot back up, you'll see two of the edges of what looks like two big flat stones fitted side by side. I think they might be part of the landing or floor around the well."

"I think Jari's right, Lars. He's uncovered built structure work. Our work has started to pay off."

Lars reached a hand down to help Nagora out of the hole. "True enough, and we have a good idea of what awaits us. I think we've earned our bath at the stream."

"You two go ahead. I'll let Jenni know you're on your way. Then I'll tend to the mules and horses. I'll have my bath later. See you at the supper table," said Jari.

Jenni's face couldn't hide it when they entered the lodge. Something was amiss. Linen strips of bandages covered Jenni's hands. "Is everything okay here, Jenni?"

"I'll be fine." Jenni pointed a trembling hand up toward the small third floor room. "I'll talk with you when she's asleep. Not before."

Nagora's eyes jumped from Jenni to the loft ladder and back to Jenni. "Is she up there? Is she okay?"

Jenni nodded twice and brushed a stray hair from her face. "Jenni?"

Jenni shook her head. "Later. Please."

Nagora climbed the loft ladder and then the shorter ladder to the small room built over the notch in the stone there. Alizarine sat cross-legged on her small rear end, rocking back and forth on the wide window seat built into the window frame. The child was looking out to sea through the open window, holding her basket in her arms and humming as she rocked. Nagora leaned on the window frame and looked over Alizarine's head.

She looked down at Alizarine. Blood stained the witch child's hands. "Have you seen any boats, Alizarine?"

"Not yet."

"Do you know when the next storm is coming?"

"In three days after they're gone."

Now what does she mean by that? I better not ask. "Do you think we'll find a treasure on the beach after the storm?"

"A dragon tooth. Maybe three."

Nagora frowned. "I'm hoping to find pieces of shells I can use to make buttons."

Alizarine carried on with her humming.

"I'll call you when supper's ready."

On the seat of the window which looked out on the rocky plain, three braided woolen dolls sat. Two of them had dried blood on them.

That evening when Nagora came down from the loft, she leaned close to Jenni. "Alizarine's asleep now."

"Can we talk outside?" asked Jenni.

Nagora and Lars let Jenni lead the way. She led them past the corner of the lodge, along the wall to where it met the huge stone outcrop. It was the farthest corner away from Alizarine. Jenni leaned against the stone wall, and moved her head back so it too touched the wall. Jenni looked from Jari to Lars and then to Nagora. "I never thought I would have to say this about a child." Her hands trembled as she brought them to her chin. "I'm terrified of her. I won't stay a day longer. I'll leave at sunrise. Jari wants the night to think about if he'll stay or not. If it were up to me, I would leave now."

"Can you tell us what happened? How did she frighten you? I know she can lose her temper easily. What did she do?"

"Those weren't words a child would speak nor any grown person right in their mind. If I'm to believe all she yelled at me, then I am cursed, doomed to die a horrible death if I stay here. Only a witch could say such things." Jenni covered her face with bandaged hands. Her shoulders shook as she cried. Her tears fell on the dried blood stains of the linen dressings.

Nagora took Jenni in her arms. "I understand how you feel, and I respect your decision. I enjoyed your company and appreciate all the work you've done for us. Jari, as much as I would like you to stay, I think you would do well to be with your Jenni."

Nagora then took Jenni by the shoulders. "Jenni, I want you to look at me. Look into my eyes. Jenni, I feel your fear. I'll give you a charm that'll protect you from Alizarine's curse." Nagora reached up into the left sleeve of her sweater until her fingers found the dolphin armband her mother had given her. She pulled it from her arm and held it out to Jenni. "You knew my mum, Tagnyoriva?"

Jenni nodded.

"Mum gave me this to give me protection in my time of need. She told me to keep it until the day I met someone in need of protection. Jenni, you are that person. I want you to wear it always for a whole year, and every day, the first thing in the morning, I want you to recite these words: 'I am the mistress of my destiny. I alone guide my future. I refuse evil's curse wished upon me.' Repeat them now so I know you won't forget them."

Jenni repeated the words to accompany the protective charm.

"Good, Jenni. Put this on your left arm now above your elbow. Do as I told you, and one year from now on this day, the curse will be no more. After that, it will be your turn to pass on the armband to someone you meet who needs protection."

Jenni wasted no time rolling up her sleeve to put on the armband. Then she hugged Nagora. "Thank you."

"There's one more thing both of you will have to do to have peace of mind. It's most important. You must tell no one of what happened this day or of what you did while you were here with us. If you are asked, say that your work with us is done. What you ended up doing was helping us put the final touches on our lodge, stable, and garden. If asked about the armband, say it was my gift to you. Understood?"

"Understood," said Jenni.

Lars offered them his hand. "Jari, I'll always remember what we accomplished this day. Thank you for that. If you wish to leave now, do so. You should make it to Skull Bay just before nightfall. Or you can stay the night."

Jari nodded. "I think Jenni will feel better if we leave now. We'll get our belongings."

Nagora, Lars, and the dogs watched them disappear over the distant hill. Lars sighed. "Looks like we're on our own from now on. Jenni truly wanted to be away from here as soon as possible."

"I know. I saw she had packed their things. I did my best to console her."

"That you thought of giving her Tagnya's armband surprised me. I thought you would never part with it. That story you made up about it ... a whole year?"

"Sometimes the stories we attach to objects give them much greater value. Believe me, she'll repeat those words even if she parts with the armband. Alizarine terrified her.

And I figured it might increase the likelihood of them not talking."

"That remains to be seen. Here we are, both of us marked as returning twins to this land that still holds our kind in fear. We're living together, away from everyone else, with a child that is not ours. Evil rumors about us as twins living here must travel faster than they can be whispered. Jenni and Jari must be strong not to speak of what happened and what we're doing here, living so close to a legendary place. Even if they keep it to themselves, their return will just fuel more rumors."

Nagora put her arms around Lars. "Well, I will not worry myself sick with what people may say about us. I want to take each day in stride and make the best of whatever I have to do on that day. You'd best do likewise."

Lars placed a hand on Nagora's cheek. "I'll do my best, but I won't leave you here alone while I'm in Skull Bay for an extended period. I'll pay Umma to put you up with Alizarine during that time."

Nagora didn't argue. Lars will keep his word on that count.

They turned to make their way back to their lodge. Alizarine was standing in the doorway holding her basket. As they approached, Nagora caught the smile on Alizarine's face, just before she turned around and scampered back inside. Do I tell Lars how she makes me feel? I won't. He must know that I wish I could rip her apart with my bare hands to get rid of her. Such is the hatred she ferments in me. He need not hear me complain.

Why am I cursed to mother this witch? Until the day my daughter helps me execute the sentence Heqet pronounced on Alizarine, she is my sworn enemy. Until then, I am slave to time and this task put on my path. May I celebrate my freedom on that day.

The morning after the storm, Nagora set out for the beach with Alizarine and Aydan. A cool wind was doing its best to chase away the last of the storm clouds, which seemed to fight back to keep the sunshine at bay. It'll clear. Until it does, I'm happy I wore an extra sweater under my vest. The valley stream was still a dirty torrent. Alizarine insisted Nagora hold her hand as they walked down the path.

"If we had left right at sunrise like you wanted, the path would have been underwater. Look how high the water was earlier." Nagora pointed to the wet grass the flow of the stream's floodwater had combed along the path. "You would have been in water up to your waist. We would have had to fight our way down through the brambles and bushes higher along the bank."

Alizarine hadn't thrown a tantrum when Nagora told her why they wouldn't leave for the cove beach right away. Nagora's morning exercises came first, and she figured that by now Alizarine realized if she had a crying fit, she would only have herself as an audience. "Cry and scream all you want. That's your right. I don't have to listen to it. You have a choice: Go cry outside where I can't hear you. Or ask me politely to leave so you can cry here all by yourself."

Alizarine had only once politely asked Nagora to leave. Nagora had left with these words: "Alizarine, so help me, if you break anything in this lodge while I'm away, I promise you I'll beat you so hard your screams will fall on the ears of the people in Skull Bay."

...

It wasn't until they were on top of the small dune of marram grass that Alizarine spoke. "Look at the beach. It's not the same as the last time we were here."

"That's what storms do, Alizarine. They change things." Nagora caught herself thinking of Alizarine as a storm. Someday, Alizarine, when your story is known, you'll be compared to a terrible storm that changed so many things for so many people. I'll savor the day I put an end to any further ravages you might cause. "See all the dulse and seaweed that mark the new high-water line? The waves pushed them all the way back here. Those big rolling waves are now on the outgoing tide. Imagine how much bigger they were when the storm was at full force in the middle of the night. No way we would've been able to stand on the beach then."

Nagora and Alizarine sat on the damp sand and pulled off their leather boots. "Which way do you want to go, Alizarine?"

Alizarine pointed to her right, toward the cliffs. "We'll walk until the cliffs, then turn around and walk to the other end of the beach."

"Okay. Here's your bag. I'll carry the lunch and the waterskin. Let's go see what you can find."

As soon as they headed toward the cliffs, Aydan led the way.

Alizarine's tired eyes stared at the three dragon teeth she had lined up on the top of the table after supper. It took her two hands to move one tooth into a position that suited her. Alizarine's hands rested flat, one on top of the other, on the table. Her right cheek lay on top of her hands. Now and then she reached out both hands to reposition the teeth, so she was looking at different sides of them.

"You know, Alizarine, I must put them back outside with the shells. If I don't, the whole place will smell fishy. Tomorrow, I'll boil them all in vinegar and then let them dry in the sun. Then you'll be able to bring them back in."

Alizarine yawned more than nodded and closed her eyes.

"Before you fall asleep at the table, I want you to climb the ladder and crawl into your bed in the loft. I don't want to risk carrying you up there. Lars would, if he were here. Up you go, please. I'll be right behind you to make sure you don't fall on the way up."

Until he was ready to leave for the Land of the Danu, Gabe had given Lars an extra free day a week to help Nagora excavate at the well. That meant they had four days in a row to work at the site. He had also promised Lars a whole month off upon his return.

Nagora had convinced Lars that she would be fine for the three days he would be absent. She would have Aydan to protect her, and she promised not to work at the well by herself while he was away. She would spend her time cooking and preparing food for them to take to the work site. And she would have time with Alizarine.

In the weeks before Gabe's departure for the Land of the Danu to visit Sagora, they had been able to clear the well rim completely as well as an armspan perimeter around it. This showed a part of the fitted stone landing that had been built around the well. They had also removed enough rubble from the well as to require a ladder to get in and out of it. With the removed rubble, they had built a high platform upon which they installed a tripod with a long lever. And they had attached a system of pulleys to the end of the lever to help them haul out more rocks and dirt. They figured sooner or later, they would have to install a second tripod on a platform of its own, with its own lever and pulleys. Future loads would be lifted out in two stages.

When Gabe left, their stay with Umma was a welcome break. Taking over from Gabe was not a strenuous task for Lars. It required tact and patience to filter petty disputes and complaints Godomor need not hear. As a returning twin to the Land of Skulls, Lars had grown used to working under the close scrutiny of those who still bore a fear of twins. That he had gained the trust of most other people in the community seemed make his job easier.

And Nagora's time with Umma helped shorten Nagora's wait for the letters Gabe would bring on his return. All I want is news about Sarah. How I miss you, my daughter! If only I could go to you. In time, though I fear the day when I'll have no choice but to go to you. Will I be able to convince you of the necessity of the task the curse has set for us?

A Place to Rest
Ayiwepowin

† NOW: *in the fifteenth year of*
rebuilding the maze in the Land of Skulls

Nagora moved to shift Alizarine in her lap without waking her. The child's eyes opened. "You and your egg are getting heavy. What if you leave your basket in my lap and lay your head on my leg? That way I'll be more comfortable, and you can still hold onto your basket."

As usual, Alizarine considered the suggestion, her eyes looking about and to the sky. "Help me up."

Nagora reached under the child's arms and lifted her. "I'll stand too so I can stretch my legs."

Alizarine leaned against the edge of the well and tried to peer over its edge. "Can we go down so I can play with the wagons?"

Nagora bent, placed both hands on one of the big stones on the well's lip, and stretched a leg out behind her. "Alizarine, we agreed about going down there, didn't we? Do you re-member?"

Alizarine nodded. "But we would be safe down there."

"What is our agreement, Alizarine?"

Alizarine pouted and turned her head away.

"Yes, I'm talking to you."

Alizarine hung her head. "I have to ask the night before I want you to bring me to play with the wagons."

"Last night, did you ask?"

Alizarine shook her head. "No."

"Do you remember why we agreed, Alizarine?"

"So you can rig a rope and pulley to lower my basket and bring it back up safely."

Nagora released the tension on her outstretched leg and extended her other for the same treatment. "Did I bring the rope and pulley and the special pole today?"

"No."

"That's right, and you know we don't want to take risks with your precious egg going down those steps and climbing back up. Instead, we'll go down some other time." Nagora stood with hands on her hips. "Do you want to rest more or head back home?"

Alizarine turned her back to the well and made a sign for Nagora to sit. "Rest more."

She sat cross-legged so Alizarine could place her basket in her lap. Once she did, Alizarine laid on her side on the smooth stone surface with her head on Nagora's thigh.

Nagora combed Alizarine's black hair back with her fingers and then let her hand rest on the child's shoulder. Nagora let her mind slip back to the day she and Lars had figured out something useful about the well.

Mysteries of the Maze
Mâmaskâc Kîkway
Âpihtâwâyihk

† THEN: *in the first year of*
rebuilding the maze in the Land of Skulls

Nagora stood on the well ladder, watching Alizarine settle her basket on the side of the mound of smaller debris of dirt and stone chips. Lyam had already claimed a spot at the top of the heap with his hindquarters. Aydan stood behind Alizarine, waiting for her to sit. He held her small wooden shovel in his mouth. Already his paws were dirty. "Alizarine, I'm going down now. Soon we'll be bringing up more stones. Don't let Aydan do all the digging. Throw the stone chips as close to the chip pile as you can."

After placing one foot on a big stone and leaving the other on the ladder that rested against the inside of the well's rim, Nagora rested a hand on her growing belly. "So what's that board for?" she asked Lars, who had climbed down ahead of her.

Lars replied, "Remember the spiral markings in the tube part of the cave below?"

Nagora nodded and looked at where Lars was now pointing. She twisted and turned as she followed his finger. Why hadn't I noticed them before? I must've been focusing on the debris at the bottom.

"So Nagora, what do you make of them?"

"They seem to spiral down. The pieces of stone seem to all be broken off at irregular angles. Could the broken pieces have been steps?"

"That's what I've been thinking." Lars bent over to pick up a slab of stone next to which he had set the wooden board. He held the slab's broken end up next to the protruding stone.

"The broken off part is a perfect fit, Lars. If it's a step, it's about the length of your arm."

Lars was smiling. "We've been bringing up a bunch of these. Yesterday, I tried matching this piece. It fits here. Now I'll try to pry the other part out and then put the board in its place." Lars already had his hands on the piece he had just showed. He was trying to wiggle it from side to side. The stone wasn't cooperating.

Lars reached for a hammer and a stonemason's chisel in the leather bucket at his feet. He went to work on the protruding stone, tapping on one side, then the other. Next he wedged a small pry bar into the crack on one side and pried. There was a slight movement. Lars did the same to the other side and got the stone to move more. After two more pries on each side, he set the tools down and pulled with his hands. Lars pulled it out a finger's length at a time.

The whole piece came out. It was half the length of the broken part. After shaving off a few chips from the wooden board with a small axe, Lars could fit it into the hole. He stood back to look at the board. Now what's he thinking? If I were coming down such spiral steps into the well, I would be trying to hug the wall. I wouldn't be comfortable on steps of that length. Wait a moment! Who were those steps made for? Not for the Little People. For the Dragon Talker? Most likely.

Lars looked up at her. "I would only come down steps like these with a pole to hold across to the other side for support. Or with a rope hanging down that I could hold on to. How about you, Dragon Talker?"

The man reads my mind. "I would be afraid to fall off steps like these. Perhaps it takes some getting used to. Your idea of a pole or a rope could work. I can see coming up by leaning forward to hold onto the steps above. Perhaps going down on a rope would be easier."

Lars pointed up at her. "I like that. Down on a rope. Crawl up the steps. Maybe we'll find clues further down."

"Are you going to make boards for the other broken steps?"

"If the other stones come out like this one, it would be worth it. As long as they don't make our job more difficult."

As a final solution for hauling bigger pieces of stone out with greater ease, which might drag along the well wall as they were brought up, Lars tied a short piece of wood to one end of each new wooden step. By inserting the shorter pieces into the step holes of the well wall, the longer steps hung down along the wall, out of the way of the loads being brought up in the cowhide bundle. This way, they could select which steps to move out of the way as needed.

Going down on a rope and coming back up by the wooden steps turned out to be most efficient. It was faster than by the ladder which they would have had to lengthen and reposition before and after bringing each load out.

...

In the month off Gabe had given Lars, their work took on a new rhythm, paced and efficient. Lars made the most of his month at the work site. Nagora uncovered the first spout. About time! "Surely we're closer to the bottom!" she said as she pointed to it.

Lars stared at the spout. His mind's working at making sense of what he's seeing, trying to piece together the big picture with what he already knows. Nagora nudged him. "What're you thinking?"

"Gold can't run out this spout. It wouldn't stay molten long enough to cover the distance from the hatching ring. At least I don't see how it could."

"It's not our problem, is it, Lars?"

"Still, I would like to know."

"Maybe we'll find out when we reach the bottom."

Lars nodded and wiped his brow.

Then, below the spouts, the well wall sweated water in small trickles. "We've reached the veins, Lars."

"So deep. I wondered when we would find them."

"How much further down do we have to go?"

Lars reached down to his feet and took hold of the rope they had come down on. He lifted the rope until his hand was well over his head. Lars pointed to the knot in the rope next to his boot. "I tied that knot at the floor level of the cave entrance. This could be how far down we have yet to go."

"So we're close. If all goes well, tomorrow we could be at the bottom!"

Lars smiled at Nagora. "I sure hope so." He put an arm around her shoulders. "The sooner I can get you in position to call the Little People, the happier I'll be. We'll need all the help we can get." Lars placed a hand on her belly. "I want our child to have a strong mother, not a stone-hauling, haggard wench."

Nagora gave Lars a jab in the stomach. "I want our child to have a strong da, not a stone-hauling husband, complaining of a sore back."

"Well, good then. Let's get to the bottom of this well." Lars slapped her backside.

Nagora shook a finger at Lars and winked at him. "If you play games like that, we'll not get much done today."

They hugged and then got back to work. Before long, they were again digging into the debris which had long ago spilled over into the cave.

Lars dug on the opposite side of the spill. "Looks like the cave continues on this side. It'll be two more days to get to the bottom and clear both sides. It feels good to know we've made it this far."

The next day, after lowering a wheelbarrow, they brought Alizarine down with them.

Near the end of the afternoon, Lars kicked the toe of his boot into the dwindling debris pile. "Tomorrow morning, we'll be done cleaning this out. Have you figured out how you'll call the Little People?"

Nagora pointed to the well wall behind Lars. "Since sweeping that wall clean, the water trickle has turned into an almost steady flow down the surface. It no longer has dirt and muck to fight through."

Nagora moved past Lars, pulled the skystone blade from its sheath, and bent down on one knee on the metal crosswalk.

She held it broadside against one of the metal bars of the grate so that the steady trickle fell against the blue metal of the blade. "I'll tie the coin to the crossguard like I did the first time I called them and then lash my blade in this position. The flow of the water will hit the coin, making it dance and ring out its calling song on the blade."

Lars frowned. "Simple as that?"

Nagora smiled up at him. "Simple as that. Then I must wait for them to come. I don't know how long it'll take. But I'm sure they'll come."

"Will you have to wait for them here?"

"Not this time. I'm sure they'll let me know of their arrival."

Lars sighed. "Okay. Once your blade's in place, do we explore the cave on that side?"

"Can you wait until tomorrow?"

Lars nodded. "We've put in a good day already. We'll bring tapers tomorrow and ropes to measure distances. We won't feel rushed."

Nagora put her blade away and walked over to Alizarine. "Okay, Alizarine. Come. Lars will carry you up on his back."

"Can I keep these stones?"

"Show me. Hmm. You found them in the pile there?"

"Yes."

"Those little golden drops are pretty, aren't they? Do you want me to carry them up for you, or are you going to put them in your basket?" asked Nagora.

"In my basket."

"Good. Let's go." Lars went down on one knee, and Nagora helped Alizarine climb up on his back. "That's it. Basket on the left arm. Let it hang there. It'll be fine if you hold on to his shirt with both hands. Don't let go until we're out and Lars sets you down next to Aydan."

"Holding tight?" asked Lars.

"Yes."

"Up we go, Alizarine," said Lars.

"I'll be right behind you two," said Nagora.

The next day, Lars lit the two tapers. He gave one to Nagora. They stopped on the middle of the hammered metal crosswalk that spanned the grate-covered well beneath their feet. Nagora lowered her taper toward the grate at the side of the crosswalk. "See, Alizarine, the water is making the coin dance on the big blade. The sound of the coin dancing on the blade will bring someone to help us rebuild the maze. The coin is made of gold, just like the small gold stones you found yesterday. If you keep your eyes open and watch where you step, perhaps you'll find more on this side of the cave today."

Alizarine held on to Nagora's hand as they moved on. The cave was round, like the section with the spiral drawings on the seaward side of the well. No water flowed on the floor of the cave on this side.

Perhaps we're on a slight incline.

So far, Nagora hadn't spotted a drawing anywhere on the walls. She asked Lars, "Do you think the drawings in the other section were meant for the dragons? I haven't seen a single drawing yet on this side."

Lars stopped and turned once, holding his taper as high as he could. "It could be. Perhaps the dragons didn't come on this side." Lars pointed to the flame on his taper. "See that? It's moving in the direction we're headed, not back toward the well shaft. There's a definite draft here."

Nagora pointed up. "So there must be another opening to the ground above."

Lars shrugged. "Hmm. If so, will we find it?"

Ahead in the distance, the cave appeared to end.

As they got closer, a drawing appeared on the wall ahead of them. It was of a dragon standing with its wings spread. Its head was in profile, looking to its right, with a stream of flames coming from its mouth and nostrils. Its big ball-tipped tail curled around one of its legs and seemed to point left.

Alizarine pulled on Nagora's hand. "Which way will we go?"

Alizarine's has a point. The cave splits off in the two directions the dragon seems to show.

Lars stopped and held out an arm. "What do you make of the drawing? Directions, or a warning?"

"I say directions. Let's go toward the flame's flicker."

They stopped in front of the drawing. Lars slowly moved his taper across it.

"Wow! Lars! The colors and details of the scales! So realistic! Almost like Danuka is before us. The drawings in the other section are all done in black and shades of gray. This one glows in iridescent tones of red and blue, like the colors on Danuka whenever the day's rising or setting sun shines on her."

The single eye looked directly inside of Nagora, as only Danuka could. It makes me feel weak and vulnerable, just like when Danuka looks at me, like she can see inside me and read my every thought. Though I have no proof of that, other than the decision I made after the first time Danuka looked at me that way. I surrendered to her, accepted she had powers beyond anything I could ever imagine possessing. When I did that, I knew I was on my way to becoming a Dragon Talker.

They headed in the direction the dragon's flames pointed.

Twenty-five paces later, the cave passage opened onto a vaulted, rectangular chamber with terraced levels on one of its walls. Many staircases climbed from one terrace to the next. Equipment covered each level. I recognize many of these pieces—the bellows, the anvils, the pulleys, the chains, and some of the other tools. They're all in miniature size, as are the staircases. And I have no clue what certain pieces of the equipment are. "Lars, I'm guessing it's a forge. Everything is the size the Little People could use."

Lars looked around the chamber and then approached the terraced area with his taper extended so he could reach it under the stone projection where the bellows lined up. The taper's flame roared to life as it got sucked upward. Lars moved the taper to the right. Its flame settled for a moment until he reached the next bellows, where again it roared to life.

"You're right Nagora. These are forges." Lars said as he pointed and counted. "Twelve of them. Their vent hoods must all connect to the same chimney."

Alizarine had let go of Nagora's hand and was kneeling next to her basket near the first terrace. She straightened up, turned to Nagora, and held up her finger. "Look."

Nagora bent to examine the fingertip. It sparkled with gold dust.

Then Alizarine turned her hand and opened her palm so Nagora could see what it held. Seven or eight little clusters of gold, smaller than the ones Alizarine had found the day before.

"Come see what Alizarine found."

Lars bent to see. "You have a good eye, Alizarine. Are you going to put them in the pouch you brought?"

Alizarine smiled and nodded before reaching for the small leather pouch which hung from her waist.

Nagora removed the candle lantern she had tied to her belt. She lit it and set it on the floor near Alizarine. "Be careful when you move it."

Lars headed for the wall to the right of the chamber entrance.

He was looking at the patchwork of shelves, all of which had ladders of different lengths leading up to them from the floor. He reached out and took something from a shelf.

"Look at this." He placed it in Nagora's hand.

It was a gold coin, the size of the one she had tied to the crossguard of her skystone blade. A dragon, like the one they had just seen on the cave wall, was struck on one side of the coin. The other side was blank.

"Strange, isn't it?"

Nagora didn't understand Lars's comment. "How so?"

"When a coin is struck, both sides usually get struck at once. That one has a blank side."

Nagora turned the coin over in her hand. "Yes. I guess that's strange. Why would that be? Are there others?"

"I haven't checked all the shelves. This is the only one I've spotted so far."

Nagora followed him back to the shelves to search for more coins. She recalled what Geirador had told her about coin making. "Maybe it was a test strike. To see if the image on the punch made a satisfactory likeness on the coin. Or a test of the block that held the dragon image. It looks like a hammer struck the blank side of the coin."

Nagora pointed to the other side of the shelving unit. "You start on that side. We'll check them all. Look for metal blocks and punches too."

All of her shelves were empty except for a coat of dust.

"Nothing." Lars stepped back and scratched his head.

"On what shelf did you find it?" asked Nagora.

Lars pointed to the small shelf in the middle of all the other bigger ones. "I could just get my hand into the shelf recess to pick it up. Take a peek. You can still see the mark in the dust where it lay."

The shelf was at the height of Nagora's chest. Nagora held her taper closer as she peered in. She stepped back to eye the shelves on either side of the small one. Then she stood on tiptoe to gaze into the recesses above. She bent to the ones below.

Nagora stepped back. "Alizarine. Can you bring your candle lantern here, please? I need it for just a moment. Then I'll give it back to you."

Alizarine stood up and shuffled over with her basket on one arm and the lantern in her other hand.

Nagora handed her taper to Lars. "Can you hold both of them up just over my right shoulder?" Nagora took the candle lantern and held it next to the small shelf hole before bringing her eye next to it to peek inside.

Lars held the tapers as Nagora had asked. "Well?"

Nagora held up a finger from her free hand, stepped back, and gave the lantern to Alizarine. "Thank you, Alizarine. You can go back to your search."

As soon as Alizarine turned away, Nagora placed a finger to her lips and held out her other hand for her taper, all the while keeping an eye on Alizarine. Once she was back on her knees searching along the terrace ledge, Nagora motioned to Lars to bend his ear to her.

"I think the Little People left the coin here to be found."

Lars moved his head back with a question on his face. His lips mouthed the word: "Explain." Then he bent to Nagora's lips again.

"It's the smallest shelf hole. The coin is easy for us to spot. What's not visible is how deep the space inside is. It's much deeper than all the other shelves around it. And at the back, I can see a handle."

Lars stepped back. His jaw had dropped and his eyes were blinking. He went back to the shelf hole and tried to reach in. "My arm's too big. I can barely get my forearm in. You try."

Nagora reached in. She was almost shoulder deep by the time her fingers wrapped around the T-shaped metal handle. She had two fingers wrapped on each side. The handle was in a horizontal position and cool to the touch.

Lars stared at her. "And?"

Nagora nodded. "I have it."

He nodded back and motioned for her to turn it.

She hesitated and withdrew her hand.

Lars made a confused face at her.

Nagora held up a finger and then pulled a small knife blade from the side strap holster under her left arm. "Come."

Lars seemed to be more confused.

Nagora stood at the left side of the shelving unit. She held the taper high and then brought it down along the wall where the side of the unit rested.

Next she ran the tip of the small blade down the corner junction. Dust and flecks of dirt flew out the path the blade plowed. Nagora bent onto one knee. She pointed to the bottom of the wooden shelf upright. It appeared to rest on the floor, but she could slip the small knife under it. Lars was blinking his eyes again as Nagora stood to make her way to the other end of the shelves. Nagora repeated the procedure and then pulled Lars closer. "Now do you see what I see?"

Lars nodded. "The shelf unit is a door."

"Do you see how it'll open?"

"Pivot at the middle where the handle is."

Nagora's eyes shot to Alizarine, then she whispered, "Do we open it now or come back without her?"

Lars stepped back and bit his lip before leaning toward Nagora to answer in a hushed tone. "I won't let you open it alone. We'll have to come back. Unless we can find something to distract her in the other part of the cave."

Nagora nodded and spoke her question aloud. "Shall we all go have a look now?"

"Yes, let's go see what's over there," said Lars.

"Alizarine, we're going to see what's in the other part of the cave. Do you want to stay here or come with us?"

Alizarine stood up with her basket and pointed to her pouch.

Nagora reached down to lift the pouch. "My! Alizarine! You seem to have found many gold specks."

Alizarine smiled, held up a finger, and made a digging motion with it. "They're all in the crack at the bottom of the step." Then she reached for Nagora's hand. Nagora bent to pick up the candle lantern.

...

As they passed the dragon drawing, the eye followed Nagora. *Whoever drew this has my admiration. They knew what they were doing. The result is so lifelike.*

Here too they found a vaulted, rectangular chamber. Nagora cast her eyes about, taking in the fleet of shallow, low-lying wooden wagons, about the length of her arm and as wide as the length of her forearm, set onto small metal wheels. She stepped closer and bent down to examine one of them. The wagon had two sets of wheels. There were twelve small wheels in all, six at each end of the wagon, on fixed undercarriages. The front undercarriage of wheels pivoted left or right, allowing the wagon to turn.

Lars reached into a wagon and held up a set of small leather harnesses fastened to the pivoting undercarriage. He bent over as he brought the harness in front of the wagon to pull it.

"I want to get on! I want to get on!" Alizarine cried.

Lars stopped. "First, let me check the wheels to make sure they're fastened well." He tilted the wagon on its side and gave all the wheels a quick spin. "Everything looks solid. Come, Alizarine. Set your basket here in front. Sit with your legs around it. I'll take you for a ride."

Nagora put her candle lantern on a wagon and took the taper Lars handed her.

With a candle lantern in one hand, Lars led the wagon toward the forge chamber with a happy passenger onboard.

While they played, Nagora investigated. One wagon had what she could only describe as eight stone boats or barges sitting in it. They appeared to all be the same size, even though they differed in color.

Nagora picked one up with her free hand. It was heavy. So many of them, and in several colors. This stone must be granite. She turned it over. Its rectangular bottom corners and edges were rounded and polished. Nagora set the stone boat down in the wagon. She went down on one knee to examine that side of it. The whole surface of the boat had a concave shape that gave way to a deeper recessed area in the center that resembled one half of an empty eggshell. She ran her fingers inside it. It too was polished smooth.

Nagora tilted the stone on its side to examine it further. She turned it over from one side to another and from one end to the other. Each top edge curved inward on a tilting plain that ran to the edge of the recessed egg shape at the center.

Nagora wiped the dust from the neighboring boat to examine it. Other than the difference in the color of the granite, its shape was the same as the first one.

They're all the same shape.

Knee-high wooden shelves with separators lined the far wall of the chamber to her left. Nagora stepped closer. Each of the cubicles housed a stone boat. Too many to count. I'm guessing close to a hundred stone boats lined up across the three shelf levels.

Alizarine's giggles signaled her return as Lars pulled her into the chamber atop the wagon.

"Sounds like you had fun!" said Nagora.

Alizarine lifted a leg over her basket and turned on her behind to bring both legs over the wagon's side. She looked up at Lars. "Thank you, Lars."

Nagora handed her taper to Lars. She pointed back across the room to where the candle lantern sat in the wagon, next to the one with the stone boats. "One wagon over there has eight of these on it," she told Lars as she walked over to the shelves, bent, and pulled a stone boat out from its cubicle. She blew dust from it and wiped it down with her sleeve, then walked back, setting it in the wagon next to Alizarine's basket.

"What's that?" asked Alizarine.

"I don't truly know." Nagora pointed along the shelves. "There are many of them here. They all seem to have the same shape, but they're not all the same color.

"What do you think they might be used for, Alizarine?"

Alizarine bent over and picked it up. "It's heavy and it's smooth. I like the color." Alizarine set it down and ran her fingers over the top surface.

Then she looked up at Nagora. "I know what I could use it for."

"Oh you do? What would you use it for, Alizarine?"

Alizarine reached over into her basket and peeled away the sheepskin and the red silk scarf that covered her egg. With both hands and great care, she pulled it out and set it on the stone boat. "That's what I would use it for. See? My beautiful egg stays put and doesn't roll away."

Lars's eyes were round as apples as he looked at Nagora.

Nagora smiled. We're thinking the same thing.

He and Nagora looked back at the egg. It protruded from each side of the stone boat. The egg was beautiful sitting there. The boat had truly been made to support the egg.

Lars was smiling at Nagora again. Yes! We've found another piece of the puzzle.

Nagora returned to the shelves and picked up another boat, holding it up with both hands. The bottom's curved edges rested in her palms and her fingers held the two long sides. "On our way back up, we should be able to confirm if it fits in the spout."

Lars held out Nagora's taper. "Looks like it'll fit."

Nagora shifted the boat to one hand, took her taper, and handed the boat to Lars.

He looked at it with care, nodding as he turned it over to stare at the bottom. "This would make more sense." Lars set it down in the wagon, next to the one with the egg.

Alizarine moved her egg onto the reddish stone Lars had just set down. "I think I like this one better. Can I bring it back with me? Can I bring a wagon back too?"

Nagora bent to one knee. "You see the small wheels, Alizarine? They roll and spin well here on the stone floor. If you bring a wagon up, it won't have a hard surface like this to roll on. It'll always be getting stuck by the uneven ground and stones. You won't be able to pull it anywhere."

Alizarine's down-turned lips showed her disappointment.

"Tell you what, Alizarine. You seem to like how your egg sits on the stone without rolling away. Why don't you choose two to bring up with you? You could have one for the loft and one for near the fireplace, where you like to play."

Alizarine's smile returned.

"If we set three candle lanterns here on the top shelf, you could use the wagon to move along the cubicles to choose the two you want to bring back. There are many colors to choose from. While you are choosing, Lars and I will go back to the other room to look at the forge tools. Will that be okay with you?"

Alizarine was looking along the length of shelves. "I can choose two? Any two I want?"

"Any two you want. We won't be gone long. When we come back, we'll give you another ride in the wagon, all the way back to the well."

Alizarine set her basket down on the floor and moved the wagon closer to the shelves.

Lars lit two more candle lanterns while Nagora went to retrieve the one on the other side of the room.

"Can I put a lantern in the wagon?" asked Alizarine.

"Yes, you can. Just don't pull the wagon fast," said Nagora.

Back in the forge room at the wall of shelves, Nagora reached in and took hold of the handle. Lars's eyes were on hers. She gritted her teeth as she tried to turn the handle first one way, then the other. "It won't budge." She pulled her arm out.

"Stuck? Let me try," said Lars.

"Even if you cut away the shelf sides, you won't be able to get your hand in deep enough into the stone hole," said Nagora.

Lars moved aside. "Grab the handle and pull on it instead of turning it."

Nagora reached back in, took hold of the handle, and pulled with all her might. Just as she was about to give up, the handle moved back with a thunk.

"It moved?" asked Lars.

Nagora nodded.

"Try turning it now."

"That's what I'm doing."

"Both ways?"

"Yes, to the left and to the right, but nothing's happening."

"Try moving it up and down."

Nagora's eyes widened. "It's moving, but not much. It's moving more side to side." Nagora pushed it back in, pulled it out, and when she tried to turn it, it did. Metal slapped against metal. "You hear that?" Nagora pulled her hand out.

Lars had stepped back and was looking at the wall of shelves.

"What side do we push on?"

Lars pointed to his right as he stepped in that direction.

Nagora was right beside him. "I turned the handle, you push it open."

Lars placed the heel of his hand against the wooden upright of the shelves at that end. He leaned against it and pushed with his legs. The wall of shelves pivoted, and then Lars took tentative steps with his hand on the upright.

Nagora followed right behind him with her taper held high.

Lars held out an arm to stop her from going any further.

"What's wrong?"

"Do you smell that?"

Nagora sniffed and breathed in deep. "Coal?"

"That's right. Let's just back out and close the door. I don't want to take a chance of setting the coal dust on fire with our tapers. We need a candle lantern."

As they backed out, Nagora did her best to see into the room. In the corner nearest them, she could make out a big pile of coal. The other corner held a huge pile of small burlap sacks. One would fit in my hand.

Once they were back in the forge room and Lars had pushed the pivoting door shut, he looked at Nagora. "It's a coal room to store the fuel they use for the forges. Like Geirador has in Cairnmase. But his is open to the outdoors."

Nagora nodded. "Aye, and it's in a stall of its own away from any sparks or flames. He carries in a bucket or two as needed."

Nagora pointed down the length of the terrace, at the fire pits lined up with the bellows. "At least they seem to know what they're doing down here. I think Geirador would be impressed by their set-up."

"Do you think there's anything else to find in there?"

Lars scratched his chin. "Perhaps there's a mine shaft that leads to coal. Other than that, I can't see what else they would keep in there."

"Shall I lock the door?"

"Sure. We'll head back."

Alizarine was humming and pulling a wagon around the room. Her basket sat at the back of the wagon bed, followed by her egg on a stone boat and a candle lantern on another one. She came toward them as they entered the room. "I chose two."

"Show us, Alizarine," said Nagora.

The girl stopped and set the leather harnesses in the wagon beside the stone boats. Next, she spread open the sheepskin and transferred her egg back into the basket before setting the candle lantern aside.

Alizarine picked up a dark red and black boat. Red was the dominant color, and black created the stone's irregular background pattern. "This one I like a lot. I want it to be next to my bed."

"Its colors are unique," said Nagora.

"You hold it."

Nagora took the stone and Alizarine turned to lift her other choice from the wagon. Most of the stone was dark green on one side and a faded lighter green on the other. "Alizarine, you've chosen well. The colors are beautiful."

Alizarine gave it to Lars. "Hold it. I'll get ready." She set the candle lantern on the floor, moved her basket to the front of the wagon, and then climbed onto the back of it before sitting down. Alizarine spread her legs. "You can put them here."

They set the stone boats between Alizarine's legs, and then Lars collected the lanterns and set them on another wagon. "Might as well make our trip back lighter." He handed the leather harnesses to Nagora. "Are you ready, Alizarine?"

"Ready."

At the well, Nagora helped Alizarine onto Lars's back. "We stop for a rest at the spouts."

"Okay. Hang on tight, Alizarine," said Lars.

Nagora pulled the stone boat from her scrip and slid it into the spout, narrow side first, as far as she could. She let go of it and pulled her hand back. Almost as fast, the stone came sliding back. "Perfect fit! We guessed right. The boat slides down the spout. That means above in the hatching ring, eggs with gold veins sit on the boats. When the eggs hatch, the gold veins melt. The gold collects in the boat's depression, cools, and is ready to be sent down the spout. If the boat's journey ends here, we have to see where in the inner circle it starts up top."

"It'll be awhile before we can figure that part out."

Nagora pointed to the small holes in the well wall between the spouts. "I bet pintles go in those holes, holding up a net to catch the boats as they come sliding out."

"Could be."

Nagora put the stone away. "Ready to continue up."

"Hang on, Alizarine," said Lars.

Going Home
Kîwewin

† NOW: *in the fifteenth year of
rebuilding the maze in the Land of Skulls*

Alizarine awoke with a start. Even if Nagora still held her in
her arms, her frightened eyes, once again, looked from
Nagora's face to the skies above the inner circle of stone pillars. Alizarine pushed herself up on Nagora's lap to see the
sky above the stone lintels that topped the pillars of the inner
circle on that side. "You fell asleep after that terrible fright
you had."

"The shadow didn't come back?"

"No, it didn't. The sky's been clear since you fell asleep.
Do you think we can head for home now? I'll hold your hand
all the way and keep my bow and an arrow ready in my other
hand."

Alizarine swallowed as she listened to Nagora and wiped
at her nose. "Okay. Hold my hand."

Nagora took Alizarine's hand in hers and helped her stand.
Then she stood up and stretched before bending to pick up her

quiver and bow. As she bent, she looked into the well. "Are you thirsty, Alizarine? Do you want to drink before we go?"

"No. I have to pee."

"Me too. How about we wait until we're in the maze path. Not even a bird will see us."

Nagora and Alizarine headed for the inner maze gate that would take them out.

"I'm afraid." Alizarine's hand trembled in Nagora's as she spoke the words. They were standing on the edge of the outer maze path. One more step and they would be out.

"Let go of my hand for a moment, Alizarine, so I can nock an arrow on my bow. Then we'll head for home."

Alizarine grabbed hold of Nagora's leg.

Nagora held her bow in her left hand and nocked the arrow. "You must hold my right hand if you want me to be ready to shoot fast."

Alizarine reached for Nagora's hand and peered out of the maze toward the sea and then to the sky.

"Let's go. We'll stay close to the wall. If the shadow comes, you'll hug the wall and I'll cover you." Nagora didn't hurry Alizarine along. Instead, she let her stumble, twist, and turn so she could keep her eyes on the sky.

When they had reached a quarter of the way along the wall, Nagora stopped and pointed. "Over there, Alizarine. See our lodge, up on the other side of the valley? We're almost at the trail down to the stream. Soon as we get past the open area, we'll be in the trees. You'll be safe. Are you ready to go? Do you want to run with me a ways?"

Alizarine held on tighter. "Walk."

They stood on the path beneath the branches of a willow tree, about twenty paces from the bridge. "We'll cross the bridge and go up through the trees until we get to the field. We'll whistle for Arm and Hand. They'll race down to us in no time and greet us with happy barks. Then they'll escort us home as we climb the grassy hill. You'll be safe there."

Nagora closed both the outside winter door and the inside summer door of the lodge. Then she lifted the lock beam onto its supports on each side of the door frame. "How's that, Alizarine? We'll let the dogs sleep inside tonight. You must be hungry. I am."

Nagora bent to pet their two wolfhounds. "You two bad boys. Did you behave yourselves today? Aye, I know. You wish you were with Lars and Dannor on the hunt, don't you?"

The dogs whined and pranced as soon as Nagora mentioned the names of her men and the word "hunt," just like their old faithful hounds, Aydan and Lyam, used to. Age had taken its toll on their health; and so Lars brought the hounds to live out their final days with Black Jack, the charcoal maker and lumberyard guard outside of Skull Bay.

Since Lars and Dannor had gone for several days to hunt deer, they left Arm and Hand with Nagora. Every time she heard their names, she had to smile.

When Lars had brought the wolfhound pups home and they played with Dannor, the same hound would always grab his hand with its mouth, and the other would always take hold of his arm. Dannor took to calling them Arm and Hand, and to Nagora's surprise, they responded to those names. The names stuck. That was what, four years ago already?

...

The next morning, Nagora completed the last of her exercises. She had used a combat staff for the fast series of one hundred repetitions of the motions which had become a part of her, no matter the weapon she used for the exercise. Now she stood with her feet spread the width of her shoulders, both hands almost at shoulder height on the staff, and her right cheek resting against its smooth hardwood surface.

Nagora caught her breath. The sea's gentle rollers seemed to come from over the horizon. This was her chosen exercise spot on the cliff above, beyond, and out of sight of the stone bluff where their lodge sat. Her son, Dannor, had adopted it too after asking her to teach him the exercises, but not until he was ready.

My Son
Nikosis

† THEN: *in the twelfth year of*
rebuilding the maze in the Land of Skulls

Dannor's decision to ask her to teach him the exercises was one of the things that had contributed to helping him over that awkward period; just like they helped her when she had asked her uncle, Dangor, to teach her. And, like it had with her uncle, her relationship with Dannor became stronger.

Nagora had been patient, never suggesting or speaking to him about the exercises unless he asked. She had waited for him to decide. Her uncle's lesson on teaching was not lost on her. To her, his words were gold: "Teaching someone who wants to learn is easy. Teaching someone who doesn't want to learn is a waste of time. Give me those that want to learn and I'll teach them for free. Give me the others and you'll owe me a hefty bag of coins."

But before Dannor asked to be taught the exercises, he had changed. It happened on the day her son brought a friend into the maze with him. Was it not being able to find his way out this time when he wanted to? Or that he had disobeyed

Nagora's specific order of no friends in the maze—ever? Or both? Or was it something else? She had kept the dogs from going in to find the lads and had a good mind to let the boys spend the night there, but Dannor finally led his friend out just before sunset. Panic was still evident on their faces.

The next day when Dannor had returned from accompanying his friend back to Skull Bay, he hurled a string of accusations at her. That he had done so in Lars's presence surprised her. Nagora had bit her lip and held back her tears through it all. That her own son used rumor-fed lies about her past, most likely spoken by signers still fearing twins, had shaken her. She had warned him about this, but that day it was as if he willfully ignored her warnings. Could she blame him? Perhaps her just being in the Land of Skulls was the reason he couldn't keep friends. Signers were obviously working their lies in the background, insinuating every imaginable evil she and even Lars, as twins, could possibly bear.

Lars had kept calm throughout Dannor's tirade, although the set of his jaw told Nagora he was angry. When Dannor finished, Lars pointed to the door and said, "Go saddle my horse and yours." As soon as their boy left, Lars took Nagora in his arms. "You're going to have to tell him all, everything. Answer all his questions. Keep nothing from him. I know it hurts you to talk of some of those things, but it will be good for both of you if you do. He's almost twelve, old enough, but first he needs a change of scene and some time to think on what he's said and why. I'll be back in two days, but Dannor most likely won't. Trust me." Before leaving, Lars had placed a finger on her lips to silence her protest.

...

Two days later, when Lars returned, Nagora had to ask. "Where is Dannor? What have you done with him?"

He looked at her with that grin she loved so much, though that day it didn't win her over. "Well, we first went to talk to two skulls on Edana's Victory Bridge to get their silent version of events as told by me as I witnessed them. Then we rode back to Skull Bay. By chance, a Moroes Island whaler was in port, docked for supplies and fresh water. Since Dannor was able to pull their bladder bow, they took him on to be their masthead archer."

Nagora's jaw had dropped at those words. From all the stories Lars had told about his life on a whaling boat, one of the most perilous jobs was that of the masthead archer. Pulling that bow, with its heavy barbed arrow tied with twine to a coil of rope with a big sealskin air bladder attached to the other end of the rope, in just about every possible sea condition, was risky to say the least. A whaler under sail, pitching on the waves and chasing a whale, relied on its archer to pin the bladder to the whale so they could more easily follow it when it swam below the surface. And the more bladders pinned to it, the sooner they could tire it out and get closer to throw their harpoons. "Lars, this can't be so."

"Nagora, I did it when I was his age. Our lad is strong. His character needs to be tested in another element beyond lifting stones to build this maze and disobeying us. He'll make new friends, learn what it is to pull his weight as a crew member, and earn some coins. He'll get an extra coin for every bladder pinned."

She controlled the fury she wanted to unleash on him. "Why didn't you ask me?"

His grin grew wider. "You would've said no. No need to ask to get that answer. The choice was his. I didn't force Dannor to go. It was an opportunity, and he took it. I'm glad he did, and in time so will you."

"How long will he be gone?"

"A month, two at the most."

"Do you know the people Dannor will be with?"

"Aye, the skipper and a few of the crew. Good people. The captain only takes on the best."

"Until my son returns, you sleep in the stable."

Two nights later, she joined him in the stable hayloft. "Reassure me Dannor will be alright."

At twilight, they walked arm in arm through the dew-coated grass to their lodge.

Just over two months later, summer's end arrived, and brought Dannor home. To Nagora, it was as if another man had just stepped into her life. Dannor was taller, leaner, and stronger. His hair was longer and sun-streaked, and the skin on his face and hands had darkened to a burnished copper. Even his voice had changed, deepening. His movements in the lodge now were calm and unhurried.

Dannor brought gifts: four pairs of sealskin boots he had made, thanks to a new skill a crew member had taught him; a skin of whale oil; and a stone lamp to burn it. He set two leather pouches of coins on the table.

Pointing to the bigger one first, he said, "For the extra bladders my arrows pinned to the whales we hunted," then, pointing to the other, "My wages. Skipper said he would be glad to have me on again next year, but to start earlier. I told him I had work waiting for me. It doesn't pay the same wages, but it's important work, and I love the people I work with."

And when he held Nagora in his arms, he said, "I've missed you, Mum." Dannor's words had melted Nagora's heart that day.

Lars had been right—telling all to Dannor and answering all his questions, turned out to be good for both of them. Now Nagora had another partner in her enterprise who wanted to understand every aspect of what she was doing and why.

Taken Away
Sipwehtahaw

✝ NOW: *in the fifteenth year of*
rebuilding the maze in the Land of Skulls

As Nagora stood on the cliff, still facing into the morning sea breeze, her thoughts remained on how her son was changing. Since Dannor's return from his time on the whaler and whenever he returns from a hunt with his father, he continues to change for the better. He is more confident, more thoughtful in his decisions, more considerate to everyone around him, even the animals, and he takes pride in doing his chores well. He is becoming more and more like his father. He even walks, stands, and sits like Lars.

I can't get over how my son takes in situations. Dannor's always on the lookout for what he can do to help. Without being asked, he jumps right in and lends a hand. In the last two years, he's grown taller than me. His clumsiness is gone as he continues to grow in strength and grace.

Dannor, I'm proud of the man you're becoming. Proud you honor the namesake of Uncle Dangor and Norbul, your da's lost twin. You don't know what that means to him.

Lars had told her he liked the name they had chosen for their son. In the language of the Moroes Islanders where he was raised after being banished from the Land of Skulls, Dannor meant "gifted." *When you were born, your da's proud face told me you were his most precious gift. Every day, you continue to be more and more precious to me too.*

Nagora filled her lungs with the sea breeze and, out of habit, was going to talk to Arm and Hand. They usually followed her here to watch her do her exercises. Today she had left them with Alizarine, who was still asleep when she left. Once again the ageless witch child she had been cursed to mother pushed away her happy thoughts of the moment.

When will I be delivered?

After one last, long gaze out over the waves, she filled her lungs with a last breath of fresh, salty air before heading back.

Nagora came around the corner of their lodge. The outer winter door was resting against the stone wall.

That shouldn't be. I know I closed it.

The closer she got to the doorway, the greater her sense of urgency grew. The inner door was open. Nagora froze as she tried to comprehend what her eyes were seeing. Arm and Hand were lying on their sides, facing each other, their heads in a pool of blood on the lodge's packed dirt floor.

Nagora forced herself to step across the threshold. Her eyes searched for something. *What?* Something that would tell her the beloved dogs were not dead. Had not been killed.

Nagora knelt and touched their heads; turning her face away, she wiped her tears. Their throats had been slit.

Alizarine? No. She couldn't have done this. Or could she? Witch!

Nagora spat out the last word between clenched teeth.

"Alizarine! Alizarine! Where are you, Alizarine?"

No answer came. Nagora stood and climbed to the loft and then to the small lookout room.

"Alizarine!"

Where is she?

Nagora climbed back down, did a last quick inspection, and then stepped outside.

"Alizarine! Alizarine!"

Nagora's eyes searched across the fields into the valley and up on the other side, toward the maze.

Where did you go?

Wait! It has to be!

You've been taken!

Calm down. Put the pieces together. What do you know?

Something had frightened Alizarine the day before.

Would she go anywhere on her own today?

Where? To the maze? Not across that open space.

The dogs are dead. If not by her hand, whose?

I can't picture her killing the dogs. Alizarine doesn't have the strength, not even to slit one's throat. The other dog would have come to its defense. There's no sign of struggle.

I didn't hear barking. They even bark when Lars returns, or Dannor. The hounds sense them before I do. Why didn't they bark?

Nothing is missing from the lodge.

There had to be two of them to dispatch the dogs that way. Why did the dogs let them approach? Who would they let approach without barking?

Alizarine said she saw a shadow in the sky and it looked at her.

Nagora's eyes jumped to the sky and then fell to the ground at her feet. She meandered toward the stable and its corral, her eyes making a sweep of the still dew-covered rye grass of the pasture before her.

Footprints! Ankle deep in the grass.

And then halfway to the stable, a large splayed-out patch of grass lay in a depression before her. Just beyond it was a telltale sign, a single narrow band of grass raked toward the lodge, leading to the depression where something heavy had weighed down the grass.

Nagora took her time. I need one more sign. No, two the same. Nagora almost stepped into the first one. She paused long enough to scan ahead. The other must be over there.

Sure enough, it was. Nagora marched over to it, bent on one knee, and spread the blades of grass away from around it before feeling inside it with her fingers. Without knowing what it was, someone stumbling across these indentations would not likely understand what had caused them.

But I know. Danuka's left wing talon put down here when she landed. The impression of her right wing talon is back there. Nagora brought her fingers to her nose. I can smell it. It was faint, yet unmistakable to her, the essence of Danuka.

Early on in those months Nagora spent in the cave with her dragon, she had called it the Dragon's Kiss. From her beginning as a Dragon Talker apprentice, that intoxicating, indescribable odor enticed, overpowered, and controlled her almost every night.

Nagora stood with her eyes still on the indentation. Danuka, you have come for your egg. Mother, who rode you here? Da and Sarah? They don't know what they've gotten themselves into. Danuka, do you? Why did they not seek me out first? Why kill the dogs?

For a moment, her eyes saw black. Don't imagine what you have no proof of. Don't make Sarah the killer of the dogs. She has no reason to. It's been fifteen years, daughter, since I last saw you, and here I am making up stories of evil deeds about you. I, who had to abandon you. How can I even think such thoughts about you? May I never do this to your face. You would never forgive me, and rightfully so.

Nagora forced back her tears and turned to face the lodge. The gentle sea breeze swept down the slope, over their home and across her face. Mother, you landed downwind. One reason the dogs didn't bark.

Nagora returned to the wolfhounds. I don't want Lars and Dannor to see you like this. I'll move you, one at a time. Then I'll bury you.

Nagora climbed to the loft and pulled the checkered sheepskin blanket from Alizarine's bed.

Nagora rolled Hand onto the hide side of the blanket, tied two corners over his hind legs, and picked up the other end to pull him outside. I'll bury you at your spot.

Her dogs would often lie down on the grassy knoll, about three hundred paces from the valley trees, waiting for Nagora to return, probably because from there they had a view of part of the maze wall and the stream bridge.

Nagora untied the blanket and rolled Hand over onto the grass.

"I'll get your brother. You ran side by side all your short lives. You died side by side. I'll bury you that way too." She wiped away tears.

Once she had finished digging the grave, she sat between them, combing the fur of their shaggy coats with her fingers.

Nagora lined the hole with the checkered sheepskin blanket and pulled her hounds into the hole to lay them to rest on the blanket. Before covering them with Alizarine's embroidered woolen blanket, Nagora arranged the dogs so they faced each other, nose to nose.

Tears of sadness blurred her vision as she shoveled dirt over them. *Arm and Hand, you were part of our family, growing in loyalty like Aydan and Lyam. If they hadn't helped Lars fight to bring back the traitors, we wouldn't be alive today.*

Two days later, Lars and Dannor came over the distant rise, almost home from the hunt. *Judging from the pace they traveled, their mule was carrying a burden. Most likely another successful hunt. You'll get no happy barks to greet you today. I'll be the bearer of bad news.*

"You're sure, Nagora?" asked Lars.

"Yes, there were no other tracks of any kind on the dew-covered grass."

"But if it was your father, why didn't he look for you? Why would he kill the dogs?"

"I don't know. That part makes little sense. Maybe it was someone else. Maybe Da trained another Dragon Rider."

"Nothing else is missing?"

"Alizarine, her basket, her egg, and her stone boat. That's it. We've nothing of real value here other than our animals, our weapons, our clothes, and our store of food."

Dannor was standing at the window looking out, quiet and sad with the news of the deaths of Arm and Hand. Only the fingers of his hands moved as they shuffled the three dragon teeth Alizarine had found on the beach many years ago. "I'm sorry, Dannor. I've taken away the pleasure of you reporting on your hunt." Nagora put her arms around him.

"No, Mum. This is serious. To do that to our dogs is sense-less. If I knew who was responsible, I would go put them in my arrows' sights."

"Your buck is beautiful. Tell me all about the hunt."

Dannor pulled away from her. "Not today, Mum. Perhaps in a few days from now." He left in the direction where Nagora had told them she had buried the dogs.

Lars watched his son walk head down across the meadow.

Then, when he looked at Nagora, there were tears in his eyes. "Those dogs were part of our family. My immediate feelings are like Dannor's, but I'm older and even though their deaths pain me, I know I have to help you make some sense of this. So Nagora. Now what do we do? Will we be going to the Land of the Danu? I expect you want to sort this out. To do that, you'll have to go there."

Nagora sighed. "Lars, I've been thinking about this for the past two days. I'm staying put. I'm not going anywhere."

"No, no. That's not you! You … "

Nagora held up her hand to cut him short and then pointed over to the maze. "Look over there, Lars. We didn't work our-selves sick on that for nothing. Even though the Little People came and gave us a hand, a tremendous hand at that. They worked from sunset to sunrise, in every weather, for years.

"The only respite we had was what? Twelve days when the two Stone Standers showed up to help the Little People erect the pillars and lay the lintels on top of them. Grim's sons completed the inner and outer rings around the well. They wouldn't let us watch, let alone help.

"You remember what it was like when we started out. One massive pile of rocks strewn as far as we could see.

"What is it today, Lars? It's a fortress that can only be penetrated by those who know the way in, or by those who fly there from the sky. As far as I know, only one dragon can do that. Danuka led me here many years ago. The reason is obvious. I am the key."

"The key to what, Nagora?"

Her face burned red with frustration. "The key that will make the maze work for the dragons of the future. Whoever came here on Danuka and took Alizarine, they don't understand who she is. And most likely they'll never find out. At least not until she has done more harm than we can imagine. Danuka needs the egg. She won't get it from the witch child, nor will whoever came here. Danuka needs me—the key."

"But ... "

She held up her hands again. "Sooner or later they, or Danuka, will come to get me or send for me. Only then will I move from here." Nagora reached into her vest pocket and pulled out the gold-handled hunting dagger Raynhard had given her over fifteen years ago.

She held it up before her face. "And when I do, it will be to reunite with my daughter to place her hand on this handle and then mine over hers, so together we can plunge it into Alizarine's heart!"

Nagora jabbed the dagger down and through clenched teeth said, "We'll end her life as a young child fascinated with a dragon egg." Again she jabbed the dagger. "We'll kill the witch!"

Lars held up his hand. "Will it work, Nagora?" His voice was calm. "Heqet's curse, as you told me she stated it, said she would grant Alizarine eternal youth, until the day a queen and her daughter join hands on their king's golden-handled dagger to pierce her heart. Nagora, you're not a queen."

Nagora waved the dagger in her fist. "I am the mother of the king's daughter! If that doesn't make me a queen, then I will do what must be done to set the queen's crown on my head for as long as it takes me and my daughter to put an end to the witch, Alizarine!"

Lars took a step back, crossed his arms over his chest, and lowered his gaze. "If I could do this for you, I would. I don't want to see you get hurt again. You'll need all your wits about you. Don't let your anger steal them from you."

As the truth of his words sunk in, Nagora's anger turned to tears, boiled over, and spilled down her face. "You're right." She swallowed. "You're right, Lars. All I ask is your help."

Lars wrapped his arms around her and held her tight as she shook and buried her face against his chest. "Dannor and I will help you. You won't be alone in this."

The end of autumn brought the last of the curious visitors come to gaze upon the maze. Bolder visitors made the trip to Nagora's door to ask questions about it. Often they were the ones who inquired if they could enter the maze. Nagora's answer was always the same. "You're welcome to visit it. If you venture in, good luck to you finding your way out. I'll not go to your rescue. Come spring, if I come across your bones, I'll bring them out and throw them into the sea."

Some came in pairs, with a long rope. One would hold one end at an entrance while the other uncoiled the rope on his way in. Once, a dozen came. All of them carried a coil of stout twine. Eleven of them came out of the exit neighboring the entrance where the twelfth waited for them. It had taken them almost half a day to get to that point. The dozen had a good laugh at themselves.

No matter from which of the highest vantage points, observers could not see in to the center of the maze. Even the high stone pillars of the inner and outer circles, connected by the stone lintels that rested on them, were not visible. Only the stone walls of the maze passages that rose up to them were visible.

Those views of the maze paths, which appeared to lead to the inner rings of the maze, only confounded the viewers who tried to let their eyes walk their way into the maze. It was an exercise in frustrated concentration whether one tried to start from the inner gates to an outer entrance or from an outer gate in.

Whenever Lars spotted one of these curious maze viewers, he would shake his head and say to Nagora. "Some people have too much time to waste."

"They're just curious." Nagora would answer. "The maze is a challenge to them. A mystery they want to solve. And it has a certain beauty. The curve of its high outer wall with the regular-spaced openings is a site to behold, especially to those who had seen the rock-strewn plain before."

...

The first flecks of snow licked the cold gray air that surrounded Maze Point. It was the name people traveling there had given to their destination, and it had stuck. Those little white, fleeting crystals also brought with them questions which ate at Nagora's sense of family.

They signaled the last opportunity for missives from her parents, her sister, and her friend Paruline to make their way to her before snow blocked the mountain passes. Those last letters she had received so many years ago and reread so many times were still in a drawer in her mind. Today she opened it.

Her Letters
Omasinahikaniw

† THEN: *in the eighth year of
rebuilding the maze in the Land of Skulls*

In the years following Nagora's announcement she was with
child, Gabe had made regular trips to visit Sagora in the Land
of the Danu, except during the long winter months. He never
lost hope that one day he too would have good news to share.

Then, when Dannor's eighth birthday was approaching, a
letter brought the news Gabe had been waiting for. He was to
be a father. He had rushed off to go get Sagora, his bride-to-
be, the mother of his child.

Nagora and her men had moved in with Umma so Lars
could take over for Gabe to deal with the pressing business
spring always brought with its arrival: common road repairs,
inspection of fortifications, bridge maintenance, repairs to the
docks, installation of the main fishing weir, food store inven-
tory, crop allocations for the planting season, and more.

But a month later, Gabe returned without Sagora.

When he came to Umma's place to deliver the letters he had brought back for Nagora, he had changed. He had lost weight and his face was haggard, like one who had not slept for many nights.

"Nagora, she'll not be coming back." He reached for her hands. Despair was in his voice. "Sagora's sure she's carrying twins. Your mother confirms Sagora has all the same signs as she had, although, at the time, your mother didn't know that it was because she carried twins. What'll I do, Nagora?"

Nagora took him in her arms. "Gabe, there's still time. She may not be carrying twins. It could just be a big rambunctious boy wanting to come out to be with his da. They'll not be certain until Sagora gives birth."

"She's said as much to me, but doesn't want to return to give birth here. Only if it's a single child will she return. What your mother had to do, she'll never do. I don't blame her, Nagora. It's just that, if they are twins, I'm still their father. I'll want to see them, be a father to them, and watch them grow. How can I do that from here? Will they ever even want to return here?"

Nagora held Gabe's shoulders and looked him in the eye. "Gabe, you're thinking far ahead into the future. Many things can happen between now and then. Try to think of the best things that could happen. If the best doesn't happen, then try to think how you can make the best out of what does.

"If you end up with twins, I'm sure Raynhard will allow you to build a lodge on the border with the Land of Skulls. Build one just on the other side of the river. You'll not have as far to travel. Sagora could meet you there so you could go to spend time with her and the children. It'll be a halfway meeting place."

"I don't know why I worry so, Nagora. Is this something that all fathers do?"

She smiled at him. "Most likely all good ones do."

"But you, Nagora, how did you know that you didn't carry twins when you were expecting Dannor? The chances you could have, I've been told, are greater. I don't recall seeing you worry when you carried your baby."

Just then Lars came through the door and saw them in the infirmary room. Nagora held up a hand to show him she wished to finish talking to Gabe. Lars leaned against the door frame and crossed his arms.

"With Dannor, Gabe, the signs were the same as for my first child."

Gabe's mouth fell open as his eyes widened in a question. He looked to Lars and then back to Nagora. This is news to him? Why is that so? It means Sagora and the others in the Land of the Danu have not spoken a word to him about Sarah, and neither has Godomor, nor Lars. Why?

She turned to her man. "Lars, you didn't tell Gabe?"

"Did I have to? I figured if you told Godomor, then he would've told Gabe."

Nagora turned back to Gabe. "On all your visits to Sagora, did you ever, both of you, visit Pare? Pare would have introduced her to you as my daughter, Sarah."

"No, Nagora. However, I remember on my earliest visit to Sagora in Cairnmase, in the fall after your return, she left to visit a mother who was having difficulty nursing an infant. She didn't say if it was a girl or a boy. Nor did Paruline."

Gabe's look became even more perplexed. "If your daughter is not a twin," Gabe hesitated and looked over at Lars, "why haven't you brought Sarah here with you?"

"I can't bring Sarah here, Gabe. It's a long story. Your da will tell it all to you. Tell him I've given you permission to ask about it. But I will tell you why. The egg Alizarine has is Danuka's egg. Danuka gave it to me to trap Alizarine. In return, I had to give Sarah to Danuka. When I return the egg to Danuka, she will give me back my daughter. I didn't know that because of the trap I had set, a curse would be placed on Alizarine. And that curse involves Sarah and I."

Again, Gabe looked from Nagora to Lars and then back to Nagora. "Who is Sarah's father?"

"Raynhard."

Gabe's eyes widened.

"Your da will tell you how that came to be. I told him everything."

Gabe looked back to Lars. "Lars, I think I understand why you haven't brought this up. You must know the whole story too?"

Lars's smile and expression were flat. Not even his hand on his arm moved when he said, "I do." Her man never made idle talk of anyone, even his friends.

After Gabe left, Nagora held the letters to her heart. *I'll wait until we return to our lodge to open them.*

For the first time, she held a letter with her father's seal on it. It was a wolf's head in profile, its tongue lolling at the side of its mouth, teeth ready to bite into an oncoming wave, like the figurehead she had seen on the Sea Wolf. *I can guess what this letter will be about.*

Paruline's letter was thicker than the others, seven pages. Her mother's was a single page, while Sagora's was two pages. Nagora would wait until the first light of morning to read them.

As Nagora climbed past the stone bluff against which their lodge rested, her mind went over the letters she had just read.

The one common thread in three of them pointed to Paruline's letter, its last two pages written in Geirador's secret code. Nagora had the key to decipher it in her head. Those two pages explained why Sagora had kept Gabe unaware of Sarah.

When Nagora reached the top of the cliff with the view to seaward and the horizon beyond, she pulled the big skystone blade from its sheath. Today she would do her exercises slowly, focus on the motions, and let the pages of the letters turn over in her mind to plan her responses to them.

—Ward off—

Mum, Da has convinced you to go to sea with him for three months. That you'll be back a month before Sagora gives birth is your condition. Mum, I hope you and Da find each other again and rekindle the spark that once united you. While you are with Da, do what you do best. Be his healer. He needs you to care for him and love him. Give him all your attention. It'll be a new beginning.

—Rollback—

Da, that Danuka is still happy with the cave you found for her is good. She and her eggs are safe there. Without even a rope bridge to get to the Isle of Smoke, access is only possible by the sea cliffs. I'm sure Danuka would take care of any intruders. You are right. A Dragon Talker needs a respite from his dragon. Now that she has a safe place, Danuka can care for herself.

—Press—

People, from all parts of the land, journey to the plain opposite the Isle of Smoke to see for themselves where Edana, the Dragon-Warrior Princess, led her warriors against Queen Raganora's troops. If only they knew what their legend is doing now, and who rides her unicorn.

—Push—

The people stand on the remains of the Isle of Smoke Bridge on the mainland side to gaze across the strait at Queen Rag's fortress on the Isle of Smoke. And they stare into the waters of the strait to spot the fallen pieces of the once great stone bridge.

—Pull—

They do this as they listen to the retelling of that day's events, as witnessed by one who watched most of it happen from one of the fortress's towers. One Rumandor, who tells of his personal encounter with Edana and of his flight on Danuka's back, bringing over the line to haul the temporary rope bridge across the strait.

—Elbow strike—

Da, I couldn't help smiling when I read that. Rumandor, may you continue to earn a good coin for your storytelling, even if you change the events to suit your version of what happened that day.

—Shoulder strike—

Sagora, you do well to trust Geirador's and Pare's hands. Their experience allows them to see what others cannot. If Pare says you are twice as big as I was, believe her.

—Advance—

If Geirador says what you feel is two boys wrestling inside you, believe him.

—Retreat—

Mum says your signs mirror hers when she carried us. Believe her. Do not return here. Keep your children with you.

—Look left—

So Pare, you say Raynhard still has not spoken clearly about what happened in the cave. Aliza struck him hard that day. It's possible the blow has left him confused about exactly what happened. You say Sagora decided not to mention a word to Raynhard about Sarah or Alizarine, other than saying I did what I had to do.

—Gaze right—

Pare, you and Sagora agreed to tell him that someday, once I had made peace with myself, I, his other Dragon Talker, would return. And Da confirmed Danuka agreed with your decision to tell Raynhard that. Someday, my reason for returning will be other than that. Only after that will I find peace.

—Center balance—

Until I return, who Sarah is will be kept a secret for her protection and mine. Pare, you say you're following my instructions as given to Sagora in my letter to her. Please clarify. What instructions did Sagora give you? Please give me more news of Sarah.

Nagora repeated the twelve exercises until she had completed the slow cycle a hundred times. All the while, she gathered the strength they brought her. Strength she would need in the days to come and on the day of her return to her daughter.

When she finished, she knelt on the ground, with the tip of the skystone blade resting in the grassy loam. Her eyes climbed from the sea to the sky. If this be the path the stars have bequeathed me, I've no choice but to take it.

Pare, I trust you with my Sarah. I know you are on my side.

A single tear blurred the horizon in the time she took to blink it away. She took a deep breath before standing to wipe her blade and return it to its sheath.

Those were the last letters I received. Almost six years ago. I answered them. No answers ever came back. Why? I wrote more letters, at least one every two months. Still no answers.

Since then, the news Gabe brought from his visits with Sagora and his boys at their halfway lodge was always general news holding little interest for Nagora. Never anything I want to know. Why? Sagora would, according to Gabe, deliver Nagora's letters, but she never returned with letters of reply destined for Nagora.

If only I could understand why. If only I could travel there to find out. But I can't with Alizarine and with my task of rebuilding the maze. Even if I were to abandon my task for the time of a visit, I would have to bring Alizarine. It's my duty to protect that egg if I ever want to get Sarah back. Of course I would want to see my Sarah. And if I did, could I leave her again? Would Sarah understand? Does she even know I'm her mother or who I am? And I'd want to bring Dannor. Would seven-year-old Dannor understand? Would Danuka let me bring Sarah back? That would break our agreement. Even if Danuka did allow me to take her back, would I be putting Sarah in danger from Alizarine? There's no telling what that little witch might do. I would constantly live in fear for Sarah's safety. Would I have the time to train her to become the warrior she needs to become? Could I do a good job of it knowing what Sarah is destined to do? Sarah's wearing the dragon-tear amulet and is destined to become a Dragon Talker. How can she become that away from Danuka? And I'm not a queen. How will I ever make that happen?

All these questions tore at Nagora's insides, churning the bile in her stomach and tearing at the wound in her heart. And every late fall since then, the first flecks of snow brought with them her uneasy feeling. Something is not right.

The Invitation
Wihkomitowin

† NOW: *near the end of the fifteenth year of*
rebuilding the maze in the Land of Skulls

The coming of spring this year brought with it more than the renewal of life in the Land of Skulls. Spring allowed the border patrol to carry missives from the Land of the Danu. Those letters bore news which left an awful taste in the mouths of their recipients.

The missives contained wedding invitations. Wedding invitations usually summoned people to the joyful celebration of the union between two people, born of the love they have for each other.

But this one was an insult, a provocation, and an unbelievable affront to Gabe, Prince Gabyndor of the Land of Skulls. It was an invitation to the wedding of King Raynhard of the Land of the Danu to Sagora, former healer from the Land of Skulls and mother to Prince Gabyndor's twin boys.

News of the invitation spread throughout the Land of Skulls like a grass fire on a windy slope. The invitation revived in an instant the old fear of twins, bringing that fear back to life like a hot coal laid bare from beneath the ashes where it had waited to be stoked with fuel. The invitation was that fuel.

Sagora, overnight, had become the twin the finger pointers and signers eagerly denounced as proof of the renewed dread she embodied. Sagora, the evil twin, had been lurking among them all those past years; and now from afar, Sagora unleashed her evil.

As if Sagora's bringing twins into the world, sired by their prince, was not bad enough, leading Gabe on all these years just to toss him aside to marry the King of the Land of the Danu was an insult beyond forgiveness.

Before long, Nagora and Lars bore the brunt of the calls for redress, which grew day by day, until the calls united and turned to a clamor for war.

Three days earlier, Gabe had warned Lars to prepare his family to leave. Gabe would come for them with an escort.

Why am I not surprised? I knew it would come to this. Lars and I are twins. I'm Sagora's twin sister. It's Dannor I feel sorry for.

Dannor's few friends had deserted him. Nagora tried to console him. "Your friends had no choice, Dannor. They were under pressure from others, ignorant crowd followers unable to think for themselves and stand up for what is right. Mark my words. If ever you return here, it will be to a warm welcome.

"Given the situation, it's best we leave. For our own safety, like Gabe said."

"Mum, we could survive in the maze. They would never get to us."

Nagora's eyes held Dannor's. I like your warrior spirit, my son. But you still have much to learn. Know which battle to choose. This one isn't for us. "We would just provoke them if we did. We're going to the Land of the Danu. I never imagined I would be called there in this way. This invitation is more than what it seems."

I don't want to alarm you, my son, so I'll keep my thoughts to myself. I fear it's a trap for me.

"Son, the three of us will be together on this journey. It'll be one of discovery for you and one of rediscovery for me and your da.

"Best we start our packing. Your da's with the animals, probably trying to decide how many we bring. Go to him. You know he likes to think out loud. Lars'll be glad to hear your thoughts. Sharing them with him will help him focus on his own. Once he's decided how many animals, come tell me. It'll help me decide what to pack and what to leave behind."

Dannor stepped out of the lodge. How does he feel? Any more ready than her when she had been banished from Cairnmase for a hundred days? Nagora was on her own. Dannor would be with his parents. Will Dannor feel like she did when headed to the Land of Skulls for the first time to reunite with a mother she had been told had died giving birth to her? Not likely, but Dannor will be headed into the unknown.

What task will you have in all of this, Dannor? I know not. I only hope I don't have to ask you to do the impossible.

However, I feel your warrior skills will be tested in ways you've never imagined. I'll have your back whenever I can, my son.

Nagora couldn't sleep. They were packed and ready to go. Gabe would arrive early in the morning. I've forgotten to pack something important. What is it? Tar piss! I'll get up. Maybe it'll help me remember.

As Nagora stood, a light at the window caught her attention. It was no ordinary light. Nagora had seen such lights before. They always came in the dark of night.

The first time was in Raynhard's secret cave and then in recent years, when the Little People came to work on the maze at night. Like in Raynhard's cave, they wanted to be left alone to do their nightly work.

In the daytime, when Nagora, Lars, and Dannor went to work on building up the maze walls, they found stones the Little People had neatly stacked along the base of the walls that needed to be built up. All they had to do was stack the stones from the piles the Little People left for them.

Some nights from their lodge, they could see the glow of lights along the upper portions of the maze walls when the Little People were setting the final top stones in place.

Now, this night before Nagora's departure, the Little People signaled they were near. In all the times they had approached her, she had only ever seen one of them once, in daylight. When he let himself be seen, he returned to her the gold coin she now wore at her neck. Nagora brought her hand to it and held it as she approached the window. It was the same coin she had used to call the Little People both times.

A circle of miniature lights had formed on the ground. The lights danced and formed the maze with its inner and outer circles. The spot in the center glowed with a light that pulsed brighter than all the others.

Then all the lights danced again and formed into a new image. It was of Nagora lying on the ground on her back with her arms out at her sides and her legs spread. A line of lights skipped around her outline. Like when they asked me to lie on the ground in Raynhard's secret cave. I remember what it felt like, as if they were measuring me.

Next, Nagora's body image stood and looked at her, motioning to her to follow. Nagora nodded, turned from the window, and went to Lars.

She shook him awake. "Shh. I'm going to the maze."

Lars was trying to blink sleep from his eyes. "What?"

"Go back to sleep. The Little People have called me to the maze. I'm going there now. With them."

"I'm going too."

"No, Lars. They've called me. Just me. I'll be fine."

Lars let his head fall back and waved Nagora away.

The lights waited in the distance. Nagora walked as fast as she could. She did not carry a taper nor a lantern. They'll be easier to follow. If I need them, there are tapers and lanterns at the center of the maze and in the well.

As Nagora stepped through the gate into the middle of the maze, the lights disappeared. Only starlight lit Nagora's surroundings. Where will they reappear? The big stone lintels stood against the starry sky. Nagora's eyes caught *The Twins*.

Dangor's voice telling her the star stories, almost every night of her childhood, rang clear in her memory. Is there a star up there for the events my path will lead me to tomorrow?

A light flickered and caught the corner of Nagora's eye. It leaped down from the lintel and danced over to the rim of the well. When it hopped up onto the rim, it became Nagora and beckoned to her to follow. It leapt into the well.

Nagora reached for the rope that hung into the well from the stout spruce-pole tripod they had set in place for the purpose. She unfastened the belayed rope at the side of the well, grabbed on with both hands, and let herself swing into the center of the well. Nagora's feet came to rest on the first knot and when they did, light shone from below.

Nagora let herself down, one knot at a time, in a steady rhythm. When her feet touched the metal plate of the bridge over the grate, light glowed in the cave leading to the forge and wagon chambers.

As Nagora approached the dragon drawing, the glowing light moved left.

To the forges I go.

Inside the chamber, six candle lanterns stood on top of the uppermost terrace level, above the small furnaces.

A single candle lantern rested on a shelf next to the small, secret door-handle cubicle. A single, wee light flashed from the shelf on the other side of the cubicle. Nagora stepped up to it. When she arrived, it went out.

That's when the voice spoke. "Open the door."

Not hesitating, Nagora reached in, pulled on the handle, and turned it.

Then Nagora stepped over to the side of the shelving unit and pushed on the wooden upright. Nagora followed the pivoting door into the coal room.

The voice spoke again. "Look on the back of the door."

Nagora took several steps to the other side of the door. Light from the candle lanterns on the top terrace of the forge lit that side of the door. I see a shelf but can't make out the objects on it. Nagora stepped closer.

One looked like a scrip. The other looked familiar. Nagora reached for the familiar one. As soon as her hands took hold of it, they told her what she held. Nagora had wrapped them herself and given them in payment to the Little People years ago in Raynhard's secret cave.

Nagora had inherited them from Dangor along with a pouch of gold coins. Now she wore a single coin from that pouch at her neck. As Nagora unwrapped her uncle's set of blades and grasped the handle of the big skystone blade, the voice spoke to her again. "You will need the blades. Give the set you wear to your son. His father will agree."

Dangor's big sheath was the same as hers, the one Danuka had instructed her to give to Sarah along with her dragon-tear amulet. And it was the same as the set she now wore, Lars's. The leather shoulder straps of all three sets of blades each held two small throwing knife holsters.

Now, having Dangor's blades back in her possession gave Nagora hope. I feel stronger, like Uncle is by my side. Nagora rolled them back up in the piece of hide and set them back on the shelf before taking the scrip.

"We made it for you. Only you can wear it and use it, because it will only fit you and no one else."

Nagora opened the scrip and reached in. Can it be? Should I trust my fingers? It's been so long since I've touched Danuka's skin. Yet the memory of it was present in Nagora's fingers as they explored the skin. The essence of the Dragon's Kiss confirmed it truly was Danuka's skin.

"This is a garment? You made this from the skin Danuka shed? I am to wear it? To do what?"

"When you wear it, it has the power to hide you from the eyes of others. It will only do so if you believe it can and you will it to do so. That is how you control it."

Nagora shook her head. Am I hearing right? "It will … make me invisible?"

"Like a dragon can make itself invisible with its skin, if it chooses. Remove your clothes and try it on."

Nagora removed her blades and her clothes before pulling the garment from the scrip. She let the fine mesh of dragonskin scales unravel before her and held it up. "How do I get into it?"

"Find the hole on the front, the belly. Your fingers will guide you."

Wow! This garment is amazing! The way it fits my body! It clung to every bump, curve, and indentation of Nagora's skin, but not in a manner that was restrictive. It was part of her, another layer, transparent, seamless, and comfortable. Looking at her hands, the fine mesh of dragon scales was impossible to detect in the light of the lanterns.

The essence of the Dragon's Kiss enveloped Nagora's body as it had the last time she stood before her dragon in Raynhard's cave. It made every muscle of her limbs come alive. It seemed to multiply their strength.

"Well?" asked the voice.

"How you managed to sew this skin of my dragon so it stretches to fit me like it does is a mystery to me. So is the way it makes me feel, like I'm bigger and stronger. Invincible. And I can see and breathe and hear and speak with it on."

"It makes you more aware of your own strength, is what it does to you," said the voice.

"Thank you. Just the same, I cannot think of how or why I might use this garment."

"If you keep it a secret, you will use it to best advantage when the occasion presents itself."

Nagora dressed, pulled the shoulder straps of Dangor's blades onto her shoulders, tightened the straps, and adjusted the small knife holsters.

She picked up the dragonskin garment scrip and Lars's set of blades. Do the Little People have anything else for me? "You have known all along my departure would come. You know what awaits me. Do you have anything else for me?"

"We have known this day would come. What awaits you has elements of the unknown. Those we cannot know. The best we can do are these weapons. They might give you an advantage. Everything else depends on trust.

"Trust you are a warrior.

"Trust you are a Dragon Talker.

"Trust you will do your best for the future of the dragons.

"Trust you will know who you can trust and who you cannot.

"Trust your heart when it speaks to you.

"Trust you will return here to see a better future."

Nagora held the scrip to her chest, lowered her gaze, and bit into her upper lip as she took a deep breath. This struggle with learning to trust—will it never end?

The light from the candle lanterns dimmed.

Time to go.

Nagora followed the glow out of the chamber. It waited opposite the dragon drawing. It knows I want to have one last look at it.

Nagora stared up at the dragon's red eye. It looked right inside her, making her speak her thoughts. "I am your Dragon Talker. Danuka, will you trust me when I go to you? I promise I will do all in my power to return your egg.

"And if it be your will, I will bring you back here and stand guard over you and your eggs once again."

When Nagora turned away from the drawing, the voice spoke to her one last time. "Dragon Talker, we are certain of one thing. It is important that you know. The egg Alizarine, the witch, holds bears a male dragon. We have one more of Danuka's eggs to examine. All the others bear females. If the last egg does too, then the future of the dragons will rest with that egg. Need I say more?"

"No." Nagora swallowed and tasted the bitterness of the realization.

Danuka, you knew all along. You chose that egg. Now I see what you have done. You value that egg as much as I value my Sarah, perhaps more. It was no accident I called you "Mother" all those days in the cave. You've been my mother in so many ways. Mother, you've controlled my destiny since the beginning. Now give me the strength to do what I must do.

With at least two full counts of darkness remaining, Nagora crawled into bed next to her man. She rested her cheek against Lars's strong shoulder and closed her eyes.

Sleep, come now. I'm as prepared as I'll ever be for the task ahead. From now on, I'll deal with each day's events as they present themselves. If I focus on the burden of this task, I'll never sleep. I've taken it one day at a time. I've made it this far by doing so. So why not continue?

They saddled their horses and tied their bedrolls, wrapped in waxed woolen rain capes, to the backs of the saddles along with their saddlebags and waterskins.

Lars had decided they would each have a mule loaded with enough belongings to set up basic housekeeping in a small hut until they figured out where they would settle in the Land of the Danu.

To that, Nagora spoke her thought aloud. "If we ever settle."

Lars seemed to ignore her words. "We're carrying enough food supplies for the journey, and we have coins to buy what we need once we arrive."

When Gabe showed up with the escort, he dismounted and asked them to go inside so he could have a word with them in private.

Gabe cast a quick eye about the main room of their lodge.

I read the pain on your face as you see what we're leaving behind.

Gabe set his hands on his hips and glanced at the floor before speaking. "Father thinks it's best you not come into Skull Bay. He'll meet us at Edana's Victory Bridge.

"Nagora, Lars, Dannor, the people's reaction to what has happened has gotten out of hand. Father wants me to assure you we're asking you to leave for your protection, so this situation can settle and we can get answers to help us understand what this is all about.

"Nagora, I'm hoping I can convince those who're calling for action against Raynhard and Sagora that you will find the truth behind what many are now calling an act of treason. You've borne truth to this land once before and showed how treason had taken root from within. As a result, you saved my father's life. He and I are forever in debt to you for that.

"Perhaps, once in the Land of the Danu, you'll be able to root out the cause of this duplicity and allow me to save face before I'm forced to take up arms to seek redress."

Nagora nodded. "Gabe, like you, I want answers. Something is amiss, and I intend to find out what. As soon as I do, I'll send word to you. Or deliver it myself if I have to."

"I trust you will, Nagora.

"Lars, Dannor, take good care of her."

"We will," they said in unison.

"I hope you'll return with Nagora. Our land needs good men like you. Best we get moving to get you on your way as soon as possible." Gabe held the door open.

Nagora gave the lead rope of her mule to Lars. "I've something to ask Gabe. Do you mind?"

She rode ahead to Gabe. "Gabe, can we talk honestly while we have the time? I have a few personal questions to ask you. If you don't want to answer, that's fine with me. I'm looking for any information that might help me."

"Ask. I'll be honest with you."

Nagora glanced behind her to make sure they wouldn't be overheard. "Tell me about the last time you were with Sagora."

Gabe frowned and bit his lower lip before answering. "To be honest, Nagora, last fall I did not feel welcome. The boys weren't their usual selves, and neither was Sagora. I had sensed it from Sagora on earlier visits, but that last time, it was palpable with the lads.

"Usually, the boys are full of questions and want to head off into the forest with me, or go to the river to fish. There was none of that this time. The twins were biding their time, waiting for me to leave. I had to ask questions. Their answers held no enthusiasm."

"I appreciate your honesty, Gabe. Were you and Sagora intimate in bed?"

Gabe looked off into the distance before answering. "Less and less, after the birth of the twins. If I didn't approach Sagora, she kept her distance. Sagora said she didn't want to risk having another set of twins. Strange though, she kept on wearing that fertility ring Raynhard had given her as a gift. He said it would help her conceive. That it did, or at least it seemed to since not long after she began to wear it, she became pregnant. I thought she would take it off, but no."

A memory of Raynhard surfaced in Nagora's mind. "Tell me about the ring. What did it look like?"

Gabe's eyebrows peaked for a moment as his jaw set. "Silver, with an amber stone that looked almost like an eye. Why do you ask?"

"Just curious," said Nagora.

Not having seen it, I can't confirm what I'm thinking. Though that description fits the ring Raynhard wore when he visited me in the cave. Something had changed in him back then.

Gabe seemed about to say something, but instead he looked skyward. Taking a deep breath, he looked back at Nagora. "Damn it! I'll tell you! Sagora asked me not to. But I will. We argued all the time about her coming back to live with me part of the year and then return to live with our sons. Sagora didn't want that. To put an end to our arguments, on my next visit, she removed her headscarf to show the brand on her forehead."

That information took a moment to settle. "A Tiwaz?"

"Yes, Nagora! Identical to yours!"

I can't believe it! "So Sagora put an end to any possibility of her returning. Now we wear the same brand!"

Gabe hung his head and shook it. "I don't know why I continued to visit them. I told myself I was doing it for the boys. That maybe someday, there would be a way for them to come here. However, the last time I saw them, I had the feeling they had to choose whether they would even return to the halfway lodge or not. I guess they couldn't say it to my face."

Why did Sagora continue to visit Gabe? Perhaps her intentions were honorable in the early days. Gabe was the father of the boys. Perhaps Sagora too had hopes for the future.

What changed, Sagora? Could it be the ring?

"Gabe, at the halfway lodge, does someone live there to care for it?"

"No. Two people, a couple, escort Sagora and the lads. They take care of the chores, mostly cooking and any repairs to the place, especially after winter."

"Is it easy to find? Do you think I could visit it?"

Gabe nodded. "You'll have no problem finding it. Remember the big stone with its two sentinel trees? You'll see it as soon as you cross the Blood River. Go right at that stone. The trail will take you up the hill to the lodge."

Nagora nodded.

Gabe added, "If you climb to the roof, on a clear day you can see down to the small cove where Outlanders had landed their boats to come invade us long ago."

"I remember you telling about that invasion the first day I met you."

Gabe looked at Nagora. "It was a memorable day for me. I took you for Sagora. Some of my men became frightened when they realized you were Sagora's twin. With your arrival, Nagora, so many things changed that day."

Nagora bowed her head and looked down at her hands.

"Nagora, please, don't take that wrong. I'm not saying that as a blame."

Her eyes climbed back to Gabe's. "I know you're not. You're right. So many things changed for me too on that day."

Nagora reached a finger to the Tiwaz brand on her forehead. I chose it that day as the price a returning twin pays and for its meaning, for a higher cause. Does the Tiwaz still hold sway over my life today?

Even before the branding, Geirador had etched the Tiwaz on Nagora's skystone blade. It was the first one he had made. He had made it for Nagora. Her uncle had delivered it to her. Now all these years later, I realize that was the moment I set foot on a path in service to a higher cause. I was chosen.

Here I am, still the chosen one, on a path not of my choice. It will bring me to my daughter. I will have to convince Sarah that she too is chosen. Chosen for a deed she cannot imagine.

Will I be able to convince Sarah to join her own mother in that enterprise?

Always the unknown. It has always been a path of unknowns. I seem to trudge along it, one bloody day at a time.

Gabe had been watching Nagora, most likely allowing her to lose herself in thought. She smiled at him. He smiled back. "Good luck, Nagora." She nodded and returned to her mule.

As they approached Godomor, he was standing next to his horse on the bridge in his great black cape, his mounted guards behind him. Edana's Victory Bridge. Today, I'm embarrassed by the bridge's name. Am I on my way to another victory, or will this be my defeat? Just as well I don't know the future. I wouldn't have the pleasure of being tormented by questions like these.

Godomor fastened his great sword in its scabbard to the saddle of his horse. Then he turned to watch them approach. As soon as Storm's hooves hit the floorboards of the bridge, Nagora dismounted and walked toward Godomor's open arms. He spoke in her ear in the language of *The People*. "*Ka Peyakot Mahihkan*, all my strength goes with you on this path. Go without fear into the face of the unknown. You will find your path on the other side. Trust your skills and your weapons. Trust your heart." Godomor was the only person who had ever called her Lone Wolf. He did so with the greatest respect.

He held Nagora close in a strong, genuine embrace. From the first time Godomor touched my shoulder on the landing of his Grand Hall in Skull Bay, just before my branding, I knew this man was connected to me in a special way. Once again, today, I know that connection is still there, stronger than ever. Nagora returned Godomor's hug. "*Ohtawimaw*, thank you for your kind words. Already I feel their strength in me. Your wise words are just what I need for this journey."

Godomor eased his embrace and held Nagora by the shoulders. He looked into her eyes. Godomor's face was grave. "*Mitanisimaw*, I will hold back my wolves for as long as possible. Be warned there will come a time when my voice will no longer be heard above their howls for the hunt to begin. I dare not predict what will stay standing once they cross the Blood River on their path of revenge, seeking blood wherever they can find it to quench the fire they will bear in their teeth. Let these words be my message to King Raynhard and Sagora."

Nagora took a deep breath. "*Ohtawimaw*, implore your wolves to give Nagnuska tykommi iyammani a chance to return with the truth again, to bring back proof of redress for this provocation. Tell them if I die trying, and that when Lars or Dannor returns with news of my death, then you will unleash your horde."

Godomor let his hands fall from Nagora's shoulders. "I will do that. It remains to be seen if my words will cause them to respect the wishes of *Ka Peyakot Mahihkan*."

"Father, I have a question."

"Speak it, *Mitanisimaw*."

"I have heard that long ago the Land of Skulls and the Land of the Danu were one land. Is that so?"

Godomor took a deep breath. "Yes, it was once one land. It is still one big island, but an island divided."

"Because of twins, like today?"

Godomor pursed his lips. "Yes. It is a long story to be told by a fire in winter. *Ka Peyakot Mahihkan*, may you return to hear it one day."

Nagora smiled at Godomor. "*Ohtawimaw*, I look forward to sitting by your fire to hear you tell that story. It is another good reason for me to return."

Godomor smiled at Nagora and looked over to Lars and Dannor. He stepped in their direction. When Godomor was near, he put a hand on a shoulder of each one and looked from one to the other. "Lars, protect Nagora. Dannor, protect your mother and your father. I am counting on both of you to bring her back."

Dannor's chest swelled. I'm sure he can feel not only the strength of Godomor's grip, but the sincerity of his command as well.

Lars looked from Godomor to Nagora and back again. "We'll bring her back to you, Godomor."

The first time Nagora saw Lars from atop the landing of the Grand Hall, he was standing in the rain with his two hounds, his face hidden beneath the hood of his shirt. Just before Sagora touched the brand to her forehead, what Nagora then called "the strange eye" had spoken to her. "Your protector," Danuka had said. Thunder, lightning, and rain in torrents had struck, dispersing all the onlookers except for Lars. He was the only one still standing in the downpour on the road below, watching Nagora. Lars, I know I can count on you.

Godomor patted Lars on the back. "Gabe and his warriors will escort you to where the trail enters the forest. You'll be on your own from there onward."

As they mounted to continue on their way, Nagora caught Trowan's familiar, warm smile. "Good to see you today, Trowan." The archer who'd fought at her side on the Isle of

Smoke Bridge had earned a posting with Godomor's personal guard. Whenever in Skull Bay, Nagora made a point of Lars and her getting together with Trowan. Dannor tried not to miss those meetings. He was always eager for more details about the campaign to free his grandda, Yogari, and Danuka, the mother dragon. And Trowan always had a valuable tip for the young bowman.

"When I heard our king had planned an escort for you today, I wanted to be part of the group."

Nagora reached over and touched Trowan's arm. "I'm glad you are." At least not everyone is out to get my hide. Nagora looked over to Lars and Dannor, then back to Trowan. "When we come back, we must get together and talk. I'll tell you how it went." Trowan's smile broadened. If I come back. On to the unknown.

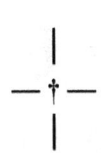

In the LAND
of the DANU

— † —

Return to the Land of the Danu
Kîwêw Askîy Paskwaskisiw

† NOW: *the first day in
the Land of the Danu*

As the three riders crossed the Blood River into the Land of
the Danu, Dannor glanced around at the weathered skulls
which sat atop the stakes twenty paces one from each other
along the riverbank on the Land of Skulls side. Those which
sat in shadier spots at the edge of the river wore manes of
green moss.

Once they were on the other side, Nagora stopped so
Dannor could turn his horse around to have a better look at the
skulls which stared back with blank eyes and jawless smiles.
"Not inviting, is it, Dannor?"

"I guess not, for those not used to seeing skulls on display
every day."

When they left the river's edge, Lars was waiting at the big
stone with its two oaks, one to a side, standing guard over it.

...

They rode up the trail to the top where the halfway lodge sat in a clearing. It was much smaller than their home lodge, round with stones all around, a slate stone roof, a single door, and a single window opening. It had been built much like Godomor's hunting lodge where they had slept the night before, their last night in the Land of Skulls.

I don't know what I'll find inside, but I want to have a look. In the least, I'll satisfy my curiosity and not feel I've overlooked something.

They entered the lodge and looked around the dim inside. "Lars, can you believe how it's set up? Only curtains separate these sections from each other." Nagora pointed. "Perhaps where the escort couple slept? It's truly not a meeting place for Sagora to welcome Gabe properly."

Lars shook his head as he looked around. "Are you thinking what I am?"

"That Sagora purposely set it up to discourage visits rather than encourage them?"

Lars exhaled and nodded. "Aye." He found candle lanterns and lit them. He handed one to Nagora and one to Dannor.

Nagora walked around the interior. The furnishings were so sparse: beds of woven leather straps empty of cedar boughs; a table with two benches and two chairs; and a firepit with its posts and crossbar, a hook, a pot, and a skillet. "They must've used mules to pack in everything else they needed."

Lars didn't reply. He stood next to her near the firepit and looked up at the wooden beams which supported the half hewn logs, upon which the roof's overlapping slate stones rested.

As Nagora stared into the firepit at her feet, she bent to one knee with the candle lantern and reached for the remains of a burnt stick to dig through the ashes. On one side of the pit, she found charred remains. They resembled pages of vellum. Nagora's stick broke most of them apart, but more pages were packed together beneath. I see written symbols on the page.

"Lars, bring your lantern here. Hold mine too." As soon as Lars took her lantern, Nagora bent closer to the pages she had uncovered. "Hold them closer so I can try to read this."

No mistaking the last word on the page. That's Pare's signature. Even if it was upside down on the edge of the pit, she could read it. The rest of the symbols were charred as dark as the pages closer to the center of the pit.

Nagora pulled a small knife from its holster and moved to the other side of the pit so Paruline's signature was right side up. With a gentle hand, she slipped the knife blade beneath the charred page and lifted it to show another beneath it. It fell apart as soon as she set it down. "Horses in the corral with fo … " Her brow furrowed. "Must be 'foal or foals'. That's all I can make out on this one."

"What was on the first one?" asked Dannor.

"Pare's signature. Pare's my dearest friend in Cairnmase. Geirador's daughter. I've told you about them before."

"Yes, I remember."

Nagora moved to slip the blade under another charred page, but Lars stopped her. "Wait. Do you think you can move the whole pack of them together and then separate them one at a time?"

"I'll need something to set them on."

Lars pointed. "Dannor, get that wooden shovel next to the door."

Nagora looked up at Lars and smiled. "I knew I married you for something other than your good looks."

"How did you know I want to hit you with the shovel?"

Nagora got the reaction she wanted. She was happy to see that teasing smile of his she loved so much.

Dannor brought the big wooden blade of the shovel down into the firepit.

Nagora reached under the pack of pages with the knife blade and the stick. She lifted the pile onto the shovel without it falling apart.

Dannor walked with the shovel. "Don't rush. Go easy. Set it on the floor in the doorway. Be gentle," said Lars.

She and Lars followed. Nagora went to her knees.

This time, she worked with two small knives to separate and lift each page. Most of them broke at the edge. By the time she finished going through the pile, there was little she could decipher as the black ink had melded with the charred vellum. "I'm sure they were letters. Why did she burn them?" It was beyond her comprehension. Nagora placed the charred remains back on the shovel.

Dannor lifted the shovel. "Shall I dump them in the firepit?"

"Yes. Thank you, Dannor."

Nagora stood and followed her son over to the pit. "Give me the shovel." She stirred the ashes in the pit. As she did so, she hooked the stone which covered the mouth of the firepit vent hole. The stone rolled aside to uncover the entrance to the small tunnel which ran beneath the floor and brought outside air to the pit. Rolling the stone away from the opening allowed for control of the draft of air to the fire.

Nagora had a thought. "Lars, your lantern, please."

Lars stepped next to Nagora as she bent down. She reached for the lantern and shone its light into the hole. Nagora's eyes widened at what she saw. Handing the lantern back to Lars, she reached into the hole. Her hand pulled out the single folded piece of vellum. Only one edge was singed, and the wax seal on the crossover fold was still intact. Had a back draft sucked it in there? How else?

"What is it?" asked Lars.

"This is my mum's seal." She turned the letter over. "For Nagora" was written on the middle section on the back of the page. "It's for me. This is my mum's writing." Nagora's heart beat faster. Mum, it's like I'm in your presence. Such was the magic letters always held for her.

Nagora stood and walked back to the doorway, holding the seal to her chest. She stopped at the doorframe. What news is in here? She looked from Lars to Dannor.

"Mum, are you going to open it?"

Nagora nodded as she reached for a small knife to slide under the seal. The seal popped up. Her fingers trembled as she fumbled to unfold the page. Her eyes read the words and in her mind, her mother's voice spoke to her.

"What does it say?" asked Dannor.

Nagora read it aloud for them:

‡

In my fifty-third year

My daughter, Nagora,

As in the letters of the past, I once again implore you for a last time. Please, it is imperative I know what happened on your last day in the cave.

There is much mystery about the events of that day. It

is leading to confusion and misunderstanding.
Raynhard is not proving to be a reliable witness to the events. What you know of the events will be of great help to us.

Sagora read a letter which you left in her care. Sagora says she is not at liberty to share it with us.

Paruline told us of the events from her visit to you at the cave.

We hope your daughter, Sarah, is well.

We look forward to news from you about Lars and Sarah.

Please, Nagora, we await your reply with great urgency.

Tagnyoriva
‡

Nagora swallowed and handed the page to Lars. "What is going on? Where is Sarah? What has Sagora done?"

"Mum, it sounds like we're headed into a nasty situation. Is there something I should know?"

Nagora took her son's hand in hers. "Dannor, when your da and I spoke to you in the days before we left, we told you everything. I've hidden nothing from you or your da. If all these letters were destined for me and they were never delivered, and if Sagora is the one who burned them, then you are right. We are headed for trouble."

"But why would she do this to you, Mum? Perhaps she is the evil twin and has been all along, like people have been saying."

Nagora placed a hand on his arm. "Dannor, please don't buy into those beliefs. There must be a reason we can't see right now."

Lars returned the letter to Nagora. "Why would she go to the trouble of burning the letters here when she could've gotten rid of them before?"

Nagora folded the letter and shrugged. "My guess is perhaps to make a show of delivering them, though judging from the pile of ashes, that's a lot of letters that were burned in one fire. How long had she been accumulating them? And when did she burn them? On her last visit here? When was that? Last fall, according to Gabe." She held up the letter. "At least, this gives us warning that something is terribly amiss. Mum wrote this letter five years ago. She's fifty-eight now. In it she mentions past letters. How many did Sagora not deliver?" Nagora placed her mother's letter in her scrip. Will I ever find out?

Visiting Three Places
Kîhokewin Nistwayak

† NOW: *the fifth day in*
the Land of the Danu

In the early morning light, on the fifth day after having left Sagora's halfway lodge, Nagora led Lars and Dannor up through the trees to the clifftop which overlooked the hamlet of Cairnmase. "Lars, I know this is a deceptive way to return, but I feel it's prudent to scout the area before just riding in."
What Nagora's eyes saw only brought more questions to mind. "What do you think, Lars?"

"It's not the same place I left years ago. It looks abandoned. There's no sign of life. See the roof on Geirador's smithy. It's sagging, almost fallen in, probably from heavy snow not removed over several winters. The corral is overgrown with weeds. The forest is reclaiming the fields all around."

Nagora spoke her thoughts out loud. "Where could they have gone to? Geirador loved this place and the people who lived here. He and Pare were supposed to raise and train Sarah here. I was expecting to find her here. If not find her, at least get news of her whereabouts from Pare and Geirador."

Lars placed his hand on Nagora's back. "Shall we go down to have a look around?"

Nagora nodded. She blinked as she looked up into Lars's face before taking a deep breath. "Yes, let's do that. I'm sorry. I don't know what to say. This was the last thing I expected."

Dannor put a hand on his mother's shoulder. "It's okay, Mum. You trusted your feelings."

Nagora dismounted and slipped Storm's reins over the corral fence nearest to Geirador's lodge. She walked the three hundred paces to the stone cliff against which Geirador's home nestled. Today she did so with an uneasy feeling.

The door was ajar. The smell of Paruline's cooking was not there to greet her. Instead, a dark dampness hung in the air as she crossed the threshold. No cheerful sing-song words from Paruline, and no hearty laugh from Geirador. In her memory, all the words and laughter Nagora had ever shared with them belonged there. Now there was only silence. That silence left a sick knot in her stomach.

Why? Why did they leave? Where did they go?

Lars stepped past Nagora, into the dim interior toward the fireplace. "Let me see if I can find a lantern." Lars had spent time here with the wounded from Godomor's Hundred Best, waiting until their wounds healed enough to allow them to make the return trip home. He knew his way around Geirador's home. "There's a stub of a candle left in this one. You'll have light in a moment."

A chair sat alone in a corner. The huge table was gone, as were the benches and the ladder to the loft.

"Lars, have a look in the cold room." He and Dannor walked to the closed door and pushed it open. They disappeared inside.

When they came out, Dannor held open his palms. They contained nutshells. "It's empty. Looks like the squirrels got the last of the nuts left behind."

Nagora shrugged. "Well, at least Geirador's cabinet with his medical implements and supplies is gone. And all of their cooking utensils. They've moved somewhere. We'll find them."

As Lars returned the lantern to its hook, the candle flame died, leaving a wisp of smoke to hang above the stub.

They mounted their horses and led their mules through Cairnmase, past empty stone huts, winding their way through the cairn peaks of the abandoned village. It left Nagora with an eerie feeling. No one spoke until they reached the forest road.

The road could take them to the town of Yhorgal or, if they stayed with the fork in the road to the right, it would take them to the sparse remains of the lodge where Nagora had lived with her uncle, Dangor. Nagora stopped her horse and turned to Dannor. "I'm going to show you where I was brought up."

Wow! The forest has reclaimed this road. Now a wagon would have to fight its way through. To think Patches pulled Uncle and me on our cart over this road. Now it's barely a forest trail, overgrown with brush and young trees.

...

What had once been a cleared field was now being invaded by stands of alder and hawthorn trees, with a scattering of young spruce trees fighting to grow taller. Their heads, known as arrows, showed signs of being repeatedly clipped by deer feeding on them in winter when the snow was deep. Those tender tips, peeking out above the snow's crust, offered the deer sustenance in that cold season. Each spring, one of the lower branches fought to become the tree's new arrow, pointing skyward. They don't give up easily.

Nagora found the stone bluff and dismounted. "This is where our lodge was. Uncle built it against the bluff." She pointed. "The sod roof reached to the top of the bluff. I slept up in the loft." Nagora paused. So much I could tell you about it. The sad memory had stopped her. "But Queen Raganora's captain came and had it torn down. Every stone was deliberately strewn about."

Nagora kicked the one next to her foot. She reached down to pick it up. "See the charring here? This part of the stone was on the inside of our chimney. Queen Rag's soldiers burnt everything that could be burned. Only a pile of ashes remained."

"Mum, it sounds like they wanted to leave a message."

Nagora let the stone drop. "Until we came upon the scene that day, I had never seen such dismay and pain on Uncle's face. They obliterated our home, but not our memories of our life in it. Yes, Dannor. That's what it was—a warning to Edana and anyone who supported her."

Nagora fought back her tears as she mounted Storm. "Let's go see what remains of the beach hut."

...

Within a count they were looking down on the remains of the hut. "I didn't expect to see any of it standing. Almost two walls of stacked stones still upright. It looks like a sea storm might've pushed in two of the walls and covered them with sand."

"Could've been a big storm, or two. Or winter ice pushed by a spring storm that knocked them in," said Lars. "I've seen that happen on the Moroes Islands."

Nagora pointed along the beach that reached out into the bay in the shape of a hook. "Dannor, that's where I played as a child growing up. How many times I ran to the tip of the hook and back. I would leave after breakfast and get back for a late lunch, starved. Uncle would have shore soup and stone-baked bread waiting for me. I didn't have a single care to worry about in those days. Play on the beach and swim in the sea. Those days seemed to last forever back then. At least that's how they felt to me. I would fall asleep and dream about the next day on the beach."

"Mum, when did you start training with your uncle?"

Nagora smiled. "You know, Dannor, that's so hard to answer. It was never formal training with Uncle unless we went to meet other people who gathered in Cairnmase to train. It all started out as play with Uncle."

"What do you mean?"

"Well, those runs to the tip of the hook. They trained me to become a runner. I only found out years later that now and then a fisher friend of Uncle's would leave something for me to find, to entice me to run all the way out there."

"Like what?" asked Dannor.

"Oh, an old boot, a belt buckle, a rusty knife, and once, an old wooden shield with brass nails and leather strapping that held it together. Imagine, I carried and rolled that old shield all the way back to the hut.

"Uncle and I always had great talks about where those objects had come from. Who they belonged to. How they came to get washed up in the stone dip at the tip of the hook."

Lars dismounted. "I think we could all do with a good swim to get some of this road dust off us. We could set up camp at the edge of the forest near the stream and make our way to Yhorgal tomorrow."

Nagora dismounted and went over to Lars. She threw her arms around him and stared up into his face. "Good idea."

Lars brought his nose down to Nagora's. "You head down to the beach. Dannor and I'll take care of the horses and mules. Then we'll join you."

Nagora walked around the remains of the hut. She found the pieces of three speckled eggs amongst the stones of the fallen walls inside the remains of the hut. I'm happy one of those funny little shore birds nested here. Though, they always seem to nest in the open for a better view of predators coming from all directions. I hope the chicks survived.

That thought reminded her of when she had awoken under one of the curraghs she and her uncle used to build on the beach. The air was stifling beneath the small leather craft when she came to. It was her first realization she had survived her swim to freedom from the dungeon sea cave and Hag's death sentence. Another reason to execute you, Alizarine. You are Hag in another body.

Who had placed her under the curragh and why had worried her then. She had peered out from under it and spotted another next to it. She had managed to prop the curragh up, roll over to the other cowhide boat, prop it up, and roll under it.

Those efforts had exhausted her and she fell into unconsciousness again. When she awoke, she realized her dragon-tear amulet was missing.

Here I am today and I'm without my amulet, again. Sarah is supposed to have it.

When I got my amulet back, I thought I was losing my mind or had died and returned. I didn't realize it was the amulet revealing its powers.

What will that amulet reveal if ever I wear it again? Do I want to know?

Danuka told her of another power the amulet had. Nagora could show another person something she had experienced in the past, but to do so required her to join in sexual union with the other and hold the amulet pressed between their foreheads.

I did that once. Why, Raynhard, did you lie about what I'd shown you? Was it to spite me? Was it out of love for Aliza? Or did she have that much control over you? Will I ever find answers that are the truth?

Nagora undressed except for her knitted shirt, which she kept on. She pulled the hood onto the back of her head as she walked to the water's edge where the cool sea breeze pushed gentle rolling waves to the shore.

The tide's on its way out.

Nagora bent to pick up a small stone in the wet sand at her feet. She held it in her palm to examine it. At the same moment, a wave washed over her feet and pulled back out, leaving foamy licks on the sand that now covered her toes.

It'll be a cool, refreshing swim.

Nagora turned the stone over again before holding it up to the sunlight.

What other powers does my amulet hold? Will I ever find out?

With the screams of warriors riding into battle, her two men, naked and laughing, ran past her into the water, splashing headlong as far as they could until they had to dive in. Nagora didn't wait for them to come back out to haul her in. She shed her sweater and ran in after them.

The water seemed colder than what her memory told her it had been. After swimming a few strokes and diving under repeatedly, it was bearable and she welcomed its cool, cleansing caress on her body.

On their way out of the water, they kicked at the waves until they set foot on the wet sand. Nagora pointed to their shriveled manhood. "That's how cold the water is."

Lars laughed. "It's not the cold. It's fear of becoming bait for the fish. They retreat into the forest."

Nagora gave him a shove. "Dannor, help me throw him back in. The fish will have their due."

A playful struggle ensued until Lars ended up dragging them both back into the waves, kicking and screaming, under his arms.

I knew we wouldn't win that one. Offer me a choice: a moment like this, or a purse full of gold coins? Gold can't buy times like this, even if they are short-lived.

...

They headed to the ruins of the hut, which would give them a windbreak from the cool sea breeze. "Dannor brought his bow. He'll try to hit a flounder. If he does, we'll make shore soup for supper," said Lars.

Nagora pointed to where the beach narrowed and the sea was closer to the cliffs. "Good, Dannor. There used to be shallow pools over that way. While you hunt, we'll dig for clams and see if we can find eggs in the nests on the cliff face."

"Let's warm up first."

Nagora fell asleep wrapped in a blanket of sunshine, her head resting in the crook of Lars's arm. When she awoke, Dannor was gone.

"I've been waiting for you," said Lars.

Nagora rolled over onto her side and draped a leg over one of Lars's knees. "You could have woken me."

"No. I rather gaze upon your face. You're most beautiful when you sleep."

Nagora ran her hand up from his stomach, across his chest, and snaked it to the back of his neck. As she pulled him to her for a kiss, her leg bent at the knee and climbed his. When her lips left his and slid over his beard to his ear, she whispered, "Do we have time? Let me check on Dannor."

Nagora gazed down the beach. Dannor was a silhouette in the distance, up to his knees in the water, holding his bow and a nocked arrow. They had time.

Nagora lined a linen sack with pieces of dried dulse to hold the eggs they might collect. Dangor liked gathering the ingredients to make shore soup. His foraging expeditions with her had been teaching moments. Nagora learned to hunt, climb, scavenge, observe, and how to be patient. She learned how to prepare and cook those ingredients.

Similar lessons took place in the forest and hills above and beyond the cliffs. The game was bigger. Tracking and hunting it required more skills and patience.

There were the other two-legged predators that competed for the same prizes.

That was the aspect of Dangor's teaching that took on greater meaning. Learning those lessons could mean the difference between living and dying.

How do you discern whether they were friend or foe? How do you read the signs they left to learn about them? Were they skillful or careless? Respectful or not of the land which provided for them?

Dangor would point to his head and say, "Think of them as enemy. What can you learn just by looking at them? How they dress. The kinds of weapons they carry. How they handle and care for their weapons. Their hands. Their faces. Where they gaze and how they glance when they are alone, with others, and especially when speaking with others. Learn by observing those you trust. Watch for changes. Try to understand what causes the changes." How many times had he spoken these words to her?

Will I see how my sister and my king have changed? Will I have to imagine them as enemies?

How many times had Uncle questioned me to see if I was seeing and learning from what I had seen? It was always in the details.

"Do you think that man at the market was a good archer? Why or why not? What did the feathers on his arrows tell you? What did the dirt on his quiver tell you? What about his bow string?" Uncle's questions were numerous.

My answers followed: "Most likely not a good archer. Dirty feathers, and some of the whippings holding them to their shafts were missing. Many frayed. Quiver dirty. Bow dirty. String frayed. A break waiting to happen. Archers with good skills take pride in their equipment. I would never pick him to fight alongside me."

He'd then ask: "In that group of men, who was the quiet one? Who was the leader? Which one was his best man? Who was his last pick? Does he trust the others completely?"

I'd respond: "The one always staring at his hands and feet. The one who talked the loudest and touched the others. The one who was always the first to agree with what he said. The quiet one. He never touched him. His sword hand was never far from the handle of his sword. Even when he drank from his mug of ale, he used his other hand. His eyes were continually watching theirs."

"If they cornered you and you had to fight them, who would you take first? What's his weakness?" Uncle would inquire.

I'd answer: "The leader. His sword is big, but he's no swordsman. The pommel is worn, but the handle's grip is not. He rarely practices with it. Get to him before he draws it, and the others will most likely flee. I see only false loyalty to him."

Will I see the details that will warn me? The unknown. Always the unknown.

Dannor had been lucky. The flounder he shot was perfect for the pot. Nagora's linen bag held five eggs secreted from five different nests found on the cliff. Lars had dug a dozen clams and caught two crabs. They climbed the cliff path with the makings of their meal in hand.

At the top, Nagora had a last look at the remains of the hut and her beach before crossing the meadow to the forest edge where her men had tethered the horses and mules, free of their saddles and packs. Nagora and Dannor took the animals to the nearby stream to drink while Lars set up the tarp they would spend the night under. By the time they finished their meal, the night sky was pulling its starry cover over them. Lars took the first watch.

Nagora slept soundly until her turn.

With an occasional look to her men and her ears focused on the sounds of the night, Nagora tried to guess what could have caused the people of Cairnmase to leave. Was it because their once secret vocation as weapon makers was no longer needed? Did they choose to belong to a larger community? Perhaps. In the coming morning, once we reach Yhorgal, I might get answers to my questions.

Nagora fed a last log to the fire before waking Lars for his last watch.

Old Friends
Kayâsi Otôtêmimâw

✝ NOW: *the sixth day in
the Land of the Danu*

"I'll ask the first person we meet. Unless they're a stranger to these parts, they should know," said Nagora. The first person was on the bridge that crossed Yhorgal River on the outskirts of the town that gave the river its name. The man held a fishing pole in one hand. He was tall with bowed legs, a bald head, and a single crooked tooth in the middle of his grin. He squinted at them and, as they approached, he leaned his pole against the bridge rail.

"Morning, kind sir."

The man gazed up at Nagora as his right hand touched his forehead and traced the Tiwaz symbol on the skin above his nose. The fisher looked from Nagora to Lars and then to Dannor. He craned his neck to see their horses and the mules. Then he turned in a complete circle. He seemed to search for something.

When he looked back up at Nagora, he asked, "Where's Danuka?"

"What do you mean?"

Now the fisher was scratching his head. "You always come here on the dragon. What are you doing on a horse?"

I won't try to explain. "I'm looking for the blacksmith, Geirador. Do you know where I can find him?"

The fisher seemed taken aback. "You mean the former smithy Geirador from Cairnmase?"

Nagora nodded. "Yes, him."

"Geirador's now Laird Geirador of Yhorgal Fortress Domain. That's where you'll find him, as if you didn't know, Lady Edana." The man winked. "Your secret's good with me. Being one of the common folk one last time before you take the crown?"

The fisher raised both thumbs and pointer fingers to his forehead and moved them back and forth across it.

What's he doing now?

"Pardon me, my Lady, but if I were you, I would wear a band or scarf to cover, you know. It gives you away." He winked again.

Nagora pretended surprise, reached back to pull her hood over her head, and folded the edge down over her forehead.

The man gave her a thumbs-up and winked again. "Do you know the way to the fortress?"

"I do. Thank you."

The man bowed, returned to his fishing pole, and dropped his line into the river.

Nagora led the men on the road which would bypass the town and bring them to the road heading to the fortress.

A guard stood outside the closed gate. "Do you have a summons? No summons, no entry."

Look at this guard, relishing in the power he thinks he has. Nagora pulled her hood back.

The guard's eyes widened. "Sorry, my Lady. Didn't recognize you. These two are with you?"

"Yes." As Nagora replied, the guard looked all about beyond them and to the sky.

Is he looking for Danuka too?

The gate guard called up to the sentinels on the wall. "Open the gate. Lady Edana and company."

Nagora glanced back at Lars and Dannor and shrugged her shoulders. I'm seeing the picture.

They dismounted, and two grooms came to attend to their horses and mules. Not much had changed in the fortress yard since her last forced visit when Nagora had been among a dozen other young girls taken by Prince Acindor's guards from the Yhorgal market square and brought to the fortress for the prince's pleasure. Acindor was looking for a virgin bride.

Nagora scanned the walls of the yard. I almost despaired when I saw the guards chain Uncle to the iron rings on that wall. They brought him along with the girls because he had asked their captain about how his men would treat the girls.

Then Nagora's eyes went to the stone staircase which led to the level of the prince's chambers.

At that moment, Geirador appeared at the door on the landing at the top of the stairs. He wasn't dressed in his usual smithy garb. His hair and beard were almost completely white. He had lost weight. The look on Geirador's face was grave.

Where has your welcoming smile gone? Nagora had rarely seen Geirador wear such a face.

Geirador paused on the landing, slowing his step until it came to a stop. He looked around the yard, to the sky, and then back to Nagora.

The look on his face changed. His mouth moved, but no words came forth. He shook his head, blinked his eyes and set his legs in motion down the staircase. Geirador found his voice. "Nagora? Lars?" His steps gained speed and when he reached the yard, he was scurrying.

Tears welled up and wet Nagora's face. She couldn't stop them. She couldn't speak his name. Nagora spread her arms and walked in his direction. Her shoulders shook when he held her in his embrace.

"Nagora, we have so much to speak of, so much to set right. Paruline has been wishing for this day for years."

Nagora could only look up into Geirador's eyes as she held onto his arms and nodded.

Geirador kept an arm around Nagora and offered his free hand to Lars. "Lars, I'm so glad to see you again."

Lars let go of Geirador's hand and placed it on Dannor's shoulder. "Geirador, my son and Nagora's son, Dannor. Dannor, we've spoken often of this man. Now you get to shake his hand."

As he took Geirador's hand, Dannor's other hand reached over his own shoulder to touch the handle of the skystone blade. "I'm honored to meet you. I wear your blades with pride."

Geirador smiled. "If your parents taught you how to use them, they'll serve you well."

My son, your confident smile pleases me, and your skills make me proud.

"Sir, if it's all right with you, I'll go to the stable with our horses?"

Geirador placed a hand on Dannor's shoulder. "I'll have none of this 'Sir' business from a new friend. Dannor, you saw where the grooms went. Take care of your mounts. I'm sure you'll find us inside." Geirador shepherded Nagora and Lars toward the stairs. "Come. We'll go in to Paruline."

Geirador led them along the hall to a chamber. It was the room where the soldiers had brought Nagora and the other girls to wash their faces and hands and comb their hair before being brought before Prince Acindor.

The narrow table and the mirrors above it along the windowless wall were still in place. Now a table with chairs around it occupied the middle of the room, whereas back then a single long bench sat by itself.

Geirador motioned them to the chairs. "Please, remove your weapons. Make yourselves comfortable at the table. Paruline will join us soon. I want to see her face when she walks in."

They did not have long to wait. Paruline appeared at the door. That's so unlike how I remember you, Pare. Nagora had never seen Paruline wear a dress this length nor a surcoat with such elaborate embroidery. Paruline held her hands before her, below her breast, her left fist wrapped in her right hand. Her face wore only the hint of a smile. She frowned as she looked from Nagora to Lars and then to her father, and back to Nagora.

Nagora stood. "Pare."

Paruline's hands went to her face as her mouth dropped open and she drew a great breath. Then she held out her arms and stepped in Nagora's direction. Paruline's face fought between twisting into a smile and holding back tears of disbelief. "Nagora!"

"Pare!"

After embracing and looking each other up and down, Paruline said, "You can't imagine how I've wished for this day!" She smiled at Lars. He was standing, waiting to greet her. "Lars," she reached over to him and pulled him to her, "it's good to see you after all these years."

"We're glad to find you. We worried about you when we showed up in Cairnmase yesterday."

Paruline shook her head and bit her lower lip. She sighed. "I wish we were back there now." She looked from Lars to Nagora. "So you've heard?"

"If you mean about the royal wedding invitation, yes. It's the first news in almost six years. Someone's been burning the missives you sent and most likely the ones I sent," said Nagora.

"Nagora, we suspected as much when you didn't reply to my wedding invitation."

"Pare! You're married!" Nagora took her friend's hands in hers.

Paruline wore a proud smile. "Aye, I am, almost five years ago in Cairnmase. Our anniversary will be on the same day the king marries."

"When will we meet the lucky man?" Nagora looked from Paruline to Geirador and back, eager for an answer.

Her friend shook her head. "Not today. He's away on business." Paruline looked to her father.

Geirador waved for them to sit. "Three years after you left for the Land of Skulls, three brothers from Dromester showed up in Cairnmase to look me up. Olen, the smith who runs a stable in Windhaven, had referred them."

"Aye, I remember Olen well. You say they're from Dromester. Do they know Bardas, the smith?"

Geirador smiled. "You're getting ahead of me. In fact two of them were working for Bardas. They were hoping to expand their business by making a line of cutlery and knives to sell at the docks in Windhaven. The two working for Bardas, Jani and Joni, were to marry his daughters that fall. You know them too, Moreena and Erin. Jani, the blind Konen brother, married Moreena, and Joni married Erin. Harri, the eldest, owns a shop at the docks. He was looking for wares to sell."

Paruline interrupted with a bashful smile. "In case Da forgets, Harri is my husband."

"As I was saying," said Geirador, smiling, "Jani and Joni were looking for recipes and techniques to make quality knives and cutlery. Harri was looking for specialty metal items to sell. When he saw the decorative hinges, latches, handles, and locks I make, he was keen on getting me to produce for him. To cut a long story short, the Konen brothers stayed for almost two months learning my recipes and techniques. Not only did Harri take an interest in learning to make my line of goods, he showed a definite interest in Paruline."

Paruline placed a hand on her father's arm. "Da likes to think Harri's interest grew over time. I knew he was to be mine from day one. Demand for the goods he sold grew to the point he had to hire extra shopkeepers to replace him when he came here to work on production."

"Wow! Pare, I'm so happy for you."

Just as Nagora was about to ask more questions, Dannor stepped into the room.

Paruline's eyes took him in and then went from Dannor to Nagora and then to Lars. "Your son?"

Nagora smiled and nodded. "Our son, Dannor."

Paruline stood and reached for Dannor's hands. Her eyes were full of admiration. "Dannor, I think your father has made a replica, except for the color of your eyes. Those are your mum's eyes. Soon, you'll be as tall as him. I'm most happy to meet you."

Paruline let go of one hand and reached for Nagora's hand. "How old is Dannor?"

"Fourteen months younger than Sarah." The look in Paruline's eyes changed. "Pare, do you know where Sarah is?"

Now Paruline held both of Nagora's hands. I see pain in my dear friend's eyes. "Sarah's with Sagora, as you wished her to be." Paruline let go of their hands.

Anger filled Nagora's chest. Sagora, what have you done? "Pare, no! I never made such a wish. You were to raise Sarah as your own. You and your da were to train her. You know that. We discussed it when you came to help me give birth to Sarah."

Paruline crossed her arms over her stomach. "That's not what Sagora said was in your letter to her."

"Did Sagora show you the letter?"

"No, Sagora said there was other information in the letter for her eyes only."

"Pare, believe me. There were only two things in that letter I wanted Sagora to know if I should not return for Sarah." Nagora held up a thumb. "Who Sarah's father is. That I had lied to Raynhard, telling him he was not the father, only because he had lied to me about Aliza."

Then she held up a finger. "And most important, I wanted her to entrust Sarah to your care so you could raise her as your own, and when Sarah was old enough, you and your da were to train her. At the time Sagora, Tagnya, and Yogari were too busy to care for Sarah. I thought Danuka would understand and not hold so strictly to her condition that I give Sarah to Sagora."

Paruline's eyes blinked as she swallowed and shook her head.

Pare wants to believe me. "Pare, you saw the blue spots on Sarah's back. You told me they were a sign one of the parents was a direct descendant of the original *First People* of the Land. Raynhard is. His black hair too attests to that, as well as his dark eyes and the color of his skin in summer. You and your parents saw me as a baby. I did not have those spots on my back. Did I, Geirador? Dannor was not born with them either."

Pare, you have to trust me.

"Please, Pare, why would I have changed my mind? I named Sarah after your mum. She nursed me when Uncle Dangor brought me back from the Land of Skulls."

Nagora reached into her scrip and brought out the letter she had recovered at Sagora's halfway lodge. After explaining how she had found it, she handed it to Paruline. "Here, it's from Mum. Read it, Pare, please!"

Paruline examined the charred edge of the page before she opened it.

Geirador approached. "Paruline, you have to tell Nagora. It'll be better if she knows all we know."

Paruline finished reading the letter then looked up to Nagora, to her father, and back to Nagora. "Very well. I know when Tagnya wrote this letter. Your mum spoke to me and told me she was writing to you one last time. She was feeling desperate with the situation.

"Nagora, you'll understand why when I explain Sagora's actions, though I doubt you will see the reasoning behind her actions."

Nagora shook her head. "Explain, Pare, I need to know."

Paruline took a breath. "Try to follow what I'll tell you." Paruline paused. "Sagora told Tagnya that Sarah was my baby. An easy lie because we had not been together since you had visited. Sagora told Tagnya that Raynhard was the father, but Sarah's existence as his daughter had to be kept from him." Paruline closed her eyes and took another breath.

I read the pain that lie causes you.

"To make sure that happened, Tagnya was to make believe to Raynhard that Sarah was Sagora's baby with Gabe as the father. Another easy lie, since Sagora had spent the winter in the Land of Skulls and did not see Raynhard until well after you left. This I only found out after Sagora had lied to Tagnya, painting me as part of the lie."

I can't believe it. "But why such lies, Pare?"

"First the facts, Nagora. Then you can conclude what you want.

"Sagora had herself branded. She said she was doing it for Raynhard and the people of the Land of the Danu. They needed their Edana. So she became Edana. The people wanted Edana at Raynhard's side. They wanted her on Danuka. They wanted to see their heroine. They wanted Edana to guide them, to inspire them, to lead them back to a new and better life.

"Raynhard had Yogari train Sagora to be a Dragon Rider."

Nagora held up her hands. "So where was Sarah all this time?"

"At the castle in Windhaven, where Sagora now lives with Raynhard."

"Why did Raynhard not marry her sooner?"

"We're guessing he had been waiting for you to return."

"Why would he have waited for me?"

Paruline looked to Lars and Dannor before answering. "To be his queen."

This is even more confusing. I've so many questions to make sense of this. "But why would he? I refused to be his queen. He knew that. He took to Aliza. When he did, he almost had no use for me, other than being his cave-bound Dragon Talker, guarding Danuka's eggs. So what changed his mind? Was it Sagora?"

Paruline was shaking her head. "We don't know. There's a new child in the castle."

Nagora looked wide-eyed from Paruline to Geirador. She said, "You don't know who that child is, do you? Do you know where it's from? Did Raynhard ever tell you what happened on that last day I was with him in the cave?"

Paruline made a sign with her hands for her father to speak to that question. "Nagora, we don't know what to believe. We've heard so many stories from Raynhard that, honestly, we wonder about his ability to rule. Look at us. Do you think we're happy to be here?"

I see so much hurt in your face, Geirador.

Paruline's shoulders sagged as she hung her head and brought her hands to her mouth. "Raynhard gifted us with the title to this fortress and its lands, against our wishes. He forced us to leave all we had built in Cairnmase. Not just us, but all our people. We had a good life in the cairns, especially with our production with Harri. It was our home. This is no home to us. Yes, we've been able to set up production here at the fortress forge, but it's not the same. Da hardly ever gets to do the work he loves anymore. It's a prison!"

Nagora reached out for Paruline's hands. She held them to her chest. "Oh, Pare. I can see the pain all this is causing you. Talking about it is difficult. Believe me. I want to help make this right. You had more freedom in Cairnmase under Queen Rag's rule than you have here. That's not what we fought for."

Paruline let go of Nagora's hands and pointed about. "This is our reward for our contribution to help return Raynhard to his throne. We didn't do it for a reward!"

Geirador held up a fist. "We knew Raynhard. We knew The Watcher. We knew Chive." The three roles our king took on to plan to reclaim his throne. "We don't know who sits on the throne and rules us the way he does these days."

I want to tell you what happened in the cave that day, and I have more questions I want answers to. Where to start? "We knew we were coming into a situation which Dannor guessed would be nasty. From what I'm hearing, the situation for our king is also a desperate one. Pare, Geirador, believe me. We are here to help."

Nagora placed a hand on Geirador's arm. "You said we have much to speak about and much to set right. Let's see if we can do that."

As they sat at the table, a servant arrived with a tray of berry bread, cheese, nuts, and tea. Paruline dismissed the maid after she had set the tray on the table.

I'll get to the point. "How long have you been here?"

Geirador looked to Paruline. "It'll be five years this fall."

Paruline nodded once. "Five years too many, against our will."

Raynhard did that to you? "You had no choice?"

"Father has the duties of a laird. He's become a recorder of levies of grain stores and livestock in the domain."

Nagora shook her head and placed her fingers on the side of her head.

"Surpluses produced here are marked for possible redistribution to needy areas in the kingdom," said Paruline.

Geirador laid a hand flat on the table and stared at it for a moment. "And to feed the garrison troops. And I'm also to collect levies on profits from merchants to pay wages to the troops."

Paruline reached for her father's hand.

Nagora had been looking at Geirador's hand. It was not the strong, calloused metal-and-coal-stained hand she remembered.

"Father feels his talents are being wasted here." Paruline's eyes were almost pleading as she spoke those words.

Paruline was right. Here was a master smithy and weapon maker who had once run a secret network of smithies throughout the land, all loyal to The Cause. A man who knew how to make every weapon. A man who tamed horses and trained riders. A man who was a healer. A man who drew people to him so they could learn to make tools or weapons of quality and become productive, with a purpose, like he did with the Konen brothers.

Now the only stains on his otherwise clean hand were the ink stains from a tribute collector's quill. Nagora's eyes climbed from his hand to his face.

Geirador took a breath. "Raynhard insisted. Said he needed someone he could trust to do the job. Said I was not to worry. That I would take to the job and title. That I deserved a rest from the fires of my forge."

"But he didn't consider what you wanted. That just doesn't seem like how Raynhard would treat loyal friends," said Nagora.

Geirador shrugged, placed his hand on the table and spread his fingers. "No. I tried to tell him. He didn't listen."

"When's the last time you saw him?" asked Nagora.

"That day when he ordered us here."

"Have you been to Windhaven since?"

"No. The wedding invitation will change that."

"So who do you deal with on these duties Raynhard has burdened you with?"

"Sagora. She flies here on Danuka."

"Sagora flies here alone on Danuka?"

"Yes. As Paruline said, Raynhard had Yogari train her as a rider."

"Do you know who trained Sarah in warrior skills?"

"Yogari and Tagnya, on Raynhard's insistence. It was his attempt to bring your mother and father back together," said Paruline.

"So they're all living in Windhaven? At the castle?"

Paruline raised her eyebrows. "Sarah was there with Sagora until she turned seven. Then Sarah lived with your parents at the fortress on the Isle of Smoke, learning to become a Dragon Talker and rider with Yogari's help. She learned warrior skills from both your mother and father.

"Now she's back at the castle in Windhaven." Paruline looked at Geirador with a frown on her face. What does she want him to confirm?

Geirador brought his hands together on the tabletop. "I'll tell. They need to know. The sooner the better. Yogari and Tagnya are away at sea on the Sea Wolf. Your father and his old crew rebuilt the Wolf," Geirador paused, "for a purpose."

Why do I think this will not be good news? Nagora reached for Lars's hand. "What purpose?"

"You remember Grallimdor? Raganora's commander at the Isle of Smoke fortress?"

"Yes. Wasn't he killed when fleeing with Raganora to Windhaven after Da and Danuka destroyed the Isle of Smoke Bridge?"

Geirador's look was solemn as he shook his head from side to side. "That wasn't Grallimdor."

Nagora's jaw dropped. "What! How can that be?"

Geirador held up a finger. "Nor was that Raganora they captured."

A million thoughts raced through Nagora's mind as she tried to understand. "But ... but ... How can that be?"

"The boat you heard Grallimdor speak to Raganora about with all the dragon gold on it, well, it sailed the night before the battle, with Raganora and Grallimdor on board, and two dozen mercenaries who had holed up in Windhaven castle."

Nagora shook her head. "That means—they knew I was listening! Raganora and Grallimdor knew of the raiders' plan to take the Isle of Smoke all along! How? Who gave them that information?" That's why Raynhard didn't want me to … Nagora swallowed. No. Hold that thought. It has to make sense. I need proof. I have to think this through.

Geirador held her eyes with his. "If you think on it long enough and play out all the possibilities as many times as I have, Nagora, you'll come up with the same name as I do. However, you'll not get to the why of it."

Geirador's right. Why? A knot tightened in her stomach. Best move on. Don't let it make you sick. Think on it later. "Is there a new bridge to the Isle of Smoke?"

"No. Danuka takes them to and from the island."

"Are her eggs there?"

"Yes, in a secret cave. Only Yogari and Sarah know its whereabouts."

And the Little People. They need not know that. And Geirador must suspect as much. I better tell them all about what happened on my last day in the cave with Raynhard and Aliza. This they should know.

Paruline and Geirador listened to Nagora and Lars long enough for the servant to have replenished the tray of food and tea twice, and for the maid to inquire, on the third trip to the table, if the guests would be staying for the evening meal. Geirador assured the servant they would, and they would also spend the night at the fortress.

"Perhaps Raynhard was still knocked out when Heqet spoke the new curse on Alizarine and maybe he only woke up as Aliza was crossing to the island. At that moment Raynhard must've believed you had killed Danuka, and that you would destroy what he thought was the last dragon egg and perhaps kill Aliza too," said Paruline.

Nagora shrugged. "That could be. Although when Raynhard crossed over to the island and saw Aliza had changed into the young girl, Alizarine, he was stunned by what he saw.

"When I told him I would take care of her, I don't know if he thought I meant I would kill her. I had my hand on the handle of the dagger when I said it.

"Perhaps, instead, he thought I would actually care for her and the egg. If that's so, and Alizarine's at the castle, he must recognize her. She hasn't grown older since that day. She has the egg with her. So he must know where she came from."

Nagora raised both hands and shrugged. "I can't say for sure he heard Heqet's curse and understood it. Aliza's hit might have left him dazed. That scene, which the Little People brought alive in his cave, was a lot for him to take in and make sense of. It looked so real. Perhaps he thought he was in a dream state?

"I'm sure Aliza, or Alizarine if you wish, had control on him. Perhaps not to the extent she had on Pug, but power over him nevertheless. Is that what we're seeing, behavior, so unlike him? Maybe Hag always had control over him, even as Chive, her idiot gatherer of herbs and forest mushrooms."

Did Pare tell Geirador what she'd told me, about her night with Raynhard in their home after she brought the freed girls back from the fortress?

Geirador sat back, scratched his chin, and pulled at his beard. "So Alizarine has not aged in all these years. And she called you 'Mother.' And even if you wanted to, you couldn't kill her?"

Nagora sighed. "That's right. Such is Heqet's curse. I tried that day. I couldn't. Believe me. If there's a witch I want to see dead, it's her. Call her Hag, Aliza, Alizarine, or any other name. I want her dead!"

Geirador brought his hands together, crossing his fingers. "But you'll need Sarah's help. How will you convince Sarah?"

Nagora bit into her upper lip as she looked at Geirador. She took a deep breath. "You're right. I wish I had the answer to your question. I don't know how I'll convince Sarah. I must find a way."

Geirador looked to Lars and Dannor, then back to Nagora. "This Alizarine, from what we've heard, has won the hearts of all at the court. She calls Sagora 'Mother' and Raynhard 'Father.' Sagora's boys are her 'brothers.' And Sarah her 'sister.' Nagora, perhaps Raynhard truly thinks Alizarine is your daughter."

Nagora held her palms up. "I don't see how Raynhard can think that even if he doesn't remember her from that day in the cave. And now he's taken by her. Because of the curse, or because of Alizarine's power over him? Or perhaps he does think I'm her mother and Lars her father. That she's the age she appears to be. She calls me mother too. But Raynhard doesn't know that. If he and the others are truly taken by her, it's because they don't know that they should be wary of her."

Nagora shrugged. "Sarah might see her as my daughter. If Mum and Da were here, how would they see her? I don't know."

What piece of information might I use to convince my daughter? "Pare, do you know who brought Alizarine back here? I can't imagine Sagora doing that on her own."

Paruline shook her head and looked to her father. "We're now just learning who this Alizarine is and where she's come from. I'm sorry. We can't help you with those details."

Geirador appeared to be thinking. "From what you've told us, I'm guessing it would be Danuka herself. Her eggs are due to hatch. Danuka must've known all along that you—I mean Alizarine, under your care, had the only egg with a male dragon, not potentially as the Little People think. Danuka took you on a flight to show you where to go in the Land of Skulls. In her own way, she gave you the map to those maze-protected ancient hatching circles, designed by the Little People for the dragons to use.

"Somehow Danuka knows of Heqet's curse. Most likely from the Little People. They were there. They witnessed it. Danuka brought Alizarine here to bring you to Sarah to carry out the curse so she can get that valuable egg back. Danuka wants to give you back your daughter in return for her egg. How will Danuka do that?" Geirador paused.

Nagora held up a finger. "So if it was Danuka's doing, who did she choose to do the task?"

Geirador did not hesitate. "The Dragon Talker or the Dragon Rider. Or both? If you were Danuka, who would you have chosen?"

Nagora shook her head. "I don't know. Why didn't they come to find me and tell me Danuka needed her egg? Sarah and I could have killed Alizarine, right there. Why kill the dogs?"

Geirador reached over to place a hand on one of Nagora's. "The curse, Nagora. You don't see it yet, do you?"

I see it, but I don't dare speak it in your presence. Before she could say anything, Geirador spoke. "You are mother to the king's daughter. You have yet to be crowned queen."

Oh yes, I see it, even if I wish it were not so. The curse invites me to wed Raynhard.

Nagora looked from Geirador to Lars and Dannor. This added dimension makes me wish I could absolve Lars and Dannor from taking this path destined for me. They are not part of my contract with Danuka.

Then Nagora looked back to Paruline and Geirador. You too have been drawn onto my path. Are all our destinies linked? Have I shackled all of you to my chain? Even our dogs?

The killing of their dogs had troubled her, and now the thought of them brought back that apprehension. "But why kill the dogs?"

Geirador squeezed her hand. "It's a warning."

A warning from Alizarine, through Sagora? Or from Sagora only? If so, what's she trying to tell me? Not to meddle in her wedding? The painful knot in the pit of Nagora's stomach tightened again. "Geirador, what do you mean when you say it's a warning?"

Geirador kept hold of Nagora's hand and pursed his lips before answering. "Whoever killed the dogs is warning you that they'll stop at nothing to get what they want. They're telling you that you'll be risking your life if you get involved."

Paruline took hold of Nagora's other hand and called her by her pet name. "Little Sister, I don't know how you'll do this. I know you'll take that risk. You've done so before. I trust you'll find a way, and when this is all over, we'll have our king back.

"Danuka will have her egg back and you'll have Sarah back. You and Sarah will take Danuka and her eggs to the safe hatching circles you've rebuilt. It'll be a new age for the dragons. A new age for you, for Lars, for Dannor, and for Sarah."

Oh! Pare! I hope you're right.

Hands came to rest on Nagora's shoulders. "Mum, Da and I are with you on this journey. We'll see you through this. We'll do whatever we have to," said Dannor.

Nagora leaned her head on Dannor's arm as her eyes found Lars's. How can I ever show you how grateful I am for your support? My son, my husband, I fear for your safety more than my own. Why do people hold on to visions of an ideal future? Why do I feel compelled to continue to fight when, with each battle, the ideal seems to move further and further away?

After they had eaten the evening meal and talked until dark, Nagora rose from the table. "I don't think my head can take anymore of this speculating on possible ways to deal with this situation. All I know it is that I need to get to Windhaven as soon as possible. Coming face to face with Raynhard and Sagora will give me a way to come up with a plan. A good night's sleep is in order so we can leave for Windhaven soon after first light."

Paruline and Geirador stood. "I so wish our reunion had taken place under better circumstances. The wedding is in eleven days. That will give you ten days to act. Father and I will arrive the day before the wedding. Until then, our duties keep us here," said Paruline. "Come. I'll show you to your rooms."

...

When they passed the door that led to the dungeon sea cave stairwell, uneasiness overcame Nagora. It increased as they turned the corner at the end of the hall.

A maid stood by an open door. Raynhard, as Chive, had hobbled out of that door over fifteen years before on the night Nagora had returned to the dungeon sea cave. She had honored her vow to the girls still held captive there and to those who had died at the hands of the prince and his jailor. It was Hag's room.

Paruline paused before the doorway. She pointed to the open door on the other side of the hallway. "Dannor's room, opposite yours. It's small, but he'll be comfortable."

Chive's room?

"You and Lars will have this room. I think you'll find it to your liking."

Paruline most likely doesn't know this was Hag's chamber. If she knew, she wouldn't put us here. No use mentioning it to her or to Lars.

Nagora's night was sleepless as she relived every detail of her ordeal in the dungeon sea cave. Lars's steady breathing was her only comfort, until Danuka spoke to her in her mind.

Danuka hadn't done so in such a long time, but there it was in the language Nagora understood so well now. *Ka Peyakot Mahihkan, miska kichewakan. Nihtâ-kitohcikêw.* Lone Wolf, find your friend. She plays music well.

Yes, Mother, I hear you.

Danuka wants me to find Moreena. Why? Danuka always has a reason when she speaks to me this way. Okay. Dromester is our destination. It is close to Windhaven. Tomorrow after breakfast, we'll keep our good-byes short. If all goes well, in five days we'll be with Moreena before nightfall. We'll ride from sunrise to sunset. Danuka, once again, you give me hope. I'll act on your words right away.

To Moreena
Natawi Moreena

† NOW: *the eleventh day in*
the Land of the Danu,
five days before the wedding

Five days of travel had brought Nagora, Lars, and Dannor closer to Dromester, and past more and more restoration work being done to the defaced dragon images on statues and bridges of the towns they rode through. Stone Stander scaffolding was everywhere. How many had come down from their high, guarded mountain plateau to work? Dressed in their white work garb, they were easy to spot. They were the ones recreating the artwork in the stones. Locals worked with them to clear debris and take care of their needs, bringing hearty meals and plenty of tea to drink.

Remember, Tars, what it was like when we last passed through here? No happy whistling from the workers in those days, right? Nagora almost laughed out loud at her words with Tars. It was as if she were still that scruffy looking lad her uncle had suggested she become to travel the land on her task. We made it though, didn't we, Tars?

...

Nagora made a point of being on the distant end of the second of the Twin Rivers' bridges at sunrise so Dannor and Lars could see the huge sculpture of the twin dragon heads facing each other in profile against the rising sun. "Here comes the sun. Watch them spit fire at each other."

The previous evening after arranging to stay with the local blacksmith for the night, Nagora had taken them to see the twin dragons up close in the town square. Stone Standers had completed the restoration work on the dragons. The details were perfect in every respect except for the color of the stone. No stone could ever replicate Danuka's colors.

Dannor's mouth hung open in awe as he took in the dragon heads silhouetted against the fiery disc of the rising sun that, for a few moments, bloomed and blasted from their open jaws.

Then, as the sun rose above the heads of the dragons, Lars tapped Dannor's shoulder with a fist. "Probably as close as you'll ever get to seeing the real thing."

"Mum, can dragons truly spit fire like you told me when Danuka shed her skin?"

"Those were the only times I've ever seen Danuka 'spit fire' as you say. But I suppose they can do so whenever they decide to. Why else would the drawing of the dragon in the maze cave show it with flames streaming from its mouth? Surely not just to indicate the forge room.

"On to Dromester. We should be there well before night-fall." They turned their mounts and, with the sun at their backs, rode away.

The riders made good time and near the end of the after-noon, they pulled up in front of Bardas's smithy. His hammer rang and clanged as it struck metal on his anvil. Nagora dismounted and stepped through the big open doors of the shop.

Lars and Dannor followed.

Bardas and another man, sensing their presence, turned to face the three. Bardas still held the hammer in his big hand. The other man held a knife in one hand and a whetstone in the other. He slipped the rectangular stone into a pocket on his leather apron. "What can we do you for?" asked Bardas.

Nagora stepped closer. "How are you, Bardas?"

Bardas crossed his arms in front of him and tilted his head. "Am I supposed to know you?"

"We've met before."

"That so?" He twirled the handle of his hammer so its head spun a few times.

Nagora pulled her hood back and took another step forward.

Bardas's barrel chest expanded further as his eyes focused on her brand. "Lady Edana? Tars, is that you?"

"Aye, Bardas. It's me. Is Moreena here?"

"Who is it, Bardas?" asked his companion.

The big man's head was shaking as his questioning grin turned into a smile and his eyes filled with tears. Bardas shoved the handle of his hammer into the leather loop on his apron, held his arms open, and took Nagora in a warm embrace. "It's Tars. The one who saved Erin!"

The man took a step in Bardas's direction. He wore a smile on his face.

Bardas took a step away from Nagora and pointed. "Tars, this is Jani, Moreena's husband. He works with me. He's the best finisher and sharpener of all the knives and blades we make."

The tools on the workbench behind Jani were in studied order, all within reach around his workspace. Jani was a strong, handsome man of medium build. He wore his long golden hair tied at the back. His beard was neatly trimmed, not a grizzled mass like Bardas wore.

"Pleased to meet you, Jani."

Jani turned toward Nagora's voice and waved. "My pleasure too. I've heard so much about you."

"All good I hope, Jani."

He smiled. "Only good things."

"Tars, you can't know how happy we were all those years ago when we got your message. That you had made it home wiped away our worries. We had heard so many stories about what happened to you," said Bardas.

Bardas looked Nagora up and down. "Moreena's with Erin in Windhaven. They're practicing with other musicians for your wedding at the Center for the Dragon Arts. Have you not spoken to her yet?"

Do I tell him or let it ride? "No, Bardas, my intention was to do so today. I've been away from Windhaven on personal business and thought I'd take a chance to see her here today. Will you attend the wedding?"

"Aye, Jani and Joni too. We'll not miss our women play on this great occasion."

Jani was smiling and nodding in agreement.

Nagora pointed to Lars and Dannor. "My escorts today. We're on our way back to Windhaven. I've been traveling in disguise again. I hope to see Moreena and Erin before nightfall."

"Aye. They'll be happy to see you. They're staying with Olen. You'll find them there."

"The same place I remember?"

Bardas gave a nod. "Aye, the same."

"Good. I'll find them. These are busy days, as you can imagine. I best be on my way. Good to see you again, Bardas. And to meet you, Jani." Both men nodded.

Nagora turned in her saddle to wave goodbye. Bardas held his hammer handle in one hand, its head resting in the palm of his other as he tilted his smiling face to one side to say something to Jani. It took a moment before Bardas waved to her with his hammer. Jani waved with his free hand.

The guards at the gates of Windhaven's great wall waved them through as soon as Nagora pulled back her hood and gave them a stern look.

Nagora led Lars and Dannor to the left on Stables Way, the first side street they came to. Six doors down the street, well away from the castle, Olen's smithy and stables were nestled alongside another long row of buildings that lined that side of the way. The stable doors stood closed, but the door leading to Olen's workshop was open. Lars and Dannor waited outside while Nagora went in.

The shop was cool and Olen nowhere in sight, but whistling came from beyond the open inside door that led to the stable. Like the first time we met. And he's whistling the same tune.

Nagora stepped through the doorway into the stable. Horses occupied most of the stalls. Olen was in the same stall at the end as the last time. I hope I won't get the same greeting. She whistled along with him.

Olen paused and continued.

Nagora walked down the row between the stalls still whistling along with him until Olen popped his head out. "Olen, I hope I smell better than the last time we met here, and that I get a better welcome!"

Olen squinted as he looked at Nagora.

"I come bearing news that one such as you should know firsthand. And I plan to share that news with Moreena and Erin."

Olen's jaw had dropped, and he fumbled for words. "Lady … Ah … Your … Lady Edana? Tars? I mean, that's how I know you."

"Aye, it is, Olen. You can call me Tars if you want, as long as you don't put me in a cart and cover me with horse shit."

Olen's arms went up. "Damn! It is you! Tars! I don't know what to say."

"Olen, first off, just answer my questions. Do you have place for three horses and three mules?"

"I do. Stalls for the horses. Mules in the yard."

"Are Moreena and Erin here?"

"Aye, in the kitchen, making soup and bread."

"Do you have place to put up three travelers?"

"I do."

"Last question, Olen. Can I trust you to keep secret all I'll tell you, Moreena, and Erin?"

"Aye, you know you can. Why?"

"Olen, the last battle for The Cause is about to be fought. It could be the one that'll decide the future of our king and his kingdom."

Olen stepped back and his hand went to his head. "Truly? I thought we had won that one. I had better be all ears to listen to what you have to tell." Olen crossed his arms over his chest, tilted his head to one side, and pointed a large finger at her. "Say, could this have something to do with what's been happening at the castle these last few months?"

I bet Alizarine's presence has changed things even more. "Could be, Olen. We must talk. We've no time to waste. Come. Open your stable doors. I'll introduce my people once we're inside your home."

Nagora held Moreena and Erin in her arms. It was an awkward yet tearful reunion once Nagora had finished explaining who she was in relation to her twin sister acting as Edana.

Moreena was still wiping away tears as she spoke. "Tars. Sorry, Nagora, it's easier for me. I've thought of you all these years by that name and we didn't truly understand, at the time, that it was you who had returned as Edana, the Dragon-Warrior Princess, to lead the fight against Raganora."

Erin spoke up. "When your sister appeared on the scene as Edana with the brand on her forehead, I couldn't help notice the resemblance to you. I told Moreena I thought she was you. Now we understand why she paid so little attention to us when introduced to us at the Center for the Dragon Arts. Had it been you, you would've spoken to us."

Erin placed a hand on Nagora's arm. "You have to come see the Center. All the stained glass windows are being restored. They're almost done the work on them. Nagora, you have to see the dragon window. No more sign of the Temple of Fire. Our Center for the Dragon Arts is back. Come see us practice there tomorrow."

"Erin, I promise I will." Erin has truly found her voice. I'm happy for her. "What instrument do you play?"

Erin wore a proud smile. "The harp. Moreena taught me. And your flute. I always play your flute."

Moreena wiped a last tear from the corner of her eye. "My little sister has become an excellent harpist. Erin even has her own harp now. Every session we play, she accompanies me with her beloved flute for six or more tunes. The flute you gave Erin has become as precious to her as Mum's harp is to me."

Nagora smiled at the sisters. "I'm glad to hear that. And I must tell you that a few days ago my dear friend, Pare, informed us of your marriage, and her marriage, to the Konen brothers. Moreena, earlier today your da introduced us to Jani. What a handsome man he is! I'm so happy for you."

Moreena's smile brightened her face. "Isn't he, Tars? And he's a good man too. I'm so lucky to have him, as is Da. With Pauline's da's help, Da's business is thriving."

"Erin, we have yet to meet your Joni and Pare's Harri," said Nagora.

Erin too seemed happy as she reached for her sister's arm and pulled her close. "Well, my Joni is the best looking of the three brothers. And he's mine!"

Moreena laughed and shook her head. "Not so! Jani is. You'll see for yourself, Tars. I mean Nagora. Once you've met the other two."

Erin leaned her head on Moreena's shoulder, grinning. It was obvious they teased each other about the looks of their men. Erin let go of her sister's arm. "Joni's at the shop down by the docks, helping Harri restock the shelves with the wagonload of wares brought back from Yhorgal.

"There will be lots of business these days. The wedding has attracted many visitors to Windhaven. There are so many trading boats at the docks that many have had to tie up shoulder to shoulder, some three and four abreast. Joni and Harri will sleep and eat at the shop, keeping it open until late each night until the day of the wedding. All the shops will be closed on that day."

Erin waved a hand. "Enough talk about our men. Nagora, you haven't introduced us to the two accompanying you!"

Nagora turned to Moreena and took her blind friend's hand. "I want you to meet my son, Dannor, and his da, Lars. Moreena, please take the time to see their faces with your fingers as you did mine the first time we met. I want you to see them better in your mind."

Nagora held out a hand to her son. "Dannor, come stand here so Moreena can … see you."

Moreena took her time, letting her fingers explore all the features of Dannor's face, even his hair. Then she held his hands and her fingers examined them and tested them. Moreena seemed satisfied as she kept Dannor's hands in hers and turned to Nagora. "Dannor is as strong as you were when I first met you. He surely has your skills with a bow. Now I want to see his da."

Lars stepped forward and submitted to Moreena's examination.

"Dannor is definitely your son. Someday, Dannor, you'll be as tall and as strong as your da and be able to wield his sword. Nagora, in all your dreams could you ever have dreamed of a warrior such as Lars, standing by your side as your protector? You were destined for each other."

"Moreena, I know we were."

Nagora smiled at her man and then looked to Erin and Moreena. "I wish I had only good news for you. Like I told Olen earlier, the fight for The Cause is not over. We still have to defeat the witch, Hag, to settle this once and for all. I'll explain ... "

Moreena reached for Nagora's arm. "I know you'll have more to tell us, but first you and your men will share our evening meal with us."

Once they had eaten, Nagora explained all that had happened since the last time they had been together. Olen let out a long whistle. "The witch is still a threat, not only to Raynhard, but to his dragon. And the warriors from the Land of Skulls stand ready to cross into our land and scorch it. We thought the good times had returned."

Olen cleared his throat. "However, like I mentioned earlier, things have been going on at the castle, strange things. They coincide with that Alizarine's arrival. The witch, Hag, is back, but in another form."

"Olen," Nagora touched his arm, "what strange things? What've your sources told you?"

Olen leaned back. "All castle servants, cooks, scullery workers, sweeps, gardeners, you name them; all them that work and are fed there no longer lodge there. They come in at sunrise and are to leave before sunset unless instructed otherwise."

Olen's thumb went up. "Castle guards. No more inside the castle proper at any of the rooms unless instructed otherwise. Those that did duty inside are now posted around the castle perimeter within Windhaven walls in rotation with those on the walls and at the gate. They have their own barracks.

"The number of visitors to the castle has dwindled, and all requests for audiences with King Raynhard have been put off until after the wedding. Only those with business about wedding preparations are gaining access." Olen leaned forward and spread the fingers of his hands flat on the table. "The king's put everything on hold. If it has nothing to do with the wedding, it has to wait."

Lars shook his head. "Business in any land shouldn't come to a halt for wedding preparations. On the day of the wedding, yes. Then it's time for celebration."

"I think we all agree on that. You're right, Olen. Something strange has been going on. This doesn't sound like the king I knew. Olen, you must've heard something else," said Nagora.

"Tell her what the room maid said, Olen. That'll give her an idea," said Erin.

Olen lowered his gaze to his hands. "I didn't get this from her directly, but from one who swears it's so. She said the maid's happy to not be sleeping in castle quarters any longer because she's afraid of the new girl child, that Alizarine, despite initially being won over by her. Now when she meets Alizarine, she avoids eye contact. She says she senses the evil in that child."

We've gotten used to it. She does well to fear Alizarine. I bet others do too. "Olen, I believe what that girl said. She's right to trust her feelings. Thanks for this information. It doesn't surprise me, but it worries me and confirms the battle with Hag is not over."

Moreena brought both hands to her chest. "Danuka talks to you, Nagora? You say she did as we stood outside beneath the dragon window those years ago and she told you to set the fire to free Erin. And now Danuka has told you to seek me out? Why?"

Lars placed a hand a Nagora's shoulder. "Moreena, that's why we are here, to find out why. You must know something or be able to do something that will help Danuka recover her egg from Alizarine."

Moreena brought her hands to her lips, shook her head, and held them out before her. "I've no idea what I could have or what I could do that would help. Believe me, if I did, I would tell you now."

Nagora reached over and touched Moreena's sleeve. "Moreena, I believe you. Whenever Danuka has asked me to do something, how is never obvious at once. It's like she points me in the direction, but not to the final destination. I know she wants me to return the egg at all costs, but exactly how to do it isn't clear."

Erin spoke up. "Danuka said: 'Find your friend. She plays music well.' Could the music be the direction? What in the music could have an influence on Alizarine, the witch who holds Danuka's egg? Think, Mo."

Moreena brought the palms of her hands together and pressed her pointer fingers to her lips as she closed her eyes and took a deep breath.

The freckles on Moreena's eyelids seemed to dance. What is she thinking? Where has she gone to in her thoughts? Moreena's eyebrows furrowed and then settled as her eyelids fluttered again, but this time, it built into a furious dance that only stopped when her eyes opened.

Moreena dropped her hands to the table and faced Nagora. "Mum's harp! Now I remember what the witch said." Moreena faced Erin. "You must too, Erin! It was on that day Hag asked for all the golden harps to be brought to the Temple of Fire. Hag's reason for wanting all the harps. We all thought it was for the gold, but it wasn't only for the gold. It truly was for the pretext she gave."

Erin was nodding. "I remember Hag's words because Mum spoke them over and over again, saying, 'Hag, if what you say be true, let me sit at my harp and play your death song.' Hag's words were, 'Any instrument that makes music to hold me spellbound must be destroyed.'"

Nagora looked from Erin to Moreena. "Is your mum's harp here in Windhaven?"

"Aye, it is. It's here. Now I always keep it near. When we go to the Center for the Dragon Arts, Olen brings it for me by hand cart and he picks it up for our return here. Olen's our escort. Though now Nagora, with the news you bring, I fear for Mum's harp."

I have to reassure her. She reached out and held Moreena's hand. "Fear not for your mum's harp. If and whenever Alizarine gets near it, Lars, Dannor, and I will be there to protect it and you. We'll not let anything happen to either of you. Trust me, Moreena."

Moreena was shaking her head. "What will I have to do? What does Danuka want me to do? To what end? What will happen?"

Erin placed a hand on her sister's arm. "To answer your questions, we have to ask what Mother Dragon wants. Danuka wants her egg back. Somehow, the music you play will allow her to get her egg back."

Erin turned to Nagora. "You said Alizarine never lets the egg out of her sight. She always keeps it near. If she goes anywhere, she carries it in a basket, wrapped in a sheepskin. That means she would have to go to the Center for the Dragon Arts to hear Moreena play the harp. Alizarine would be so taken by the music that you could take the egg from her. Could that be what Danuka wants to happen?"

Nagora tilted her head from one side to the other as she bit her lower lip. "Yes and no. It won't be that simple. I would rather not even try to imagine what would happen when the music stopped. The fit Alizarine would have. There's no telling what she would do, even if she's in the body of a six-year-old child with a mind the same age. Alizarine is still the witch, Hag."

Nagora sighed. "Yes, Danuka wants her egg. There are only two ways I can see that happen." A chill covered her from head to foot in the warm kitchen. Get on with it.

"The first way: It would be an occasion to switch the egg with another. That would mean Danuka would sacrifice a female egg for the only male egg. Will she do that? If she does, it'll mean less dragons for the future. Every single offspring from those eggs will influence the future of the Land of the Danu.

"The second way: ... " Nagora swallowed and looked at the faces around the table. "It would be an occasion to carry out Heqet's curse on Alizarine. That would mean several conditions would have to be satisfied first. One, that I be crowned queen. Two, that Sarah be convinced to take part in this execution with me."

Olen was standing now. "Can you imagine the second way take place in the Center for the Dragon Arts? In public view? I can't! If it were still the Temple of Fire under Raganora's rule with Prince Acindor playing his perverted games, then I could swallow it. No way now! The invited guests wouldn't understand what they would be seeing—the execution of the witch, Hag. Even if you told them after the fact. Would they believe it? Would they believe their beloved Edana?" Olen sat.

Nagora bowed her head. "I wasn't trying to sell that possibility." She lifted her head. "Just laying it out for what it is. For the occasion to make a switch to happen, we'd need an egg. That means I have to meet with Danuka."

Dannor spoke up. "I don't want to spoil the speculating going on, but I have a question. If the egg is switched, will Alizarine notice?"

Nagora's eyes held Dannor's. "There's always the unknown. Always. We can't plan for it. When confronted with the unknown, we can only trust ourselves and our weapons to deal with it."

Lars cleared his throat. "I too have a question. Well, perhaps more than one. My understanding is the wedding will take place at the Center for the Dragon Arts. Olen, Moreena, Erin, do you know what's supposed to happen before and after the actual wedding in the Center?"

Moreena and Erin turned to Olen, who was nodding. Olen pointed to himself. "The information I have is that after the wedding reception, the wedding procession will leave the castle at the end of the afternoon and go down Castle Way to Center Square. Invited guests will wait inside the Center. People of Windhaven and those from outside will fill the square and the surrounding streets. The wedding itself takes place as soon as the king and bride-to-be arrive, followed by the crowning of the queen, princesses, and princes. After the ceremonies, the procession goes down to the harbor by Main Gate Way and then back up to the castle by Castle Hill Way."

The hair on the back of Nagora's neck stood as she recalled helping the rebel, Maton, rescue his young sister, Ilma, and then Acindor's cruel judgment of them in his abominable trial by barrel. *I should have killed the prince before he even sentenced Maton and Ilma. They wouldn't have rolled down Castle Hill Way to their deaths.*

Olen continued. "Invited guests go into the castle yard for a final toast to the king and queen before returning to Castle Square outside the castle walls for a night of festivities with the people of Windhaven and any come to celebrate."

Lars leaned an arm on the table. "Moreena, my understanding is you'll be playing harp in the Center during the wedding, but not at the castle. Is that right?"

"Yes, Lars. Erin and I and the other musicians will play pieces before and after the vows, and before and after the queen is crowned."

"Who crowns the queen?" asked Lars.

"King Raynhard does, as neither of his parents are alive to pass on the title," said Moreena.

Lars nodded. "My last question. Have the king and his bride-to-be been invited to listen to the music you'll play at their ceremonies?"

Erin answered, "In two days, they're coming to listen to the songs we propose to play. They'll choose from those. It'll be a private concert in the evening for them and whoever they bring along. If they bring Alizarine, it would be a perfect time to switch the egg."

Nagora smiled at Erin. "True. It would. If we can get another egg by then, it would be worth the try."

Nagora smiled at Lars. That's good to know. I'm glad you asked your questions, my man.

Lars made a hand signal. Dannor might have caught it too. It meant "Later. Remind me." I will. Something the others need not know.

Nagora placed her hands on the table. "This has been helpful. Does anyone have something else to add that might help? I don't know how this will all play out. That's in the future. What I would love to hear right now in the present is Moreena and Erin play for us. Would you?"

Moreena reached out for Nagora's hand. "On condition you play with us."

Nagora turned to her son. "Dannor, would you like to join me?"

"Sure." Dannor stood and walked over to the rack where they had hung their quivers and bows. He reached for his flute on the outer pocket of his quiver and pulled Nagora's from hers.

"Will we be three flutes and a harp, or two flutes and two harps?" asked Nagora.

Erin said, "Both. I still love playing your flute Nagora. I bring it everywhere I go."

Olen was up and moving his chair to the nearest wall. "We'll make room for the harps. Best we move the table."

Erin went to the neighboring room and returned with two small stools.

Olen returned with the golden dragon harp. "Here it is. The most beautiful harp in the land." Olen set it down on the stool before Moreena.

The proud dragon, made entirely of gold from its rearing head down along its neck and belly to its clawed feet, seemed to stand, clutching Moreena's stool. Its gold, spread-back wing tips joined behind it at the wooden board of the harp's long sound box which rested on Moreena's shoulder, slanting down to the dragon's back claws. Gold strings, strung from the joined winged-edge to the middle of the long board, resembled a dragon's wings completely pulled back.

Exactly as I remember it. The first time I heard the dragon chord sound, it was unforgettable.

"Dannor, Lars, I've told you about the sound of this harp hundreds of times."

"No, Mum. Thousands of times!" Dannor smiled.

Erin pulled her chair next to Nagora's. She held her harp with her knees and her flute in her hands. "See? I've taken good care of it."

"Erin, I'm happy that you have. My uncle, Dangor, made it for me from the leg bone of an elk."

"Who made the one you're holding?"

"Lars did when he showed Dannor how to make the one in his hands."

Lars smiled at Erin. "I love to make them. I'm more of a listener than a player. Looks like Olen and I will be your audience this evening."

Erin shook her head. "Oh, no. Olen, get the bohdrans."

"I haven't played one of those since being on the Moroes Islands," said Lars.

Olen handed the bigger one to Lars. "Here you go. We'll keep time with them. Give the beat, you know."

Moreena pulled her harp to her, splayed her small and pointer finger along with her thumb, and played the dragon chord. Lars and Dannor looked to Nagora with eyes and mouths open wide. Nagora smiled. "I told you. Now do you believe me?" Your faces tell me you do.

For several counts, Nagora had forgotten what awaited her, but as soon as they put away their instruments, the urgency of her task returned.

To the Center for the Dragon Arts
Mêtawêwikamik Paskwaskisiw Naspasinahikewin

† NOW: *the twelfth day in*
the Land of the Danu,
four days before the wedding

The next morning found Nagora, Lars, and Dannor on Stables Way along with Moreena, Erin, and Olen headed for the Center for the Dragon Arts. Nagora walked hand in hand with Moreena and Erin.

Erin squeezed Nagora's hand. "Promise you'll keep your eyes closed as we enter the Center. Only open them when I tell you."

"I promise, Erin."

They stopped on the edge of Center Square. The towering walls of the Center came into view. Stained glass art now filled the once empty tall windows. I can't wait to see them from inside the Center.

This is not the same square I stepped into years ago. Today it's alive. Even at this early hour, vendors with hand carts have their goods on display. People are smiling and laughing. The sweet smell of fresh baked goods fills the air. Flowers in boxes and pots surround Center Square. Paintings and decorations cover the walls of the buildings. Banners hang from staffs.

Erin pulled on her arm. "Come, Nagora. We'll go around this way to the main entrance." They skirted the tiers upon which the Center for the Dragon Arts sat and rounded the last corner.

"Close your eyes, Nagora. The doors are open. I don't want you to see the part of the window that's visible from here."

Nagora did as Erin instructed and let herself be led up the stone steps, over the top tier, and inside the center.

"Stop here. Wait 'til I tell you."

If I remember right, this would be where the cauldron of the Temple Of Fire was, at center stage. What are they doing? We've come early, before the other musicians arrive.

"Ready." It was Moreena's voice.

"Open your eyes," said Erin.

The dragon chord sounded from Moreena's harp and she began to play *As Dragons Soar*. Colored light bathed the stage where Nagora stood, and as she looked up, she felt her chest swell. For the briefest moment it was Danuka in all her shimmering iridescent glory before her with wings spread back and her tail curled twice behind her. Danuka's head seemed to come at her because of the way her eyes stared. She appeared to be flying on a colored background that could only be a most beautiful sunset or sunrise. A frame made of red rectangles, squares, and triangles, interspersed with diamond-shaped pieces of blue, green, amber, and white glass surrounded the background on which the dragon flew.

Okâwîmâw, I am here. I have arrived to do your will. Hear me, Mother. Come to me as soon as you can. Many years ago I stood looking at the other side of this window. You spoke to me. I need you to help me so I can help you.

The last notes of *As Dragons Soar* faded. *Okâwîmâw*, will you be the last dragon to soar in our skies? Let it not be so.

Erin tugged on Nagora's sleeve. "Look at Lars and Dannor. They're as rapt as you."

Slowly, she turned to take in the other windows as Lars and Dannor were doing.

Other musicians had arrived and were setting up.

After listening to several songs, they approached Moreena, Erin, and Olen to shake their hands and give them brief hugs before setting off on foot on Castle Way to seek an audience with King Raynhard. Your true Edana is back.

To the Castle
Kihci-Okimâwikamik

† NOW: *the twelfth day in*
the Land of the Danu,
four days before the wedding

Will Sagora be there? Will I see Sarah? How will I approach them? What welcome awaits me this morning? What about Alizarine? What does she hold in store for me? I've never felt this uncertain about a situation since setting foot on that chain-link bridge to cross into Stone Stander territory. That was what, Tars? Almost eighteen years ago? It seems like it was only days ago. Tars, we never walked up Castle Way the last time we were here.

"Lars, last evening you signaled you had something you wanted me to remind you of. What is it?"

Lars stopped and held her arm. "You remember the day I gave you Aydan. I told you Sagora could show you some of the other hand commands I used with my dogs since she had so often seen me use them."

"I remember it well. On the way back to Mum's, Sagora showed me four or five other hand commands. What are you getting at, Lars?"

"Arm and Hand didn't bark to warn you when Danuka came for Alizarine. We taught them the same commands as we did Lyam and Aydan. Who knew the command for them not to bark?"

Nagora's stomach turned as the image flashed before her eyes. "Sagora! Sagora slit the throats of our dogs! What evil is she up to, Lars?"

"Nagora, be on guard. Their deaths were a warning. We can't trust Sagora, or anything she says."

"Why, Lars? What is she doing? Does she realize what she's done?"

Lars bit at his upper lip and shook his head. "For her to be acting this way, a voice of reason must be absent from her life. That voice is Tagnya. Tagnya and Yogari are not in Windhaven. Tagnya would never have let her daughter do what she's done to Gabe. What nest are we about to step in-to?"

Nagora swallowed. "I fear it's a nest of vipers."

"Mum, look." Dannor pointed, as they came into the square before the castle. Workers were busy hanging banners with the royal crests from the eaves of the buildings surrounding the square. Gardeners were tending to the potted plants set on the highest steps of the viewing stands, set along fronts of those same buildings. Workers swept the cobblestone surface of the square.

All is in motion for the big day. Dare I even try to stop it? Not if I'm to become queen. One day at a time. One step at a time. Can I get an egg from Danuka?

The three of them stood in the middle of Castle Square, facing the rising way that led to the castle gates. Dannor took Nagora's hand. "It's just like I imagined it when you told me about it, but so much bigger! So this will be your first time inside it?"

Nagora squeezed his hand. "Aye, Dannor, it will, and I'm glad to be going in there with my men at my side. If the guards will let us in." Nagora checked the edge of her hood over her forehead and made sure it still folded next to each ear.

The way narrowed the closer they got to the moat and castle bridge. Eight soldiers standing abreast could cross the bridge. On the other side of the bridge, the outermost gate, a huge grate of wooden beams strapped with strips of iron blocked the way. Four armed soldiers guarded the grate's small door that allowed a single person through. It stood open.

The two soldiers standing at the threshold crossed their spears as Nagora approached. A third guard raised his hand. "Good day to you. State your calling."

"We've come from the Land of Skulls bearing messages from King Godomor. Please tell his majesty, King Raynhard, that Nagora and Lars, and their son, Dannor, seek an audience with him as soon as possible."

"Give me the messages, and I'll deliver them to my king."

"It is King Godomor's wishes we deliver the messages in person, ourselves, as he sends no written missives."

"I'll deliver your request to my king today. Come back tomorrow for his answer."

"I imagine you are following orders. I respect that, but the nature of our messages is of utmost importance. Even a delay of a single count in King Raynhard receiving this information could cost you your life, and King Raynhard his country."

The soldier crossed his arms and spread his legs. "Is that so? I stand by what I told you I would do. Come back tomorrow."

"Take a good look at me." Nagora pulled her hood back and pointed at her brand.

The soldier's mouth fell open, but then he stepped back, regained his composure, and placed a hand on the pommel of his sword. "I know who you are trying to impersonate. It's not going to work. My words stand. Come back tomorrow." Two other soldiers at the door were placing both hands on their spears as they stared at her with eyes open wide and mouths hanging open. A fourth, as stupefied as the others, fumbled with the scabbard of his sword.

Nagora reached behind her, flipped the latch on the sheath of her big blade, and pulled it out. "If I have to kill the four of you louts and every other guard beyond this gate to get to the king, believe me I'll do so or die trying." Dannor pulled his big blade and Lars his great sword.

The soldier stepped back.

Nagora reached into the pocket of her vest and pulled out the sheathed royal hunting dagger. "Take this. Place it in the hands of your king. Now go announce us. I've started counting. If you're not back by the end of my count, there'll be blood on this bridge. If the king will only see me tomorrow, I want him to tell me so to my face."

"Mum, archers above have us in their sights."

"Stay as you are, Dannor. Don't move. If they've heard what I said and have some soldierly sense, they'll not shoot unless ordered to. Should they dare to shoot us, the king will have them executed."

The soldier had disappeared through the door of the inner gate set diagonally across from where Nagora stood.

Halfway through Nagora's count, someone yelled orders from the other side of the inner gate. The archers from the wall above disappeared, and the message-carrying guard re-appeared, out of breath, through the door of the inner gate. The guard stumbled through the outer door, handed her the gold-handled dagger, and managed to say, "Follow me."

Raynhard sent the dagger back. Is he afraid I would not take it back from him, that I would no longer be duty bound to him? Or does he know I'll have to use it? Although, if he only recovered from Aliza's blow after Heqet spoke the curse, he wouldn't know unless someone who did know, told him.

Nagora, Lars, and Dannor sheathed their weapons and followed.

Inside the courtyard, guards had assembled in two lines leading to Raynhard who was standing at the door opposite the gate they had just come through. The king waved them forward, stepped into the yard, and strode toward them with arms outstretched. "Nagora! Lars! And Dannor."

Nagora walked into his embrace. "Raynhard! I almost had to fight my way in to see you."

Raynhard held her shoulders. "Nagora, it's been too, too long. You can't imagine how I've missed you!"

So much so you've replaced me with my sister who you're going to marry. If only you knew what's in store for you. I'll feed you some of it and watch how you react.

Nagora reached out to Dannor. "It has been a long time. This is my son, Dannor. In my eyes, he's a man. Here he stands before you as a measure of most of the time we haven't seen each other."

Raynhard held out a hand to Dannor and looked at Lars. "You must be a proud father, Lars. Welcome to Windhaven, Dannor. I owe so much to your father and your mother."

All those jeweled rings of gold and silver must make for a heavy hand. Such trappings don't become the man I once knew, the man who wanted to ease the hunger of his oppressed people.

Raynhard let go of Dannor's hand and shook Lars's. "Good to see you again, Lars."

Lars's face barely carried a smile. "Raynhard, as you say, it's been too long."

Raynhard showed them to the door behind him. "This way. I've been told you come bearing urgent messages from King Godomor?"

As if you can't guess what they might be. "We do. Are Sagora and Sarah here?"

Raynhard stopped near the door. "They left with Danuka early this morning. They should be back by noon. I'm anxious to hear the messages Godomor sends."

I bet you are. They'll not leave you indifferent. "Raynhard, will we be able to speak to you in private?"

Raynhard nodded once. "Follow me."

...

The three followed Raynhard along a wide corridor. Most of the doors were on the left-hand side. The only door to the right stood open next to the single door at the end.

They stepped into a high vaulted room. It was empty except for a throne of carved wood, which rested on a dais at the far end to their left. Two long tables, each with four chairs on one side, stood on each side of the dais.

Three sets of three stained glass windows decorated each of the chamber walls two thirds up, each bearing different scenery. The forest, mountain and lake, and coastal scenes all contained animals. People and dragons were absent from all the scenes. Who had decided that? Which king or queen? Or was it the artist?

On each wall, two taller windows separated the stained-glass scenes and shed light into the throne room. Their clear glass panels of patterned squares and rectangles were interconnected by rondelles. The lead lines of these panels and the rough texture of the glass gave a distorted view of the sky.

Raynhard led them past the throne to a door about twenty paces away directly behind it.

Dannor had slowed as he pointed to the carved taloned armrests and the folded-back dragon wings that formed the throne's backrest. From the seat of the throne, the dragon's neck curled down, under, and back to the front so the dragon's chin rested on the surface of the dais. The king's feet would rest on each side of the head.

A dragon throne for the king. Where's the queen's throne? Did Queen Julianna have a throne? Did Raganora sit on this throne? To show she had subjugated the dragons? Where will I sit after I am wed to Raynhard?

"In here. This is as private as I can control." Raynhard ushered them into a square room.

So that's where the light is coming from. Nagora looked up. Judging from the structural separations in the stonework, the room's four windowless walls rose for three floor levels to a pyramid-shaped skylight made of clear leaded glass panes. The skylight took up most of the ceiling area of the room. Whoever cleans those panes must have access to that part of the castle roof.

A big round table of polished oak, with twelve oak chairs that sat directly below the glass pyramid, benefitted from the light it let in.

"Shall I lock the door so we have no interruptions?" asked Raynhard.

It was the only door to the room, a stout one at that. Nagora looked from Lars to Dannor and back to Raynhard. "Yes, Raynhard. Please do."

Raynhard pulled on the door's long, twisted wrought iron handle with both hands and then pushed it shut, revealing the big key on its inner side. He turned the key, pulled on the handle, and faced them, pointing back to the key in the lock. "We're locked in. Please be seated." Raynhard stood with arms crossed.

Our king's waiting for us to sit. I'll sit here. Where will he sit?

Lars and Dannor sat on each side of Nagora.

Raynhard walked to the chair opposite Nagora, pulled it back, and sat. He laced the fingers of his hands together and rested them on the table before him. The king waited.

Is this a game? Who gets first move? Nagora leaned back in her chair, glanced around the room, and noted several pieces of wooden furniture. Each held a stack of at least a dozen thin but wide drawers. I could ask what they hold. That might throw you off your game.

Raynhard unfolded his fingers. "I'm listening."

Too bad King Bernhard and Queen Julianna died before their time. They could have taught you how a king behaves. Nagora held Raynhard's gaze. "Here is King Godomor's message, in his words: ' … I will hold back my wolves for as long as possible. Be warned there will come a time when my voice will no longer be heard above their howls for the hunt to begin. I dare not predict what will stay standing once they cross the Blood River on their path of revenge, seeking blood wherever they can find it to quench the fire they will bear in their teeth.'

"King Raynhard, what have you done?"

Surely you remember the fearless archers from the Land of Skulls on your battlefield, holding three and sometimes four lit fire arrows with their teeth as they advanced with another nocked on their bows. They were on your side then. Imagine them against you.

Raynhard's eyes remained passive, but his knuckles turned white. Then he took a great breath through his nose, spread his fingers flat on the table, and straightened his arms so he leaned back in his chair. "Nagora, please dispense with the 'king' title." He waved a hand and stared at her. "I did what my people wanted. They clamored for Edana. I gave them

Edana. The people clamored for her to ride Danuka. I gave them Edana on Danuka's back in the sky. The people now clamor for Edana to be at my side. I will give them Queen Edana at my side. The Land of the Danu needs Edana. Edana gave them hope in the darkness. Now Edana inspires them in the light."

Nagora shook her head. "Did you ever ask Edana what she wanted? Did she want to be used by you? Did Edana have a choice in her duty to you?

"Or are you carrying out Sagora's wishes? Making Sagora's dreams come true? Ignoring the cost of what you do? Well, now you know the cost!" Nagora jabbed a finger in Raynhard's direction, "And when I meet Sagora, so will she! Raynhard, this is your last chance to call off the wedding and send Sagora back to the Land of Skulls to apologize to Gabe before it's too late. Otherwise you risk watching your country burn to the ground all around you. That's one thing I don't have the power to stop."

Raynhard's face had flushed red, and he pushed his chair back.

Nagora pushed her chair back and pointed a finger at him. "Is that the fame you seek for the future? Every time two or more survivors in this land gather around a fire, it will remind one or both of them of the folly of their king who let their land be scorched and bled. Is that what you want, Raynhard?"

Raynhard was on his feet, clenching his teeth and glaring at Nagora, his fists on the table, leaning in her direction.

Nagora stood, leaned against the table, and pointed at Raynhard again as she spoke. "Continue on this path, Raynhard. Believe me! You'll never see another dragon fly in these skies again!"

Raynhard slammed a fist on the table. "Is that a threat, Nagora? Has Godomor sent you here to threaten me? In my kingdom? In my castle? Are you, yourself, threatening me? Are you questioning what is right for my people?"

Nagora opened her mouth, but Raynhard raised his hand. "You've had your say, Nagora. It's my turn."

Dannor sat just like his father with one hand flat on the table, fingers spread, staring at Raynhard.

Raynhard stood straight. "Nagora, I asked you to be my queen. I begged you to be my queen."

You made me to be your queen for one night. Sarah is your daughter from that night, though I doubt you know it, thanks to my lie and the lies Sagora concocted. Nagora bowed her head.

"You refused, Nagora." Raynhard inhaled a great breath. "But Sagora did not."

Slowly, Nagora brought her head up and locked her eyes on his. "You are blind, Raynhard. You do not see. Like the time I called you to the cave to warn you about Aliza. What is it that blinds you?"

Raynhard shook his head. "No, Nagora. I am not blind. I see all too well. You are jealous because you missed out on the opportunity Sagora has taken."

Oh, my poor, blind king. If only you knew what I have done for you and your dragon. No matter if I tried to explain, I know you would not understand. Where is the man of reason I once knew? What is it that blinds you to the obvious? What is it that is using you to its own ends? What in the past caused you to use me? Is there a way I can reach you? Can I play along with your game even if I don't know its rules?

Nagora sat back in her chair. "I'm sorry, Raynhard. You're right." She lowered her gaze and signaled to Lars and Dannor. "Read my hand signals."

Nagora's gaze returned to Raynhard. "I am jealous of Sagora. Of all she's accomplished with you. Of all she's done for the people of the Land of the Danu. I chose another man and another path. I was afraid of what being Edana entailed as a responsibility and what it would lead to—becoming your queen, and the responsibilities that come with that title." Nagora shook her head.

"Raynhard, I beg you forgive my threats. May the words I spoke to you in anger in this room never leave it. As a pledge to my apology, I will not be present at your wedding to Sagora. That way you'll have no fear I'll spoil that day for you.

"Instead, I offer to hasten my return to the Land of Skulls to bear a message of your choosing to King Godomor in the hopes it will appease him and his people.

"Please, Raynhard, take the time to think of the message you wish me to deliver."

As Nagora apologized, Raynhard was standing with his hands on his hips. Now he stepped around to the back of his chair and placed his hands on its backrest. Nagora remained seated and bowed her head.

Lars's hand on his leg, like Dannor's, signaled: "I follow."

Nagora stared up at Raynhard.

He pushed his chair to the table. "Very well, Nagora. I accept your apology. I admire you for admitting your motivations and the decision you've come to." Raynhard placed an elbow in the palm of one hand and brought the other hand to his chin, touching the amber jewel of his ring to his lips. "I will consult Sagora on the message I'll send to Godomor.

"In the meantime, you are welcome to stay here in the castle with us. Sagora will be pleased to see you and Lars again, and to meet Dannor."

Nagora smiled at him. "Thank you, Raynhard. You are most gracious. Are Mum and Da here?"

Raynhard cocked his head to the side. "Perhaps that news didn't make it to you? Oh, well. Better late than never. They're at sea, hoping to track down Grallimdor and Raganora, who sailed away with a boatload of dragon gold."

Make this look real. Nagora let her jaw drop, turned to Lars, then to Dannor, and back to Raynhard, letting her jaw move without words coming out. Nagora shook her head. "But ... but ... how can that be? I thought ... "

Raynhard pointed at her and then at himself. "That's right. As did many others, you and I both thought that Grallimdor was dead and Raganora captured, until we found and questioned the remaining mercenaries who gave themselves up here at the castle. Then the one who acted as Raganora on the day of the battle on the plain opposite the Isle of Smoke confirmed it. Raganora, Grallimdor, and two dozen mercenaries sailed from our harbor here the night before the battle."

Nagora placed a hand to the side of her head. "So Raganora knew all along of our plans? A spy was among us? Who?"

Raynhard dropped his gaze to the table. "That's what Yogari and Tagnya are trying to find out. They hope to recover the dragon gold, my gold. Yogari and his old crew rebuilt the Sea Wolf. Then he vowed to find the gold and bring it back with Raganora so I can serve justice on her."

Nagora looked to Lars and back to Raynhard. "They've been gone for how long?"

"It'll be five years soon."

Pieces fell into place. Sagora couldn't have acted as she's done with Mum and Da still here. They most likely don't know about the wedding. What better way to get Mum's voice of reason out of the way. Send her on the chase with Da. Has Mum truly reconnected with the Yogari she once knew? Has she helped Da heal from fifteen years of captivity with Danuka? Is this chase a last hope effort in the healing process, to give Da a meaningful goal?

"Was Mum happy to leave with Da?"

Raynhard smiled. "In Tagnya's words, happier than she had been in a long time. 'Excited' was a word Tagnya used many times to say how she felt. Yogari was confident he would succeed in his mission."

"Any news from them, Raynhard?"

"None so far. Nevertheless we're hopeful."

"So they don't know you and Sagora are to wed?"

Raynhard held his palms open, pursed his lips, and sucked in a breath. "Perhaps they do. Soon as we decided to marry, we sent out word via the traders where such information is posted and shared in ports that are hubs on routes common to most traders and seafarers. For all we know they could be headed back for the wedding. Our coastal lookouts have their eyes to the sea for the Wolf."

Another piece. "Did Da tell you where he would sail to?"

Raynhard's smile broadened. "I can show you a map Yogari left. It shows his destination."

Raynhard walked to the chest of wide thin drawers, pulled the top drawer open, pulled out a big sheet of vellum, and returned to the table.

Raynhard laid it on the table, turned it so Nagora could read it, and pointed. "You'll find his course marked in red and the destination, 'Kemet', known as the 'Black Lands.'"

Lars and Dannor stood with Nagora. She leaned over the map and took it in, first as one big piece of information. She placed a hand on Dannor's shoulder. "I've seen a rough likeness of this map. Uncle drew it once on the wet sand of our beach. One of my great-great-granddas, on Da's side, traveled to this inland sea. He saw wonders there. Uncle said he had taken inland rivers to get there. Da's route is by sea then through a narrow strait into the inland sea."

Nagora pointed to the words "Black Lands" and the drawings of three pyramids. She looked to Lars.

Lars was nodding. "In the Moroes Islands, an old captain on a whaler I worked on spoke of this 'Middle Sea' and the desert land where a big river carries rich black soil all the way to the sea. Said he couldn't believe how hot it was in that land. The captain spoke of strange animals like horses with long necks and a single big hump on their backs. At the captain's home lodge, he had hung on his wall a sword and a spear from that country."

Dannor's fascination was clear.

"Uncle spoke of those things as well." Nagora pointed to the map. "Great-great-grandda must've taken these rivers." Her finger traced over the inland rivers. "They would take him to Kemet that way."

Raynhard cleared his throat. "That's where Yogari and Tagnya have gone. All based on interrogating mercenaries here. Yogari granted them safe passage home if they would guide him and his crew and help find Raganora and the gold."

Mum, Da, may you return safely. Nagora studied the map further. After a long moment, she looked up at Raynhard. He had set the thumb of one hand under his chin as his lips rested on a finger. Something bothered Nagora. "Raynhard, is there another map?"

Raynhard's mouth opened, and he blinked his eyes. "You said?"

"Is there another map? One of Kemet, the country? Did Yogari leave you another map?"

"Why yes! I'll get it."

Raynhard took his time walking over to the chest and pulled a map from the same open drawer. It was on a piece of vellum as big as the other.

He laid it on top of the first. "You'll find the port where they'll dock and from there, three possible locations the mercenaries suggested he search."

The location names had little meaning for Nagora. Each place had several names listed alongside it. Probably spelled as her Father heard them spoken. He had written the estimated time of travel to each place from the port of landing, as well as time of travel from one location to another by various connecting routes.

Nagora looked up at Raynhard, then to Lars and Dannor. "If I read this right, they'll be on an extensive land expedition, crossing mountains and deserts from one watering hole to another to get to those locations. They'll need guides they can trust. I wouldn't want to be in their boots."

Acindor's face appeared in the back of her mind. "What about Prince Acindor? Is he dead?"

Raynhard stared at her, brought a hand to his mouth, and coughed. "Oh, yes! We're certain of that. Edana cut his head off."

Sagora? That would have been Sagora. Why can't I believe that? "You saw the head, Raynhard?"

"I did. Your sister brought it to me."

For a moment the room darkened. They all looked up to the skylight. Light poured down again. "Wait," said Raynhard.

A shadow plunged the room into darkness again. Longer this time.

When it left, Raynhard was still looking up and smiling. "Danuka's back. Soon you'll be meeting Sagora and Sarah. Have you finished with the maps? If so, we'll go greet them in the courtyard."

Dannor held his mother's arm. "Mum, will we see Danuka?"

Nagora looked over to Raynhard.

His smile was almost childlike. "Of course, Dannor. Let's go."

In the throne room, Danuka rippled across the panes of the clear glass windows. Iridescent shades of red, blue, and green light fractured and ricocheted from the fine mesh scales of Danuka's skin as she glided by.

Raynhard had a hand on Dannor's shoulder and as he pointed from one window to another, he turned the boy to follow Danuka's flight. "Look, Dannor, she's gliding now, slowing her flight as she circles nearer and nearer. Come. You'll see Danuka land in the courtyard."

...

Nagora and Lars followed. As they stepped into the shadow of the courtyard wall, their eyes climbed to the sky. "There!" shouted Dannor, his arm pointed at Danuka.

"Danuka will circle one more time. We'll stay where we are. Give her room to land. Sarah has the reins," said Raynhard.

My Sarah. Will I even be able to call you that when you step down from Danuka's wing? How will Sagora introduce you?

A door on the adjacent wall slammed open and two screaming boys tumbled out into the sunlit part of the yard. The first one rolled and stood up, wagging a finger at the other who was jacking himself up with both arms. "I beat you! I beat you! I'm first again!"

Gabe's boys? Must be.

Once on his feet, the second lad pushed the first. "Shut up! I beat you yesterday! So!"

Both turned to walk back to the door. Each held out a hand. The basket squeezed out of the shadow first, dragging Alizarine with it. The lads were at her sides locking their arms in hers. Alizarine limped into the sunlight and squinted at the sky.

Nagora's skin begged to be scratched. Somehow, soon, I'll rid this scab from my life.

"Watch out!" Dannor stumbled back. Danuka must've glided down into the square outside the castle to come up with wings spread wide over the top of the wall. For a moment she seemed to hang in the sunlit air. Danuka flapped her great wings once, rose, and glided forward, clearing the wall to land in the courtyard. The sunlight rippled in a thousand colors on the scales of her wings.

Mother, you have grown since I last saw you. How many times have you shed your skin since?

Danuka was looking at Nagora as she folded her wings back, brought their talons forward and down to the cobblestone yard, and moaned, long and low. A young woman, who could only be Sarah, sat in the forward saddle on the dragon's back. She seemed to wear a puzzled look as she patted Danuka's neck. Sagora slid out of her saddle first and stepped onto Danuka's raised wing and unfastened a satchel tied to the back of the saddle. The dragon lowered her wing, and Sagora stepped off. Then it was Sarah's turn.

Sagora had set the bag down and bent to one knee to open it. She seemed to search for something. Sarah headed in Alizarine's direction.

"Sister! Sarah!" The two lads raced in her direction.

Nagora swallowed and blinked back her tears.

The one who had been second was first this time, but looked back at his brother, tripped, and crashed to a stop on the cobblestones.

Raynhard laughed. "That's Baerik, the second born, all thumbs with two left feet these days. Can't seem to keep up with Raean."

"Na, na, na, na ya!" bleated Raean as he marched by, one thumb to his nose and the other to his bum.

Raean hopped on ahead and threw himself at Sarah. She caught him, swung him around, and turned him upside down, bending to one knee and rolling him over onto it. She gave him two whacks on his backside. "Now go help Baerik up. Stop being such a brat."

Raean high-stepped to Baerik with one hand in the back of his pants and his other jabbing in his brother's direction, grimacing with each step.

Alizarine had limped on behind the boys and was waving. "Sister Sarah!"

Sarah walked faster.

Nagora closed her eyes for a moment. When she opened them, Sarah was on one knee. She had an arm around Alizarine's waist and a hand on her leg, touching it. Then Sarah brought her hand up, held Alizarine's chin, and kissed her on the cheek as Sagora walked toward Alizarine's waving hand. Sagora held a leather bag in her hand behind her back.

Nagora turned her head away. Danuka's red eyes were still on her. Mother, how will I convince her? I'll need your help and the amulet Sarah wears. Danuka moaned again. Familiar hands came to rest on her shoulders.

Dannor leaned forward and looked into her eyes. "Don't worry, Mum. We'll find a way."

Nagora pulled Dannor and Lars to her and held them tight. "Yes, somehow, we'll find a way. Wait for me here."

Nagora stepped out of the shadow and walked to Danuka. Danuka pushed up on her wing talons to raise her belly off the ground. Once her tail was in place to give added balance to her legs, she drew back her head and raised her wings. Nagora stepped closer. "Speak, Mother."

"Look, Mother!" It was Alizarine's voice from behind her.

Danuka lowered her wings and crossed them behind Nagora as she set her talons on the ground, making a tent around Nagora. Then Danuka brought her head down over Nagora's head until the tip of her snout touched the Tiwaz brand on her forehead.

Nagora inhaled Danuka's scent. Indescribable and unforgettable, especially its effect on her. It was so powerful that Nagora had called it the Dragon's Kiss. Now it seemed to give her strength. Nagora was relaxed and at peace in her dragon's embrace.

It was like the last time she had stood before Danuka in the cave, and not what she had experienced all the previous times when it had excited her and filled her with lust like she had never felt before. Each time it had been a battle to satisfy and control those feelings.

Now Nagora basked in a sensation that left her calm yet feeling strong and fearless as every muscle in her body came alive.

Danuka spoke to her in the language of the dragons. "Yes, Mother. I will. You want me to bring my son. I will. Then we will talk over there. Not before. I understand, Mother."

For a slow count of ten, the dragon held her snout to Nagora's brand without speaking a word. Mother, you give me strength. I feel it course through me.

Danuka lifted her head away, pulled back her wings, and spread them wide.

Nagora stepped back. Thank you, Mother. Yes, we'll be ready when you return for us later.

Danuka folded her wings and brought her talons back to the ground.

Nagora turned to face the others.

Sagora strode toward her, followed by Sarah.

Raynhard was crossing the yard on a course that would take him to Sagora.

Lars and Dannor were in a slow run to Nagora. They arrived first, followed by the twin boys who had scooted past the others. "Who are you? Why do you look like our mum?"

Nagora smiled at them. "For the same reason you two look like each other."

The twins scrunched up their faces, grabbed a lock of hair on their heads, and wound it around their pointer fingers. "You and Mum are twins?" Is that Raean?

"I'll let her tell you."

"Nagora, what are you doing here?"

"Glad to see you too, big sister."

Sagora held up her hand. "I'm sorry. I wasn't expecting to see you until the day of the wedding." Sagora held open her arms.

Nagora stepped into her embrace. "Well, I won't be here for your wedding. Raynhard will tell you all about it. I'll be leaving as soon as he's discussed an important issue with you and come to a decision as to what message I'm to return to Godomor. It's one of those sooner-the-better situations.

"In the meantime, Sagora, face-to-face introductions are in order. Let me start. This is our son, Dannor. Dannor, my sister and your aunt, Sagora."

Sagora held out her hand to Dannor and looked at Lars. "Dannor, there's no denying whose son you are. Welcome to Windhaven." Sagora let go of Dannor's hand and moved to embrace Lars. "Good to see you, Lars. Welcome to Windhaven."

Lars's demeanor was neutral with barely the hint of a smile. "We've been too long without news from you, Sagora. We have some catching up to do."

Sagora stepped back, bowed her head, and brought a hand to her chin. Her lips rested on the amber stone of the silver ring on her hand. Sagora looked up to Raynhard and back to Lars. "Yes, we do." Sagora's ring is the same as the one Raynhard wears. Promissory rings? Promise to wed?

Sagora pulled her sons to her, looked from one's face to the other. "This is Raean. This is Baerik. Lads, meet your auntie, Nagora. Your uncle, Lars. And your cousin, Dannor."

Baerik shook Dannor's hand. "Cousin, are you going to live with us? You could teach us how to fight."

Dannor set a knee on the ground and smiled at Baerik. "That's not my business on this visit. Perhaps another time. Do you have practice swords?"

Baerik nodded.

Raean said, "But they're heavy. Da says we have to grow some more muscle first."

"Dannor! Dannor! I thought I would never see you again!" Alizarine had pushed past the twins with her basket and was reaching an arm around Dannor's neck.

"Well! Alizarine! Here I am. I've come to visit you to see if you've been taking good care of your egg. No cracks on it I hope?"

Alizarine shook her head. "Oh! No! Not a single crack, Dannor."

"You make me proud, Alizarine. You always take good care of it. I bet you still clean it every day with your little brush."

"Always before going to sleep, Dannor."

Dannor sat on the ground and crossed his legs so Alizarine could sit on his knee. "You know, Alizarine, I sure miss having a peek at your beautiful egg. It's been many days since the last peek I had. I won't bother you now with all these people around, 'cause they'll want to see it too."

"Dannor, I can let just you have a peek." Alizarine pulled the sheepskin aside and then the red silk scarf.

"Alizarine! You amaze me! Your egg looks as beautiful as ever! You take such good care of it. I bet the other side is as shiny as this one."

"It is, Dannor. Look." Alizarine reached in with both hands and with difficulty turned the egg over. "See?"

"Oh! Yes! I see, Alizarine! That side shines just like the other. Now I can truly say you've taken excellent care of your beautiful egg. Do you still sing to it, Alizarine?"

"I do, Dannor."

"What about music, Alizarine? Have you found anyone to play the flute for it, like I used to?"

Alizarine's face became sad as she shook her head from side to side. "No."

"Well, don't worry about that, Alizarine. Living in a big town like Windhaven now, I'm sure you'll learn about places where you could bring your egg so it could hear music. Like you always told me, 'A happy egg makes for a happy Alizarine.'"

Raean stepped near Alizarine. "I know a place where you could bring your egg to hear music, Alizarine."

Alizarine's eyes opened wide. "You do? Where, Raean?"

Raean wore a smile that dented both cheeks. He licked his upper lip. "At the Center for the Dragon Arts." He looked over at Sagora. "Isn't that so, Mum?"

Sagora nodded. "You're right, Raean."

Alizarine held out her arms to him. "Oh! Raean! You know everything! I'm so lucky to have you."

I'm so lucky to have you, Dannor. Thank you for planting the seed.

Sarah had been looking from Sagora to Nagora and back. She seemed to be waiting for Sagora to introduce her. With each moment the ache in Nagora's chest grew. *Piwi Mahihkan*, my Little Wolf how you have grown since the day you were born! Nagora bit into her lower lip to stem her tears. *Ka Peyakot Mahihkan*, if ever there was a time for you to stay strong and hide your feelings, now is the time.

Raynhard stepped forward. "We must not forget, Sarah, Sagora's eldest. And of course, you know this dear strange child, Alizarine, brought here well in advance of the wedding. Needless to say, Alizarine has adopted us, as is clear in how she has chosen to address us. I'm sure you understand."

We understand, but do you?

Sagora placed a hand on Sarah's back. "Sarah, though we've never spoken of them to you, it's never too late to meet your aunt, Nagora, your uncle, Lars, and your cousin, Dannor."

Sarah stepped forward. "I recall Grandma Tagnya and Grandda Yogari speak of Aunt Nagora. It was a long time back."

Nagora swallowed. I wonder what they told you. She smiled, opened her arms, and pulled Sarah to her. "Sarah, you don't know how long I've waited for this day. You don't know how happy I am to hold you." Nagora rubbed Sarah's back on each side of the sheath of her skystone blade. Then Nagora brought a hand to the back of Sarah's neck. The tips of her fingers brushed against the four eights knots of the fine leather lace. Good. The dragon-tear amulet hangs on this lace. You are wearing it. I wore it for eighteen years. Has it begun to reveal its power to you?

As Nagora released Sarah from her embrace and Sarah turned to Lars, Nagora said, loud enough for Sarah to hear, "*Piwi Mahihkan, mâcikôtân. Niya kikawiy.*"

Sarah's eyes, framed with the frown of a question, shot back to Nagora's.

Little Wolf, you will see for yourself it is so. I am your mother. Nagora smiled and nodded. The amulet is revealing its power. You do already understand the language of the dragons. However you doubt yourself as I once did, thinking I was hearing a voice speak strange words I understood yet could speak them as well as my own language.

Uncle was right—if he had told me what power my amulet held, I would not have believed him. Sarah, Da must have taught you many things a Dragon Talker needs to know, but the power of the amulet only reveals itself over time. Thank you, *Piwi Mahihkan*, you give me hope.

Sarah looked up into Lars's face.

Lars gave her one of his grand smiles as he placed both his hands around the one she offered. "Finally, I get to meet you, Sarah, the daughter I wish I had."

"Uncle Lars." Sarah blushed and turned to Dannor, who wore the same warm smile as his father.

Dannor held her hand as his father had. "Sarah, finally I get to meet another member of my family. I can't wait to tell my friends back home about you. They'll not believe a beautiful girl such as you can ride a dragon." *Dannor, you charmer. What else has your da been teaching you on those hunting trips?*

"Cousin Dannor, your friends won't believe you until they meet me and judge for themselves. Thank you for the compliment."

Now Dannor sported a smile to match Sarah's. *He's right though. Sarah is beautiful, especially when she smiles. I hope what I must ask of you will not wipe away your smile forever.*

Raynhard held out his arms. "Well, that takes care of introductions. It's nearing time for our midday meal." He gestured to Nagora, Lars, and Dannor. "Please, join us. The lads will lead the way."

"Come, Alizarine." Baerik and Raean locked arms with hers and picked up their knees in a slow march to match Alizarine's limping gait.

Nagora took Sagora's arm in hers. "Big sister, what happened to Alizarine's leg?"

Sagora smiled and glanced to the sky. "She fell in her haste to climb down from Danuka's saddle. Nothing broken from what we can see. A bad sprain. At least she's up and walking again."

"Mum, look!" It was Dannor. Nagora turned with Sagora to see him and Sarah pointing to the dragon who was flapping her wings and lifting from the ground.

Yes, Mother. When you return, we'll be ready.

Nagora turned to her sister. "It's all new for him, Sagora. Dannor's heard plenty of talk about Danuka, but to see her with his own eyes must be even more fascinating." The dragon was now climbing higher and higher and beginning to circle above the castle. "I couldn't believe my eyes the first time I saw her."

Nagora placed a hand on her man's arm. "Lars, you go on ahead with Dannor and Sarah. I want a moment alone with my big sister. Do you mind, Sagora?"

Sagora shook her head and brought a hand to her chin. Her lip twitched. "No, not at all."

That's a forced smile and your hand trembles. I can guess why.

As soon as Lars crossed the threshold of the doorway, Nagora held out her hands. "Take my hands, Sagora. I'll keep this short and not make any threats. I just want to be sure you have the same information I gave Raynhard earlier. That way, the two of you can decide what message I'll bring back to Godomor."

Sagora swallowed and her face paled like cream about to sour.

This might ruin your appetite, but right now I couldn't care less. "Sagora, here are Godomor's words: ' ... I will hold back my wolves for as long as possible. Be warned there will come a time when my voice will no longer be heard above their howls for the hunt to begin. I dare not predict what will stay standing once they cross the Blood River on their path of revenge, seeking blood wherever they can find it to quench the fire they will bear in their teeth.'"

The shudder that shook Sagora's body rippled through her hands and her face.

"Sister, you know what actions spawned Godomor's words. Think well on the message you and Raynhard will have me bear on my return to the Land of Skulls."

Sagora closed her eyes and turned her twisted face away, pulling her hands away to hold her sides. Your hands once healed. Today, can they soothe the aches and quakes you now feel inside? I doubt it. If only I knew the why of your foolish actions, I might forgive you.

Sagora had turned her back to Nagora and was bent over, retching.

Nagora went to her and placed a hand on her back, but Sagora struck it away. "Leave me. Go in. Tell the others I'll join them shortly."

Raynhard had barely eaten, and Sagora joined them only after the servants had cleared the table.

To the delight of Raean and Baerik, Dannor had questioned Sarah about how she had learned to ride Danuka and what it was like. Sarah obviously enjoyed recounting her most memorable flights on the dragon's back.

Dannor, I don't know if your conversation with Sarah was out of pure interest or if you were seeking information. From what I've gathered, Sarah was not on Danuka's flight to the Land of Skulls to bring Alizarine back.

Sarah's longest flight was to what was once the secret cave where I had taken Danuka. Sarah, you flew along my beach. Someday, I hope to be able to tell you that.

Dannor, you learned more things about your grandda, Yogari. I hope you meet him someday. What you don't know is that you're in for a big surprise today.

Nagora stood. "Raynhard, Sagora. I thank you both for this meal. Earlier, in the courtyard, you saw me enfolded in Danuka's wings. She told me she would return this afternoon.

She wants to bring me—and Dannor—to inspect her eggs on the Isle of Smoke."

"Luuuckyyy!" said the twins in unison, as they crossed their arms. "We never get to go."

Sagora spoke for the first time since excusing herself for being indisposed and not sharing the meal with them. "It's dangerous. When you're older. You don't want to get hurt like Alizarine."

Alizarine wore the same glum face since the conversation had turned to dragon riding.

Sarah had one hand on Dannor's arm and another on his shoulder as she shook him. "You heard well, Dannor. You're going for a ride on Danuka. You're not scared, are you?"

Dannor closed his mouth and looked from his father, who was smiling proudly, to his mother. "It's true? Danuka wants you to bring me?"

Sarah hugged him. "It is! That's what she said! You can't say no."

"No, I can. I mean no. I won't say no. Of course I'll go!"

"Lars, it'll be another time," said Nagora.

Lars shook his head. "I've had a turn on Danuka's back already. I'll wait for you here."

Sarah stood. "Uncle, I'll show you around the castle."

Now Dannor was standing. "Da, you have? You never told me about riding on Danuka."

Lars smiled and pointed at him. "I will, Dannor. It's a flight I'll always remember." Then his smile settled on Sarah. "Thank you, Sarah. I'm happy to have you as my guide."

Raynhard cleared his throat as he stood. "Shall I make arrangements for you to spend the night?"

Nagora shook her head. "That won't be necessary, Raynhard. We've found lodging in town, with an old friend."

"May I ask where?" asked Sagora.

"At Olen's. He's a smithy and also runs a stable on Stables Way. Our horses and mules are there. Our rooms are comfortable," said Nagora. You seem pleased, sister. We'll be out of your way. Have your discussion with your husband-to-be. I wonder if sleep will find you this coming night.

Raynhard was nodding. "I know the place. The smith, Olen, has a good reputation. Dannor, you are a lucky young man today. Enjoy your ride with your mother. Danuka should arrive at any moment now." Raynhard looked from Dannor to Nagora. "You'll want to use the latrine before you go. One of the lads will be glad to show you where."

Sarah stood nearby in the yard with Raean and Baerik, watching Nagora and Dannor prepare for their flight on the dragon. The lads' fascination with the dragon and their envy of Dannor seemed to keep them quiet for the time being.

"Watch me, Dannor," Nagora instructed. "Once I'm in the saddle, Danuka will lower her wing. Step on and place a hand on her side to steady yourself. Danuka will raise her wing. I'll be watching and will take hold of your left hand and guide it to the saddle-hold loop. Once you're high enough, swing your right leg up and over. You'll land in the saddle behind me. First, I'll check her bridle and saddle straps."

Dannor nodded and stood back.

The dragon lowered her head and opened her mouth.

Nagora patted Danuka's chin before running a finger over the chain links of the bit in her mouth. Then she ran her fingers over the bridle straps around the dragon's snout and along the straps of the reins also. "Good, *Okâwîmâw*. Up now. On your talons, Mother, so I can check the saddle straps."

If you're listening, Sarah, you should understand when I speak in the language of the dragons. Da taught you the hand signals and you use a rider's goad. If you understand, you should be able to guide Danuka with your thoughts. You don't know you have that power yet. Da didn't tell you because you didn't tell him about the voice. Perhaps you only started hearing it after Da left.

Nagora crouched at the base of Danuka's neck where the first strap crossed her breastbone. Its buckle and the leather were fine, well-oiled, as was the metal ring that held the belly strap leading to the waist strap. Nagora could just reach its buckle. It too was fine.

Nagora turned to waddle out from under the dragon. Dannor's wide open mouth and eyes told her he was worried for her. Don't worry, my son. Mother won't crush me.

Nagora patted Danuka's neck. "Down, *Okâwîmâw*. I will check the straps on your back and the saddles."

She stepped onto the wing. As it rose, Nagora slipped her fingers under the strap and ran them along it until she came to the saddles. Nagora pulled and lifted along their entire lengths. Geirador's brand was on the back of the strap fixed to the rear end of each saddle seat, three rune symbols within a circle.

Were these the last saddles he made? They're so much better than the first ones he had quickly pieced together for me. Da's suggestions and mine have all been taken into account. I like the rings at the back for tying on bags. The back strap, where it joined the waist belt, was layered, thick and solid with more attachment rings for tying on whatever a rider would want the dragon to carry.

Nagora grabbed the front saddle-hold loop and swung up onto the saddle. She tested the footholds. They were short. She lengthened the adjustment straps at their buckles by two holes. Perfect. Sarah was watching.

Nagora bent and patted Danuka's neck. "Mother, I love your saddles. I am sure they please you too. Lower your wing."

Dannor looked at Sarah before stepping onto the wing.

"Up, Mother," said Nagora.

Dannor landed in the saddle behind Nagora. "Dannor, do you see the three rune symbols on the strap at the back of my saddle?"

"In the circle where Algiz appears to hold Raidho on one of its arms and Jera on the other? I've never seen them arranged like that before," said Dannor.

"That's Geirador's brand. The circle is for the wheel, one of the most useful items a good smithy can make and repair. The three symbols inside it mean *Courage* on the *journey* brings *reward*. I thought you would like to know that for your first flight on Danuka." Geirador, keep your courage. Somehow, if I can, I will make it so your path brings you back to your calling.

"Right now I feel like I've used all my courage just to climb into this saddle," said Dannor.

"Let go of your saddle-hold loop. Keep your arms around me. There's a moveable woven leather belt from my saddle hold for you. I'll put your hands on it. Have your feet found the foot holds?"

"Yes, Mum."

"Are you comfortable in your saddle, Dannor?"

"I'm fine like this. I don't think I could be more comfortable."

Nagora glanced over her shoulder at Dannor's smile. My heart swells when I see you smile that way. "Repeat after me. *Okâwîmâw.*"

"*Okâwîmâw.*"

"That means 'Mother.' Now: *Kitatamihin.*"

"*Kitatamihin.*"

"That means 'Thank you, you make me smile.' Say again: '*Okâwîmâw, kitatamihin.*'"

"*Okâwîmâw, kitatamihin.*"

"Reach with me and we'll pat her neck. You thank her."

As Dannor patted Danuka, the boys had moved back. Sarah remained where she had been standing. She held the fingers of both hands before her mouth. Her face trembled as her eyes blinked at the pools of tears spilling from them.

"*Okâwîmâw, kitatamihin,*" said Dannor.

"We are ready, *Okâwîmâw.* Take us to your eggs," said Nagora.

Danuka pushed up on her talons and spread her wings.

The boys moved back some more, flapping their arms.

Sarah stumbled back, one hand over her mouth, the other trembled as it reached up. Is she nodding? What has Sarah realized? My *Piwi Mahihkan*, let it be so. Let me prove it to you with the amulet.

Danuka flapped her wings and pushed off with her powerful legs, lifting Nagora and Dannor with her out of the courtyard.

To the Cave
Yâwâtakan

† NOW: *the twelfth day in*
the Land of the Danu,
four days before the wedding

"Woooo hoooo!" Dannor screamed as Danuka rose higher and higher and then tilted and turned in a great arc that spiraled up above the castle. The walls of Windhaven receded as Danuka pulled out of her circular climb over the town to fly over the inlet waters of Windhaven's long bay.

Now Danuka pumped her wings with a steady beat, carrying them forward faster and faster. Dannor held the loop tight and pressed his arms into Nagora's sides. His cheek pressed into her left shoulder.

Nagora glanced at his squinting eyes.

He lifted his head and moved his lips.

She shook her head. "I—can't—hear—you."

Dannor smiled, nodded, stuck his cheek back on her shoulder, and lifted his arm to point. Soon they would be over the sea.

...

When they were, Danuka slowed the beat of her wings, tilted them left so she now flew along the rocky coastline. She glided in a slow dive and then let herself climb until almost slowing to a stop before pumping her wings again. Danuka seemed to do this in a rhythm that matched the beauty of parts of the coastline's evergreen forests, farmland fields, and rocky outcrops.

Once, she veered inland toward a mountain to skim along its jagged slope.

At one point, Dannor let go of his loop and wrapped his arms around Nagora's waist and hugged her hard as he rubbed his face against her back. Like my happy little boy used to do.

When he took hold of his loop again, Nagora tapped his arm and pointed ahead. A plume of steamy smoke stood like a limp truce flag above the Isle of Smoke's sleeping volcano. A rare calm for this time of day. Usually by now, the wind has picked up. Gentle swells from far away waves are the only disturbance on this sea of glass.

Far away over Nagora's right shoulder, in the quarter where the guiding star stood and the morning sun rose, dark clouds gathered low in the sky. The thunder mason's building a sky of gray and black clouds. The fine weather of these past days has just about run its course. When the clouds gathered like that, her uncle used to say: "Soon they won't be able to hold it any longer, and we'll be drenched in piss." The rainstorm will be here by tomorrow night at the latest.

...

Now the timber fortress was visible. Do Mum and Da leave a caretaker there while they're gone? Probably not with no bridge back to the mainland, and they would have to be someone trusted, someone who would not hunt for Danuka's eggs.

Danuka veered left inland, followed the road below for not even half a count, and then cut further inland, skimming over forest trees until she soared above the vast plain that lay opposite the Isle of Smoke. The plain no longer bore the scar of the V-shaped ditch Raganora's troops had dug as a defense against Edana's announced attack. Now wheat covered it.

Danuka circled back and flew onward toward the fortress.

Nagora pointed to her right at the vestiges of the once great Isle of Smoke stone bridge.

Danuka climbed left, up the slope of the volcano to its ridge high above the fortress, crossing over the mouth of the volcano and disturbing the smoke plume with a single beat of her wings.

The dragon dove to the right down the other slope along the sea coast cliffs. She veered out to sea in a long graceful arc that brought her back to an opening on the cliff face that required her to glide in sideways then level out, pull back her wings, and land.

Dannor was leaning against his mother with arms around her waist. "We made it! This last part was the scariest. Mum, what an experience!" He leaned forward and reached out to pat the dragon's neck. "*Okâwîmâw, kitatamihin.* Even if I got the fright of my life, I'm smiling now."

Danuka moaned as she folded in her wings, brought her talons onto the cave floor, and lowered her belly. "You're off first, Dannor."

"Mum, how long did it take Danuka to fly here? I'm guessing three counts."

"I would say you're right, Dannor." As soon as he stepped to the floor, Nagora eased out of her saddle. "Go see if you can find a taper or a candle lantern nearby. We have barely enough light. More won't hurt."

Nagora stepped off the wing, and Dannor appeared with a taper in one hand and a candle lantern in the other. "There are two more tapers and three more lanterns over on the rock shelf on that wall." He pointed back and to his right. "Which do I light?"

"Light the taper first, but move back near the wall. We'll explore the cave."

Nagora turned to Danuka. "*Okâwîmâw*, you have found a good cave beyond that crack in the cliff face. The only chance someone will find it is if they see you fly in or out. You will not let that happen."

Danuka looked down at her and spoke. Her words rang clear in the mind of her Dragon Talker. "*Ka Peyakot Mahihkan*, first you and your son will hold my eggs for my inspection." What Da and the Little People said is true. I'm a true Dragon Talker. Mother, I hear you well, like your last words to me in Raynhard's secret cave.

In Nagora's mind Danuka said, "After, Lone Wolf, we will talk. We will plan. I need the egg. Hatching time nears. It cannot be delayed."

Mother, I understand. We will make a plan that works.

Dannor had been waiting with the lit taper. "Mum, did you ask Danuka to bring me with you?"

"No, Dannor, she asked me—ordered me, in fact. Believe me, son, she has her reasons. I don't always know what they are. First she wants us to hold her eggs so she can examine them"

Dannor frowned.

"Don't worry. Just do as I tell you. It won't hurt." Even so, I worry. What will the Dragon's Kiss do when she folds her wings around us? Will her essence overpower me and excite my senses like in Raynhard's secret cave? What will it do to Dannor? Please, Mother, not with my son, do not do that to me. I beg you. Please, don't.

In Nagora's mind Danuka said, "Lone Wolf, worry not. Trust Danuka. You are no longer an apprentice. You have proven yourself. Now the power is in you. It is no longer necessary for me to control you. I trust you will do what you must. You are prepared for the ultimate sacrifice."

Is my path taking me there? Am I truly prepared? Mother, if you say I am, then I trust you. I will do whatever it takes to give you back your egg. All I ask is my daughter in return so Dannor can have a true sister and Sarah a true brother.

"Mum. Mum! What's wrong?"

Nagora shook her head and smiled. "I'm sorry. Believe it or not, I was speaking to Danuka. My mind to her mind. A Dragon Talker who's no longer an apprentice can do that."

"Truly? Then where are her eggs?"

"She wants us to try to find them. Let's get a taper for me and then we'll try our luck."

They had walked the length of Danuka's winding cave, but the only eggs they found were the feeder eggs for the hatchlings, piled in a dark recess of the cave. They had not spotted a single pouch with baby dragon eggs. "She must've hidden them on a high shelf that we can't see from here. It must be hidden in the shadows cast by the light of our tapers striking the rocky projections."

They returned to Danuka. "Mother, we cannot find your eggs. Show them to us."

Yes, Mother, we will wait near the entrance for you to return.

"Come, Dannor."

"She's being extra careful, Mum. Doesn't she trust you?"

Do I tell him? Does he need to know?

Nagora stopped and turned to him, reaching for his hand. Her eyes fell to her boots before climbing back to his. "Can you blame her, Dannor? Those eggs contain the last of her kind. They are more than precious. They are the future. The future of her kind. The future of the Land of the Danu. She trusts me and she trusts you too, Dannor. Otherwise we wouldn't be here."

Danuka returned with four pouches and set them on the floor where they sat near Nagora's sheepskin vest. Nagora had laid it fur-side up before Dannor at the spot in the cave entrance with the most light.

Dannor sat cross-legged on the floor of the cave, his back to Nagora between her spread legs. "Pull the vest closer, up into your lap. Good. Now can you reach the straps of the pouches?" She kept a hand on his shoulder as he bent forward. "Good. Pull them closer. Wait for Mother to place her wings."

The dragon faced them, came closer, and spread her wings, bringing one over and behind Nagora so her talon rested on the floor to Nagora's left side. The other wing crossed over the first. Its talon rested to the right of Nagora.

Nagora whispered in Dannor's ear. "Don't be afraid. She won't fall on us. For almost a full year she had me do this every day."

Danuka sat on her hindquarters and curled her long tail around them. Its bulbous tip carried a vertical fin that ran back from the top of her tail. The fin pointed out past the tip of the tail and curved underneath. Two longer side fins stuck out from the tip's round sides. The ball-shaped finned tip came to rest on the hind claws of Danuka's left hind leg.

"Keep your eyes on her head. Wait until she brings it down and touches her snout to your forehead. Then open a pouch and pull an egg out with both hands."

Dannor's shiver rippled through his shoulders to Nagora's fingers as the dragon touched his forehead. He took a deep breath and pulled one of the four-pocket pouches to his side, unbuckled the leather strap, and flipped the cover flap back. Each pocket held a single-egg pouch with a buckled flap. He pulled one out and removed the egg. "Wow! It's heavy. It's a wonder you-know-who can carry it."

Nagora's cheek almost touched Dannor's. "I know what you mean. Hold it over your lap. One hand on the smaller end. The other on the bigger end. Turn it slow so she can eye it and smell it."

Danuka smelled the entire surface of the blue egg with its red and gold veins. Then she examined it with one of her big red eyes. The eye was without eyelashes and the size of Nagora's two fists held together.

"Good, Dannor. Replace the egg. Take out the next one. Twelve more to go."

Dannor had just pulled the ninth egg from its pocket when he said, "Mum, this egg isn't like the others. It's different. It's lighter, I'm sure. And the color of the gold is not the same."

"Are you sure?" Nagora kept a hand on Dannor's shoulder as she reached over to the last four-egg pouch, unfastened the buckle, and pulled back the flap. "Two eggs! She's supposed to have only thirteen. Could ... "

Danuka cut her short.

"I will, Mother. Dannor, Danuka wants to know if Alizarine would notice."

"I'm sure she would. If I noticed, Alizarine would. What's wrong with this egg?"

Okâwîmâw, you are wise.

"Well, Dannor, now we know why she wanted you here. The egg you hold is a feeder egg. It's one of the eggs I gilded with gold leaf, many years ago, to trick an egg thief. Danuka thought we might switch the gilded egg for the one Alizarine carries. Now you've proven we must use one of the female eggs. Mother was hoping we wouldn't have to."

Danuka's lips curled back as she reached for the gilded egg, giving Dannor a glimpse of her teeth. Again a shiver ran through him and he pulled his hands away as soon as the lips of the dragon grasped the egg. Danuka set it on the ground and gave it a nudge so it rolled over to the wall.

"Only four more to go, Dannor."

When Danuka had finished inspecting the last egg, her big red eyes stared at Dannor.

"Son, Mother wants you to choose which egg to switch."

Dannor looked to his mother. "She does?"

"Yes, Dannor. Choose."

Dannor did not hesitate. He reached for the first four-pocket pouch, unbuckled the strap, flipped open the flap, and pulled out the third single-pocket pouch. He removed the egg it held and placed it in his lap. "I can't say why it's this one. It's a feeling I had earlier when I pulled it from its pocket. The feeling told me this one is just like the one Alizarine has, its true sister egg, the one laid right after Alizarine's was."

Nagora hugged him. "Mother says you chose well, for the reasons you spoke. You trusted your feelings. That is why she trusts you to make the switch."

"Me? Make the switch?"

"If she says she trusts you to do it, Dannor, do so."

Dannor sat with his back straight, reached out his hand, and rubbed Danuka's snout. "*Okâwîmâw, kitatamihin.*"

Nagora hugged her son and Danuka moaned as she always did while raising her right wing. "Mother says she will speak with me now. Go to the lip of the cave entrance and gaze out to sea."

Dannor stood, handed Nagora her sheepskin vest, and stepped over Danuka's tail. "I'll wait for you there, Mum."

...

After Danuka had folded her wing back over Nagora, her big, calm red eyes stared into hers before speaking. She's searching for something inside me. "*Ka Peyakot Mahihkan*, our king is not our king. Evil possesses him and Sagora, who he would make his queen. You must remove the evil."

"Remove the evil? How? What evil? *Okâwîmâw*, I want to help, but I do not know of what evil you speak. How can I remove what I do not know is the evil? Mother, sometimes you speak in riddles. Is it because you don't have the words to tell me outright what I have to do?"

Danuka tilted her head for a moment as one of her eyes seemed to look deeper into Nagora. "Lone Wolf, take the skystone blade. Look at it. Remember. It removed evil from this island many years ago. It can remove the evil again."

Nagora reached behind her beneath her hooded shirt for the handle of the big skystone blade. She flicked the latch that locked it in her sheath, pulled it free, and held it before her. Remember? On this island? This blade is identical to mine. What did I do with my blade? She squeezed the layered walrus hide grip. Come on, Tar piss! Remember! I held it against Rumandor's back.

Wait!

"Mother, you said 'It' removed evil from this island. 'It ... 'It?' Yes!"

The flash of that moment surfaced from her memory of being with Hag in the vent shaft cave all those years ago.

"Mother! 'It!' I remember! Hag held my blade!" Nagora raised the skystone blade as Hag had held hers. "I held Hag's amber-eyed staff with its three intertwined silver snakes. As

Hag struck at me, I jabbed the staff at the blade. It was as if lightning had struck. There was an explosion. It threw me back onto the floor of the cave. Where Hag had been standing was a cloud of black smoke that disappeared into the crack in the ceiling. All that remained of Hag's staff was a burnt stub of a stick."

Nagora pointed to the skystone blade. "'It removed Hag. No more Alizarine on the island. Mother, I can't kill Alizarine with the skystone blade. The curse, Mother. Surely you know about the curse?"

Danuka moaned.

"You do. Well, then ... what?"

Not Alizarine, but the evil they wear.

"The evil they wear?"

It is what they wear that allows evil to control them?

"Mother, I do not understand."

You say the evil makes them act on their secret thoughts, what they would not act on if the evil did not possess them. The evil controls them like you controlled me in Raynhard's secret cave, to test me and teach me and give me the strength of mind to do the unthinkable.

But Raynhard and Sagora have no control over the evil they wear. You had to fight to control me with your essence, and I always regained control of my actions. And I saw the consequences of my actions. Raynhard and Sagora cannot see the consequences as long as they wear the evil.

Nagora set her blade on the sheepskin vest and brought her hands together at her lips. "Mother, give me a moment to think on this."

What am I not seeing? It must be obvious, plain as day. Raynhard is not the Raynhard I once knew. He's a changed man. Sagora too has changed. They aren't behaving as themselves, as the persons I once knew. They have not thought out the consequences of their actions.

"Mother, Sagora brought you to find Alizarine and the egg. Was that of your choosing?"

It was not.

"Mother, why would Sagora do that?"

Yogari told Sagora about the missing egg. As a Dragon Talker it was in my care. Sarah, as apprentice Dragon Talker, would care for the other eggs while he was away. Later, when Sagora wore evil, she wanted Sarah to have all the eggs to care for as Dragon Talker.

"Mother, did Sagora kill our dogs?"

You did not know she would do that. You say that is an example of her acting on her secret thoughts. That it was a warning to me.

Nagora's shoulders shook as a chill ran through her, like on the day she found Arm and Hand dead on the floor of her lodge. Sagora, would you even think of doing the same to Lars and me?

What is it you wear that lets you act out those deep, dark desires? Something obvious, easy to see with the eye like … like … the amber eye on Hag's staff. The evil they wear! Yes! Mother! They both wear rings with amber stones like the witch's staff!

"Where did those rings come from, Mother?"

You say they are the same rings King Bernhard and Queen Juliana wore when the evil began its attack on them, when Hag controlled them.

"Mother, does Alizarine control them?"

Not yet because she has to relearn how.

"Mother," Nagora picked up the blade, "this can destroy the rings? I must find a way. Trust me, I will find a way."

Nagora returned the blade to its sheath. "Mother, I need your help. How do I convince Sarah, my *Piwi Mahihkan*, she is my daughter and must help me carry out the curse to rid Alizarine from the Land of the Danu for all time? Can it be done with the amulet, without joining with my daughter like I did with Raynhard to show the past? With your help instead?"

Danuka reared her head and looked at Nagora. "Yes, Lone Wolf, *Piwi Mahihkan* is your own blood. You can do this with the amulet and golden-handled dragon dagger you carry." The dragon lowered her snout and touched Nagora's right thigh. "And this. Place the hand of Little Wolf here. My help is unnecessary. You have all you need."

Nagora reached out to touch Danuka's snout. "*Okâwîmâw, kitatamihin*. Mother, you give me great relief and great hope."

Dannor sat at the mouth of the cave, staring out to sea. Just like your da. My mum too loves looking out to sea.

I've only been on the Sea Wolf once, but I can see what the draw is to those who've been to sea before. A life of exploration with a good crew on a trusty vessel you believe you can control leads to adventure, no matter the whims of the winds and waves and tides.

"You see anything, son?"

"Two finback whales in the distance."

Dannor stood and pointed up along the tall, narrow entrance. "How can Danuka fly out of here? The only way out I can see would be for Danuka to jump or push off from that ledge up there. Once clear of the crack, she could glide out to sea. How will she get up there with us on her back?"

Nagora rested a hand on his shoulder. "She wouldn't have brought us here if she couldn't take us back. Come. It's time we leave." She handed him the well worn, single-egg leather pouch containing the egg he had chosen. "It'll be a rough ride out of here. Danuka trusts you with this egg. Tie it well to the rings on the back of your saddle." Nagora adjusted the leather strap on her left shoulder and patted her scrip. "When we get back to the castle, I'll put your egg in here with the gilded egg."

They took their places in the saddles on the dragon's back, and Danuka had warned them to hold on tight as she walked to the entrance.

The dragon brought her folded wings up as high as she could and with her strong wing talons, she grasped the rock on each side of the crack. She lifted with her right wing, found a foothold for her right hind claws, released her right talon, and lifted with her left wing talon, allowing the right talon to clamp onto a rock further up. Her left hind claws took hold.

In two more alternating climbs, Danuka reached the ledge where she let her hindquarters rest while positioning the talon of her right wing high above her perch. She hooked her left wing talon well below on the other side of the crack.

Her tail snaked out of the crack. It must have found a spot on the cliff face above her left talon.

"Hold tight, Dannor. Yes, *Okâwîmâw*, we are ready."

Danuka pushed with her powerful hind legs and pulled with her wing talons. In the time it took for Danuka to shoot sideways out of the crack into the air above the sea, they had slid sideways in their saddles. They almost fell out of their saddles, only to be whipped up and over to the other side before plunging forward in them.

"Whooo hoooo!" screamed Dannor as Danuka dove, picked up speed, and spread her giant wings to pull up just over the water. She glided and rose until her speed slowed. Then she pumped her wings in long, slow sweeps that carried them higher and further out to sea.

Then the dragon tipped right and began a gentle glide as she arced back to the coast. With the cliffs in view, Danuka tipped left and for the rest of the flight, she took them along the coast until they came to the inlet leading to Windhaven's harbor.

From there, Danuka flew straight on to the castle and over it before circling around and down into the courtyard.

Dannor reached forward to pat Danuka's neck and hug his mother at the same time. "*Okâwîmâw, kitatamihin.* Mum, I'll always remember this day."

Nagora turned to hug him back. If you could see your smile, my son. "Nor I, Dannor. I'm so happy to have shared it with you."

Dannor leaped from the wing and ran to his father before Danuka had completely set her wing talon down. Lars stood with arms crossed on his chest. He wore his best smile, relishing in Dannor's excitement.

Nagora slipped from the saddle, untied the leather pouch from the ring at the back of Dannor's saddle, and slipped it into her scrip.

As she stepped from Danuka's wing, the look on Lars's face changed to the opposite of Dannor's. It expressed deep concern. Now what?

As Lars hugged Nagora, he whispered in her ear. "Alizarine has the amulet."

"What?" She threw her head back to search his face. "How?"

He held her close again. "The twins took it from Sarah in a tussle and gave it to Alizarine." He let go of her.

Nagora's hands went to her lips as she read Lars's face. Alizarine won't give it back. Is there no end to the pain you cause me, Alizarine?

The Amulet
Kanawisimowin

† NOW: *the twelfth day in*
the Land of the Danu,
four days before the wedding

"Dannor! Dannor! Tell us about the ride!" The twins poured out of the door into the yard, pulling and pushing each other as they raced to Dannor.

Alizarine followed with her basket. Sarah was at her side. She seemed to plead with Alizarine who stopped her limping procession to purse her lips shut and shake her head from left to right. You're wasting your time, my daughter. You'll not win it back from Alizarine with words. It'll take more than words. Yes, more than words, but what?

Sarah left Alizarine standing near the door and rushed over to the twins. She grabbed each by an arm. "The amulet's mine. You had no right to take it from me and give it to her." She let go of Raean's arm and pointed at Alizarine, who was a pouting statue with both arms threaded through the handle of her basket. "She won't give it back to me. I want you two to go get it and give it back to me. It's mine. I'll tell Mum and you'll see what she'll do."

Raean scrunched up his face at Sarah. "We already asked, and she won't give it back. Mum asked too, and still she won't give it back. What do you want us to do?"

Sarah spoke through clenched teeth with repeated jabs of a finger at Raean. "Take it back like—you—took—it—from—me!" Sarah turned away, crossed her arms, and then placed her chin in one palm. Her shoulders shook.

Dannor went to her side and put a hand on her back. He whispered something in her ear. She looked at him, nodded, and placed a hand on his shoulder.

Whatever you promised her, son, I hope you can make good on it.

Lars squeezed Nagora's hand. "And?"

"I have a lot to tell you later. Right now, I can tell you Dannor had an unforgettable ride."

Lars smiled. "That's what his face told me when he jumped from Danuka's wing."

"How about you? Did you get a tour of the castle?"

A slight smile returned to his face. "After you two left on Danuka, Sarah dried her tears and had a rest before giving me a tour. We had just finished the tour when they ambushed her."

Nagora shook her head. "I see why the people in the Land of Skulls have beliefs and rituals about twins. They wouldn't put up with these two for long.

"Did you find out what Sarah had been crying about?"

Lars raised his eyebrows and shrugged. "I didn't dare ask. I'm not good with young ladies in that respect."

She nudged him in the ribs. "Raynhard and Sagora?"

Lars made a discreet thumbs down sign. "They kept to themselves most of the afternoon. Sagora showed up for a few moments to see what the ruckus was about. She didn't help the situation any."

"Do we stay for the evening meal?" Nagora leaned her head on his shoulder. Her eyes were on Sarah and Dannor.

"Only if you think staying will give Dannor a chance to approach Alizarine."

The twins were skipping around Alizarine, singing. "Please! Please! Alizarine. Give it back, please!"

Alizarine's eyes were shut tighter than her lips as she shook her head no. If you could, little witch, you would cover your ears too.

"I think we would be wasting our time. I would like to speak to Sarah before we go. Then we'll leave them to their games."

Dannor left Sarah and headed for the twins.

Sarah turned to face Nagora and Lars. She lowered her gaze, took a slow step toward them and stopped. Nagora walked to her with a hand outstretched. Sarah looked up and took several steps to meet her.

"I hear Alizarine has something that belongs to you and won't give it back. She has upset you." Nagora took Sarah's hand.

"Yes, she has my amulet. I've always worn it since I can remember. It's just a stone, but I feel so connected to it. I don't feel complete without it."

I've had the same feeling. "Do you know who gave you the amulet?"

"When I was a little girl I used to ask Mum who had given me the amulet. She would say: 'Someone who loves you very much.' I would ask: 'Who is that?' She would smile and say: 'Your mum.'" A hidden truth. Why, Sagora?

"Sarah, you're an apprentice Dragon Talker. I know my da, Yogari, has given you some training. Did he ever mention the amulet when training you?"

"Only once. He said it had powers, and that with time they would reveal themselves. When I asked what powers, he said if he told me I would not believe him and they would stay hidden."

Sarah stared at Nagora. "You ask these questions about my amulet. You seem to know about it. What can you tell me about it?"

"Right now, Sarah, I can only ask you about it. Earlier this afternoon, as we were leaving on Danuka's back, I saw you cry. Can you tell me why you cried?"

Sarah looked at the ground.

Nagora squeezed Sarah's hand. "I think you cried because you realized something, and you don't trust yourself in what that is. Inside, you feel you are hearing a voice speak in a language that is strange, yet as familiar as the one you speak."

Sarah looked up at her. Her mouth moved, but no words came out at first. "But ... but ... how do you know this?"

She smiled at Sarah. I guessed right, my daughter. "Well, Sarah. I, like my da, am a Dragon Talker. I once was an apprentice, like you, but I didn't know it. For many years before you were born, I wore that same amulet."

Sarah's mouth now hung open as she appeared to be making sense of the connections she was making.

"Today, Sarah, probably for the first time, you heard someone speak out loud in that strange language. Still, you don't trust that you truly understood what you heard. Do you, *Piwi Mahihkan?*"

Tears filled Sarah's eyes. She swallowed and the words spilled out. "Little Wolf. You called me 'Little Wolf.' And," Sarah sniffled, "what you said when Rayhnard introduced us—after you hugged me—is true? Am I to believe that? I'll need proof."

"*Piwi Mahihkan, asici kanawisimowin, mâcikôtân. Ka Peyakot Mahihkan kikawiy.*"

Again Sarah swallowed, repeated the words, and then translated them. "Little Wolf, with the amulet, you will see for yourself it is so. Lone Wolf is your mother."

Sarah threw her arms around Nagora. "*Okâwîmâw.*"

Now, daughter, I have to fight back my tears. "*Mitanisimaw*, you called me 'Mother.'"

Sarah pulled away and grabbed Nagora's hands. "Make it so. Please, make it so." She pointed around her. "I no longer understand what goes on in this place. It's not a home. Something terrible has gone wrong here." Sarah pointed to Alizarine. "And it's only gotten worse with her arrival. From the day my grandparents sailed away, things changed." Sarah pulled Nagora's hands to her chin. "Today you bring me relief. I'm not losing my mind when I hear and understand those words."

Nagora squeezed Sarah's fingers. "Sarah, you are not. You are on your way to becoming a Dragon Talker. You speak and understand the language of the dragons." Will you believe what I will show you with the amulet and the dagger? The

task that awaits us? Will you join me in carrying out our cursed duty as Dragon Talkers?

Lars put a hand on Nagora's shoulder and pointed.

Dannor sat cross-legged on the ground with Alizarine on
one knee and Baerik and Raean sitting just opposite him. His
thumbs were crossed, palms facing him, as he moved his
hands up and about. He's telling of his flight on Danuka.

Nagora placed Sarah's hands in Lars's. "Wait here,
please." She walked over to listen to her storyteller son.

Dannor held out his left hand just above the cobblestones
and moved it over them with a slight fluttering motion of his
spread fingers. "We skimmed right over the sea. If there had
been waves, Danuka's wing tips would've touched them."

"Did you see any fishes?" Baerik asked.

"Ha! Better than fishes. Whales!"

"Whales?" asked the twins.

Dannor held his forearm up with wrist bent so he was
looking over it at the boys. He placed the fingers of his other
hand behind his arm to make the dorsal fin. "Two great finback whales." He moved his elbow and fin fingers to make
the whale dive. "The two of them swam side by side. They
dove together side by side. They surfaced together side by
side. Their fins were like black flags on their backs."

"Luuucky!" said Raean. "Did you see their teeth?"

Dannor pretended surprise. "Raean, Baerik, did you know
most whales don't have teeth like we do?"

"What do you mean? How do they eat?" asked Raean.

"I'll tell you what my da told me. When he was young, he
worked with the whalers from the Moroes Islands. They hunted plenty of whales on the boat he was on."

"What did he say? What did he say?" Baerik hollered.

Dannor held up a finger. "Imagine this. Instead of the teeth you have in your mouth now, you had a big horsehair brush in place of your top teeth and another big horsehair brush where your bottom teeth are. And! Imagine you could open your mouth so wide you could pour a whole pot of chicken soup inside. That would be a lot of broth, wouldn't it?"

The twins and even Alizarine nodded.

"Now remember, you don't have teeth. You have brushes. And you don't want all the broth, but you do want all the pieces of chicken and vegetables. What would you do?"

Raean had his two hands in front of him, fingers curled and spread as he brought them together so the crossed fingers closed the spaces between. "I would close my brushes together and bend forward so all the broth spills through the brush hairs back into the pot, but all the chicken pieces and vegetables stay in my mouth."

Dannor clapped. "Raean, you said it so well. You're ready to become a whale!"

Raean lifted his whale-mouth hands up to his wide smile and acted out the part. Baerik did the same. Alizarine only smiled.

"Do you have any other whale stories?" asked Raean.

Dannor held up both hands. "I started telling you about flying on a dragon. I wound up telling you about whale teeth, but that's not what they're called. Da says the whalers call them 'baleen.' And by the way, Raean, they only have it on the top of their mouths. I could get back to dragons and tell you about dragon teeth."

Alizarine lifted one arm loose from the handle of her basket and placed a hand on Dannor's shoulder. "Yes! Tell us about dragon teeth."

The twins' eyes were saucers waiting to be fed another of Dannor's tales.

Dannor looked from one child to the next and spoke in a quiet voice, close to a whisper. "What I'm about to tell you has to be kept secret. I won't tell you why right now. I'm pretty sure by the end of my story you'll understand why. Can I trust you three to keep this for yourselves?"

The three nodded solemnly.

He pointed to each one in turn. "You promise, right?"

Again they nodded.

"Good. I'm counting on you to keep your promise, because what I'm about to tell you comes from what my mum told me. Now, if you didn't know already, she's a Dragon Talker, like your grandda, Yogari. You saw her fly away with me on Danuka earlier today." He turned and pointed to where Danuka had landed in the yard.

He saw Nagora leaning against the wall not far from them. "Oops! There she is. Mum, is it alright if I tell them you-know-what?"

Nagora drew a finger across her lips and nodded. *As if you needed my permission to weave a tale with inventions and half-truths of your own creation. Go ahead. Perhaps it'll bear fruit.* As soon as Dannor turned back, Nagora signaled to Lars to come over with Sarah to listen.

"How did she become a Dragon Talker?" asked Raean.

Dannor pointed at him. "Exactly what I was about to tell you. Dragon Talkers are chosen and most times they don't know they've been chosen."

Lars and Sarah stood with Nagora.

"Why is that?" asked Baerik.

Dannor pointed to Baerik. "I'm glad you asked. I was going to forget that part. Well, Baerik, it's because they're too young when they get chosen. Most times they get chosen within a few days of being born." He leaned toward Baerik. "Do you remember anything from those days?"

Baerik shook his head no.

"How do they get chosen?" asked Raean.

Dannor pointed with both hands. "You lads sure have all the right questions to keep me on track. You don't want to miss a thing, do you? Dragon Talkers get chosen by another Dragon Talker who gives them a special stone, like I said, close to the day they were born. Oh! To you and me, it might look like an ordinary black stone wrapped in cat sinew, hanging from a leather lace, but that's not what a Dragon Talker sees. Oh! No!" Dannor paused and looked from one child's face to the next.

"What do they see?" asked Alizarine.

Baerik and Raean were nodding yes to Alizarine's question.

Dannor pretended he was taking an amulet from around his neck and holding it up to the sun. "What a Dragon Talker sees is the inside of the black stone. Inside, there is a red glow. And inside the red glow there is a pink filament, like a curled thread that moves. Yes, it moves, Alizarine. It's alive."

Sarah put a hand to her mouth and whispered, "Yes, that's true!"

I can confirm that my daughter.

"Even if you were able to hold the amulet up to the sun, you would not be able to see what a Dragon Talker sees.

There's no way you could, because you haven't been wearing it around your neck since you were a baby, because you weren't chosen to wear it."

"Well, what would I see if I was?" asked Alizarine.

Nagora clenched her teeth. *You would never be chosen. Don't get any ideas you can start wearing it now.*

Dannor held up a single finger, paused and spoke his next words slowly and softly. "What a Dragon Talker, who is pure of heart, sees is a single blood tear from a dragon inside that black stone."

The twins sucked in a breath between their teeth and their shoulders shivered.

Sarah took Nagora's hand and squeezed it.

"That's right, a dragon's blood tear. Now don't ask me how that blood tear got inside that stone, I can't say for sure. I've heard, not from my mum, but someone who heard from someone else who heard it from another someone else who said, a long time ago a sad dragon was imprisoned in a cave inside a mountain volcano and it cried blood tears." Dannor's fingers drew imaginary tears on his cheeks.

"The tears dripped down to the molten rock of the volcano, and because the tears were so cold the volcano spewed them out in pieces of molten lava that fell to the ground as black stones. Friends of that dragon collected those stones, which were destined to be given to future Dragon Talkers."

Dannor squinted and pointed at his young listeners. "What is special about these stones, or dragon-tear amulets, is that, because they contain a dragon's tear, they have certain dragon powers. Not my mum, but others have said the amulets contain the fire powers of a dragon."

"Wow! Fire powers! How would they know that?" asked Raean.

Dannor held both hands open. "Again, this is not from my mum, but from others. There's a story of someone who once killed a Dragon Talker to steal an amulet, thinking if they wore the amulet it would give them the fire powers of a dragon."

Dannor looked from one to the other. "I don't want to scare you, but I'll tell you what those others told. Soon as the murderer put the amulet around their neck and it touched their skin, it burned a hole right into their chest and melted their heart." Dannor paused. "That's how the dead murderer was found lying on the ground." Dannor grabbed the sides of his chest with spread fingers. "The fingers of both hands dug into their own chest."

Dannor turned his face into a grimace. "And their face twisted into a silent scream of pain. Yes, lads, the amulet had the fire power of that Dragon Talker's dragon, all right. Fire power strong enough to burn a hole right through the thieving murderer."

The twins had their hands on their chests, and Alizarine squirmed on Dannor's knee.

Dannor scratched his head and looked from one twin to the other. "I've gotten off track again. What was I supposed to be telling you about?"

Raean spread his lips with two fingers from each hand. "Duh dwagon's teef."

Dannor snapped his fingers. "That's it! I went from flying on a dragon, to seeing whales, to whale teeth, to the Dragon Talker amulets, and now on to the truly secret stuff of dragon teeth."

Dannor grinned to bare his teeth. "You've surely seen Danuka's teeth before, haven't you?"

"They're bigger than mine," said Baerik.

"Of course. Think of the biggest animal you've ever seen, besides Danuka," said Dannor.

"A horse!" said Raean.

"Or a cow!" said Baerik.

Dannor snapped his fingers twice. "Good, lads! So how much bigger would you say Danuka's head is compared to a cow or horse head?"

Right away Baerik yelled, "Ten times!"

Raean punched Baerik on the shoulder. "Not that big!" He spread his hands and was expanding their spread, obviously trying to give himself a reference. "I say four times as big, maybe five if the horse is small."

Dannor held up a thumb. "I think you're close Raean. What I'm getting at is the dragon's head is much bigger so its teeth are going to be much bigger than the teeth of a horse or a cow."

"But that's not a secret. Is it?" asked Raean, obviously disappointed.

Dannor shook his head. "I'm getting to the secret. Have any of you ever found a dragon tooth?"

Alizarine said, "I have. I found three."

"No way!" said Baerik.

Raean clubbed his brother's arm again.

"Ask Dannor, he'll tell you," said Alizarine.

"It's true. Alizarine did find three dragon teeth. Believe me. They're not found just anywhere. She found them because back home we live near a special place, a dragon maze.

I know you know what a maze is. I saw the one on that side of the castle when I was on Danuka's back.

"Well, this dragon maze is ancient, and people believe old dragons came to die on the seaside cliffs near the maze to pay back the crows and ravens for sharing the sky with them. Once crows and ravens finished picking over their bodies, other dragons pushed their skeletons over the cliffs into the sea. That was long ago." Dannor had made a pushing motion before crossing his arms.

Dannor leaned toward the twins. "Not far from our lodge, there is a sandy cove close to where the dragon maze is. When there are big storms at sea, the waves come crashing into our cove, and all kinds of things get washed onto our beach." His arms made the tumbling action of the waves.

Dannor pointed at the witch sitting on his knee. "Alizarine went to the beach with my mum one day after a big storm and found three dragon teeth."

"What's secret about that? I don't believe it. Show us the teeth," said Baerik as he held up his hands to ward off another hit from his brother.

"Let him finish, Baerik. You're such a baby. Always jumping ahead, asking dumb questions," said Raean.

"Alizarine can't show you the teeth because she left them at home. But I can show them to you tomorrow because I brought them with me. They're in my saddlebags at the place we're staying at."

"That can't be the secret. Why did you bring the dragon teeth with you?" asked Baerik.

"Of course not, Baerik. I brought the teeth because I thought Alizarine already knew the secret I only discovered recently and I wanted to share it with you, Baerik, you, Raean, and Sarah," said Dannor.

"Not Alizarine? They're her teeth," said Baerik.

"True, Baerik, but I figured she already benefited from their secret and had left them behind for me to use. If she hadn't benefited, why would she have left them behind?" asked Dannor.

Raean pointed at Alizarine then Dannor. "Maybe she didn't know about the secret."

Dannor brought a hand to his head as he looked to Alizarine and then Raean. "I never thought of that, Raean. You have a point."

Dannor placed a finger on Alizarine's shoulder. "Did you know about the secret of the dragon teeth?"

Alizarine shook her head. "No. No one told me about any secret. What secret?"

Dannor held his head with both hands. "Well, then. That changes everything, doesn't it? The teeth would go back to you if you didn't use the three wishes. I thought you knew. That you had made your three wishes."

"What three wishes?" asked Alizarine.

"Aye! What three wishes?" asked Raean.

Dannor held up his hands. "That's the secret. The wishes. I was told by an old fisher back home about the wish a dragon tooth accorded its finder. Now he said, whoever found a dragon tooth was granted one wish. Right away I said: 'Oh! How lucky Alizarine is. She found not one, but three teeth!' Now mind you, I hadn't seen those teeth in a long, long time. Anyway, a few days after Alizarine left, I found the three teeth."

He pointed a thumb at his chest. "So I said to myself, 'Dannor boy, here's your chance to make three wishes.' And so I did."

"What did you wish for?" asked Baerik.

Dannor held up a finger. "Number one, I wished to go on a long, long journey out of the country where I lived. When I made that wish, I didn't know we would be coming here."

A second finger went up. "Number two, I wished ever so hard to meet the other members of my family. Here you are! You're not all here, but most of you are, so I consider that coming true."

His third finger went up, "Wish number three, which, honestly, I never ever thought would come true, but it did today. That was to ride on a dragon!"

Dannor pointed at his three fingers. "So there you have them. My three wishes granted. Aren't I lucky?"

"Wow! Luuucky is right!" said Raean.

"Oh! Aye! Lucky for sure!" said Baerik. "Will Alizarine get three wishes too?"

Dannor took a deep breath and lifted his shoulders. "That's the thing. I asked the fisher if someone could get more than one wish from a tooth. He told me this: 'A wish on a dragon tooth works under special conditions.'" Four of Dannor's fingers went up again.

"One, that the person who finds the tooth makes the wish.

"Two, if the person loses the tooth unintentionally and has not made a wish on it yet, but then finds it again, they can make a wish.

"Three, if a person made a wish, they can hide the tooth for another finder to make a wish. If that second finder makes a wish and hides the tooth, and the first hider finds it again without cheating, then and only then can the one who finds the tooth for a second time make a second wish on the tooth. This, said the fisher, works for up to three wishes on a single tooth for a three-time finder. Can you imagine how lucky that person would have to be?"

The twins were shaking their heads.

Dannor wiggled his little finger. "Alizarine, lads, there's a fourth and final condition. If the finder of a dragon tooth can truly say they left it behind and didn't know about the wish before someone else found it ... "

Dannor held up his two pointer fingers. "The tooth, I warn you, will know if this is true." He glanced at Alizarine.

He continued. " ... then the first finder of the tooth can pay," Dannor paused, "with something of value," he paused again, "to the second finder and ask them to hide the tooth as a," he took a breath, "treasure," and he glanced around at the rapt faces, "in a place where the first finder stands a chance of finding it before the sun sets on the day of the treasure hunt!"

Dannor looked from one twin to the other and then to Alizarine. "Since I have three dragon teeth, I will have a treasure hunt here in the castle, tomorrow. You three each stand a chance of finding a dragon tooth. Or with much greater luck, find two! Or with the greatest of luck, find three dragon teeth!"

"I know what I'll do if I find one! I'll wi ... Oops!" Raean put a hand on his own mouth. His eyes shifted from Alizarine to Baerik.

Dannor laughed. "Now here's something to think upon given all I've told you. Truly, what would you prefer to find on the treasure hunt tomorrow? A dragon-tear amulet, or a dragon tooth?" He held a finger across his lips. "Something else to think upon—what'll you wish for?"

Dannor turned to Alizarine, placed his hands around her waist, and stood her on her feet. "And finally, Alizarine, you must think upon this since you were the first finder. What of value in your possession will you give for this treasure hunt to take place here at the castle tomorrow?"

Alizarine bit her lower lip and her eyes shifted back and forth from the twins to Dannor and finally settled on her basket before she limped toward the door.

Nagora held Sarah's hand. She'll not surrender her egg. The amulet, possibly. She squeezed Sarah's hand. There's hope, my daughter. More than words. A way with words. Well done, Dannor.

Dannor stood, held out a hand to each twin, and helped them up. "Off you go. Think well about what you'll wish for." Already they seemed hard at work with thoughts of possible wishes. Each seemed to be so lost in thought that neither spoke a word nor ran for the door. Instead, they were lost in a pensive amble.

When Dannor turned to Nagora, she hugged him and whispered in his ear, "Well done, my son."

As Sarah hugged him, his father patted him on the back.

Once Sarah let go of Dannor, she turned to Nagora. "Are you staying for the evening meal?"

"Sarah, obviously the king and his bride-to-be have many important matters to discuss. And I'm tired. So we'll go to our lodgings, eat with our friends, and be early to bed. I suggest you find your bed early too. Please offer our apologies to … Raynhard and my sister." I almost said "your da." There'll be a time for that news. Enough for one day. "Tell them we'll come for breakfast so Dannor can prepare the treasure hunt."

Sarah smiled and hugged Nagora. "Until tomorrow. Thank you, all of you."

They finished their evening meal at Olen's and cleared the table. Nagora was completing her telling of the day's events, except for what had happened to Sarah's amulet.

Olen had listened attentively and now wore a smile he could fit a horse's bit into. "Tars! I mean Nagora. I knew you would find an egg! Now all you have to do is make the switch."

Nagora smiled at Olen. "You make it sound so easy. Have you ever seen a dragon egg?"

Olen laughed. "No, never. And probably never will."

Nagora pushed back her chair, stood, and lifted the strap of her scrip over her head, handing it to Dannor. She removed her sheepskin vest, set it on the table, and bunched it up to make a nest for the egg. She rested her hands on the table and looked around at the group. "Friends, it's important you see what you'll be dealing with tomorrow evening. I ask you to look, but please don't touch it. Moreena, you can touch it."

"Dannor, place the egg here, please." She moved over next to Lars.

"Wow! Blue with red and gold veins!" said Erin.

Olen's eyes, big as cups, stared and followed the egg's journey to the sheepskin nest. "It seems to be heavy, Dannor. It must be six times the size of a goose egg."

"It is heavy."

Nagora touched Dannor's arm. She held out her hands palms down and indicated he should take Moreena's hands.

Dannor turned to her. "Stand, Moreena. Give me your hands. I'll place them on the egg."

Moreena did as Dannor told her. Her fingers were like spider legs, tentatively feeling their way over the veined surface of the egg. When they finally settled, their tips explored the embossed gold veins. "I'm touching the gold veins, aren't I?"

"Yes, Moreena," said Nagora.

With her fingers spread at each end of the egg, Moreena lifted it slightly. "My! It is heavy. As heavy as my iron pot. This Alizarine, a six-year-old, carries an egg that weighs this much?"

"Yes, Moreena, the witch is cursed with a beautiful burden," said Nagora.

Moreena lifted her hands from the egg and stood straight. "Dannor, earlier you said you used to play the flute for Alizarine's egg. Did she uncover it when you played?"

"Yes she did, and she would sit her egg on one of what we call her 'stone boats,' a stone with a flat bottom and a depression on the top deep enough to keep the egg from rolling."

Moreena reached out and touched Dannor's arm. "Do you think she'll uncover her egg and set it on that stone pedestal?"

Dannor raised his eyebrows. "I think so. One of the stone boats was missing when Alizarine was taken. I'm guessing she brought it or convinced Sagora to bring it for her. It's heavier than the egg. Then again, we can never tell with Alizarine and her moods."

Moreena's eyes were closed and she was nodding ever so slightly.

Nagora went over to her. "Moreena, what are you thinking?"

Moreena placed her hands on Nagora's. "It's just a thought about how this egg switch will go. I was wondering if in some way, we musicians could help make it happen other than just playing our songs."

Dannor spoke up. "Pardon me, Moreena, Mum. Danuka asked me to make the switch. I've had time to consider how I might best do that. What Moreena has just said gives me an idea. A way the musicians can make the switch happen. They might even create several possible moments where it could happen."

There was definite excitement in Dannor's voice. Moreena surely heard it as well. "Go ahead, Dannor. Tell us your idea."

Dannor nodded and held up both hands. He took a breath. "Yesterday we learned Hag was spellbound by the golden harps. Chances are, so will Alizarine. She's Hag after all. Moreena will be playing her golden harp. Erin will be playing her wooden harp and her flute. And there'll be other musicians. Am I right?"

"Correct," said Erin.

"So what I was thinking is this." He lowered his hands and shook his head. "It might not be possible, but I'll speak it anyway. Would it be possible to have Moreena sit and play her harp from one side of the stage, and Erin sit and play her harp from the other side of the stage?" His hands indicated their places on the stage.

"Are there songs in which one harp plays a part of a song and then the other plays the next part, back and forth?"

Erin nodded and made sign with her hand for him to continue with his idea.

"Now if Alizarine were to be sitting in the middle, between the two harps, in such a place as she'd need to want to turn to face each harp as it plays its part of the song, I could be sitting next to her and offer to move her egg on its stone pedestal each time so it too faced the music. If she agrees, then each move to face the other harp becomes an occasion to make the switch."

Erin had been nodding and looking to her sister. "Moreena, the other musicians already sit between our harps. Perhaps we could just sit even further apart?"

Moreena's hand went up. "Yes, we could. And if the children were to sit up front, right on the stage in front of the musicians, that would help too. The adults will sit on the tiers above the stage.

"And in two of our songs, Erin and I play alternate verses." Moreena's eyelids fluttered. She must be counting how many. "In those two songs, eleven changes in all."

Dannor clapped his hands twice. "Everyone's eyes will be on the musicians. It'll be up to me to make the switch."

Olen pointed at the egg. "That's a big egg to hide. Where are you going to put it, Dannor?"

Lars spoke up. "If you could shorten the strap on that pocket pouch and tie it to one of the bottom corners so the flap opens sideways like this, it would be easier to slip one egg out and the other one in. Do that and I'll let you wear my sheepskin vest. You'll have room to hide the pouch under your arm at your side."

Dannor looked at his father. "What'll you wear?"

"Yours!" He smiled and laughed. "I packed my old one too. You wear the new one."

Olen slapped the tabletop and the egg jumped. "Oops!" He looked at the egg. "Sorry about that.

"What'll it be? Music or mead before bed tonight?"

Nagora slapped one hand onto another. "Olen, you have mead. Do you have honey?"

"Aye, I do."

"Cream?"

"Aye." He gave her a quizzical look.

"Stone rolled oats?"

"I do have all of that. Anything else?"

"That'll do. Bring it along with a pot and a big bowl to the counter near the fireplace. I'll make a potion that'll have us all sleeping like babies tonight. Now it'll take awhile for the oats to steep. If the flute players would be so kind as to charm us with a few tunes while we wait, I'll get busy."

The Hunt Begins
Mâcîwin Mâcipayin

† NOW: *the thirteenth day in
the Land of the Danu,
three days before the wedding*

It had been a night of both mead and music after all, thanks to Geirador's recipe which Nagora shared with her friends. The Potion, as Geirador liked to call it, did make them sleep. Luckily, Moreena had stopped after one cup, otherwise Nagora, Lars, and Dannor would still be sound asleep and not on their way to the castle for breakfast.

Dannor had made quick work of adapting the pouch as his father had suggested. And he carried in his scrip the three dragon teeth.

They walked in silence, choosing this day to go by Stables Way. The day was gray, as Nagora had predicted the day before. Would the rain hold off until tonight? Lars didn't think so. He had rolled their waxed woolen rain capes into one tight roll around which he had wound leather lanyards and attached a leather carry strap. Now he carried the bundle slung over his shoulder.

What will this day at the castle bring us?

Sagora, have you and Raynhard come to a decision? Have you found words that will hold Godomor's wolves at bay? Have you come to your senses? How will I rid you of the amber stones you wear?

Sarah, will Dannor win your amulet back today? If so, will we be able to join with the amulet and the dagger to give you proof of who you truly are, and the task you and I have been cursed with? Will you believe it? Will you join me in its execution or refuse?

Always the unknown. One day at a time. One moment at a time.

This morning, the castle guards played no games. One led them in and sent a page ahead to announce their arrival.

"Dragon teeth! Dragon teeth! Dragon teeth!" The chants of the twins reached their ears fifty paces from the dining room and well before the aromas of meat pies and fresh-baked bread fell upon their noses.

Lars put one hand on Nagora's shoulder and the other on his son's. He looked from one to the other. "All of a sudden, I'm hungry."

Nagora returned his smile.

"Let the games begin," said Dannor.

"Right on time!" Raynhard was standing near the dining room table with arms spread wide. "Come, come join us."

Sagora stood, wearing a warm smile. What message for Godomor have you come up with, big sister? You seem pleased with yourself this morning. Sagora showed the chairs to the left of where Sarah stood. "Welcome to our table. Please sit here."

After hugging Sarah, they took their places.

Opposite them sat the children. The twins flanked Alizarine and did their best not to squirm on their chairs. Alizarine was serene as she held onto her basket in her lap.

Nagora reached into Sarah's lap and took her hand. I'll fall off my chair if she hands her egg over to Dannor.

He sat opposite Alizarine. Lars sat to his left, near Raynhard.

The twins stared at Dannor, obviously fighting to contain their excitement.

"Good morning, Alizarine." Dannor looked to her right. "Baerik, did you sleep well?"

Baerik kept his lips pursed and nodded energetically.

"Raean, I can tell you spent the night thinking about the wish you would make," said Dannor.

"Wishes!" His eyes bulged and Raean slapped a hand over his mouth as he looked over at Sagora.

She gave him a look of ice, then looked over to his brother. "You may speak now."

It was a tangle of exclamations, questions, and demands all rolled into one as the twins unleashed their excitement about the treasure hunt.

Dannor looked from one to the other, scratched his head, and pushed his chair back. Then he looked under the table, before standing. He lifted his chair and looked under it. When he put it down, he looked under his father's chair and then his mother's.

When the twins finally shut up, Raean said, "What are you looking for, Dannor?"

Dannor pointed at him and kept pointing as he sat. "That, Raean, I understood. I was looking for all those other people I heard talking. I couldn't understand a single word you two good lads were saying." Dannor peeked under the table. "I guess they've gone away as quickly as they arrived. Now we'll be able to talk."

Raean raised his hand.

Dannor nodded at him. "Yes, Raean, you may speak."

"Did you bring the dragon teeth?"

"I have."

Baerik's hand shot up. He waited for Dannor to nod. "Will you show them to us now?"

"Only after we've eaten our meal and Alizarine has delivered an object of significant value that will allow the treasure hunt to take place. And ... when I show them to you, I will place them on this table once it's empty, and you will not touch them. I alone will move them to show all their sides. And ... I warn you, if you touch a tooth, it will lose its power to grant you a wish. Fair warning to you. Now you know. Only a *found* tooth has the power to grant a wish."

I'm as anxious as the twins for the treasure hunt to start. But my men aren't. Lars, that's your third portion of meat pie. Dannor, you're slicing up a second apple. Will you have enough cheese and honey to top onto those slices? Sagora must think Olen didn't feed us an evening meal. And here I am sipping from another bowl of forest tea listening to your small talk with Raynhard and Sagora. One good thing has come from it though—an invitation to join them at the Center for the Dragon Arts for a private concert after the evening meal. Good. That game piece has fallen into place.

Sarah's been quiet this morning. Waiting to see if she'll get her amulet back? What of value will Alizarine give? She has nothing else I'm aware of. Will Dannor's moves cause Alizarine to put that piece into play in this game?

The servants cleared the table, and the twins pulled their chairs closer. Alizarine seemed to be waiting for her moment. Dannor looked around the table, rubbed his hands, and reached into his scrip. "The time has come to show you the chicken teeth."

The twins and Alizarine didn't find it funny. Baerik and Raean shook their fists at Dannor while the others laughed. Dannor made like he was placing invisible, pinhead-sized teeth on the table. "Do you see them, lads?"

They rolled their eyes.

"Of course you don't. Chickens don't have teeth."

Dannor, you're a teaser like your da.

Alizarine, with effort, hoisted her basket onto the table and stood. "I have my object of value to give so the treasure hunt can begin."

It can't be!

Dannor stood and looked Alizarine in the eye, his face no longer a joker's. "What object do you offer, Alizarine?"

"You'll find it next to my egg wrapped in the red scarf."

Dannor pointed at the basket. "You want me to take it?"

Alizarine nodded.

Nagora and Sarah locked their hands together.

Dannor leaned over to the basket, pulled the folded sheepskin aside to reveal the egg. The red silk scarf sat next to it, rolled into a ball. He took it from the basket, laid it on the table, and slowly unraveled the long red scarf to show the amulet.

That's it, wrapped in its intricate pattern of cat's sinew, waiting to hang from Sarah's neck on its leather lace with the four eights knots.

Dannor glanced from Sarah to Alizarine. "Are you sure this is what you want to give, Alizarine?"

"Yes, because it has great value for a Dragon Talker."

And you're afraid of the amulet. You've always feared it, so much so you wanted the sea to drown me and take me and my amulet to its deepest depths.

Dannor held the amulet by its leather lace as he gave it to Sarah. She smiled as she pulled it over her head and let it fall at her neck. Then Dannor draped the red silk scarf over the egg, folded the sheepskin over it, and looked from Alizarine to the twins. "Within a count, the treasure hunt will begin." He sat in his chair.

Alizarine pulled her basket from the table and bent to set it on the floor at her feet. Then she joined the twins who had leaned their forearms on the table to rest their chins on them. She placed one hand over the other and laid her cheek on it.

Dannor set the first dragon tooth on the table so it rested at an angle on its three long roots. It was taller than the width of his hand.

"Wow! So big!" said Baerik.

A hand's span from the first one, Dannor set the second on the table in a like manner so it tilted toward the first. It was smaller.

The third was the smallest of the three, and he also rested it on its roots.

"There's green on the small one's legs, and the other two each have brown legs," said Baerik.

"How come you don't have any sharp ones like Danuka has at the front of her mouth?" asked Raean.

Dannor pointed to Raean. "I'll tell you what the old fisher told me." He lifted the smallest tooth. "The sharp teeth at the front of a dragon's mouth don't have three legs like this back tooth. What happens in the sea is that the sharp teeth drill down deep in the sand because they have only one leg."

He made the small tooth walk on its three legs. "Teeth like these can walk on the bottom of the sea when pushed by waves. This one with the green on its legs probably stood in seaweeds for a long time. Its spread legs don't allow it to drill down."

Raean's mouth hung open as he nodded. "That makes sense."

Alizarine lifted her cheek from her hands. "Show them the tops."

Dannor set them on their sides, waiting a few moments before turning each one once and then again a last time.

"Tell them what the chips on the tops are," said Alizarine.

Dannor picked up the biggest one and pointed to where a chip from the tooth had broken off. "You see here where a piece of tooth is missing?" He held it closer to Baerik then to Raean. "That's caused by a dragon grinding stones between its teeth to make sparks so it can breathe out fire."

"Reeealllly?" asked Raean.

"How else would a dragon be able to breathe fire?" asked Dannor.

Raean and Baerik twisted their mouths and scratched their chins.

Dannor held up a finger. "I'll tell you how it works, but then I must go hide the teeth so the treasure hunt can start. Lads, is that okay with you?"

They nodded.

"You see, lads, when dragons eat, the food in their bellies makes gas. Dragons can breathe that gas out. When they want to breathe out fire, which is not often from what I've heard, they have to grind small stones with their teeth to make sparks."

"Like flint stones," said Raean.

"Exactly! The sparks set the gas on fire as the dragon breathes out." Dannor brought his fingers to his mouth. "Crunch! Sparks!" Then he threw his fingers out at the twins before him. "Fire!"

Baerik clapped. "I would like to see a dragon do that!"

Dannor stood, pulled the teeth to him, and placed them one by one in his scrip. "As soon as I come back, you can start hunting." He looked to Raynhard. "I have the run of the castle, your Majesty?"

Raynhard nodded. "Any chamber with an unlocked door is yours to use as a hiding place."

Dannor bowed. "Thank you most kindly." He left by the door they had entered.

Now if only I can get away with Sarah to somewhere private. Here in the castle or away. I must be sure we won't be interrupted. I know where. If Danuka comes this morning, I'll take Moreena's offer and still be able to keep her mountain cave a secret.

"Lars, your son is an imaginative storyteller. We had such a quiet evening yesterday. The only thing they told us was

Dannor would have a treasure hunt for them today in the castle," said Raynhard.

Lars leaned an elbow over the back of his chair and smiled. "Well, he's always loved a good story. Nagora and I have told him many, some more than once. He often told stories to Alizarine."

Lars turned to Sagora and pointed to her twins. "I think he enjoyed having Baerik and Raean for an audience. You lads sure know how to ask the right questions. You made sure Dannor gave you proper answers."

He turned his gaze to the witch. "Alizarine, would you like Dannor to take care of your egg while you hunt for dragon teeth? I'm sure he wouldn't mind."

She shook her head no. "I think my egg will help me."

That was worth a try, my man. It would have been a first if she had said yes.

"In that case, Alizarine, you're better off bringing it with you," said Lars.

Raean and Baerik wore frowns as they looked at Alizarine.

Sagora cleared her throat, and her eyes bored into twins as she held a finger to her lips. Once she had their attention, she smiled. "Alizarine went to bed soon after the evening meal. Usually she's the last one in bed. I think she wanted to be rested for today. I bet she'll find a tooth."

Nagora touched Sarah's hand. *Time to make my move.* "Sarah, will Danuka return this morning?"

Sarah smiled wide. "Oh! Yes! She'll be here soon to see if we need her to take us somewhere." Sarah turned to Sagora. "Mum, do you have a visit planned for today?"

Piwi Mahihkan, who will you continue to call "Mum" after we join with the amulet?

Sagora shook her head no. "No visits until after the wedding." She looked to Raynhard and smiled. He smiled back. *Put those smiles away. They're too good to be true.*

Sarah took Nagora's hand. "Well then, I'll take Nagora for a ride on Danuka. I'm sure she would enjoy that even if she went with Dannor yesterday."

"Sarah, I truly would." She squeezed Sarah's hand. *I know where I'll take you. You won't be the same person when you come back.*

Dannor stumbled into the dining room. He had obviously been running and was out of breath. He bent over and put his hands on his knees. When he stood straight for a moment, he said, as he pointed to Alizarine and the twins, "I hope you find the teeth, because I don't know if I'll remember where I hid them! You have until sunset. Go to it! Good luck on the hunt."

The twins left in a dash, leaving Alizarine behind. She stood in place, slowly turning to the left and then back to the right. With a definite nod of her head, she left the dining room, her basket leading the way.

Dannor stood with his hands on his hips. "Coming through the throne room, I saw Danuka fly by. She'll be landing any moment now."

Nagora stood. She was holding Sarah's hand. "Dannor, Sarah and I are going for a ride on Danuka. I trust you'll keep your da out of trouble until we get back." She got what she wanted, a grand smile from each of her men. Their smiles gave her strength for what she was about to do. *How you'll react, my little wolf, I have no way of knowing.*

Denial
Ânwehtamowin

† NOW: *the thirteenth day in*
the Land of the Danu,
three days before the wedding

Danuka carried a mother and her daughter out of the courtyard in an ever-growing spiral. Nagora was happy to sit in the saddle with Sarah behind her, holding on to her waist and pressing her cheek to her shoulder. Sarah had agreed to let Nagora tell Danuka where to go. On the last arc of her spiral up from the castle, the dragon followed the main road out of Windhaven toward Dromester, Moreena's home hamlet.

For now, Nagora kept Danuka below the cloud cover so she could get her bearings to the base of the mountain.

The mountain came into view. The cart trail along the farm field was below them. They followed it to the forest until they came to the clearing across from the scree pile at the base of the cliffs. Here, Danuka climbed skyward into the mist. The canopy of trees below was barely visible through the fog of the clouds. Above the tree line, they crossed to the stony slope of the mountain.

Danuka slowed and landed alongside the three boulders near the entrance to Moreena's secret cave. "You can open your eyes now, Sarah. We'll be safe here, and sure no one will bother us. I spent four days here eighteen years ago with a friend. I promise, someday, I'll tell you all about it."

Like Moreena had done back then, Nagora asked Sarah to find the cave's entrance. Sarah too could not locate it.

Sarah followed Nagora's lead, sitting on her bum to let her feet find the footholds that took them into the dark hole. "Wait right there, Sarah. I'll find a taper and light it." Milkweed silk from her scrip and the edge of her belt knife against her flint created a flame from which she lit the taper. "Follow me, Sarah." How I love to say your name. If only you knew all the images it brings to the front of my mind.

Nagora led Sarah around the hidden corner of the cave's interior entrance. "Oh! I see! Another room here," said Sarah.

Nagora found the candle lanterns and lit three of them. She placed one on the small table, one on a wall hook near the bed frame, and hung the last one from the ceiling just before it sloped upward above the firepit. "We'll make a fire and spread hides on the floor. We'll be comfortable."

Side by side on their knees, the two women watched the kindling burst into flames that licked at the logs. A shiver went through Nagora. Godomor, will I get to you in time?

Sarah put her arm through Nagora's and pulled her closer. "I'm afraid and anxious."

"Sarah, so am I, for I know what the amulet will show you." She reached into her vest pocket and pulled out the golden-handled dagger still in its sheath. "And what this too will show you. Take it. Look at it."

Sarah's eyes grew wide. "The sheath bears the royal coat of arms." She pulled the dagger from its sheath, resting the blade in one palm and the handle in her other. "The detail in the handle is beautiful. The dragon's wings and body curl around it. Yet it's comfortable to hold. The dragon's mouth holds a crown at the pommel. Its tail loops out on each side of the blade to form the cross guard." Sarah looked at Nagora. "This is no ordinary dagger. This is a king's dagger."

"It is, Sarah."

"Was it given to you?"

"Yes, Sarah, by your da."

Sarah's hands trembled.

Nagora took the dagger before it fell.

Sarah's right hand balled into a fist that she held with her left. "With the dagger too, you will give me proof?"

Nagora reached for the sheath in Sarah's lap and returned the dagger's blade to it. "Trust me, Sarah, I will. I showed you the dagger so you'll better understand what the amulet shows you and then what the dagger itself will show you. Are you ready to go on with this, Sarah?"

Sarah swallowed. "Yes. I must. I want to know."

Nagora laid two more logs in a peak over the fire and backed away. "Come, give me the amulet and lie on your back. It'll be easier." Nagora focused before pulling the leather lace over Sarah's head. Only images from when I wore this amulet. If Sarah wishes I see something from when she wore it, let it be her decision. The amulet hung free at Nagora's neck.

Once Sarah had lain on a hide, Nagora brought the amulet to her lips and closed her eyes. *So many events to show you. Too many. Only enough to give you proof. One at a time. If you want more, I'll call them forth.*

She moved closer to Sarah's right side, took her arm, and placed it along her left thigh. "I will place the amulet on your forehead and then lean over and place my forehead against it. In that position, I will show you images of events the amulet witnessed as I wore it. If you wish to hold me, you may. I'll take you from one event to another to show you what you must know. And I'll try to show you my thoughts and feelings at those moments."

"I'm ready."

As Nagora's forehead came to rest on the stone, she closed her eyes to summon the first event:

> She was on the bridge, leaving Twin Rivers, when she, as Tars, encountered the witch, Hag, for the first time … nearing the halfway point on the bridge, a cold gust of wind licked at her neck. At the same moment, the words *Kiskwehkan Iskwew* entered her mind. Their meaning was clear—Witch. … All, from Hag touching Nagora's arm to Hag leaving, played out.

Through it all, Sarah held Nagora's sides.

How Nagora discovered Hag's poisoned apples.

How Nagora tried to kill Hag with fire arrows at the

Temple of Fire, now once again the Center for the Dagon Arts.

Nagora's encounter with Hag in the prince's fortress:

> How Hag stepped closer, and the prince stepped aside … Hag lowered her staff. Its amber head, seen from head on, looked like an eye. Hag directed it between Nagora's legs. "She is armed. Strip her." … Everything, from Hag sentencing Nagora to death to her escape from the dungeon sea cave and her rescue by Raynhard, played out.

Sarah cried through most of it.

> Raynhard giving Nagora his father's golden-handled hunting dagger.

> … Raynhard's words, from when Nagora had put her amulet back on, rushing into her mind. … "Soup fit for a king and his queen. Let's go see if my queen is awake." … And Nagora's reaction: Was my head playing tricks on me? Am I right in my mind? I've heard strange words and understood their meaning. At least I think I do. Am I in the same world as I was before? …

How Nagora saved Danuka's eggs from Hag in the cave in the vent shaft on the Isle of Smoke:

> Hag revealing herself as the beautiful temptress, Alizarine, Nagora's battle with Hag, and the destruction of Hag's amber-headed staff, all played out.

A painful event for Nagora:

> All, from Raynhard's arrival on his second visit to Nagora in his secret cave where she guarded Danuka's eggs to his departure, played out.

Was this a rape or not? Sarah, I'll let you decide.

How Nagora realized Raynhard's love interest, Aliza, was in fact Alizarine, and how she tried to prove it to Raynhard.

Finally, from a most joyful to a most painful event, Nagora's agreement with Danuka in exchange for a dragon-baby egg:

> Sarah's birth at the cave with Paruline's help, giving up her blades, handing Sarah over to Paruline, and placing the amulet around Sarah's neck, all played out.

Sarah's sobs were such that the amulet fell away from her forehead as she pulled Nagora to her, almost choking on the words as she cried, "Mother! Oh! Mother! It's true! You are my mother. Never abandon me again!"

Nagora pulled back from Sarah and wiped tears from her cheeks. "Yes. Now my daughter, you know. There is more to know, but I'll let you rest awhile before I show you."

"Mother, you've been through so much!"

Nagora placed a hand on Sarah's soft cheek as she looked into her dark eyes. "You don't know the half of it. Someday, Sarah, you will. Right now, you need rest. I can boil some forest tea, or we can go out for a count or so."

"Make tea, Mother."

On a shelf that held Moreena's supplies, Nagora had even found a chunk of honeycomb wrapped in waxed cloth inside a stone crock. She hoped it would not only sweeten their tea, but Sarah's mood as well.

...

They sipped tea in quiet, each in their own thoughts.

No amulet to show you what next I must. Danuka said all I needed was the golden-handled dagger and my scars. Will this work? Somehow it aligns with the curse. Will you believe it? Will you doubt what you see? Will you believe what the curse demands?

I doubt you've killed. No training can truly prepare one for that. Battle has not tested you, and the task that awaits you will not seem a battle. You'll most likely see it as the murder of one by two, one child killed by two women with one dagger.

What will it take to convince you? A million times I've tumbled this question in my mind. A million times I've come up with no answer. I can only show you what I know, and beg you to see Alizarine for what in truth she is and not what you see before you. In the end my Sarah, the choice will be yours. I'll not be able to force your hand in this.

"Mother. Mother."

Nagora shook her head and looked at Sarah. "Yes?"

"Shall we get on with it?"

"Yes. Let's do that."

Nagora stood and brought the candle lantern close to the edge of the table. Next, she pulled her chair beyond the side of the table and pointed. "I want you to place your chair here and sit."

Sarah sat and Nagora unfastened the ties which held her legging to her underpants at her right hip. As Sarah sat,

Nagora pulled the legging down below her knee, moved her chair into position so when she sat facing Sarah, her right thigh resting against Sarah's right thigh.

Sarah was staring at the scars on Nagora's thigh. "Mother, what happened?"

Nagora blinked away a tear, took a breath, and said, "Give me your left hand."

Sarah extended it, and Nagora took it and placed its palm against the scars. She kept her hand on top of Sarah's. "It's part of a map, Sarah."

Nagora pulled the dagger from her vest with her right hand and held it by the sheath. "Take the dagger's handle. I want your thumb near the pommel." Sarah did as told. Nagora placed the sheath on the table and then wrapped her hand over Sarah's.

In her mind she willed the dagger to show: from the moment Raynhard arrives with Aliza to witness me kill his dragon to the time he leaves the cave. Nagora closed her eyes and brought herself back to that moment, trying to see it as clearly as the events she had shown Sarah with the amulet.

"Mother, what am I supposed to see? I'm not seeing a thing."

Nagora's eyes fell open. "Danuka said this would work. What am I doing wrong?" She pulled her right hand away from Sarah's, took hold of the four-eights knots of the leather lace, and slipped the amulet off her neck and then onto Sarah's.

She covered Sarah's hand with hers, "Let's try this again." She recalled from the moment Raynhard arrived to the time he left the cave.

"Still nothing, Mother. What's wrong?"

Nagora shook her head. "Let me think." What did Heqet say? ... Alizarine, I am come to witness what you do not see. I am come to grant your due, eternal youth for as long as you find beauty in that which you wish to destroy. Mark, Alizarine, this will hold true until the day a queen and her daughter join their hands on their king's golden-handled dagger to pierce your heart. Only on that day, Alizarine, will you truly see what now you do not see. ... Tar Piss! Do I have to be queen to be able to show her? Or ... or in that order? Worth a try.

Nagora held out her palm. "Sarah, place the handle in my hand. Don't let go until I have a good grasp."

"Like this?"

"Yes! Good! Now spread your fingers over my hand and close your eyes." Nagora took a deep breath.

Sarah's fingers gripped the back of Nagora's hand When she did the shaking began, moving from her hand to her arm, causing Nagora to tighten her grip on the dagger's handle. The shaking stopped and gave way to a slight continuous tremor that now seemed to run from Nagora's arm to Sarah's.

All was so clear for Nagora, as if she were back in the cave at that moment, watching the scene unfold from above. The transformation of Aliza into Alizarine stood out, as did Heqet's spoken curse.

When the scene ended, Sarah dropped her hand to her side and leaned back in her chair, breathing hard as if she had run a great distance.

With a trembling hand, Nagora brought the dagger to the table and let it drop there.

Sarah brought her arm up and covered her eyes with it. "No!" She shook her head. "I can't! There's no way I can do that! You can't make me do it! I can't! I won't!"

Nagora brought her own trembling hands to her face and looked at her daughter. I won't ask you to do it. I can't do that to you. I've already done the cruelest thing a mother can do and for the wrong reasons. Damn you, Raynhard! Why do I still serve you? May your kingdom burn!

Sarah, you must truly hate me now. At least you know the curse. A day may come when you'll change your mind. Will I be there to help you? Will Raynhard be there? Not for long if Godomor's wolves attack. Once again, I have failed in my duty to my king.

Well, Danuka. Let's hope we don't fail you tonight. If we succeed, you and your eggs will have a safe place.

Sarah had pushed her chair back. Her crying told Nagora she wanted to be left alone. Is she beyond consolation from this person she called "Mother" moments ago? Will she ever call me that again? Probably not. The curse has seen to that. It is a two-edged sword. One edge to carry out the curse. The other edge to prevent its fulfillment. And that edge has severed the momentary mother-daughter bond we had.

Nagora reached for the dagger on the table. She slid it back into its sheath and placed it in her vest pocket. She gazed at the sets of identical blades on the table; her uncle's, which she had been wearing and her own set, which Sarah had worn. An icy chill settled on her shoulders.

They're not the same. My set is different. I know the difference. No one else does. Nagora swallowed. Is this a last call to duty for my king? Will Sarah notice? She reached over, picked up Sarah's set, and left Dangor's set on the table. Just two buckle adjustments to make. Sarah will not notice.

Nagora slipped her own blades on, loosened the side strap buckles of the big sheath so it hung comfortably on her back, and then readjusted Dangor's set to the buckle holes Sarah had set hers.

Then she doused the embers of the fire with water from her waterskin, rolled up the hides, and set them in their place alongside the shelves before taking down the candle lantern from the ceiling and the one from the wall hook.

She lit a taper from the candle lantern on the table and kicked Sarah's chair. "We're leaving. I can't and I won't force you to kill anyone, not even the witch. The choice to kill will always be yours, Sarah. However I will ask you to help me in another way. No killing is involved. We may just save this kingdom from burning to the ground."

Sarah wiped her face. "I don't understand."

The seed of the idea had only moments earlier materialized in Nagora's mind and had germinated and sprouted leaves. All it needed was a blossom. "If you care about Danuka and the Land of the Danu, you'll do what I ask you to do when the time comes. No killing. You'll be saving lives. You'll be a hero." You'll be the blossom if you do that for me. "I'll only tell you more when the time comes. Promise me now you'll do what I ask you. Not a daughter's promise to her mother. One warrior's promise to another."

Sarah hung her head.

Are you the daughter I think you can be? If not, I'll have to do it all myself and it'll be a mess.

Sarah stood, reached for the set of blades on the table, and slipped them on her shoulders. "I promise."

"Thank you. Now we stand a chance. Let's go."

Outside the cave, cold drizzle and foggy mist shrouded the mountain. They found Danuka lying curled around herself, like a cat. A single great red eye followed them as they approached.

Yes, *Okâwîmâw*, that is how it went. You suspected as much, but it was necessary.

I wonder, Mother. I thought I would gain a daughter, but now *Ka Peyakot Mahihkan* feels she has lost her *Piwi Mahihkan* forever.

Mother, you tell me not to despair, for the path of *Piwi Mahihkan* is not mine to know. You tell me to hold no blame in my heart, not even the blame I hold for myself, but to keep my heart always open.

Mother, your words are wise. They echo those of my spirit father, King Godomor: *Ka Peyakot Mahihkan, kitimakeyimiso*. I told him I would be kind to myself. I try my best to live by those words. It is difficult.

The Hunt Ends
Mâcîwin Kisipayin

† NOW: *the thirteenth day in
the Land of the Danu,
three days before the wedding*

Nagora and Sarah landed with Danuka in the castle courtyard. Mother and daughter were soaked and shivering. The raindrops pearled on Danuka's fine mesh of scales.

Sarah stepped from Danuka's wing. "Come, Nagora. I'll get you a change of dry clothes." They were her first words since leaving the cave.

Nagora patted Danuka's neck. Thank you, Mother. You will come again tomorrow morning? Early? Good.

Nagora followed Sarah inside, past the door leading to the throne room and on to the last door at the end of the hall. The door took them to a long, wide staircase.

At the top was a large hall with a ceiling not as high as the throne room. The hall was as long and as wide. Of course! We're above the throne room. This is a reception hall. Bare tables and chairs waited to be set up, stacked along the opposite wall.

To their left, another staircase would take them up to a third floor where the resident rooms could be found. Along the wall on the other side of the reception room, a second, identical staircase also led to the third floor. A raised stage stood between the staircases. Most likely for musicians.

Just as they set foot on the first step, screams from the third floor above reached their ears. They stopped to listen. The treasure hunt must still be on. Now the screaming was clear.

"Give it to me! Give it to me, Baerik!" Alizarine was yelling. The tone in Alizarine's voice sounded like a warning to Nagora. The little witch will have a fit.

"Let me go! Alizarine! I found it! It's mine! Let me go!"

Nagora and Sarah turned back onto the landing and ran past the stage to the opposite staircase. From the bottom of that staircase, they saw Alizarine and Baerik at the top.

Alizarine had Baerik by the collar of his shirt, twisting and yanking on it with both hands.

Where's Alizarine's egg?

Baerik pulled at his collar with one hand while the other clutched a dragon tooth, holding it out of Alizarine's reach.

Alizarine hauled Baerik back and pulled him sideways so his head hit the corner of the wall at the top of the stairs.

Sarah gasped and grabbed Nagora's arm, stopping her stride.

"Ouch!" Baerik's hand holding the tooth flew up to the side of his head as Alizarine yanked him back and slammed him against the stone corner again. "Aaaah!" Baerik tried to brace himself with his now bloodied hand still grasping the tooth.

"Stop Alizarine!" Nagora shook free of Sarah's hold and climbed the stairs.

Alizarine kicked the side of Baerik's knee. As he went down on it, Alizarine slammed Baerik's head against the wall again and again. Something clattered to the floor. It had to be the tooth. Alizarine kneed Baerik in the back twice.

Baerik arched his back in a silent scream, one hand at his collar, the other at the side of his head.

Alizarine let go of Baerik's collar. "You little bastard! It's mine, now!" Alizarine placed a foot on his back and pushed. Baerik pitched forward and rolled halfway down the staircase to Nagora's feet. When Nagora looked up, Alizarine had disappeared. Nagora turned to her daughter. "Sarah!"

Sarah stood frozen on the steps below. Her mouth hung open. Her eyes were open wide. *You still don't believe, do you? We do not see others as they are. We see them as we are. Are you a warrior? Perhaps today, you'll choose to be one.* Nagora pointed at Sarah. "Quick! Go find Sagora! Tell her to bring her medical scrip."

Nagora bent to Baerik. He lay twisted across two stairs, one arm under him, and the other hung limp in front of him. Baerik's head wound was bleeding where the corner of the wall and the roots of the dragon tooth had made contact. Nagora pulled her shirt up away from her belt, took her knife from her belt, and cut into the hem of her shirt, tearing off a strip all the way around.

Baerik moaned.

"Baerik, hold on, lad. You'll be fine. Your mum's on her way." Nagora folded the strip and pressed it against the wounds with one hand while she pulled his arm out from under him. Doing so brought a groan from him, but didn't stop his moans. As gently as she could, she pulled his hips and legs down onto the same step as his upper body. Baerik stopped moaning. Now and then a short moan escaped from his throat. Poor lad. What Alizarine has done to you is unforgiveable.

Nagora caressed Baerik's cheek. "Hold on. Mum's coming. She'll take care of you." Come on Sagora! Move it! Where are you? Your son needs you!

Lars, Dannor, and Raynhard arrived first, followed by Sagora and Sarah.

Sagora set her scrip on the step next to Nagora. "Did you move him?"

"Aye. I pulled his arm from under him and brought his hips and legs down to this step. He stopped moaning when I set him there."

"Show me his wound."

Nagora pulled back the pad of linen.

Sagora sucked in air between her teeth. "What … the dragon tooth?"

"And the corner of the wall up there." Nagora pointed.

Sagora looked around at their faces. Something seemed to take hold of her. "Where's Raean? Find Raean! Now!"

Lars put a hand on Dannor's arm. He pointed up. "I'll take the second floor. You take the third. Raynhard, the ground floor. Whatever we find, we meet back here. Nagora, stay with Sagora. Sarah, go with Dannor."

...

Once the others had left, Sagora unraveled the linen strip and tied it around Baerik's head. "Can you bring him down to the nearest table over there?"

Nagora did and Sagora followed with her scrip.

After laying him on the table, Nagora removed the golden dagger from the pocket of her sheepskin vest, stuck it in her belt under her shirt, and pulled off her vest. Nagora shook what she could of the wetness from it and folded it to make a pillow for Baerik.

Sagora had removed her bracelets and rings, except for the amber one. As much as she tried, it would not come off.

"Big sister, do you want me to help with that?"

Sagora held out her hand. "I don't know why it's not coming off. It's so tight suddenly."

Nagora dribbled a gob of spit on the finger, twisted, turned, and pulled. The amber stone truly resembled an eye. The ring did not come off. "Better see to Baerik. I'm worried."

Sagora lifted the lid of her scrip and set it down with the inside up to use as a tray. There she placed clean rolls of linen, pinches of milkweed silk, a pot of salve, scissors, and several short sticks, pointed at one end and flat at the other.

Next came a bottle of disinfectant with a cork stopper on it. Sagora uncorked it to drip several drops onto the fingers of one hand and then the other. "Can you remove the linen pad from his wound for me?"

As Nagora did, another moan escaped from Baerik's throat.

"Now gently turn his head and hold it that way." Sagora had wadded a clean strip of linen into a pad over which she poured disinfectant. "Keep his head still. This will sting. Most likely he'll want to move."

As soon as Sagora pressed the pad to one of Baerik's wounds, his eyes sprung open for a count of three then squeezed shut. "Good sign! Baerik you're going to be fine. Mum is taking care of you," said Sagora as she continued to clean the blood away from his scalp above his ear. Fresh blood boiled to the surface with each pass of disinfectant. Soon four blood-stained pads sat on the corner of the table.

Sagora made two fresh pads big enough to cover the wounds. She placed one over them and then lifted a finger's worth of salve onto the flat end of a stick. As she lifted one part of the pad at a time, she spread the salve over the wound. Once she had covered them in salve, she spread milkweed silk over the salve, and set the last clean linen pad over the wounds.

Sagora took a new roll of linen from the cover of the scrip. "Can you reach under to lift his head by his neck so I can wrap this around his head?"

Nagora did so, and Sagora wrapped and tied the linen strip in place, securing the pad over the wound.

"Will he be all right?" asked Nagora.

"Hard to tell. It could depend on how long he takes to come to. The sooner the better. I must keep an eye on my dear Baerik to see how he reacts when and if he comes to." Sagora took Baerik's hand in hers and kissed it. "Mum is with you, son. You'll be fine."

"Young boys are tough, Sagora. Sometimes in a fall that would break a man, they bounce back up. I hope he comes to soon."

"Thank you, Nagora. Thank you for acting so quickly."

I should've yelled. What I saw took me by surprise. My eyes didn't believe what they were seeing. It happened so fast.

Now my plan may be in jeopardy.

Raean came running down the same stairs that Alizarine had pushed Baerik down. He held both hands to his chest.

Soon Lars followed behind him.

"Mum! Mum! What happened to Baerik?"

Sagora caught him as he skidded toward the table. "Slow down. Baerik's been hurt."

"I want to see! I want to see!"

Sagora held a finger to her lips. "Shhhh. He hurt his head. He needs quiet and rest now. What do you have there?"

Raean held out his blood-stained fingers to show the bloody dragon tooth in his hands.

"Where did you get that, Raean?" Sagora seemed to do her best to keep her voice even.

"Alizarine gave it to me. She traded it for the small tooth I found."

The little witch knows we saw her hurt Baerik. Even so Alizarine's trying to put the blame on Raean.

"Ooow! Mum! It hurts!"

Raean pointed to Baerik.

Baerik had a hand on his bandage and was trying to lift up on one elbow.

Raean pushed forward to the edge of the table. "What happened, Baerik?"

Baerik laid his head back on the vest. "Alizarine took my dragon tooth. She hurt my head and stole my tooth. It's not fair! Alizarine cheated!" Baerik closed his eyes and rolled his head from side to side.

Sagora took Baerik's hand in hers. "Stay calm, Baerik. Mum put a bandage on your head. You'll be getting better, soon. I'll give you some willow tea. It'll help calm the hurt in your head."

"I want my dragon tooth." Baerik's eyes blinked open for a moment.

Sagora held a finger to her lips and glanced from Baerik to Raean. "Don't worry, Baerik. We'll get your dragon tooth back."

Baerik swallowed. "Okay."

Nagora went to Lars. "Alizarine?"

Lars bent to her ear. "Locked in her room. I found Raean near a window at the end of the hall examining the tooth."

"You're sure she's there?"

"That's what Raean says."

Sarah and Dannor arrived at the top of the staircase. She had a hand on Dannor's arm and was pointing to the corner of the wall. It must be stained with blood.

Sarah came down as fast as she could and went to Baerik's side. "Is he okay?"

Baerik's lifted his hand. "Sarah, my head hurts."

"I know, Baerik. Mum has taken good care of you. You'll feel better soon. Won't he, Mum?" Sarah looked at Nagora as she spoke the last word.

You know it pains me. It's not the word as much as your intentional use of it as a weapon to disown me. You are young and do not know better. Blood is a stronger bond than you think.

Sagora patted Baerik's hand. "He'll be up and bouncing about soon, won't you, Baerik?"

"Aye, with my dragon tooth!"

Raean held the tooth to his chest and shook his head no, ever so slightly.

Raynhard appeared at the top of the staircase leading up from the ground floor. He crossed the floor with brisk strides, slowed, and raised his arms when he caught sight of Raean. "Good! You've found him! How goes our Baerik?"

Again Baerik attempted to lean on his elbow. "Mum says I'll be better soon. My head still hurts. I want my dragon tooth back."

"That's good news, Baerik." Raynhard took his hand. "We'll get your tooth back."

Raean backed away from the table.

"And we'll punish Alizarine. No concert for her tonight at the Center for the Dragon Arts," said Raynhard.

Lars took a step forward. "I don't want to meddle in your discipline. I want to warn you. Earlier you made a promise to Alizarine and the boys. Perhaps Nagora or Dannor could tell you what you risk if you break a promise to Alizarine."

Dannor was shaking his head. "You don't want to see Alizarine throw one of her fits. When she was with us, we learned the hard way. You can't imagine what she's capable of destroying. A fit can last for days."

Lars held Nagora's hand up. "Tell them about the stable."

Nagora bowed her head for a moment and took a breath before speaking. "The first stable we'd built held our three horses, three mules, seven milking goats, six ewes, a ram, two dozen hens, and a rooster. Timber-framed stone walls with a slate roof. Ship planked doors on iron hinges." She paused.

"We saved the horses and mules and goats. Three hens. All the rest she killed. She left not a stone nor a single piece of timber standing. She took seven days and seven nights to destroy it, all because of a broken promise. There was no way we could get near her without risking our own lives. You don't have to believe me. If you break your promise, we won't stay around to witness what happens." Nagora stopped and looked from Sagora back to Raynhard. "I give you fair warning. I know Alizarine could bring this castle down. She is a witch after all. Raynhard, I'm surprised you didn't recognize her the first day Sagora brought her here." Although, I can guess why.

Lars gave her hand a squeeze. I bet he's biting the inside of his cheeks so as not to laugh.

Sagora glared at her.

Raynhard seemed to ignore her comment about Alizarine being a witch. Why would he? That ring on his hand is the answer. The first finger and thumb of Raynhard's right hand worked at the amber ring on the finger of his left hand. "In that case Alizarine will come, but she'll not sit next to the boys."

Dannor took a step forward. "I've grown up alongside Alizarine. I know how to handle her. Allow me to escort her to and from the concert and guard her while she's there. No harm will come to the lads. I promise you so long as they keep away and do not talk to her. Let me deal with her in my way."

Raynhard looked to Sagora and then back to Dannor. "Well then. I'll have a separate carriage for you and Alizarine. You'll leave before us."

Dannor bowed. "Thank you. That'll be most helpful."

"Sarah, we were on our way to change into dry clothes. Can you lead me to them?" asked Nagora.

"Mum, I was taking Nagora to your chambers to lend her a change of dry clothes. Is that all right?"

Sagora's glare softened. "Yes, do so."

Lars stepped forward. "Sagora, would you like me to take Baerik somewhere for you?"

Her glare melted into a smile. "Aye, please, Lars. Bring him to my chambers. Follow Sarah. I'll be up in a moment."

Lars pointed to Sagora's medical scrip. "Dannor, bring the scrip."

On the way up the stairs, Dannor climbed the steps next to his mum with the scrip under one arm. Nagora took his free hand in hers. "Is the treasure hunt over?"

Dannor raised his eyebrows. "I guess so. I never thought it would turn out like this. Raean has the big tooth Baerik found. Alizarine has the small tooth Raean found and she has the middle-size one she herself found. Alizarine has made a mess of this."

More than a mess. We're only beginning to see it.

The bed in Sagora's room was even bigger than the one Nagora had seen years ago in Prince Acindor's chambers at the fortress in Yhorgal. Does she go to Raynhard's bed, or does he come to hers? Why would I even think of such a thing?

"Do you want a dress, or garb such as you're wearing?" Sarah seemed impatient as she stood with a fist on one hip, looking at Nagora.

"Something to replace what I'm wearing, but dry."

Sarah rolled her eyes and pulled aside a curtain to show a small room lined with shelves and hooks and forms that held a variety of dresses and garments. Had I tried to imagine such a number and assortment of clothing, I would have fallen short.

Sarah pulled out leather leggings, underpants, shirts, a sweater, socks, and a pair of boots, all from different shelves. She set them on a bench in the small room. "Leave your wet clothes on the floor in a pile. A servant will tend to them. Your clothes will be clean and dry by tomorrow." Sarah left before Nagora could say thanks.

When Nagora came out of the clothes room, Sagora was sitting on the bed next to Baerik whom she had propped up with several pillows. Sagora was washing his face with a wet cloth. Her medical scrip was on a small table near the bed.

As Nagora approached the bed, she made quick work of tying off her braid with the leather lace. "Baerik, you're look-ing better. Did you drink some willow tea?"

Baerik nodded. "I'll feel better when I get my dragon tooth back. I know what I'll wish for when the half moon comes. Then I'll count the days until it comes true on the next half moon. I won't sleep on that night to see it happen." I won't ask about your wish, but I can imagine what it'll be.

"Well, little sister, you are out of your wet clothes. Are those to your liking?"

"Yes they are. Sarah chose them for me. Thank you for lending them. My wet ones are in a pile on my vest on the floor of your clothes room. Sarah said a servant would take care of them."

Sagora nodded and continued wiping Baerik's neck.

"So you have to wait until the half moon to make your wish?" asked Nagora.

Baerik nodded. He pursed his lips in a scowl. "That's what Dannor says."

Nagora bit the inside of her cheek. My son the storyteller doesn't want to be around when the wishes don't come true. Neither do I.

Do I ask what message she and Raynhard have decided to send? Sagora will not answer me in Baerik's presence. Perhaps she wants Raynhard to be present to deliver it.

"Get well soon, Baerik. Sagora, again, thank you for the loan of these clothes. Excuse me. I'll go find the others."

Nagora found Raynhard in the dining room with Lars and Dannor. The table was set minus two places. Raynhard stood as she approached the table. "Nagora, how's our Baerik doing?"

"He drank some willow tea. He's wide awake, propped up on a pile of pillows on Sagora's bed, and she was washing his face. Baerik's a tough lad. He's eager to make his wish on his dragon tooth if he can get it back in time for the next half moon."

Raynhard smiled. "That's what Lars and I have been discussing with Dannor. Your son thinks he might get Alizarine to surrender the tooth she did not find." He looked to Dannor.

Dannor shrugged. "Perhaps by tonight, I can convince her that a tooth not found cannot grant a wish. I'll use the same argument to get Raean to give Baerik back his tooth. If they come to the table to eat, I'll plant the seed. I hope Alizarine will think it over and hand over the small dragon tooth. If she does, I'm sure Raean will do the same."

Nagora smiled at Dannor. "That would make sense. You're right. Alizarine will need time to think on it."

Lars lifted his hand from the table. "The other thing I reminded Dannor of is not to accuse Alizarine of having done something wrong. Dannor must word it so as not to point a finger at her. If there's one thing she hates, it's that. Alizarine knows what she's done. She won't stand to be accused in front of others."

Nagora nodded. "That's so true. Good thinking."

Then Raynhard spoke to her unspoken question. "We've sent Sarah to explain this to Raean so he won't ruin the chances of Baerik, and himself, getting their wish teeth back. Sarah will also speak to Baerik and Sagora."

Dannor held up a hand. "I asked Sarah to make it clear to the boys that it might take until tomorrow morning for Alizarine to do the right thing."

Nagora smiled at him. "Good, Dannor. You make me proud, my son. Perhaps this situation will mend itself."

Nagora turned to Raynhard. "So Raynhard, now you see what Alizarine is capable of. I'm surprised in the months she's been with you, nothing like this happened before." Why do you not see her as the witch, Hag, she is? Why do you not recognize her as the child Aliza became in your cave? What is it that blinds you? Was it Aliza's hit to your head that removed your ability to see? You're not the man I once knew.

Raynhard seemed to be lost in thought as the thumb and finger of one hand played with the amber-stone ring on his other.

I've nothing to lose. "Raynhard, I noticed you and Sagora both wear rings with amber stones on the same fingers of the same hands. Are those promissory rings?"

Raynhard smiled as he held up his hand and looked at the amber ring. "Yes, Nagora, they are. In four days, on our wedding day, we'll have worn them for five years."

"Isn't it custom to remove the silver promissory rings three days before the wedding day to make way for the gold rings that will wed you?" asked Nagora.

"We will take them off tonight."

"Earlier when Sagora was tending to Baerik, she could remove her other rings, but not her promissory ring. Can you take yours off?"

Raynhard smiled and pulled and twisted and turned it and pulled again, but the ring did not come off. He chuckled and sat back. "I guess it's not meant to come off until later."

Lars touched Raynhard's arm. "Before trying tonight, wash your hands, rub a piece of lard on that finger, and then hold your arm straight up above your head for a full count. The ring should come off."

"Thank you, Lars. We'll try that."

If that doesn't work, I can cut your fingers off. I've done that before. If I have to do it again, twice more, I will. Whatever it takes to destroy those rings.

The Concert
Miyometawestamâkewin

† NOW: *the thirteenth day in
the Land of the Danu,
three days before the wedding*

The carriage with Alizarine and Dannor had already left for the Center for the Dragon Arts.

Nagora and Lars were the last to get on Raynhard's carriage. Baerik sat between Sagora and Sarah. He was holding his big dragon tooth. Raean, who didn't look pleased at all, sat with arms crossed, between Raynhard and Sagora, biting his upper lip with his lower front teeth.

Lars held their rolled up waxed rain capes across his knees and had his eyes to the sky. "We'll be more than lucky if the clouds hold back the rain until the concert's over. The wind's been stacking up those clouds black and tight. As soon as one bursts, they all will."

Nagora leaned her head on his shoulder. "You're not at sea, so don't worry."

"Skies like this carry heavy rain and hide hammers that'll throw more than sparks. Those on land will do well to heed those black flags," said Lars.

Nagora poked him in the ribs. "Have you been hanging out with Godomor's bard?"

The wind ushered them up the steps to the open main doors of the Center for the Dragon Arts. Unlike the other stained glass windows, no colors showed from the window above the door still undergoing restoration.

Just inside the Center, the snapping sound of a tarp overhead drew Nagora's eyes up.

Center attendants had rigged big canvas tarps near the roof opening. They had strung a rope with a hook on its end from the middle of one side of each tarp. The rope ran all the way down to one of the grates in the narrow drain canal surrounding the main stage.

An attendant was wrestling the rope of the last tarp to hook it to its intended grate. To direct the rain off the tarps? Will this work in a heavy downpour? The attendant succeeded in setting the hook, silencing the snapping tarp.

The musicians were setting up to Nagora's right on the long side of the stage. Further down the left side of the stage, opposite where Moreena's golden harp stood, sat Alizarine and Dannor. She pulled Lars to her. "We'll sit on the tier just behind them and to their right, in case something goes wrong. Follow me."

Alizarine, with a dragon tooth in each fist, sat crosslegged, with one arm through the handle of her basket which rested on her legs. Just in front of her crossed legs sat her empty stone boat. Nagora whispered to Lars, "How's she going to place her egg if she holds on to those teeth?"

He whispered back, "Maybe she'll let Dannor move it. He's right at her side."

Could that work in his favor? No doubt.

Nagora turned to see where the twins were sitting. They were with Sarah, center stage, opposite the other musicians. Raynhard and Sagora sat on the tier behind them.

Beyond, Erin stood near her harp with Moreena. No other guests were present beside the musicians, Center attendants, guards, and servants from the castle.

Attendants closed the big main doors. The candle lanterns all flickered at once. Other attendants lit the remaining candle lanterns on the stands near where the musicians sat or stood. When the attendants finished lighting the candles, Erin stepped forward, leading Moreena on her arm. Under her other arm, she held a thin, leather-covered book.

At center stage, Erin left Moreena, walked around Sarah and the twins, and offered the book to Raynhard.

Once Erin had returned from Raynhard's side, Moreena spoke. "Your Majesty, you have in your hands the list of the songs in the order we will play them for you this evening. It is unnecessary to decide anything today. As long as you let us know the day before the wedding which songs you would like us to play and in what order, we will be prepared. Enjoy this concert."

Erin and Moreena bowed. Erin led her sister to her harp before walking all the way back to hers.

Alizarine handed the teeth to Dannor, unwrapped the egg, and set it to rest on the stone boat. She kept two fingers of each hand on the boat.

Moreena seemed to look in Nagora's direction. Had Erin told her where we sat? She positioned her fingers to play the dragon chord on her harp. For a moment, she held it away from the strings. The other musicians had been watching and had readied their instruments. Moreena plucked the strings, and the beautiful sound of the dragon chord flooded the stage.

Alizarine's back straightened. Her fingers left the stone and came to rest on her knees. She was almost in profile to Nagora. Her little mouth hung open as Moreena continued to play *As Dragons Soar*. She's playing that one so we can see the effect it's having on Alizarine. As the first verse ended, a flute played the bridge to the second verse and all the musicians joined with Moreena. Again, a lone flute played the bridge to the third verse. Then Erin's harp sang out solo at the other end of the stage.

As Alizarine turned to face Erin's harp, so did Dannor while moving the stone-boat-mounted egg. Where did he put the teeth? Alizarine held one in each hand.

So it went for three more verses of the song, switching from Erin's harp to Moreena's and back to Erin. So too Dannor moved the stone boat. All present, except for Alizarine, clapped when the song ended. Although, her mouth hung open as she sat with eyes closed.

Do you see that Dannor?

The sixth song had ended. People were still clapping. Nagora leaned against Lars. "Did he make the switch yet? I can't tell."

"I don't think so. If he did, I didn't see it happen."

All the musicians seemed to adjust their chairs and their hold on their instruments at the same time. Both Moreena and

Erin were holding a hand high in the air. The stage became quiet except for the gentle bobbing of the tarps above.

Moreena's fingers took the dragon chord position. After a silent count of three, she plucked the chord. At the same time it also resonated from Erin's harp.

Alizarine turned from one to the other, but settled on Moreena's as soon as all the other musicians joined in.

Nagora had never heard the song. It built and built. The lone drummer beat his drum faster and faster. The harps and all the other instruments followed. "It's a storm!" No sooner had Nagora spoken her thought, a clap of thunder fell on the Center for the Dragon Arts, shaking it. It was louder than the one that rang out above Godomor's Grand Hall on the day of her branding. The musicians played on as if calling the storm to them. Flashes of lightning and rolling thunder outside answered. Rain fell, pelting the tarps overhead and racing down the ropes in wild torrents that spun spiraling out of control, spraying the surrounding tiers and stage area.

Still the drum beat on and the musicians followed.

Then the wind came. It sucked the wet tarps up and spit them back down.

"They'll not hold!" Lars yelled in Nagora's ear as he untied their rain capes. He handed her one. "Take it. I'll get this one to Dannor."

The next blast of wind blew the tarps from the ropes that held them, and the rain poured in like a thousand buckets being emptied at once. Lit candles in lanterns drowned in the downpour, which also knocked over the ones on stands. Bright lightning flashed above in the wind-driven sheets of rain.

In one of those flashes Lars was bent holding a flapping rain cape over Alizarine while Dannor scooted after what had to be Danuka's egg. It was rolling in Moreena's direction.

Then it was black again except for one candle lantern near the main door which flickered out of control. How long would it hold on?

Nagora gazed up into the black rain, squinting. The music hadn't stopped. How could that be? The drum beat had slowed, but remained steady, almost as if an army was marching across a battlefield. Are Godomor's warriors already on the move?

Again, lightning lit the interior. Dannor was holding an egg out to Alizarine who held out her basket. His lips were moving. What's he saying to her? Lars still held the rain cape. The image died and as it did, the wind howled and seemed to come down on them from all directions, bringing with it a familiar sound. If I were one to bet, all my coins would say that was Danuka's moan.

Mother, I would also bet Dannor has your egg. Tonight you will have your egg and more. Stay close by.

The music stopped, and the storm's fury faded along with the distant rumble of thunder, leaving behind it a cold, steady downpour. Two attendants who had found and lit a dry taper were going from one candle lantern to another, lighting them.

Most of the musicians, who now huddled together at center stage, stared at Moreena. She still sat at her harp. Erin huddled over her, her arms on Moreena's. Were they crying? The last song they played was nowhere close to a wedding theme. Had they done so with intention? Two words surfaced—*Death Song*.

So much rain had fallen inside the Center that water still covered most of the stage. The drains in the canal all around the stage had not been designed for such a deluge.

Alizarine and Dannor, wrapped in a rain cape, walked to Nagora. Lars followed them. He was wearing one of his grand smiles. Yes! Confirmation!

"Are you okay, Alizarine?" asked Nagora.

Alizarine wiped raindrops from her nose with her free arm and nodded. "But I'm wet and it's getting cold."

Nagora unrolled a rain cape. "Come. I'll wrap just you in this one. It's hardly wet. It'll help keep you warm until we get you back to the castle and help you out of your wet clothes. We'll be leaving soon."

Alizarine's free hand pulled on Dannor's sleeve. Then she pointed. "Go. Bring it to Raean now." Dannor smiled at his mother as he turned his hand over to show the small dragon tooth it held.

Nagora smiled back. "Best do as Alizarine asks."

Raynhard, Sagora, Sarah, and the twins had all moved up to the top tier, out of the rain. Attendants were placing blankets over their shoulder, and castle servants were listening to what must've been Raynhard's instructions. Dannor was climbing the tiers diagonally. He held his hand high as he called out Raean's name.

Raean obviously didn't understand what Dannor held in his shadowed hand until he got closer to the candle-lantern stands attendants had set nearby. When Raean saw the tooth, he was on his feet jumping, then shaking Baerik's shoulder and pointing to his dragon tooth. For a moment, he'll forget he's soaked. You have your tooth. Dannor has Danuka's egg. This night I'll have the rings and destroy them.

The rain had let up. Nagora stood with Lars, Alizarine, and Dannor on the top tier outside the main doors of the Center for the Dragon Arts, waiting for the carriage to pull up. Alizarine's fingers clutched the two edges of her rain cape close to the handle of her basket.

Sarah approached. "Are you getting on with us or Alizarine?" She shivered under her wet blanket. My daughter, your teeth will chatter soon if you don't get out of those wet clothes.

Dannor stepped forward. "Alizarine's cold. She wants to sit between Mum and Da on the way back to help keep her warm."

Sarah nodded. "Fine. See you at the castle. Here comes your carriage."

Lars tapped Nagora's shoulder and pointed back inside the Center for the Dragon Arts. She turned to look. Moreena and Erin were standing together with blankets over their shoulders. Erin had been watching and when she saw Nagora, she waved her fingers and smiled. She said something to Moreena, who waved and smiled. Nagora smiled back at them. The tear on her cheek would be mistaken for a raindrop.

One For Another
Meskociwepinikewin

† NOW: *the thirteenth day in*
the Land of the Danu,
three days before the wedding

As the royal carriage pulled into the castle courtyard, a single great red eye greeted them. Danuka lay in a corner, her wings folded over her and her tail curled around her. Her red eye stared at Nagora.

Lars stepped from the carriage first and lifted Alizarine down. When he saw Nagora hold back Dannor, he led Alizarine toward the door.

Nagora pulled Dannor close. "Quick! Before the others arrive. Take the pouch to Danuka. If she doesn't take it, tie its strap to the ring on the saddle. Danuka can untie it."

Dannor ran to Danuka.

Mother, when you return to your cave tonight, you will have an extra passenger.

Then Nagora rushed after Lars and Alizarine.

...

Inside, servants greeted them. The one who had been serving their meals seemed to have taken charge. Her hair was still wet, but her frock and apron were dry. The others were still in wet garments. "We've fires going in the dining hall fireplaces. There are warm blankets and hot tea waiting for you. Fresh biscuits are in the oven. We've also set out robes and slippers so you can change out of your wet clothes."

"Thank you." Nagora bent to one knee in front of Alizarine. "Do you want me to go with you to your room? I can help you dry off and change into something warm. Then I'll bring you down for tea and biscuits. Would you like that?"

Alizarine nodded. She held out her free hand and let the double-wrapped rain cape fall from her shoulders. Her basket hung from the crook of her other arm and her fist clutched the dragon tooth.

As Nagora took Alizarine's hand, Lars picked up the rain cape and took the one Nagora held out to him. "We won't be long."

Just then, Dannor bounded through the doorway. He had one hand on his chest and his mouth was open as if he were about to speak. He wore a wide smile and winked at his mother. Good, my son. Danuka has it. Dannor spread the fingers of his hand and made a fluttering motion with them as he reached above his head. Good. Danuka's already in flight.

"Alizarine, this belongs to you." Dannor lifted the flap of his scrip to show the edge of the black and red stone boat. "I squeezed it in." He had to work it out by moving it from side to side as he pulled on it. "It went in easier when it was wet."

Finally, it came free. "There. Do you want Mum to take it, or should I bring it to your room?"

Alizarine pointed to Nagora.

"Thank you, Dannor. I'll bring it. Change out of those wet clothes. Your da'll show you where."

When Nagora returned to the dining hall, Raynhard sat at the table with Lars and Dannor, sipping hot tea. Their wet clothes hung from the perches of wooden stands the servants had brought for the purpose.

The twins lay on their bellies on a blanket before the fire. Their identical bare bums bathed in the firelight. A plate of steaming biscuits and two mugs of tea with milk sat between them. Their heads twisted from one side to another as they held up the dragon teeth for examination in the light of the fire.

The blue spots on their lower backs and buttocks made Nagora wonder for a moment. Is Gabe truly your da, or is Raynhard? Both come from a line to the *First People* of this island land. Is there another telltale sign?

Raynhard stood. "Is Alizarine not coming down? It's not like her to pass up tea and biscuits."

Nagora stood near Lars's chair. "By the time I got Alizarine's wet clothes off and wiped her dry, and after she wiped her egg dry," Nagora said, glancing at her men, "all she wanted to do was curl up in bed with it. Alizarine drew up her knees, pulled her egg against her belly, and asked me to throw on another blanket. She's probably asleep by now."

"Good," said Raynhard.

Lars was smiling, and Dannor wore an even bigger smile. The switched egg had passed inspection.

"Where are Sagora and Sarah?" asked Nagora.

Raynhard had just sat down, but now he stood again holding up a finger. "Oh! That's right. Sarah was supposed to go and get you so you could change with them. I was to tell you in the event you returned before she went to you." Raynhard waved his arm. "There, I've done it. They'll be pleased if you join them."

Nagora took the mug from Lars's hand and took a long sip. "I'll do that. Save some tea for the ladies." She set the mug back in his hand.

Lars's other hand reached under the hem of her sweater and squeezed her still damp buttocks.

She squeezed his shoulder. "I can't wait to get out of these wet clothes."

Sagora and Sarah ignored Nagora as she walked in. Sagora was sitting in a chair before a mirror. Sarah kept on brushing Sagora's damp hair without even looking up. Sagora was in a huff about the storm ruining the concert.

The musicians hadn't played three of the songs on the list, and what seemed to upset her most was the last song they played. "Definitely not a song for a wedding! Why did they even play it? It was as if they called the storm to unleash its fury on us. The boys were frightened. I've a mind to call off the music."

Sagora saw Nagora standing three paces from the mirror. Sagora lifted her arm and pointed. "Over there. Same closet as earlier. Choose whatever you want. Leave the wet ones on the floor."

Sagora gazed at Sarah in the mirror. "What would you do, my sweet Sarah?"

Nagora almost stopped in mid stride. She bit her lip, clenched her fists, and moved on. That's not my sister speaking. Not the Sagora I knew.

"Go with the five songs previous to that last one, if you liked them. Mum, you have to think of the guests. They want to hear music. Let them hear music. That's it," said Sarah.

Nagora pulled aside the curtain. The single candle lantern hanging from the ceiling lit the small room. Their wet clothes were strewn all over the floor. If Tagnya saw this, she would have a fit. No, she wouldn't. Tagnya would not believe Sagora could do this.

"I can't even read the list anymore. The vellum is soaked. The ink ran. We were supposed to choose seven," said Sagora.

"Then choose two more from the three not played. Mother, it's that simple."

Nagora shut their voices from her mind as her foot shoved their wet clothes into one pile. She found another set like those she had been wearing. Before putting her blades back on, she grasped the end of the cherrywood handle of one of the small throwing knives that lay snug in its sheath. This one, the one that hangs from the strap under my right arm.

Carefully, she pulled out the knife and placed the handle between her teeth before tipping the mouth of the sheath over her open palm. Nagora tapped the sheath. Out it came, a small waxed cylinder. There you are, the last of the four I made so long ago. She slipped half of the small blade into the sheath, placed the wax cylinder on the blade. Back in your hiding place you go. She shoved the throwing knife back in place and slipped the straps of her blades onto her shoulders before putting on the green woolen sweater she had taken from a shelf.

...

Nagora left her pile of wet clothes on the floor, pulled the curtain shut, and unraveled her damp braid as she walked over to stand near Sarah. Both Sarah and Sagora had watched her approach in the mirror and remained silent.

Nagora took her comb from her scrip and set it to work, her eyes locked on her twin's in the mirror. Then she combed her hair back, pulling it into a tight bunch which she fastened with a knot of her leather lace. Nagora combed out the tail, separated it in three, and braided it. With the braid done, she rolled it in a bun at the back of her head. Easier to slip on the armor this way.

Nagora was about to speak when her eye caught the silver ring with the amber stone sitting next to the other gold rings on the shelf below the mirror. "Your promissory ring came off, Sagora?"

Sagora held up her hand. "Yes, it did. My hands were so cold when I sat here, I pulled it off without thinking before rubbing my hands together. I still don't know why it wouldn't come off this morning."

"Well, big sister, one less thing to worry about."

Sagora's and Sarah's eyes stared back at Nagora in the mirror. How long will you side with Sagora? "Are you two coming down for tea, or will you curl up in bed like Alizarine?"

Sarah rolled her eyes.

Sagora said, "Tell Raynhard we'll be down shortly. And Nagora, before you leave tonight, Raynhard and I will speak to you."

So you've made up your minds. I can't wait to hear your message. "Good. See you downstairs."

The twins had dressed and were sitting at the table, munching on biscuits and still examining their dragon teeth. Lars and Dannor were tending the clothes on the wooden supports, obviously making sure the wetter garments faced the fire. "Where's Raynhard?" asked Nagora.

Lars and Dannor turned to face her. Lars pointed at the doorway opposite the one Nagora had come through. "He went that way."

"To have a shit." It was Baerik speaking with his mouth full.

Raean slapped Baerik on the back. "Good thing Mum's not here. She would pull your ear."

Dannor shook his head.

Baerik stuffed another biscuit in his mouth and shrugged. Pointing to the tooth he held, he said something only Raean seemed to comprehend.

"Mind if I join you lads at the table?" asked Nagora.

Raean pointed to a chair. "That one's free. You have a cup." He pointed to the pot on the table. "Tea's there. Milk there." Then he set his dragon tooth down and pointed to the two plates in front of him. "Biscuits here." One had a single biscuit on it, and Baerik was reaching for it. Raean slapped his hand. "Leave some for Mum and Sarah."

Before Nagora could sit down, Dannor approached and took her hand. "Bring a cup. There's fresh tea on the fire. I've something to show you and Da." What's he smiling about? Nagora reached for a cup on the table and let Dannor lead her over to Lars near the fireplace.

...

Dannor placed Nagora's hand on his chest at the opening of his robe and bent to her ear. *"Okâwîmâw, niya isihtwawin asici kanawisimowin."*

Her hand felt it and her ears heard the words. Nagora took hold of it and stared at it. A single tear fell from her eye onto the stone. "Look, Lars! Dannor called me 'Mother' in Danuka's language. He said, 'I am gifted with an amulet.'"

She placed a hand on Dannor's cheek. "Danuka gave you this?"

"Yes, Mum."

Lars put a hand on his son's shoulder and the other on Nagora's as he looked from the amulet to Dannor. "She rewarded you, my son."

"Yes, Da." He looked to his mother. "She wants me to fly with her this night to help her, and you."

She knows my plan. You were not part of it, Dannor. My son, you make me cry. *"Nikosis, kîya môskomêw."*

"Don't cry, Mum. Danuka wouldn't have chosen me if I couldn't be of help. Don't be afraid."

"It's not fear that makes me cry, but the pride I have for you. You truly are gifted." Old Mother on Ice Island gave Yogari his amulet. What did Da do to earn his reward? We've been chosen to serve a purpose we cannot fully fathom. Why my da? Why me? Why Sarah? Why Dannor?

"Ha! Mum's here! Now we have two sets of twins in the room," said Raean.

"And two dragon tooths," said Baerik.

"Teeth," said Sagora as she strode past the table over to Nagora.

Nagora let the amulet fall back inside Dannor's robe and made like she was adjusting it.

Sagora spun around once on her heel. "Just like the old days in Skull Bay, dressed the same, hair combed the same," she paused, "identical faces," and she pointed to the Tiwaz brand.

Nagora let her eyes bore into Sagora's. If we were in Skull Bay right now, the signers would be lined up warding off the evil we twins represent. Perhaps I'll be able to put our identical appearance to good use here. All I'll have to do is mimic your speech and mannerisms. "Luckily, you have that silver ring to set you apart from me."

Sagora looked at the amber-stone ring on her hand. "It'll come off tonight, I'm sure." She truly looks confident, almost cocky. I've seen that look before, long ago.

Why is she dressed like this anyway? Is she going somewhere on Danuka tonight? "So big sister, you were dressed like this when you stepped off Danuka's wing yesterday. Are you going somewhere tonight?"

Sagora turned to look at Sarah, then back to Nagora. "As a matter of fact, we are. Sarah and I are going to get some dragon eggs."

What? Sarah, you've taken Sagora to Danuka's secret cave? Why? What's in it for you? Are you being controlled too?

Sarah had her hands on her hips. "From the pile of feeding eggs Danuka has in her cave. Grandda Yogari said she had more than enough for her hatchlings. Besides, Alizarine loves them. She's been eating some since her arrival. She ate the one we brought yesterday. We thought she had more, but were mistaken."

To give her strength for the treasure hunt? You haven't changed. Deep inside you are still Hag, aren't you, Alizarine?

"So when are you two leaving?" asked Nagora.

Sagora looked around. "Where's Raynhard?"

"Gone to have a … " Baerik clamped a hand over his mouth.

Raean laughed.

Sagora waved a finger at Baerik who was staring at her over his shoulder with one hand on his ear. "Soon as we've had some tea and biscuits, and Raynhard and I have spoken to you, Nagora."

Upon Raynhard's return, Nagora followed him and her sister to the map room near the throne room. Nagora stood on one side of the round table, they on the other. Raynhard was smiling and motioned she should sit.

Might as well. Let's get this done.

Raynhard sat, pushed aside the maps he had left on the table, and glanced up at Sagora who remained standing, looking down at Nagora.

What have they come up with?

"My dear sister, you will be the messenger and the message, not only to Godomor, but to Gabe."

What is she getting at? "The messenger and the message? Please, my dear sister, explain."

"It's simple, Nagora. You will return to the Land of Skulls as me."

I can't believe what I'm hearing. This is not the reasoned thinking of the sister I briefly got to know. Does she truly think I would do such a thing? What ... ? Stay calm. Play along. Nagora nodded.

"You will apologize to Gabe for sending the invitation. Tell him it was your way to get," Sagora pointed first to her sister then to the king, "Nagora to come to Windhaven for Raynhard, since he so badly wanted to make Edana queen and have her at his side for the benefit of his people."

You truly think they'll accept that? They know I would never toss Lars aside to marry Raynhard. No, it can't be. You would leave it up to me to invent some story about Lars's demise?

"And you'll tell Gabe that, as soon as the boys turn twelve, they will travel to the Land of Skulls where one of them will have the honor of being branded. Until then, his sons are to stay here in Windhaven."

And if I do that, I'll be branded a second time? More likely killed.

"And you'll tell Gabe that, in the meantime, you prefer to live here with the boys to see to their proper upbringing and education. I'm sure he'll understand, and you'll be sent back."

You're not in your right mind, Sagora. That ring has more sway over you than I can imagine. The Sagora I met and knew in the Land of Skulls would never even think to do such a thing, let alone ask me to do this. I doubt Tagnya brought you up that way.

"Well, Nagora, what do you think?"

"This is an outright lie. It's deceit. You're lying to the father of your children. How can you do this?"

"Nagora, I'm not lying to the father of my children." Sagora looked at Raynhard. "I'm going to marry him in three days from now."

Raynhard smiled while his thumb played with the amber stone of his ring.

There it is—the only fact that makes sense. That you reveal it, Sagora, surprises me. Or is it a lie? A lie you fed to Raynhard and are now feeding me, hoping to win me to your plan? "But why didn't you tell this to Gabe in the first place? Why did you lead him on all these years?"

"Nagora, I couldn't. I didn't want the poor man to lose hope. Gabe said he would end his own life if I didn't come back with his sons. What do you think he would've done if I had told him he was not their father?"

If this be true, he would probably be better off for it now. No use in me trying to tell you that.

Sagora held her hands open. "Look, this will calm Godomor's wolves and it'll give me time to figure out how to break the news to Gabe."

"What if he doesn't send his Sagora back?"

"Come now, Nagora. You're a mother. I'm sure you can play the tearful mother longing to be with her sons, to better prepare them for their return to the Land of Skulls."

If I say I won't do it, what'll you do, Sagora? You surely have another twisted plan to take the place of this one. No, I'll stick to my plan. You'll tell Gabe yourself.

"Okay, Sagora, I'll do this for Raynhard so he won't have to watch his country turn to ashes and his people suffer. I won't have time to get to the Land of Skulls on horseback. The only way I stand a chance of getting there in time is to go with Danuka, if it's not already too late."

"Of course, little sister, do so."

"Soon as you come back with Sarah, I'll be waiting in the courtyard to take Danuka. While you're gone, I'll tell Lars and Dannor what I'm doing. They'll decide if they'll stay or not."

Raynhard looked to Sagora, pushed his chair back, and stood. "Nagora, once again, I'm in your debt. That you are ever-loyal and duty-bound impresses me to no end. You'll not regret your actions. I and my people will be forever in your debt."

This body that stands before me is only the shell of the man I once knew. I don't know if I can reach inside to save you. If ever you awaken from this spell cast on you, you might not think so highly of me.

Raynhard and Sagora left the map room without another word.

Nagora had shared her plan with her men.

Lars was shaking his head. "In the end, Nagora, your plan might be the best way to stop this. Let's hope you're right."

Dannor had been listening to all the explanations and discussion. So far, he had not spoken. Now he reached for his mother's arm. "Mum, one thing bothers me about your plan— Sagora's ring. What if it doesn't come off? Will you cut her finger off to get it? Will I have to convince Gabe or Godomor to do it? Or will I have to do it to bring it back?"

Nagora held up her hand, but Dannor went on.

"You said Sagora sounded confident her ring would come off, that she even said she was 'sure' it would. That tells me she's experienced the ring not coming off before. If Alizarine somehow uses that ring to control Sagora, then it not coming off is connected to Alizarine—somehow."

Lars placed his hand on Dannor's shoulder. "I think Dannor's right, Nagora. I'm guessing it has to do with the dragon eggs Alizarine likes to eat. Why else would Sagora and Sarah fly off in the night to get eggs when they could wait until tomorrow? They're supposed to remove the promissory rings tonight."

Nagora took her men's hands in hers. "In the past, when Hag ate the eggs, doing so allowed her to appear much younger. She did that with Prince Acindor. And it was one of the reason's she was able to convince Pug to come steal Danuka's eggs in the cave I guarded. But now that she is so young, the eggs must give her power over the rings she uses to control Raynhard and Sagora. Perhaps when she feeds on the eggs, she has more power to control the rings to make them stay on or come off the fingers of Raynhard and Sagora. Sagora's ring came off after the concert. Alizarine was asleep and hadn't been fed an egg. Perhaps that's why it came off."

Dannor shrugged. "Danuka said it was important that you destroy the rings because they control Raynhard and Sagora."

She looked from Dannor to Lars. "Do the rings control them even when off their fingers?"

"Perhaps when they're off and nearby, the rings can still control Raynhard and Sagora," said Dannor.

Lars crossed his arms and let one hand play in his beard. "That makes me wonder about Sarah's behavior as you've described it. It's different whenever Danuka is present compared to when Sarah's in Sagora's presence inside the castle. Could it be Sarah is also under the control of the rings even if she doesn't wear one? I can understand Sarah doesn't want to help you kill Alizarine. I don't know how you'll change that. Will destroying the rings allow Sarah to see who Alizarine truly is? Sarah saw what Alizarine did to Baerik. Has that changed anything in her way of thinking?"

Nagora shook her head and shrugged. "I wish I knew. I truly do."

Dannor rubbed his hands together. "Wishing and speculating won't get us anywhere. We have to act on what we know and what we think we know. We know we need to destroy the rings. We think Alizarine having a dragon egg to eat will somehow allow the rings to come off. I say we wait before acting until after Sagora has delivered the egg to Alizarine to see if the rings come off. Once the rings are off, then you can take care of Sagora, and I'll bring her to Godomor. The wait for Sarah and Sagora to return will probably be a count or so longer."

Lars pointed at Dannor. "It'll be more difficult to get Sagora's body down into the courtyard onto Danuka. How do we do that?"

Nagora looked from Lars to Dannor. "You're both right. I think I have an idea that'll work."

The Switch
Mîskotinam

† NOW: *the thirteenth day in*
the Land of the Danu,
three days before the wedding

Nagora stood six paces from Dannor in the courtyard, wearing the dragonskin armor that rendered her invisible. Moments ago she had walked around Dannor, and he did not see her. You are patient my son, waiting for Danuka's return with your aunt and Sarah.

Before that, Nagora had gone to Sagora's chambers to change. She hid her blades and the clothes she had been wearing on one of the top shelves of the garment room. In a quick search of the dresser drawers below the mirror, Nagora found a bundle of vellum missives. As she flipped through them, she spotted, among the unopened seals, her own seal. She would have to get to them later. What was Raynhard up to?

...

Nagora found Raynhard with the twins in their room. He was sitting on one bed, telling a story, while his audience of two was under the blankets in the other bed. Baerik had already fallen asleep, and Raean's sleepy eyes did their best to focus on the dragon tooth his hands held to his chest. As soon as Raean's eyes closed, Raynhard bent and kissed both boys on their foreheads. He then stood and stretched before walking right past her. Nagora followed him to the hallway on the other side of the staircase.

Raynhard stopped at Alizarine's door, opened it wide enough to stick his head in. "Your eggs are on their way," he whispered before quietly closing the door.

Nagora followed Raynhard to his room where he pulled from his robe a key, tied to a silk cord. Did he wear it over his shoulder or around his waist? Nagora had not had time to see. Raynhard unlocked the great oak chest at the foot of his bed and lifted its lid so it rested on the wooden rail of the bed. He grabbed the handles on each side of the top tray to lift it out and set it on the bed. It contained vellum sheets in assorted sizes, each in their own walled sections; bottles of ink; quills and brushes; a row of seals of various sizes; and bars of red, green, and blue seal wax.

Raynhard lifted the biggest stack of vellum sheets. There lay a key, smaller than the one on the silk rope. He set it aside and returned to the trunk. Both hands reached in and pulled out a small chest that appeared to be heavy despite its size. It too he placed on the bed. He pushed the top tray further onto the bed and sat near the small chest.

Raynhard placed one hand on the cover of the chest and stared at it, hesitating before reaching for the key. As he put the key into the lock, he took a deep breath. Raynhard turned the key and reached for each side of the lid. Again, he breathed in hard from his nose before opening it. When he did, he turned his head away.

On the pile of golden rings, necklaces, bracelets, and cut gem stones lay two skeletal hands. Their bones, from above the wrists to their finger tips, were held together with silver wires, similar to the hand Vorpinger's brother wore over own his hand. I have it. I hid it deep under the floor of our lodge. I don't need it out in the open as a reminder. To know it's there is reminder enough.

Each of these hands wore a gold ring on its ring-finger bone. Mine wears no rings ... although it has silver rings attached to each finger bone and a silver chain at the wrist bones. I'll never wear that morbid ornament.

One skeletal hand was bigger than the other. By the rings I would say one hand is a woman's, the other a man's. Whose hands are these? Raynhard's parents? Why would he even keep such remains? Mine is a reminder of how I uncovered the plot to kill King Godomor. What dark secrets do you hide, my king?

Raynhard's hand trembled as he pulled the gold ring from the man's hand and set it on his bed. His hand trembled even more as he reached for the gold ring on the woman's hand. Raynhard stopped, made his hand into a tight fist, and sucked air in between his teeth as if to give himself strength. He held his breath and with shaky hands, pulled the ring from the woman's hand and set it next to the other.

Raynhard turned away, squeezed his eyes shut, and closed the lid, keeping both his hands on it as he exhaled. When he regained his breath, he turned the key in the lock of the chest. Raynhard's hand still trembled as he pulled the tray closer and fumbled with the vellum sheets to hide the key.

Back at the trunk, he set the small chest on the floor and set about making place for it by moving aside some of the folded garments. Only when he had put away the chest, covered it with clothes, set the tray on top of them, and closed and locked the trunk did his hands stop shaking.

Raynhard took a ring in each hand and pulled back the bed covers and a pillow. He placed the rings where the pillow had lain. Then he picked up the pillow, brought it to his face, and inhaled. Does it smell of Sagora? Do I care? Raynhard held it to his cheek with his eyes closed. What am I not seeing? Do I even want to see it? Best I go to the yard and wait with Dannor. They should be back soon.

You seem cold, my son. I stand here unseen, watching you blow into your hands and rub them hard against each other. This dragonskin armor wraps me in a strange warmth. An even wave of heat pulses over every part of my body with each beat of my heart. In this armor, each heartbeat is a distinct echo.

You heard something, Dannor? Aye, now I hear it. The gentle flap of Danuka's wings.

There you are, Mother. Danuka glided up over the wall, tilted her wings, and settled on the cobblestones. She moaned. Yes, Mother, I wear the suit the *Mêmêkwêsiw* made for me from your shed skin. Yes, Mother, you have time to return for your egg pouches. I know how fast you can fly without one of us on your back. It will give me time to do what I must.

Dannor approached the dragon as Sagora looked around the yard. I see you big sister. You don't see me.

"Where's your mum? Nagora said she would be here to take Danuka." Sagora, you look so impatient.

"Mum's locked up in the map room. She's talking with Da. I should say arguing because I heard screaming before. She told me to tell you not to bother them, that she would be out and leave by daylight at the latest, whether Da likes it or not."

Sagora slid out of the saddle with a bag strung over her shoulder, listening to Dannor.

"I wish I knew what was going on. I'm supposed to wait in the kitchens." Well done, Dannor.

Sagora slipped the bag off her shoulder and handed it to Sarah, who had just climbed out of her saddle. Sagora stepped off Danuka's wing and went to Dannor. "If I were you, Dannor, I wouldn't worry. It's just a misunderstanding. Your mum can be a hothead when she doesn't get her way." That's you, Sagora. Not me. "Help yourself to bread and cheese in the kitchen. I'm sure your parents will work it out. There's a cook's napping chair in one of the pantry corners. You can sit there while waiting. I'll show you."

Sagora led Sarah and Dannor inside. Nagora followed. Looks like you've got a few eggs in that bag. Five at least, if not six. Now let's see what happens.

...

Sagora pointed to a shelf on the kitchen wall. "Here you are, Dannor. Light as many candle lanterns as you want from that one." Sagora pointed to a door. "The pantry. Plenty of food in there. And a chair. Don't be shy. Help yourself." Then Sagora placed a hand on his shoulder and the other on Sarah's. "Dannor, I don't know if we'll be seeing you tomorrow or not. In case we don't, well, good luck." Sagora hugged him and so did Sarah. You're the one who'll need good luck, big sister. If only you knew what awaits you.

He barely had time to say thank you, and they left.

Nagora followed. Sagora and Sarah weren't wasting time. Will they go to Alizarine's room? Or will they go check the map room? If they do, Lars won't open the door, but will speak loud enough to make a show of arguing. Not to the map room. Who do I follow? Sagora, I pick you. You're headed toward your room.

Sagora hurried to her small garment room, stripped, left her clothes on the floor, and slipped a hooded, white woolen robe over her head. It had a round collar with a slit down the front to just above her navel. Its bell sleeves draped over her hands, and its hem hung just above her bare feet.

As Sagora walked over to the mirror, she pulled the sleeves back and unraveled her braid. Standing at the mirror, she took a brush to her hair, pulling it through its length with strong, even strokes. Several times Sagora leaned her head back to shake her hair out and brush again. After she set the brush on the mirror's shelf, she examined herself in the mirror, turning her head from side to side, tilting it up on one turn and down the other.

Sagora stood still for a moment, looked at her mirror image, and then lifted her ring hand to stare at the amber eye. She brought it to her lips, kissed it, and turned away from the mirror as her thumb played with the amber stone.

Where to now?

Sagora did not knock. She opened the door to Raynhard's room and swept in on bare feet. "We're back. Sarah will meet us there with Alizarine. Are you ready?"

Raynhard had been sitting on the bed. He wore a robe similar to Sagora's, and he too was barefoot. "Yes." His reply was a whisper. Raynhard stood and took her arm. Nagora followed them out the door they left open. He thinks they're alone in the castle and doesn't lock his door.

Sagora and Raynhard stood at the foot of the bed the twins slept in. They didn't say a word. They only watched and waited. Nagora waited in the hall. Well before Sagora and Raynhard, she heard Alizarine's limping gait approach as she carried her basket.

Nagora backed away to the wall opposite the door to the twins' room.

Sarah walked at Alizarine's side, dressed and combed like Sagora, and carrying a blue-and-red-veined feeder egg pressed to her stomach, one hand on the bottom of the egg, the other on top.

Alizarine's robe was black. She also was barefoot, and her hair was combed free like Sagora's. The red silk scarf from her basket snaked out, up, and around Alizarine's neck.

What are they going to do? Will the witch perform a ritual?

Sarah and Alizarine walked into the room without a word. They went to stand at the side of the bed. Alizarine set her basket on the bed behind her and she nodded to Sarah. Sarah walked behind Sagora and Raynhard and stood between them. Now both Sarah's hands were on the bottom of the egg as she held it out before her.

Together, Sagora and Raynhard placed their ring hands on the egg and closed their eyes. Alizarine spoke words Nagora did not understand. When Alizarine stopped her chant, Raynhard lifted his hand from the egg, stepped over to the witch, and removed his amber-stone ring, placing it in Alizarine's palm.

Alizarine leaned against the bed and held out her hand over Baerik's hand. Baerik let go of the tooth, and his hand rose as if being pulled by an invisible thread. Alizarine slipped the ring on Baerik's finger. Nagora's insides trembled. Will it come off? Baerik's hand went back to the tooth.

Raynhard returned to Sarah's side and then Sagora did the same as Raynhard had done. Now both Raean and Baerik wore the amber rings. Will they come off? Nagora let the procession leave the room of the sleeping boys and disappear down the hall.

Nagora went to Raean's side of the bed and picked up his hand. The ring wouldn't come off. How can that be? The ring would have had to shrink. She reached for Baerik's hand. The ring stayed put. Now what do I do? Nagora's hands trembled.

Get a hold on yourself. One thing at a time. Don't panic. You'll find a way.

What are they up to now? Will Alizarine perform another ritual? They must be in Raynhard's room by now. Tar piss! What if they closed the door? Nagora ran down the hall. Thanks to Alizarine's limp, they had just made it to the top of the staircase. Nagora was able to catch up with them. I'll squeeze inside before they go in.

Alizarine and Sarah came in first. Sarah stood at her side as Alizarine set her basket on the trunk.

Standing across from each other at the sides of the bed, Sagora and Raynhard slipped out of their robes and bent to pull back the bedclothes. As soon as they did, Sarah set the feeder egg down on the middle of the bed. Raynhard and Sagora then lay on their sides with their bellies against the egg.

After Sarah had covered them, Alizarine held out her hands and chanted words Nagora did not understand. What strange ritual is this? To what end?

Seemingly entranced, Raynhard and Sagora began to press against the egg until sweat covered their brows and they were panting, out of breath. What spell is she casting?

When Alizarine pointed to Sarah, she tore back the blankets to reveal their hands pushing, pulling, and rotating the egg as they slid it between their wet bellies. Their writhing stopped when Sarah reached a hand over the egg to touch it. Looking at Alizarine, she nodded. Have they warmed the egg for Alizarine?

Alizarine motioned with both hands. Sagora and Raynhard sat up cross-legged, facing each other. Sarah let her robe fall to the floor and climbed onto the bed. A long-handled silver spoon hung from a red silk ribbon around her neck. Her amulet! Where is it? Sarah sat facing the egg and pulled it into her lap.

Alizarine, now naked except for her red silk scarf which she wore wrapped three times around her neck, both arms, and the palms of her hands, climbed onto the bed and reached under the pillow with both hands. She's dressed like Hag when she appeared to me the first time as the dark haired beauty, Alizarine, in the cave on the Isle of Smoke, but now she's in a child's body.

Sitting across from Sarah with closed fists, Alizarine looked first to Raynhard, holding out a fist, she opened it and offered him the ring it held. He took it. Alizarine did the same for Sagora. Both held their palms out with a ring on display.

As Alizarine placed her red silk-covered palms over the rings and began to chant, Sagora and Raynhard took hold of her small hands. Is she placing a spell on the rings? Are they to be the wedding rings? I'm helpless watching this. If I interfere, I could ruin the plan.

When the chant ended, Alizarine indicated a finger on each of her hands. Raynhard and Sagora slid the rings onto those fingers and then kissed the rings.

Alizarine smiled and nodded to Sarah who, with the round back of the spoon, tapped the jagged red seam that wound its way around the bigger end of the egg. Alizarine stared with eyes round as bowls, grinning and licking her lips as Sarah pried open the cracked seam with the lip of the spoon until the shell cap popped up.

Raynhard and Sagora were still holding Alizarine's hands and kissing the rings.

Sarah stuck the spoon into the egg and stirred as fast as she could. Blood-red drops of the egg yolk spilled out. Sarah's mixing it with the thick egg white, turned it to the color of the setting sun. Sarah, with your amulet, I showed you feeding on such a mixture at your birth. What hold does Alizarine have on you? To see you do this, Sarah, worries me.

Alizarine stuck her tongue out and kept her mouth open as she leaned forward. In no time, Sarah's feeding of the witch turned into a messy frenzy as Alizarine gulped down the spoonfuls faster than Sarah could fill them.

Sagora and Raynhard only stopped kissing the rings when Sarah held out the egg shell to Alizarine. Alizarine leaned forward, grabbed it with both hands, and lifted and tilted the shell over her open mouth to drain the last of the mix. Alizarine couldn't swallow fast enough. The orange mix dribbled from the sides of her mouth and down her neck. Who'll believe me if I ever tell what I am witness to this day?

Alizarine set the shell down and licked at her chin, her lips, and even her cheeks. It's not natural her tongue can reach so far. Alizarine's fingers scraped the dribbles on her neck and chest to bring them to her mouth where she sucked them clean. Then Alizarine ran her hands over her swollen belly. What can you people be thinking when you see her like this?

Sarah slipped from the bed and walked to the curtained doorway on the wall of Raynhard's room opposite the bed. She returned with linen and a large ceramic bowl that held a pitcher. After setting them on the trunk next to Alizarine's basket and pouring water into the bowl, Sarah soaked three cloths in the water, wrung them out, and brought them to the bed. Sarah gave one each to Raynhard and Sagora before leaning over to clean off Alizarine.

After several trips to the bowl, Sarah and the others were clean. As she returned the bowl and cloths to the curtained room, Sagora climbed out of bed and dressed.

When Sarah returned, she retrieved the egg from Alizarine's basket and placed it on the bed between Raynhard and Alizarine.

Then with Sagora's help, they placed the bedclothes over Raynhard and Alizarine. Alizarine laid her head on the pillow and closed her eyes. Sarah folded Alizarine's hands on top of the blankets. Then she bent and kissed each ring.

Sagora had gone to the other side of the bed and rested a knee there to help Raynhard get comfortable as he moved closer to the egg and Alizarine. Sagora lifted the blanket enough to place his hand so it rested just below Alizarine's distended belly. She made a final adjustment to the blanket, leaned over him, and kissed him on the lips. "Sleep well, my king. Peaceful sleep to you and Alizarine. As you wished, you'll not be disturbed. Come wake me in the morning," she whispered.

Sagora pivoted off the bed, walked around to the other side, and bent to kiss the rings on Alizarine's hands. When Sagora stood, she nodded to Sarah. They set about blowing out the candle lanterns except for one.

I dare not stay the night to witness what more will happen in this room. Alizarine, you still hold Raynhard in your witch's reins, as you did when you were Aliza. Will I ever be able to cut those reins? Now it's my turn to act.

Nagora followed Sarah out of the room, slipping past the door before Sagora closed it.

She followed the two down the hall. Still, they walked as if in a slow procession, not with a regular stride, but as if a master puppeteer controlled their steps. No, the witch controls you. Soon, I will play a trick on the witch.

Without a word, Sarah went on to her room.

Nagora followed her sister.

Sagora had gone straight to her mirror to brush her hair.

Nagora pushed past the curtained doorway of the clothes room where, in the dim light, she gathered up and folded the leggings, underpants, socks, and the woolen sweater Sagora had discarded earlier. Nagora wrapped them in a neat bundle in Sagora's vest and set it on the leather boots. Then she found and put on a simple linen robe that fastened at her waist.

Nagora pulled the curtain aside for a peek. Sagora was standing and blowing out the candle lanterns on each side of the mirror. The one in the recess of the wall near the head of her bed remained lit. Then she went to her bed, pulled back the covers, and let herself fall on the bed. Sagora appeared to be staring at the dark ceiling and mumbling something inaudible. Sagora's hand shot up as if reaching for something invisible.

Then she sat up, reached for her pillow, and pulled it closer before lying on her side to rest her head on it. She pulled a blanket over herself and closed her eyes. How long do I wait?

Soon Sagora's breathing took on the regular rhythm of one asleep.

Nagora picked up the bundle of clothes and the boots and crept out of the small room. She paused at the chamber door, gently lifted its latch, and pulled the door open just enough so she could slip into the hall. Nagora ran toward the staircase, holding the bundle of clothes ahead of her.

...

Nagora paused at the door to the kitchens to will herself visible from beneath her suit of dragonskin armor. The press of the fine mesh of scales against her skin defined every muscle and bone close to the surface of her own skin. Nagora held the bundle under one arm as she pulled on the door's handle.

"Dannor! Where are you?"

"Here, Mum. Do you have the rings?"

"No, not yet. You'll not believe what I'm going to tell you." Nagora handed him the bundle and the boots. "Sagora's clothes. We'll dress her for the trip."

Quick as she could, she gave him a brief account of what she had witnessed.

"So how will you get the rings?"

"I'll try something. Give me more time before I get Sagora to come down here. You know what to do."

"Aye, Mum."

Lars stepped from the pantry into the kitchen.

"What ... ?" Nagora pointed to him.

Lars held a finger to his lips. "I was hungry. Besides, I want to help."

He held up a coil of rope. "I spoke to the Captain of the Watch and placed a gold dragon in his palm. He will let the guards on the walls know we're preparing a surprise for Raynhard's wedding. The guards are not to breathe a word about our actions in the yard until after the wedding."

"I knew I married you for a good reason." Nagora placed a hand on the coil of rope. "Good! You found one." Then she took his ring hand in hers. "Lars, I know we don't wear our wedding rings, but I need your understanding in what I'm about to ask you."

Lars's eyes narrowed. "You know I'll do anything to help you. Anything. What about our rings?"

"Will you give me yours so I can wed Raynhard, as Edana, without fear of placing Alizarine's spell-cursed gold bands on our fingers?"

Lars did not hesitate. He reached into his scrip for the ring woven mariner style from the fine tip of a skinned willow branch. He placed it in Nagora's hand and folded her fingers over it. "If it can make your plan work, use it."

Nagora kissed him and held him close before placing his ring in the pocket of the robe she wore. I'll put it with mine in my scrip later.

Then she turned to her son, dabbing at the tears that wet her cheeks beneath the dragonskin. "Dannor, you're going to have an extra passenger."

He looked surprised. "One of the twins?"

Nagora shook her head. "Sarah. I can't explain now. All I can tell you is Alizarine has control over her, too much for my liking. I hope if we can get her away from Alizarine, she'll become herself again."

Nagora turned to Lars. "Once I've brought Sagora here and put her out, and once we've changed her clothes, I'll go get Sarah."

Lars held open his arms. Nagora stepped into his embrace. He reached over and brought Dannor close. He hugged them to him. "Both of you, be careful. I don't want to lose either one of you."

Dannor said, "Don't worry, Da, I've got Danuka on my side. Count on us."

Nagora put a hand on the back of Dannor's neck. "Tell Godomor everything I told you, but don't do it in Sarah's presence. If Godomor wants to speak to her, let him." Nagora kissed his cheeks and his forehead and then took Lars in her arms for a long kiss. "Thank you for supporting me in this trial. Let it be the last battle I ever have to fight." Nagora let go of him, looked to Dannor, and took a deep breath. "Best I get moving and set my plan in motion."

Out of their sight, Nagora willed her armor to make her invisible and left for the twins' room.

In the hall before going into the room, Nagora slipped out of the linen robe. Inside, she stood at the side of the twins' bed. I hope this works. She leaned over, took the dragon teeth from their hands, and tiptoed to the foot of their bed with a tooth in each hand. She tapped the teeth on the wooden rail, making them dance. "Raean! Raean! Awake! Awake! Baerik! Baerik! Awake! Awake!"

She kept up the tapping and the repeated calls to awake, until Raean sat up and rubbed sleep from his eyes. "Raean! Laddie! You're awake!" she said in a high pitched voice. "Wake your brother, Raean, so he can tell you what you see is so. Wake him, laddie! Pinch him! We've important news for both of you."

Raean was trying to focus, most likely looking for a body attached to the voice he heard, even though the teeth must seem to talk to him. "Baerik. Baerik!" He shook Baerik. "Wake up, Baerik. You're not going to believe this." Raean pinched his brother.

Baerik sat up and struggled to open his eyes, one hand striking out from the side Raean had pinched.

"Baerik! Wake up! Look at our dragon teeth! They're talking to us!"

"Huh?" Baerik rubbed both eyes and looked around.

"Baerik! Laddie! You're awake! Listen to the news we have for you!"

Baerik grabbed hold of Raean and pointed. "It's the teeth talking!"

Raean was nodding. "So we're not dreaming. We're awake. We both see them."

"Raean! Baerik! Look at your hands! What do you see?"

The boys looked. Raean said, "Rings like Mum and Da wear!"

"How did we get these?" asked Baerik.

"Alizarine put them on you. Laddies, do you know what that means?"

They shook their heads no.

"It means you'll lose your wishes if those rings don't come off."

They grabbed the rings and pulled and twisted and pulled harder. "They won't come off!" said Raean. "What'll we do? I want my wish!"

Nagora set the teeth still on the rail for a moment, made them appear to look at each other, and then she had them look back at the boys and hop from one root to another in a dance. "Laddies, here's what you do. Every time you see Alizarine or your mum or your da, alone or together, no matter where and no matter when, you yell and holler and bang us hard on any piece of wood nearby and demand the rings come off."

Nagora lifted the teeth high and floated them back down to the rail. "If the rings come off before the wedding, nine more wishes each will be your reward. But only if the rings come off and stay off."

"Nine more wishes to be made, like Dannor told us?" asked Baerik.

"That's right, laddies! Nine more wishes each to be used just as Dannor explained."

"Wooow!" They held onto each other and bounced up and down.

"One more thing, laddies! You hold on to us with all your might and let no one take us from you. Understood?"

Both nodded.

"Good! Now lay your heads on your pillows, close your eyes, and hold your hands open. We'll hop back into your hands."

Nagora propped the teeth in their palms and blew out the candle lantern on the wall. Your turn, Sagora.

Nagora snuck back into Sagora's chamber and tiptoed into the small clothes room where she replaced the linen robe on its shelf before willing her armor to make her visible. She struggled to snake out of it. Her body chilled once it was free of the fine scale mesh of tailored dragonskin. She folded it over and over onto itself to later be able to fit into the bottom of her scrip.

Nagora reached for her blades, clothes, and scrip on the top shelf. Before she dressed, the dragonskin went into the scrip followed by Lars's willow wedding ring which she placed alongside her own in the inner ring pocket.

Next, she pulled a throwing knife from its holster on one of the carry straps of her big sheath and tapped the holster until the small wax cylinder tumbled out into her palm.

It seems like only yesterday I prepared three more like this, but it's been years. Inside the small wax cylinder was a thorn from a hawthorn shrub, the tip of which she had barely touched to the liquid in the vial of her mother's "healer's secret," as Sagora had called the poison. Nagora had used the tweezers from her mother's medical scrip to hold the thorn, placing it inside a piece of bark from a twig before filling the surrounding space with wax. Not enough to kill you, Sagora, but close.

She put the throwing knife back in its holster and slipped the straps of her big sheath over her shoulders.

Nagora crept back to the chamber door, pulled it open, and stepped out. As soon as she closed it, she rapped hard with her fist. "Sagora! Wake up! Sagora! Hurry! Wake up!" Nagora opened the door and rushed in. "Sagora! Wake ... "

Sagora was sitting up in her bed. "What is it? What's wrong?"

"Sagora! Come quick! With your medical scrip! It's Dannor. He's on the kitchen floor. He's not conscious. He's bleeding from an ear."

"Nagora, what happened?" Sagora threw aside the blanket, pulled herself to the side of the bed, and stood.

"Lars and I were arguing. Dannor tried to hold Lars back because he was threatening me. Sagora, he struck Dannor so hard. Dannor fell to the floor and didn't get up. Lars left. I don't know where to. Dannor's bleeding. You've got to help him!"

Sagora found slippers at the side of her bed and her medical scrip in a drawer in the dresser beneath the mirror. "Let's go."

...

Nagora banged open the door at the end of the hallway that led to the kitchens. *Dannor, I hope you heard that. We're coming.*

Nagora pushed past the kitchen door. "Quick! This way, near the fireplace." She stopped where Dannor lay. As Sagora knelt to place her scrip on the floor near Dannor's head, Nagora, with great care, broke open the wax cylinder to expose the tip of the thorn.

"Hold that candle lantern closer," were Sagora's last words that night as Nagora pricked the thorn into the back of her neck. Her sister's body went limp and crumpled on top of Dannor. Nagora reached under Sagora's arms and lifted her.

Dannor rolled away and stood to help. "Da! We need you now. Bring her clothes."

While they finished dressing Sagora, Nagora reminded Dannor of what he was to do. "Most important is to send for Umma and explain what I've done to Sagora. Umma will know what to do. Oh! Be careful. I don't know if Sarah speaks the language of the people of the Land of Skulls. Sagora may have taught her. Beware of what you say to others in her presence."

"I'll be careful, Mum."

Nagora placed a hand on his. "I know you will."

Lars had tied two loops together in the coil of rope he held before him. "Help your mum hold her up. I'll pull her legs into these." With the loops pulled to the top of Sagora's thighs, he crisscrossed the rope over Sagora's back, then around her waist, across her back again, and finally under her arms.

Lars bent to one knee. "Now lean her over onto my shoulder."

They did and Lars stood. "Let's go."

In the yard as they approached Danuka, Nagora took hold of Dannor's arm. "Are you ready to climb onto the saddle so your da and I can tie her to you?"

"Aye."

Dannor sat in the saddle and Nagora helped Lars lift Sagora into place behind Dannor.

Lars passed the ends of the rope over Dannor's shoulders and threaded them through the rings at the front of the saddle, where he tied them together on the ring in front of the loop handle. "Just pull on this big knot if you bend forward and want her body to follow. It shouldn't be a problem with Sarah in back of her."

Nagora placed a hand on Dannor's forearm. "Good luck, son. I look forward to your return."

Dannor gave her a thumbs up.

Lars hugged Nagora. "Go get Sarah. I'll be hiding by the time you get back."

Nagora took the candle lantern from its recessed resting place in the wall near the head of Sarah's bed.

Sarah was asleep on her stomach. Nagora pushed Sarah's hair aside. The four eights knot in the fine leather lace rested on the back of her neck. Looks like she's wearing her amulet now. Does she remove it for the rituals with Alizarine? Most likely. Alizarine's afraid of the amulet. Somehow, she must've convinced Sarah to remove it.

"Wake up, Sarah! Wake up!"

Sarah rolled over and looked up, blinking her eyes open. "What is it?"

"I need your help, Sarah. Something terrible has happened to Nagora!"

Sarah rubbed the heel of a hand to one of her eyes. "What … what happened?"

"Nagora's ruined my plan. Actually, Lars has. He's poisoned her. Sarah, I don't know if she'll live. Nagora had agreed to go back to the Land of Skulls as me, but Lars wouldn't hear of it. Now my only chance is to send her there unconscious to Umma."

"Umma?"

"The healer Mum left her infirmary to. Tagnya trained Umma. Umma will know what to do. I've tied Nagora to Dannor on Danuka's saddle. I need you to fly her to the Land of Skulls to get her there before Godomor attacks. I told Dannor what his mum had agreed to do. He said he would make sure she did it if Umma can reverse the effect of the poison. Sarah, we've no time to waste! This will be our only chance to stop Godomor's horde from attacking. Please do this for me if you still want to become a princess. I know you can do it."

Sarah lifted her legs out of bed and stood. "I'll do it. Let me get dressed."

"Oh! Thank you, Sarah! Dress warm. It'll be cold. Take a small blanket to put over Nagora's shoulders."

Sarah pulled off her night frock. Good! She is wearing her amulet.

"Is Lars still here?" asked Sarah.

"No! Thank the stars! He's left the castle. Can you believe he was so mad he even struck Dannor?"

Nagora checked that Danuka's passengers were secure and comfortable for the long flight. "Remember, Dannor, your mum is supposed to be me. Don't call her 'Mum' in front of others."

"I'll do my best," said Dannor.

Nagora stepped off Danuka's wing and backed away to the yard wall. Take good care of my children, Mother, and my sister. Danuka lifted her belly off the ground with the help of her powerful wing talons. She began the slow rhythmic flap of her wings, only increasing it as she lifted off the ground. Oh! Mother! Are those your egg pouches I see in your claws?

You will bring them to the maze. The time is near. I understand, Mother. The *Mêmêkwêsiw* are waiting. Mother, your eggs will be in good hands.

I will do my best to bring you the last egg as planned.

Danuka disappeared into the night.

Now I'll rest before the battle with the witch. Not much of this night remains.

Lars had been standing in the dark doorway. He stepped into the yard and took Nagora in his arms. "Let's hope they arrive in time. Godomor can only hold back his warriors for so long. Hopefully, with Sagora's return and depending on what she tells him, he might be able to stop his wolves from invading. Try to sleep. Tomorrow, I'll be waiting. If not tomorrow, the same time the day after. Be careful."

"I have a feeling they will. Did you see the pouches Danuka had in her claws?"

"Aye. Her eggs?"

"Yes. Our work on the maze will truly have a purpose. Thank you for sticking with me through all of this. Get some rest too. Tell Moreena and Erin I will send a carriage for them in the afternoon."

They kissed.

Confrontation
Nôtinikewin

† NOW: *the fourteenth day in
the Land of the Danu,
two days before the wedding*

The next morning, Nagora's eyes opened with the knocking on the door. She sat bolt upright in Sagora's bed. Her hand found the royal hunting dagger as Raynhard walked in with Alizarine at his side. Nagora shoved the dagger further down under her knees.

Alizarine stared at her. Does she see me or Sagora? Beneath a black sweater, Alizarine still wore her black robe, the red silk scarf at her neck, and the gold rings on her fingers. Had Raynhard combed her hair and tied it off in two tails at the sides of her head? Who else? Raynhard wore the robe from the night before.

"Good morning, Sagora. Did you sleep well?" asked Raynhard.

"Look at me! Can't you tell? I've hardly slept!"

Raynhard moved to approach Nagora's side of the bed.

"No! Stay right where you are. I have news that might not turn in our favor. Then you'll understand my tired face."

Nagora blurted out the events almost exactly as she had told them to Sarah.

"Why did you not wake me?" asked Raynhard.

Nagora looked from him to Alizarine with hands held out. "To respect your wishes to not be disturbed in your peaceful night of sleep."

Raynhard shook his head.

"If you don't believe me, go to Sarah's room. You'll not find her. I watched Danuka fly away with them.

"Raynhard, I can't imagine how this will turn out for us. I'm worried. What if Nagora's son slips up and calls her 'Mum'? Will Dannor be able to pass that off as a credible slip because we look alike? What if Umma can't reverse the effects of the poison Lars gave her? Nagora won't be able to play the part she said she would for you.

"Do we call off the wedding?"

Raynhard flinched and pulled his hand away from Alizarine's as he looked down at the witch. Alizarine's dark eyes stared back at him. He rubbed his hand and looked away. "Of course not, Sagora. We must go on with it. All our planning. It's only two days away. We've promised Alizarine. She's to carry our rings. Baerik and Raean are to offer them. You're to be crowned queen. Then I crown two princes and two princesses." Raynhard paused and glanced at Alizarine.

So this wedding is under Alizarine's control.

"Will Sarah return in time?" asked Raynhard, as he seemed to just come to that realization.

"That's why I asked about calling off the wedding."

Alizarine took hold of his hand.

"Well, I suppose, if Sarah's not here on the day of the wedding, I could crown her when she returns."

"Raynhard, put yourself in Sarah's place. It wouldn't be the same, not as regal as being crowned Princess Sarah at a royal wedding where her mother is crowned Queen Edana and her brothers crowned Princes Baerik and Raean."

Again, Raynhard flinched, almost bending to one knee this time, as Alizarine's wide-eyed stare bore into him.

"But all the guests, Sagora, on such short notice. Some are already traveling here and won't be able to be reached."

My poor king, Alizarine has you under her thumb. "True, Raynhard, true. You are right. We can only hope Sarah will be back on time. Surely, she'll be able to convince Gabe and Godomor, even if Nagora, acting as me, has not yet come to. They'll want Sarah to attend Nagora's wedding with King Raynhard to get that problem out of the way. They wouldn't deny Sarah the chance of becoming a princess. Would they?"

"No, Sagora. Those savages wouldn't dare." Raynhard smiled at her and then at Alizarine.

"Raynhard, what do we do about Lars? He's caused all of this."

Raynhard looked back to Nagora and then to Alizarine again, who still held his hand. He raised his other hand in a fist. "He'll pay for this! As soon as the wedding is over, I'll have him arrested and punished. Right now with all the guests arriving, a manhunt would just cause undo concern.

"We'll leave you now to get dressed and see you in the dining room." Alizarine led Raynhard out the chamber door.

Why does Alizarine want the wedding to happen on that day? What am I not seeing? Has Raynhard promised Alizarine something if she becomes a princess? Why on that day?

...

"Off with these rings! Off with these rings! No more rings! No more rings! We don't want these rings!" Their rhythmic chanting and banging reached Nagora's ears as she walked down the hallway to the dining room. It didn't let up. It became louder as she stepped into the room.

"Boys! Baerik! Raean! What is this? Calm down this moment!" Nagora did her best to give a stern Sagora stare, but to no avail. The boys kept up the banging as the dragon teeth had instructed. "Just take them off and stop your banging and screaming!"

They set the teeth down and showed how they weren't able to pull the amber-eyed silver rings off.

Alizarine sat with the gold rings on her hands pressed to her ears. Her basket rested in her lap against the edge of the table.

Raynhard kept closing his eyes and shaking his head. He had obviously tried to silence them and had not succeeded. His patience seemed to be running out.

Nagora walked over to him. Play the part. "What's gotten into them? Why won't they stop?"

Raynhard held his hands open, pointed to his own bare ring finger, and shrugged. "They want the rings to come off. If they don't, they promise to not stop. I have a good mind to send them to their room for the day, but they won't move. Shall I get guards to move them?"

The twins weren't letting up. How long could they keep it up before losing their voices?

Alizarine's hands reached for the edge of the table. "Call the guards!"

Nagora dropped a fist to the table. "No! Alizarine, you have to let them remove those rings!"

Alizarine's eyes narrowed as she stared back at Nagora.

"If I had known that taking them from us and putting them on my boys would have caused this, I wouldn't have allowed it. Please, Alizarine, let them take the rings off. We can put them somewhere else for safekeeping."

Alizarine covered her ears again and then she closed her eyes, shaking her head no.

I won't play this game for long. I'll make my move. Nagora skipped over to Alizarine and yanked the basket from her lap.

Alizarine screamed, "Noooo! Give me back my egg!" Her hands shot out to grab the basket.

Nagora was ready. She pulled her big skystone blade from its sheath and held its blade between the tips of Alizarine's fingers. "Stay right where you are."

The twins had stopped chanting and banging. Baerik's and Raean's mouths hung open as they stared wide-eyed, each with a dragon tooth in a hand frozen just above the table's surface.

Raynhard stood up.

Nagora flashed him a stern look then shook her blade at the witch. "Alizarine, I've had enough of your rituals. You crossed the line when you struck my Baerik and pushed him down the stairs. If you want to see this beloved egg of yours again, you'll do as I say."

Alizarine's fingers closed into her palms to make two fists. Her eyes glanced up at Raynhard.

"Not one word from you, Raynhard, if you want me standing at your side as your queen, I will not stand by and watch Alizarine torment my sons.

"Alizarine, get those rings off my boys now! Or so help me, you'll never see this egg ever again!"

Alizarine's face was turning red.

"I warn you, Alizarine. If you have one of your fits like the one my sister told me about, I'll have you hanging from shackles and chains in this castle's dungeon until you rot. The choice is yours. Get the rings off my boys, and I'll return this egg to you on the day of my wedding. As Queen Edana, it'll be my goodwill gift to you as the new Princess Alizarine.

"My boys don't need those rings. If they don't obey me in the days up to the wedding, I'll have them shackled and chained in the dungeon." Nagora pointed her blade at them. "Is that clear, you two scoundrels?"

They nodded. Baerik was close to tears.

Nagora waved her blade. "Do it now, Alizarine!"

Alizarine slid off her chair to go stand between the chairs of the twins. She held her hands out, palms down before her. "Place your ring hands beneath mine."

The boys did as asked.

Alizarine closed her eyes and chanted words Nagora did not understand. A spell of some kind. It had better work. Alizarine pulled her hands back, crossed her arms so her hands rested on her shoulders, and returned to her chair. She pointed to Raynhard and then to Nagora. "Remove the rings."

Tar piss! Is this going to work? I didn't wear one of those rings.

"Stay where you are, Raynhard. No, Alizarine." Nagora pointed with her blade. "You placed those rings on their fingers last night. Today, you remove them. When you do, set them on the table."

Alizarine's lips pursed and her mouth turned down into a sour scowl as she took a deep breath while standing up. She limped back over to the boys' side of the table and looked over at Raynhard before removing the ring from Raean's finger. Before she removed the ring from Baerik's finger, she gave Nagora a long, smoldering look. Little witch, you don't scare me.

Nagora pointed to a spot near the middle of the table. "Set them here." She glanced at the twins. "Don't touch the rings, boys!" Nagora waved her blade. "Stand up. Go stand against the wall behind you." Baerik and Raean obeyed without hesitation.

"Raynhard, the same goes for you, to the wall behind you."

Nagora waved her blade up. "Alizarine, go stand against that wall."

Nagora looked around at them. "No one move. Stay where you are." She set the basket on the table to one side, leaned across the space between her and the silver rings, and pulled them to the middle of the table. Nagora set them on edge so their amber-stone eyes looked to the ceiling.

Nagora reached for the basket handle and took a step back from the table. Again Nagora glanced from Raynhard, to the twins, and to Alizarine. She moved the basket so it hung from her hand behind her.

Then, as fast as she could, Nagora smashed the flat side of her skystone blade down on the amber-eyed silver rings. A blinding flash of light was followed by an echoing explosion, a shower of bouncing, charred splinters, and a cloud of black smoke.

As the cloud of smoke settled around Nagora, she found the others.

The twins cowered on the floor with their arms folded over their heads.

Alizarine was bent over on her knees, her arms outstretched, as her fingers tried to dig into the floor. "Noooooooooooooooooooo." Alizarine's splinter-covered shoulders heaved as she looked up with fury in her eyes.

Raynhard leaned against the wall on one arm while his other hand batted away at the surrounding smoke. Charred splinters covered that side of his body.

The blast had shot down and out from the underside of the skystone blade, leaving a hole in the tabletop three times the size of Alizarine's head. The walrus hide handle of Nagora's blade still carried vibrations from the blade's tang into her hand and up her arm. Tar piss! How did I manage to hold on to it?

Nagora blinked, lifted the blade from over the smoking hole in the oak table to see the spot on the blade where it had struck the rings. Nothing. No dent. Not even a scratch. Only the reflection of the Tiwaz on her forehead above the one etched near the crossguard of her blade. Yes! I did it for a higher cause. A higher cause!

Raynhard moved through the smoke along the other side of the table, an arm outstretched in Alizarine's direction. May you someday see what I've done for you.

Two servants rushed in, slid to a stop, and stared in disbelief.

Uncle was right, if you're going to surprise your enemy with an attack, best do it before their morning meal. Nagora shoved her blade into its sheath on her back and looked at the two maids. "I think it was lightning." Nagora pointed at the hole in the table and turned on her heel to leave through the door behind her.

The corridor Nagora took brought her to a turret that hung on the outer castle wall which was part of the great wall of Windhaven. Lars had been right. Not only did it contain an ingenious latrine seat, but a narrow spiral staircase up to the next floor. Thank you, Sarah, for giving my man a tour of the castle.

First to the latrine.

It was down five narrow, straight steps to the bottom level of the turret. To her left, past the open door, daylight streamed in from the open latrine seat hole in the far corner. She closed the door and slid the wooden lock plate in place. Nagora set the basket on the floor and stood before the hole. Just below it hung a metal cage. To the right of the seat hole on the same panel were two square wooden doors, a forearm length to a side, set on hinges.

A chain hung from a big metal hook protruding from the wall above her head and ran through a hole where the two top corners of the doors met. A rope, hanging from a pulley also attached to the big hook, passed in the two worn-out spaces where the edges of the doors met. Nagora lifted both wooden doors and saw the rest of the metal cage just beneath.

The chain ran to the bottom of the outer castle wall to its anchor point in the stream.

A pail handle was tied to one end of the long rope on the pulley, with a counter weight on the other end. An iron ring fastened to the rope above the bucket allowed it to travel along the chain. Lars was right. Reach down through the metal grid. Shove the pail in place. Take a seat. Take a shit. Pull the bucket over. It lowers all by itself. The pail hits the stream, empties, fills, and comes back up with a tug on the rope.

Nagora closed the two doors so they again made contact with the chain and the rope. She looked at the latrine-seat hole on the panel next to the doors. Now can I squeeze the basket through that seat hole? No way. Nor through the open doors because of the chain and the rope.

Lars said the whole panel has its own hinges at the back. I see them. He said by lifting it from the front and holding the two doors ajar at the same time, I can clear the chain and the pulley rope so the whole panel rests against the back wall. Looks easy enough without a bottom door frame piece.

Lifting with her left arm and using her right fist to keep the doors apart, Nagora heaved the panel up against the back wall.

Plenty of space now. Easy to grab the bucket from here. Nagora pulled it over, lifted it to gauge its weight, and set it back down before lifting the basket. Better empty some of the water. She tilted the bucket, poured some out, and compared again with the basket. More. That should do it.

Nagora set the basket next to the bucket on the metal grid. She fished in her scrip for the spare bow string she always kept there, found it, and cut it in half. I better tie the sheepskin secure to the basket and then the basket to the bucket handle. Half of the string did both jobs. The other half went back into her scrip.

Nagora paused to look to the door and listen. Has Alizarine enlisted help to find her basket, or is she searching on her own? Would she think of looking here? I better hurry.

It was not an easy juggle to pull the bucket over the edge of the metal grid. But Nagora managed get the basket to follow without hooking. She managed to maneuver the basket away from the edge of the grid.

Nagora controlled its descent and stopped the bucket from reaching the stream. Has Lars been watching and waiting? If not, I'll wait. Now I see it. Movement in the bushes on the other side of the stream. You'll have to get wet, my man.

Lars stepped into the stream and untied the basket, waved to Nagora, and disappeared with it into the trees.

Nagora let the bucket fall to the stream and fill. The counter weight's descent pulled the pail back up. Now, Alizarine, you can hunt for your basket all you want. You'll not get it until after my king crowns me.

When Nagora returned to Sagora's chambers, questions awaited her. "What got into you? Why did you do that to the rings? You didn't have to threaten the child. She would've relented sooner or later. Have you seen her? Alizarine's searching the castle like a dog for its bone. You should give her back her egg." Raynhard was pacing the room from the wall near the foot of the bed to the wall of the doorway.

Now and then Raynhard paused behind Nagora as she sat combing her hair at the mirror. Finally she looked up at him. "I was angry. I wanted to flatten the rings. Nagora always said these blades were magic. Anyway, Raynhard, I made

Alizarine a promise. I'll keep it. Until then, let her search. As long as she keeps out of my sight, I don't mind."

"These two." Raynhard pointed to the twins sitting on Sagora's bed. "What about them? You've scared the wits out of them. They follow me everywhere. They won't let me leave them out of my sight. They won't play on their own."

Nagora turned to gaze at the boys. "You'll get over it, lads, won't you? You didn't know your mum had magic in her big blade. And I got the rings off your fingers, didn't I?"

"We rarely ever see you wear your blades. Now you keep them on all the time like Auntie Nagora," said Raean.

Nagora stood and went to sit on the edge of the bed. "Give me your hand, Raean. I have something to tell you."

He did, but with reluctance.

"You see, Raean, your Auntie Nagora swore an oath one day to never ever again be caught without her blades. Why? Because each time she didn't have them, she was harmed by terrible people who did horrible things to her.

"After what happened to Auntie Nagora last night, I decided to do like her so I wouldn't fear something terrible would happen to me too. This morning, when I saw what those rings were doing to you, I had to act to protect you.

"Tell me true, Raean, do you think I did the right thing or no?"

He swallowed. "You did the right thing, Mum."

"I believe I did, Raean, and sometimes the right things we do can scare others. I'm sorry I scared you, but I had to protect you."

Raean leaned his head on her arm.

...

That afternoon, Nagora met Erin and Moreena at the yard door with a stern face and a cold follow-me greeting before leading them inside to the map room. Once she had closed the door, she hugged them both. "I can't thank you enough for your performance and courage. Your last song ripped open the sky above us! Those present will remember it forever. You surely composed it."

Moreena put an arm around Erin's shoulders. "It was Erin's idea. She said we had to honor Mum's wish to play Hag a death song. We call it *The Witch is Dead*."

Nagora hugged them again. "I hope I can make that so for you. To be honest, I can't say for sure when it will happen. I've done all I can to convince my Sarah. So far, she'll have no part in the killing. I can't do it without her. I'm hoping Sarah returns here for the wedding with a change of mind."

"Lars said the same thing. He's hopeful since not only did Dannor make the switch, but somehow you were able to get the other egg back too. He's eager to find out how. And, he said to tell you Dannor will get it to Danuka," said Moreena.

Nagora sighed. "Well, I can hardly believe how I did it myself. For now I'm keeping that for myself, unless one of the others present speaks."

"Is it true lightning struck the royal dining table and completely charred it?" asked Erin. "That's what we've heard."

Nagora smiled. "Castle gossip travels fast. I'll only say there's a wee element of truth in what you've heard." She paused. "Tell Lars the rings are no more. Now that's a piece of truth for your ears only."

Erin reached for Nagora's hand. "Oh! Lars said he would have the basket ready for you by sunrise tomorrow."

"Thank you, Erin. Tell Lars I'll be waiting."

She turned to Moreena. "Have you brought the list of songs? I liked the first five you played. I loved the sixth one, but obviously you won't play it. I trust you for the choice of two more from the remaining four. Tell me which, and I'll pen them as my choices, Sagora's choices, and show the list to Raynhard."

Moreena handed the leather sleeve to Nagora, turned to Erin, and placed a hand on her arm. "The last two, Erin?"

"Aye," said Erin.

Nagora pulled out the list. The last song was *No Longer In My Eyes, Always In My Heart*. "Oh! Moreena! I'll cry at the wedding when I hear it. I'm so happy you'll play it."

"We put it last on the list. We figured it would get refused because they hadn't heard it," said Moreena.

Nagora had tears in her eyes. "Not by me, Moreena. I've heard it and know how much it means to you. To hear you play it in the Center for the Dragon Arts will be the best part of that day.

"I'll not keep you longer. I have to make this meeting seem businesslike. Thank you for bringing the list. Forgive my stern-sister face as I lead you out."

"We understand," said Erin.

As soon as Nagora opened the door, it was obvious Alizarine had searched Sagora's room. The big drawers on the dresser near the mirror had not been pushed completely shut. Slippers that were under the bed had been pushed out to the side. The corner of a blanket stuck out from under the partially closed lid of the trunk at the foot of the bed.

Before going to inspect the clothes room, Nagora set the tribute ledgers on the bed. These contained all the information on the levies collected by the lairds in the domains of the Land of the Danu. Sagora collected levies from the lairds when she visited them. It was Nagora's intention to study them in preparation to greet the lairds invited to the wedding.

In the clothes room, dresses had been pushed aside on their hooks. Sweaters had been pulled from their shelves and stuffed onto others. Boots and shoes on the bottom shelf were all a jumble. Wow! Alizarine, you even climbed the shelves in that corner. Did you get a good peek at the tops of the others from there?

Nagora left the curtain open and went to the mirror, sat in the chair, and opened the drawer that contained the bundle of missives she had found the day before. Do I read through them now? I risk being interrupted. Tonight then, when all are to bed. Now I'll study the ledgers instead. At least they'll give me information I can use tomorrow—I'll compliment the lairds who've collected on time and inquire after those who still have levies owing.

That night Nagora read through the letters, placed them in order of their writing, and read them again. Was there some piece of information Sagora found to be of value? Was there a common thread among them? Were questions asked in them Sagora did not want answered? Were sentiments expressed that made Sagora jealous? No matter the way she sifted through them, she could not find answers to her questions.

Sleep came and went with dreams of Nagora's mother and father, and her friends, Paruline and Geirador, sitting before pages of vellum. They spoke to her as they wrote on those pages that did not get to her. Why had Sagora kept these? Why hadn't she burned them like the others? Perhaps she could not without being seen? Sagora could've burned them here. Why keep them? Dare I ask her someday?

Daughter
Mitânisimâw

✝ NOW: *the fifteenth day in*
the Land of the Danu,
the day before the wedding

Again, all these questions ran through Nagora's mind as she waited for sunrise in the turret latrine. She had opened the doors alongside the chain and ropes that hung through the metal grid. Her eyes had adjusted to the twilight and were fixed on the rope for any movement.

It came as a ripple on a fishing line. She peered down, but it was too dark below to see. She gave a gentle tug to raise the bucket, but whatever was on the end bit back. He's smiling most likely and saying: "Give me a chance to tie it on proper."

Nagora kept two fingers either side of the rope as she waited. It vibrated, but did not signal to pull. Soon. Ah! Ha! There it is! She tugged twice, raising the basket at least two arm lengths. No resistance. Good! Up you come. The counterweight took over, and the basket rose at a steady rate.

As Nagora lifted the whole latrine seat-hole panel to rest it against the back wall, below a shadow disappeared into the trees on the other side of the stream. Lars had tied the basket onto a climber's knot he had made well above the basket handle. Thank you. I'll have no problem pulling the basket onto the grid first.

Once Nagora had released the basket from the knot, she set it on the floor, pulled the bucket onto the grid, and closed the seat panel and its doors. Now to hide this basket.

Nagora hurried down the hall and through the dining room, where a smaller temporary table now stood in place of the one she had destroyed. She rushed out the opposite door, into and down the hall to the side door to the throne room, and past the throne into the map room.

Nagora locked the door, pulled two chairs aside, and crawled under the large round table to the structure that supported it. From the perimeter of the underside of the tabletop, eight beams spread out in pairs around the table. Each pair angled down to the central four-sided wooden block recessed in the stone floor of the room. Each side of the block had two joint spaces cut into it to receive a pair of support beams that held up the top.

Nagora lifted the basket up between two beams and over the corner of the main block, setting it on top of the block. Alizarine will not find it unless she crawls under here with a candle lantern. Now back to my room to prepare for regal duties.

"Is Alizarine not coming to breakfast?" asked Nagora as she pulled back her chair. Raynhard and the boys were already seated and eating.

"Alizarine," Raynhard paused, "told me she would be spending the day in her room and have her meals there too." You mean Alizarine ordered you to have her meals brought to her room. Suits me fine.

"Raynhard, I went over the ledgers so many times yesterday, I fear I'll mix up laird names with faces when they come into the throne room today," said Nagora.

Raynhard smiled. "Fear not. They won't all be coming at once today. Anyway, they'll be announced and I'll be at your side to remind you of who's who."

That'll help. I'll not recognize any of them; however they'll know me as Lady Edana from her travels to their domains. Even if they're announced, I won't have any conversation details other than compliments and a couple of inquiries. All except for two had collected the required tributes. According to the ledger notes, they're supposed to bring them today. I'll mirror what Raynhard says in my own way and hope for the best. Anyway, they'll be more interested in speaking to Raynhard.

Nagora had survived the first wave of guests who offered wishes and gifts. Thanks to her study of the ledgers, the guests being announced, and Raynhard's comments, she had been able to make a credible show of the soon-to-be Queen Edana.

Raean and Baerik, the princes-to-be, had brought a board game to keep themselves occupied as the guests filed by. When the subject of children came up, Nagora occasionally brought a guest over to the game table to introduce them to Raean and Baerik.

The greeting of guests had continued to go well that afternoon until Raean spotted Danuka's silhouette flash past one of the tall windows of the throne room. Had she returned with Sarah? Baerik said he was sure he saw her riding the dragon.

It didn't take long for confirmation.

Sarah strode into the throne room unannounced ahead of other waiting guests. She stepped right up to Raynhard who was conversing with a Windhaven official. "Please excuse me."

Sarah turned to Nagora. "We have to speak. Now! In your chambers." Her face was one of a volcano about to erupt. Sarah did not wait for a reply, but headed straight away for the staircase.

Nagora bowed to Raynhard and the official. "Excuse me. The matter seems to be urgent. Forgive my sudden withdrawal from this conversation."

Sarah had disappeared up the staircase.

Nagora found Sarah in Sagora's room, standing legs spread, arms crossed on her chest, and her face painted with a scowl. "You!" A hand shot out, and a finger jabbed in Nagora's direction, as Sarah took a step toward her. "You tricked me! You tricked my mother!"

Stay calm. "Daughter, don't insult me by calling Sagora your mother when you know I stand here before you. How is your Auntie Sagora?"

Sarah brought her hands up near her face. They shook as Sarah balled them into fists and bared her clenched teeth. Daughter, you don't dare strike me. Although, I won't blame you if you do. What I did was for your benefit and Sagora's. And for the king and his kingdom. You don't see that yet.

Sarah's eyes filled with tears as she struck at her own shoulders again and again until she bent and turned her back to Nagora. Sarah's shoulders heaved as she moaned and cried out, "Why? Why me? Why? I can't do this! I won't kill a child! No matter what you've shown me! No matter what I've witnessed!"

Nagora stepped closer to Sarah, reaching out to her shoulder with one hand as she placed the other on Sarah's back and rubbed it. "Sarah, even if Alizarine is no ordinary child, I will not ask you to kill Alizarine. I never will. I can't force you to do something against your will. I've shown you what the curse is. Take it for what it is. Don't take it as a command you have to carry out."

Nagora pulled Sarah up into her arms and held her close. Daughter of mine, these are desperate times, and I'll speak bile-soaked words to you in a bold attempt to sway you, though I feel the strength and conviction of your refusal so far.

"Someday, from somewhere, another queen and her daughter might come along and put an end to Alizarine's eternal youth. Or Alizarine could live on forever in that six-year-old body and continue to play with and nurture the evil inside her until she gains full mastery of it.

"Who can say what evil Alizarine will be capable of by then? We'll be dead and long gone. The curse will be forgotten."

Sarah pulled back and stared at Nagora.

"Or perhaps it won't. And people will wonder why, long ago, that first queen and her daughter did nothing about it when they had the opportunity. Will those people understand the choice the daughter made? Will they forgive the daughter?

Or curse her too? Whatever, we won't be there to hear of it, will we, Sarah?" Nagora wiped tears from Sarah's cheek.

"Tomorrow, King Raynhard, your own father, will crown you Princess Sarah! A big day for you."

Sarah pointed at Nagora. "Why do you go on with this ruse, knowing I won't help you?"

Nagora looked long at Sarah before answering. "*Piwi Mahihkan*, I do not know your path. My path is drawn. It is my duty to follow it. I will not fail in that duty. Denounce me if you will. When you tell the king who I am, you will see Raynhard will be most pleased to take me as his bride and queen for I am the true Edana, the one your father has always wanted as his queen.

"And Sarah, believe me. I will bear Raynhard another daughter, and I will train her to be a warrior like me. Think on what I've told you."

Sarah took two steps back, almost tripping as she did. Her mouth hung open and her jaw moved, but no words came out. Sarah swallowed and pointed as if showing some distant place. "King Godomor told me of your path—in almost the same words."

Nagora smiled. "*Piwi Mahihkan*, my spiritual father is wise. He knows his daughter well.

"Now, Sarah, tell me. How is my sister, Sagora?"

Sarah sat on the trunk and placed her hands in her lap. Taking a deep breath, she gazed at Nagora with resignation before speaking. "Sagora is filled with guilt. She confessed to Gabe and his father, King Godomor, what she and Raynhard had done and what they intended to have you do. That confession pleased the king. He looked relieved.

"Sagora says she feels differently now than when she was here. She spoke of the rings she and Raynhard had been wearing for the past years. She can't get over the growing control the rings had, especially since Alizarine's arrival. The things Alizarine made her and Raynhard say and do made her feel ashamed.

"However Sagora doesn't want to use that as an excuse for what she's done. Now she realizes she should have seen it happening, but couldn't. Sagora says she regrets having hurt Gabe like this. She wants Gabe to return with her to get Raean and Baerik and bring them back to the Land of Skulls, if Gabe and Godomor will forgive her."

Sarah held out her hands. "Mother, I'm so confused. I feel different. I realize what I've done since Alizarine's coming here. And I'm ashamed that I took part in those things. Alizarine had control over me too. I don't know how. I fear she still does."

You are right to fear Alizarine's control of you. "Sarah, you can protect yourself from Alizarine's control."

"How?" Sarah spoke the single word almost in desperation.

"Wear your amulet so Alizarine can see it. Believe me, Sarah, Alizarine fears it. It protects you."

Sarah reached into the neck of her shirt and pulled the amulet out to let it rest on her shirt.

"Good, Sarah. Stay away from Alizarine. She'll stay away from you as long as the amulet is visible."

Wedding Day
Wîkihtahiwewin Kîsikâw

† NOW: *the sixteenth day in
the Land of the Danu,
the wedding day*

Nagora had fallen asleep in Sagora's bed with Sarah in her arms. When daylight woke them, all Nagora remembered was they had both been holding the amulet as she told Sarah about her namesake, Paruline's mother.

Guests had arrived for the copious midday meal at the castle which would stretch on until the early evening, after which the guests would make their way to the Center for the Dragon Arts.

Outside, in the square before the castle gates and in the surrounding streets, citizens of Windhaven were already celebrating and preparing to follow the evening procession to the Center. There, invited guests and the stars in the sky would witness the king take Edana as his wife and queen.

That evening, Sarah helped Nagora change into Sagora's floor-length wedding dress of the finest and whitest linen in the land. Its pleated skirt was gathered in a point just below and between her breasts, where bands of golden, embroidered flowers crossed at the front and back. The buckle of a delicate jewel-studded belt rested on her left hip. The rest of the belt's tongue hung along her left leg to her knee.

Nagora stood before the mirror with the gold-handled hunting dagger in her hands. Her fingertips traced the embossed outline of the royal crest on the leather sheath. They traveled up to the gold dragon tail that looped out on each side of the blade to form its crossguard. The tips of her fingers stepped over the curled tail, body, and wings of the dragon that wrapped most of the handle's grip. From there, her fingertips climbed the dragon's winding neck to its head with its open mouth holding a crown.

She touched the crown. *Raynhard, you gave me this years ago as a reminder of my duty to you and as a symbol of the trust you have in me.* She stared at her reflection in the mirror. *Do I wear it on this jeweled belt, or do I conceal it?*

Wear it. It's the only blade you wear today. The voice of Tars spoke to her in her mind and it made her smile.

You're right, Tars. I feel vulnerable without my skystone blade. This dagger has one last destined use. However the fateful curse does not allow my hand to point it at the intended victim yet.

Sarah joined her at the mirror. "The procession leaves at sunset. The carriages are waiting for us in the yard."

"Daughter, let's not keep them waiting any longer."

Sarah placed a fine white woolen shawl over Nagora's shoulders. "You are beautiful, Nagora, my mother."

Nagora kissed Sarah's forehead and touched the amulet that hung between her breasts. "You, my daughter, Sarah, are more beautiful. Give me your shawl so I can wrap it around your shoulders." Sarah did and turned so Nagora could dress her shoulders with it.

The carriages crept out of the courtyard. Twenty mounted guards led the carriages, and another twenty followed. Crowds lined both sides of Castle Way, cheering their names and waving to them. Nagora did not disappoint them. She waved back.

The twins followed her lead, as did Sarah.

Alizarine sat by herself, her back pressed to the seat above which the driver and the footman sat. Except for the white woolen shawl she wore over her shoulders, Alizarine wore a long-sleeved, ankle-length black dress. Her red silk scarf wound around her neck and the palms of her hands. Its ends cascaded below her knees where she rested her hands. Her gaze seemed to be fixed on the gold rings she wore on her hands.

The procession came to a halt. The footman turned in his seat to speak to Raynhard. "My Lord, the street's blocked with well-wishers. Horsemen are doing their best to clear the way. Shouldn't be long."

Raynhard smiled and acknowledged the message with a two-fingered salute to the footman.

Nagora took Raynhard's hand in hers and leaned close to his ear. "It's custom for the king to grant his new queen a wish on the day he crowns her, is it not?"

"Aye, it is. What is your wish, my queen-to-be?" He patted her hand.

"A simple wish, my Lord." She reached into the small silk purse, attached to her jeweled belt she wore, and pulled out two rings. Lars had woven them mariner fashion from the fine tips of skinned willow branches on the day Godomor pronounced them husband and wife. Now she was ever grateful Lars had allowed her to use them in place of the spell-cast gold rings.

"I wish we be wed with these rings today and that, in three days time, Alizarine place our gold rings on our fingers. Will you grant this, my only wish, my Lord?"

Raynhard glanced at the rings and smiled. "Of course, I grant you your wish."

By the time their carriage pulled up to the steps of the Center for the Dragon Arts, twilight had waned and the torches around the square had been lit. As Nagora looked up at the stained glass window above the main door, she froze. Why didn't I notice it before? It was daytime and scaffolding draped in canvas stood before it inside. The canvassed scaffolds were still there on the night of the concert. She stared at Raynhard.

He smiled at her, winked, and looked up at the window. "Do you like it?"

Nagora couldn't speak. She gazed at the window and nodded. What can I say? It's the warrior Edana on the top tier of evil Queen Raganora's infamous Temple of Fire, bow in one hand, her other held high in the dragon-chord salute. A flaming arrow was stuck in the door frame, another in the door. Inside, behind the warrior, the young virgin Edana hangs in silhouette from the bar lowered onto the furnace against the background of the burning curtain. The crowd below the steps is returning Edana's salute. It's me in a moment in time, captured and frozen in the stained glass window.

The chant of "E-da-na! E-da-na! E-da-na!" rose from the crowd in the Square all around her. Nagora turned to look at them. If only you knew. Edana's battle is not yet won. The witch is still among you.

Raynhard took her hand and held it high. "Now you truly get to play the part of Edana for the people."

The crowd cheered and waved their hands in the air with the dragon-chord salute.

Nagora pressed the two middle fingers of her other hand into her palm, splayed her other fingers and thumb, and returned their salute. Raynhard, if only you knew the true Edana stands at your side.

Raynhard stepped from the carriage and helped the passengers down. Alizarine, followed by the twins and Sarah, climbed the Center stairs ahead of Raynhard and Nagora.

On the Center's top tier, Nagora held up her arms and motioned for quiet. As the crowd settled down, she held her hand ready with the dragon chord over her heart and gazed out over them. Her eyes settled on the two hooded figures standing next to the column that held the torch from which she had lit her fire arrows all those years ago. Both held a dragon chord over their heart. My men! Lars, Dannor, I love you! She threw her salute to them. They returned it, as did everyone in the crowd in the Square.

Sarah took Nagora's other hand and brought it to her lips. "I love you, Mum." Sarah had tears in her eyes. She pulled her shawl over her head and motioned Nagora do the same.

She did, waved to the crowd, and turned to take Raynhard's hand.

As they stepped inside past the open doors, the guests joined the applause from outside. Nagora smiled and bowed to acknowledge their greeting. To her right, her eyes found those of Paruline. One of her arms held her father's, the other held the arm of the one who must be Harri, her husband. Geirador's free hand pressed the dragon-chord salute to his heart.

Bardas stood next to Geirador with his two sons-in-law, Jani and Joni. Joni was leaning toward Jani, obviously giving him a running account of the procession. Nagora smiled at the three of them. She looked back to Paruline and gave her secret hand signal. It meant, "I love you, big sister." Paruline's smile broadened as she let go of her father's arm and signaled back, "I love you, little sister." *Pare, I'll never say this aloud, but I think your Harri is the handsomest of the Konen brothers.*

In the tiers on the other side, Nagora spotted Ardal, the captain of the Guard she had met more than fifteen years ago when his uniform was not so splendid. Still a captain. The two women at his side were wiping their tears. Ardal had his arm around his daughter, Edana, a grown woman now. She was biting her lower lip. *You've come with your mum to see your namesake wed the king. I wish I can make this the happy ending to the story of Dragon-Warrior Edana.* She swallowed. *If only I knew how this will turn out.*

Further up behind Ardal stood Coyle and Brin. Their uniforms today made them look like proper officers, not the huntsmen who had ambushed her years ago. For a moment, as Nagora looked to them, she brought her open hand next to her cheek and silently pretended to caw like a crow. Brin tapped Coyle's shoulder and pointed at her. Their smiles broadened as they clapped louder.

The guests had filled the Center, and all were still standing and clapping as Nagora, Raynhard, Sarah, the twins, and Alizarine walked up the stairs leading to the second and third tier seating steps below the stained glass window of the dragon.

As the royal group took their places, the musicians assembled. This time, Moreena's and Erin's harps were center stage.

The first song was *As Dragons Soar*. Before it ended, to the joy of all present except for Alizarine, Danuka glided out of the starry sky and perched on the Center's roof opening above the main door. Her wings spread across the opening to the two long sides of the roof where her talons took hold. Her long tail wrapped around her legs and belly. Mother, this building was surely designed so dragons could attend.

When the song ended, cheers rose from outside the Center as the guests inside stood and applauded. At the same time, Danuka moaned.

Raynhard bent to open the wooden box with intricately carved knotwork on it. It rested on the fourth tier between two standing guards with swords on their belts, holding spears. The box contained six crowns sitting next to each other in order of size, from the biggest to the smallest. He lifted out the biggest and set it on his head.

Raynhard turned to Nagora and took her hand in his. He looked around at the guests and finally to Alizarine. "The rings, please."

Alizarine removed one ring, gave it to Raean, and then she removed the other and gave it to Baerik. As the boys climbed the steps leading to Raynhard's tier, Nagora reached into her purse beneath her shawl and took out the willow-branch rings. Raean gave a gold ring to Raynhard. Baerik gave the other to Nagora.

In her right hand, Nagora held the two willow-branch rings. As the lads returned to join Alizarine, Nagora held out her left palm holding the gold ring. Raynhard placed the other next to it. Then Nagora dropped a willow-branch ring into his palm and slipped the two gold rings into the small purse that hung on her right hip.

Raynhard held up the willow ring. "Today, before all assembled here and before our star ancestors above, bear witness that with this ring, I, Raynhard, King of the Land of the Danu take you, Edana, to be my wife." Nagora held out her hand, and he placed the ring on her finger.

Nagora held up the willow ring. "Today, before all assembled here and before our star ancestors above, bear witness that with this ring, I, Edana, who you have chosen to be your wife, take you, Raynhard, King of the Land of the Danu to be my husband."

Had Alizarine noticed from where she stood? Possibly. Alizarine had balled her hands into two small fists and was rubbing them against each other.

Raynhard and Nagora embraced, and the guests stood and clapped. They both bowed to the guests to acknowledge their applause.

...

After the musicians played their second song, Raynhard stood and took the next crown from the box. As Sarah removed Nagora's shawl, Raynhard's eyebrows rose. He was staring at the dagger that hung from her left hip. His voice was a whisper. "Did Nagora give that to you?"

She smiled at Raynhard and held his gaze. "The one you gave it to stands before you. She is your wife. Will you make Nagora your queen?"

Raynhard's eyes grew wide as they searched her face. He's trying to make sense of the events. What will he do? His eyes went to her hands, and his astonishment held him until he gazed at the crown in his hands. Slowly, Raynhard raised it until his eyes were again looking into Nagora's.

Raynhard's eyes brightened as the smile on his face broadened. "Today, before all assembled here and before our star ancestors above, bear witness that I, Raynhard, King of the Land of the Danu, crown you, Edana, Queen of the Land of the Danu and in so doing, invest you with the power to rule this land at my side, until my death and thereafter, in my name." Raynhard placed the crown on Nagora's head. She bowed before him and then to the guests who cheered, "Long live Queen Edana! Long live King Raynhard!"

The musicians played the third song.

Now what is he thinking? He has two princes and two princesses to crown. Does Raynhard truly believe the twins are his true sons? Sarah his true daughter? Does he know that? Do I even try to understand who he believes Alizarine to be?

...

When the song ended, Raynhard stood and motioned Raean and Baerik to come up to his tier. He had Baerik stand to his right and Raean stand to his left. He turned to retrieve two crowns from the box. Raynhard held them above the twins' heads. "Today, before all assembled here and before our star ancestors above, bear witness that I, Raynhard, King of the Land of the Danu, crown you, Baerik and Raean, nephews of Queen Edana, Honorary Princes of the Land of the Danu, titles you may wear for as long as you stay in the land until your mother's return." He placed the crowns on their heads. So they are Gabe's sons! Nagora smiled.

Raean looked up at Raynhard with a puzzled face. As the guests clapped, Raynhard bent to Raean's ear and spoke briefly. When he finished, Raean nodded and then looked up at Nagora.

Nagora smiled and nodded at Raean as she bent to his ear. "Don't worry. We'll explain when we get back to the castle." I'm eager to hear what Raynhard will tell them.

The musicians started into the next song.

When it finished, Raynhard stood with his hand held out to Nagora. "And now the Queen of the Land of the Danu will carry out her first royal duties, the crowning of the princesses."

Tar piss! I wasn't expecting that. Are you regaining your sense? Since you've been truthful, so will I.

...

Nagora stood, reached for the biggest crown left in the box, and motioned for Sarah to climb to the tier.

Nagora looked around at all the guests. "Today, before all assembled here and before our star ancestors above, bear witness that I, Edana, Queen of the Land of the Danu, crown you, Sarah," she looked past Sarah at Raynhard, "daughter of King Raynhard and Queen Edana ... "

Raynhard's eyes widened and his lips inaudibly spoke. "You lied in the cave."

Nagora placed the crown on Sarah's head. " ... Princess of the Land of the Danu, with all the power and recognition you inherit with this title." *True, I lied to you, Raynhard, in exchange of your lie to me. Not today, my king. A good queen does not lie to her king.*

Sarah was smiling as she turned to hug her father, whose eyes flooded with tears as he embraced her. *Now you know, Raynhard. The truth is my gift to you this day.*

Guests were clapping, and many were bending their ears to those who had grasped the successive revelations and put them into historical context.

Princess Sarah stayed on the tier, and as the musicians played the fifth song, she sat between her parents, the King and Queen of the Land of the Danu. All in the Center were focused on Moreena and Erin as they played their harps in unison, especially Bardas, their proud father, and Jani and Joni, their husbands.

...

When the music stopped, Alizarine climbed the stairs between the tiers and stood before Nagora, who held the crown in her hands. *Hag, you are in the body of Alizarine. If it were not for the curse, instead of placing this crown on your head, I would plunge a dagger into your ear right now to reward you for all the evil you've done.* "Today, before all assembled here and before our star ancestors above, bear witness that I, Edana, Queen of the Land of the Danu, crown you, Alizarine ... for this day only ... Princess of the Land of the Danu, so I may later carry out my promise to you. This title comes to you in name only, for this day only, without power or privilege." Nagora placed the crown on Alizarine's head.

The quiet in the Center for the Dragon Arts was palpable.

Alizarine glared at Nagora. She pressed her red silk-covered fists together and twisted them back and forth as if wringing blood from them. *Little witch, glare as much as you like. You're losing your hold on my king. You've lost it on my daughter and my sister. Before the day is done, I fear you'll lose it on yourself.*

Erin played her flute, a slow meandering introduction to the second last song, which brought Nagora back to the middle of the high meadow where she had once picked a bouquet of daisies.

The memory of her thoughts that day was as fresh as the music now in her ears. *This is what freedom feels like—alone, at peace, in the sunshine in a field of flowers, doing something of my own choosing. I placed that bouquet on Uncle's blades. It was the day I failed in my duty to my king.*

Nagora looked up at the starry sky beyond Danuka's silhouette. Uncle, will I ever again taste a moment of freedom like I did on that day and not be guilty of neglect of duty?

The musicians moved to the sides of the stage to play the last piece, *No Longer In My Eyes, Always In My Heart.*

The princes led the procession along the stage, followed by the princesses and the newlywed king and his queen. As the royals walked across the stage in time to the music, the guests in attendance clapped politely. Once they reached center stage, Danuka moaned, spread her wings, and began to flap them slowly until she rose from her perch and disappeared into the night. Nagora let her tears roll down her cheeks as she stared at the stars and listened to the music.

Outside, beyond the open main doors, the crowd cheered and clapped. A chant of "Queen Edana! Queen Edana!" rose from the crowd as the royals reached the doorway.

Raynhard held Nagora's hand high.

Nagora acknowledged their cheers with a dragon-chord salute, which she threw to Lars and Dannor.

The carriage ride back to the castle was even longer than it had been to go to the Center for the Dragon Arts, for it took a new route. The well-wishers and merry-makers had control of the street intersections. Accepting and acknowledging their cheers and wishes helped make their progress faster.

In Castle Square before the gates, the press of happy revelers was so great that not even the mounted guards could make headway. Only when Nagora took Raynhard by the hand and stepped down from the carriage did the throng clear a path for them.

...

Before the newlyweds slipped into the castle, they offered a final drink to toast their wedding night to any of the guests who had been able to follow them into the courtyard. The partying in Castle Square was well under way, and most guests leaving the yard would most likely join the crowd in the square for music and dance, and for shows put on by jugglers, fire eaters, and acrobats.

Once inside the castle and the door closed behind them, the quiet that greeted them was a comfort to Nagora. All the castle servants lined the entrance hallway, waiting to greet the new queen, princesses, and princes. Most were probably eager to take part in the festive celebrating in Castle Square. To that end, Nagora shook each hand, offering a warm smile and a quick thank-you.

Nagora stood at the end of the hall with Alizarine at her side, waiting for Sarah and the boys to finish accepting the wishes and bows of the servants. Details of the marriage and crowning proclamations she and Raynhard had made most surely reached the servants. It was clear in the sincerity and warmth of how they had addressed her but ignored Alizarine who had followed right behind her, keeping her hands to herself and her eyes to the floor.

The bows Princess Sarah received were as deep as those the servants had given Nagora. The servants gave the young princes the polite yet curt bows reserved for guests, like they had given Nagora on her first visit. Raynhard closed the line by dropping two silver coins from his purse in the hand of each servant before dismissing them.

Raynhard led the royals into the throne room. Mixed smells of the roasted sheep, venison, and wild boar still wafted down from the ongoing afternoon feast in the reception room above. Candle stands and lanterns lit the area around the throne, the two staircases, and the landing at the top where decorative ribbons and banners still hung from the railing.

The wooden box of intricately carved knotwork, which had held the crowns at the Center for the Dragon Arts, now sat on a table next to the dais of Raynhard's throne. He opened it and placed his crown in it. "This is where I keep my crown until the next official ceremony. I suggest you do likewise for safe keeping. You'll be amazed at how much lighter your heads feel once you remove them."

I'll wait. Let them put theirs away like Raynhard. Alizarine placed her little crown in the box. *I hear the witch spell you chant. It's barely audible, but it's the same as the other night. And I see the subtle wave of your red, silk-covered palms over the crowns.*

Nagora stood before the box, lifted the crown from her head, and brought it down over the others. *If only I had some way of removing the spell Alizarine cast on these crowns.* She placed her crown next to Raynhard's.

Raynhard sat on his throne. "Come here, lads, my young princes." He lifted Baerik onto his right knee and Raean onto his left.

How much thought have you given to what you'll tell them?

Raynhard looked from one to the other. "I know you must be worried. Let me assure you, lads. Your mother is fine and she can't wait to come back to bring you back home to the Land of Skulls with your true father, Gabe."

"But why did she leave and Auntie Nagora take her place?" asked Raean.

"That's a long story. You'll learn all about it one day, but I will tell you this. Your mum helped me to get Auntie Nagora here so I could make her Queen Edana. You see, lads, Auntie Nagora is the true Edana. She is the one in all those stories you've heard. She's the one who did all those heroic things for me, for Danuka, and for the people of the Land of the Danu."

Raynhard pointed to Nagora. "Your mum just happens to be her twin and was able to act like the real Edana. That's why she got branded to look exactly like Edana. Your mum did that to help me bring your auntie back so I could convince her to be the true Queen Edana."

How much truth is woven in your words?

"Mum was making believe all this time?" asked Baerik.

"Aye, Baerik, she was. She did it to help me."

"Mum won't become a queen?" asked Raean.

Raynhard placed a hand on Raean's shoulder. "Well, Raean, if she marries Gabe, she'll become a princess. And when Gabe's father dies, Gabe will become King of the Land of Skulls. On that day, your mum will become Queen of the Land of Skulls. And you lads will become true Princes of the Land of Skulls, not honorary princes like you are now.

"But let me tell you this," Raynhard reached over and pointed to their crowns in the open box, "You wear these honorary crowns because of what your mum did and the role you played in helping her do it."

"How did we help?" asked Baerik.

Raynhard gave the twins a grand smile. "Quite simply by being you and believing she would marry me. If we would've told you why she was pretending, you might have made a slip up and revealed our plans. So your mother had to make it look real when she pretended she no longer loved Gabe, your father. Believe me, lads, it was difficult for her to do that."

More half-truths?

"What about Uncle Lars and Cousin Dannor? They and Auntie Nagora make a family. What happens to them?" asked Baerik.

How will you answer that one?

Raynhard held out his hand in Nagora's direction. "Queen Edana will answer that question."

I should have known. I'll answer with the truth.

Nagora stepped closer to the throne. "Baerik, Raean, unlike you young lads, Lars and Dannor are men. They're old enough to understand the whys of my actions and not slip up to give me away. They know and understand, as Edana, I am bound by duty to my king. Lars and Dannor accept I will be by the king's side until I fulfill that duty. Someday you'll learn what that duty involves and then you'll understand."

Nagora tapped their shoulders. "So don't worry about Lars and Dannor. They're still near and dear to my heart."

"Can I have my basket now? You promised." Alizarine was tugging on Nagora's sleeve.

Nagora turned to Alizarine. "Yes, Alizarine, I promised, and I will keep my promise. First however, I would like to change into something more comfortable. Perhaps you and Sarah would as well." Nagora glanced at Raynhard. "Perhaps you too, my king. Why don't we wear the robes we wore at Alizarine's last feeding?"

Raynhard's jaw moved, but no words came from his mouth.

Alizarine wore a smile. "That's a good idea. I'll wear my robe."

Sarah had taken a step back. She was obviously trying to understand. I haven't revealed all my secrets, my daughter. Play along, Sarah. Read my smile of encouragement.

"Umm. Aye, a robe would be comfortable," said Sarah, and she looked to Raynhard.

Raynhard was nodding as he lifted the twins from his knees. "Yes, I'll change too. How about you, lads?" He pointed to the landing above. "Then we can all meet at the table the servants set for us. There are pies and biscuits and apples and berries and milk and tea. We'll sleep so much better after eating."

"Good! I'm hungry!" said Baerik. "Come help us get changed. What are we supposed to call you now?"

Raynhard looked from Baerik to Raean to Nagora and Sarah, and back to Baerik. "Uncle. Call me Uncle. Come along, lads."

Sarah followed Nagora to Sagora's room. "How did you know about Alizarine's feeding?"

Nagora smiled at Sarah. "You'll not believe me if I tell you."

"Tell me." It was more an order than a request.

Nagora winked. "The Little People told me all about it."

"I don't believe you."

"Where did you get that long-handled silver spoon hanging from the red silk ribbon around your neck? Why weren't you wearing your amulet?"

Sarah brought her hands to her mouth, which hung open.

"Do you believe me now, Sarah?"

"Alizarine gave me that—spoon. I was to wear it and only it when I fed her." Sarah clenched a hand into a fist at her chest. "That's how she controls me!"

Nagora reached out and took hold of her daughter's hand. "Sarah, never remove your amulet at someone else's request unless it is me, your Grandda Yogari, or Danuka herself that asks you. The amulet is your protection. It saved my life. It could save yours too someday." Nagora pulled Sarah to her and held her tight. "You don't know how much you mean to me."

Sarah hugged Nagora and then pulled back. "I'm realizing you've come into my life at the right time. Thanks to Dannor, I got my amulet back. How much control would she have over me if I didn't get it back?"

"Sarah, go to your room and change. Bring the spoon back with you. When I come to join you and the others with Alizarine's basket, I don't want her to see you give it to me."

"I will."

As soon as Sarah left, Nagora removed the dagger and the small purse from her jeweled belt. She removed her wedding dress and set it on the trunk at the foot of the bed. Then she laid the jeweled belt on top of it.

Her fingers lingered on the belt and then on the dress. *Even with the crown on my head, I didn't feel like a queen.*

How is a queen supposed to feel? Powerful? Ready to rule? What do I know? I'm a warrior. I'm here to do battle.

Nagora combed her hair and made a single long braid which she wrapped tight and pinned to the back of her head. Then she picked up the small purse and went to her scrip in the clothes room. She shoved the small purse deep into the secret bottom of her scrip. Next she took out the remaining half of her spare bow string and set it on Sagora's robe.

Now my blades and my clothes. She stood on tiptoe to pull them from the top shelf where they lay spread along it. Alizarine, you didn't see them laying there when you were looking for your basket. Nagora set her blades on her boots, then added her socks, leather leggings, underpants, hooded linen shirt, sweater, and sheepskin vest in a neat pile on top of them. Her toe brushed against the leather of one of her boots. Will I even make it back here to put these on again? One moment at a time.

Next, she pulled the dragonskin armor of invisibility from her scrip. She found the hole and squeezed into it. Sarah, I just might be able to do something that will make you want to help me. It's worth a try. Then again, there's always the unknown.

Before putting on the hooded, white woolen robe, Nagora brought it and her piece of string to the bed. She tied the royal dagger's sheath to her forearm with her bowstring.

Nagora slipped the robe over her head and stood before the mirror. The bell sleeves fell over her hands. If she held the sleeve's edge against the pommel of the dagger with her ring finger, no one would notice the dagger. With both hands held in front of her, hidden by her sleeves, she could easily grasp the golden handle of the dagger.

Nagora pulled the robe's hood over her head and willed herself invisible. The robe moved in the mirror. She pulled the dagger from its sheath and held it before her face. It seemed to float in the air on its own. Its sight chilled her. She willed herself visible and returned the dagger to its sheath.

She stepped to the room's window and opened it to the night sky. Mother Danuka, *Ka Peyakot Mahihkan* is ready. I cannot speak for *Piwi Mahihkan*. She is one of the unknowns. If I call for help, you know what to do. Yes, Mother. I will be careful.

Now to the basket.

Nagora took the spiral staircase down the turret tower to the level of the dining hall. Crossing the dining hall into the hallway, she reached the throne room door. All seemed quiet on the landing above. She rushed past the staircase and the throne to the map room door. It was open.

Nagora stopped to listen. Voices. Raynhard. Raean. Baerik. Alizarine!

Nagora slipped the hood of her robe over her head and stepped into the room.

Alizarine was sitting in one of the big chairs, her chest resting on the table's edge. One arm was on the tabletop. Her pointer finger was tracing a line on a map. Her other arm was hidden by the tabletop.

Raean and Baerik were standing with Raynhard at the chest of map drawers. One of the drawers was open. "The map of your Grandfather Yogari goes in this drawer. I'll hold it open, and you lads slide it in carefully."

"Yes, I'm sure! The house I lived in was here!" Alizarine was pointing at a crossroads near a river on the map of Kemet. Alizarine released the trailing end of the red silk scarf she held in her palm. It spread over the map like a blot of blood.

Nagora's stomach turned.

"I don't believe you. That's far, far, far away. You wouldn't even remember when you left there. You're too young," said Raean.

"No, I'm not! Even if it's far away and it was a long time ago, I remember!"

May you not live to remember this night, Alizarine.

"So here you are," Nagora said.

Raynhard and the boys turned to look at her. "The lads helped me bring in the box of crowns." Now it rested on top of the chest of map drawers. He placed his hand on its cover. "We're putting the maps away. Soon as Alizarine finishes, that one will go in the same drawer."

Alizarine stared at Nagora. "Where's my basket?"

Nagora looked from Alizarine to Raynhard and the boys and back to the little witch. "I wanted to make sure everyone was at the table," she pointed back and up through the doorway, "before going to get it."

Alizarine brought her other hand up onto the table and placed its pointer finger next to the other. "Do you believe I lived here a long time ago?"

Nagora held Alizarine's questioning gaze. "I do, Alizarine. You told me so once before. You worked as a dyer, dying silk scarves the color of the one wrapped around your hands."

Alizarine's smile grew as she pushed away from the table and slid off the chair.

"Are you done with the map, Alizarine?" asked Raynhard.

"Yesssssss," Alizarine hissed as she kept her wide-open, staring eyes on Nagora, pulling the map from the table and holding it behind her to Baerik who had already made his move to retrieve it.

You don't scare me, Alizarine.

Baerik brought it over to the map chest. He and Raean slipped it into the drawer on top of the other map.

Raynhard closed the drawer. "Thanks for your help, lads. I don't know about you, but I would like to put a piece of pie under my tooth." He took their hands and led them around the table. "Come, Alizarine. You must be hungry too. We'll let Edana go get your basket."

Nagora backed out of the room and stood next to the throne.

"There you are!" Sarah waved from the stone railing of the landing that connected stone banisters of the twin staircases.

"I'll be up in a short while. Start without me," said Nagora as Raynhard walked by.

He looked up at Sarah. "We're coming to join you."

Alizarine trailed her red silk-covered palm along the banister as she climbed the steps and kept her eyes locked on Nagora.

When the group was out of sight and the sounds of chairs being pulled closer to the table had settled, Nagora returned to the map room.

She moved two chairs aside, lifted the hem of her robe, went to her knees, and crawled under the table. She reached beyond the two support beams over the corner of the main block and grabbed hold of the basket handle. For a moment, I thought Alizarine had found it.

Nagora placed the basket on a chair before taking her time to straighten her robe and check the dagger tied to her forearm. She took a breath. Now to retrieve the spoon.

Nagora set the basket on the third step from the top of the landing and walked over to the table.

Alizarine glared at her. "Where's my basket?"

"It won't be long. You'll have it."

Nagora placed a hand on the back of Baerik's chair. "That pie looks tasty, Baerik. Do you think there'll be a piece left for me?"

Baerik nodded with a full mouth, pointing to the pie and then to her.

Nagora went around the table to Sarah. "Is that goat cheese? I see you like it with honey on bread, just like I do."

Sarah slipped the spoon into Nagora's hand.

Nagora placed a hand on Raynhard's shoulder and pointed to the pot of tea on the stand with the lit candle beneath it. "Still enough tea in the pot?"

"Oh! Yes! Plenty! Won't you join us?"

Nagora looked at Alizarine. "In a few moments."

Nagora went to get the basket. She slipped the silver spoon under the sheepskin next to the egg before returning to the landing where she sat on the wooden bench that had been set against the stone railing.

Nagora placed the basket on the bench seat, next to her hip.

Alizarine had her eyes on the basket and was standing.

"As promised, Princess Alizarine, here is your basket with your precious egg."

Alizarine rushed over to the bench and stood before her basket.

Nagora clasped her hands before her within her sleeves. Her right hand took hold of the golden handle of the dagger.

Alizarine pulled back the sheepskin. Her left hand reached for the long handle of the silver spoon. Ever so slowly, she unraveled the red silk ribbon Sarah had wrapped around its handle.

Nagora tensed and moved her right foot further away from her left foot as she tightened her grip on the handle of the dagger, ready for Alizarine to strike out at her.

Alizarine let the red ribbon slip through her fingers back into the basket. She picked it up again and let it slide along her fingers. The third time she did this, she tilted her head and smiled at Nagora as she reached out to touch the egg with her right hand.

Nagora looked from Alizarine's smiling face to the pudgy little fingers that caressed the surface of the egg and back to Alizarine's face. Where is your fury? I'm ready for it. When will she unleash her storm on me? I see only peace, acceptance, and resignation.

Alizarine released the spoon's ribbon from her hand and lifted her fingers from the egg. She unwound the red silk scarf from her left hand and then from her right. She took her time and hummed to herself. Then she reached into her robe and pulled the ends of her scarf out of her sleeves. All the while she smiled at Nagora. Alizarine's big round eyes were so soft and tender, like on the day she had fallen in love with the egg.

Alizarine bent her head and lifted one red silk loop from around her neck, then another, and then the last loop. The scarf lay in a pile over the egg in her basket. Alizarine tied one end of her scarf to the handle of her basket.

Then she pulled the rest of the scarf through her fingers until she found the other end. She doubled the loop of ribbon tied to the spoon before tying the end of her scarf to the double loop.

What is Alizarine doing? Is it possible she hasn't noticed?

Next, with the spoon still in her hand, Alizarine reached up for the top bar of the bench's backrest. She lifted one knee onto the seat and then pulled her other knee up. Her left hand was busy pulling her red scarf out of the basket. When done, Alizarine stood up and turned to sit, her bum on the backrest. "Who wants to sing a song with me for my egg? It missed all the songs today."

Baerik was up and slapping his spoon on the table as he spewed pie crust pieces from his mouth with his scream, "I do! I do! I said it first! I want to sing! Let me drink some milk first." In no time, he downed the mug of goat milk and wiped the mustache from his upper lip.

He rushed over to the bench. "Move over, Auntie. Go sit with the audience. Clap loud for us."

Can this be? After hurting you like she did? Nagora looked from Baerik to Alizarine. Has he forgiven her so soon? Surely he hasn't forgotten.

Alizarine was smiling at him, the spoon in one hand clapped her other hand as she rocked from side to side. "Sit here on the other side of the basket, like me."

Or does Alizarine have control over you too?

Nagora stood up to make way for Baerik.

"Sit with the audience, Auntie!"

Nagora reluctantly let go of the dagger's handle and backed over to the table to sit next to Sarah.

Baerik sat his bum on the backrest and wiped his sleeve across his mouth. "What do we sing?"

"Remember the first song at the Center? It went like this. Tam-Tam-Ta-Tam-Tam ... " Alizarine waved her spoon as she sang the beats.

Baerik clapped. "The march! But there's no words! I know! We could make marching sounds on the bench with our feet as we sing the Tams!"

"Okay! Wait!" Alizarine slipped the double loop of the spoon's ribbon around her neck before bending to lift her egg from the basket. She cradled it to her chest. "Okay! Ready!"

They sang and they stomped their feet in time.

Baerik was up on the bench marching on the spot and clapping in time. When they stopped, he yelled, "Again!"

I can't believe what I'm seeing. What am I missing?

Raynhard and Sarah clapped. Nagora joined in.

Alizarine was laughing and smiling.

When Raean stopped clapping, Alizarine reached over to Baerik and placed the egg in his hands. "I know you won't drop it. We'll do the march again. The egg likes it too. Wait."

Alizarine removed the spoon's ribbon from around her neck and slipped it over Baerik's head. "Now we're ready. Tam-Tam-Ta-Tam-Tam ... "

Baerik was singing Tams as loud as he could as he lifted his knees in time to stomp out the beats of the march.

Just as Baerik's foot farthest from Alizarine was in the air, she reached over, grabbed, pulled, and then pushed him back over the railing of the landing. Alizarine jumped down from the bench and ran for the staircase. The scarf unraveled and pulled on the basket handle, pinning it to the bench backrest against the stone railing.

Baerik screamed.

Nagora was on her feet, pulling at Sarah's sleeve. "Quick! Cut the scarf!"

At the same moment Baerik's strangled scream died.

Alizarine had started down the staircase.

Nagora slid to a stop at the landing's edge. Her fingers caught air as Alizarine bounded down the steps just ahead of her. Nagora lifted the hem of her robe and skipped down the steps on Alizarine's heels. She lunged at Alizarine just as the little witch let go of the banister and jumped to the throne room floor.

Nagora froze when her own feet touched the floor. Baerik hung from the spoon's red ribbon, above the throne and out of her reach, even if she climbed onto the throne. His neck had snapped. The gilded egg had broken on the folded-back dragon wings that formed the throne's backrest.

Tar piss! Alizarine is headed to the map room. Nagora sprinted after her and slammed her shoulder against the heavy door just as Alizarine closed it, but it was enough to keep Alizarine from locking it. "Witch! You won't keep me out!"

Nagora pushed with all her might. "Sarah! Come quick! Sarah!"

...

The door gave way and Nagora burst into the room. Alizarine ran to the other side of the big round table. "Alizarine, your time has come. You've gone too far."

Alizarine pointed at Nagora. "You stole my egg. You tricked me and lied to me. Give me my egg!"

"All is fair in a war with a witch."

Sarah ran into the room past Nagora. She glanced back at Nagora, then pointed a fist at Alizarine. Sarah's face was red with rage. "You murdered my nephew! I should have listened to my mother. He would still be alive." Sarah looked back at Nagora. "Bar the door! She's not getting out of here alive!"

Nagora pushed the door shut, turned the big key, and pulled it from the lock. "Good luck finding it, Alizarine." Nagora hurled the key with all her might so it broke through a pane of glass in the skylight.

Only two candle lanterns lit the room, one on the wall near the chest of maps and the other on the wall next to the door. Alizarine can't reach them unless she climbs on a chair. Even then she would have to stretch.

Alizarine looked from Nagora to Sarah.

Nagora moved to the table and began to pull the chairs away from it as she made her way around it. Sarah took her lead and did the same thing on the other side.

Alizarine moved a single chair so she could climb up onto it and then onto the table. She looked wildly around the room and then from Sarah to Nagora. Finally, she looked up at the skylight.

Nagora did too. You'll not fly out of here. The stars disappeared from the sky and a sound almost like distant rolling thunder stumbled across the roof above. Nagora smiled, and so did Sarah as they climbed onto the table.

Alizarine's eyes blinked big and round as her face took on the pleading look of a child caught doing wrong. Her little hands clutched at her robe. "Please! No!"

Sarah crouched as Nagora stood. When Alizarine looked up at Nagora, Sarah dove. "For Baerik!" She caught Alizarine by the thighs and pulled her down.

Nagora pulled the dagger from its sheath, knelt on one of Alizarine's arms and pinned her neck to the table with her other free hand. Sarah straddled one of Alizarine's legs and pinned her other arm down.

Nagora placed the dagger over Alizarine's heart. Sarah's hand joined hers on the handle, and together they pushed down.

Alizarine's back arched and her mouth opened wide in a silent scream. Her body split open the black robe as she grew into Aliza, the raven-haired beauty Raynhard had fallen for years ago. Blood seeped from the corner of Aliza's mouth. She licked at it, breathed deep once, and coughed up more blood. "I failed in my duty." Aliza's words came out almost as a gargle as she bared her teeth in a grimace that squeezed her eyes shut.

Aliza's back sunk onto the table as her arms and legs trembled and her shoulders shook. Her breasts withered and sagged to the sides of her chest. Her face wrinkled and her hair turned white and thinned. For a moment Aliza's sunken eyes opened as she smiled a toothless grin and uttered a last word, "Eternal." Her eyes closed and her head fell to the side.

All around the dagger, Alizarine's body decayed and fell to dusty ash on the table.

The skylight crashed open. Shards of glass burst down around them.

As promised, Mother. I am all yours for the hatching. Nagora willed her armor invisible as she pulled away from the dagger and Sarah's hand. Nagora slipped out of her robe, stood on tiptoe, and reached up. As soon as Danuka's head was within reach, Nagora grabbed onto the red scaly lip of Danuka's mouth.

Danuka lifted her up, out of the room, and set Nagora on her wing so she could climb into the saddle. I am ready, Mother. Tears stuck to her face beneath her armor. Alizarine killed Baerik. I thought she would attack me, and Sarah would come to my rescue. Sagora will never forgive me.

You are right, Mother. Always the unknown. Take me to Sagora's window.

Yes, Mother, to get my blades. Then to my men for a quick word with them. Yes, Mother, I have kept my promise. We will be just in time to care for your eggs. They will be your first hatchlings. Yes, I promise to protect them and you.

Nagora untied the royal hunting dagger's sheath from her forearm and set it on the shelf below the mirror. Then she found the small hole in her armor, stretched it back over her head onto her shoulders, and pulled her arms free, then her legs. She dressed, checked to make sure the gold rings were still in the small purse, and stuffed the armor into her scrip before buckling the flap of her scrip. She lifted its strap over her head onto a shoulder.

As Nagora made her way to the window, she slipped her arms through the straps of the sheath of her skystone blade and adjusted the holsters of her throwing knives on the straps.

As soon as Nagora climbed onto Danuka's wing and took hold of the saddle loop, the dragon released her wing talons from where they had hooked onto the wall. Danuka pushed away with her powerful hind legs, gaining space to turn away and glide out over the forest below.

Nagora swung into the saddle as Danuka leveled out. Now she flapped her wings to carry them back up and over Windhaven's wall to the Center for the Dragon Arts. The streets and ways were still filled with revelers. Danuka slowed to a glide that took her around the Center for the Dragon Arts. Lars and Dannor should be waiting beneath the stained glass window of the dragon, but they weren't.

Too many people, Mother. To the bridge. Danuka pumped her wings and took them over Windhaven's main gate, along the main road to the nearby bridge. Do you see them, Mother?

Danuka slowed her flight and set down in the field to the right of the bridge, near the trees. Now I see them. A candle lantern came to life. Dannor held it above his horse's head so Nagora could see him and his father.

They dismounted and ran to Nagora as soon as she stepped from Danuka's wing. When Lars took her in his arms, she broke into tears that shook her. She managed to explain what had happened.

Dannor rubbed her back. "It's not your fault, Mum. Look at what you've accomplished. You killed Alizarine, just like the curse demanded, even if you didn't make it happen as you had planned. In war there's always a cost. Isn't that what Uncle Dangor taught you? Those who pay the cost we call heroes. I know in your heart, you'll hold little Baerik as a hero. So will Da and me. And we'll hold you and Sarah in that same league."

Lars held her shoulders. "Sagora won't be in a position to hold Baerik's death against you. Gabe will understand. If he holds it against someone, it'll be Sagora. And you're Edana, Queen of the Land of the Danu, now even more of a hero."

Nagora wiped the tears from her cheeks. "No. Edana was Queen of the Land of the Danu. Not me. I'm Nagora. If you'll have me as your queen, Lars, I'll be happy. Again I owe you so much." She reached up, pulled his face to hers, and kissed him.

When Nagora released him, Lars still held onto her shoulders. "What of Edana's King Raynhard?"

"Hopefully, he is purged of Alizarine's hold on him. He has to find his old self and rule as the king he can be. But that remains to be seen, for his record doesn't show him as fit to rule. He must prove otherwise.

"His first job will be a funeral for Queen Edana and Prince Baerik. Both died in the fight to kill the witch who almost brought him and his kingdom to a sorry end. Will he even acknowledge how close his country came to being invaded? Dare he share that truth and how it came about?

"As for Edana, she will live on as she was born—a legend." Nagora gave the dragon-chord salute.

"Mum, what'll Sarah do?"

Nagora placed a hand on Dannor's shoulder and took a breath. "Well, Sarah is Princess of the Land of the Danu and a

Dragon Talker like you, like me. She knows where to find us. There'll be plenty of work for three of us. Perhaps Raynhard will convince her to bring back a few dragons to the Land of the Danu. This is the land of the dragons. It will only be fitting that Princess Sarah, the Dragon Talker, have dragons in her land. Who knows, Sarah might be queen of this land someday."

"Mum, are you not going to come back here?

Nagora took Dannor's hand in hers. "I'm going home, Dannor, but I have a few dear friends here that I'll come back to visit now and then. It'll easy with a dragon."

"Mum, I'm worried about Raean. Is there anything we can do?"

"So am I, Dannor. Sagora loves him. I know Gabe will. They'll be broken-hearted with the news of Baerik's death. Raean might help ease that pain and heal the wounds caused by Alizarine. When I bring the sad news to Gabe and Sagora, they'll most likely want to come to bury him, or they'll bring his body back to the Land of Skulls for burial. Whatever they decide, perhaps you and your da could offer to escort them back. I'm sure Raean would like to ride Storm for that journey."

Danuka, moaned.

Yes, Mother, please give me a moment more.

"Here, Mum. Wear this. It's a long, cold ride home. I put the pouches that tie to Danuka's saddle and the letter pouch on the table in our lodge." Dannor placed her sheepskin hat in her hand.

The moss green embroidered dragon with wings spread seemed to smile at her. Nagora put it on and tied the ear flaps under her chin. "Thanks. Lars, tell Geirador and Pare to in-form Raynhard that they have orders from Danuka to resettle in Cairnmase so that they might expand their business, because young dragons will need saddles and bits and bridles from the best saddle maker in the land. And dragon riders will need excellent weapons. Dannor, tell Moreena and Erin I'll come to visit as soon as I can."

Nagora threw her arms around her men. "Thank you for all your help. I couldn't have done it without you. I love you. Come home soon."

Just then, there was a distant grumble. As the three looked to the sky, the ground beneath them trembled and shook. In the far distance on the horizon, an orange glow pointed to the sky like a beacon.

Danuka stood on her hind legs, flapped her wings, and moaned the words *"Wacikâpahkitek saskitêw."*

"Mum, did I understand right? The volcano is on fire?"

"Aye, Dannor, the Isle of Smoke is burning."

Mother you knew, and so did Alizarine. It was part of her evil plan to kill you and destroy your eggs. She failed. Yes, Mother, we will go now.

The ground tremors ceased as Nagora climbed into the saddle and waved to her men. Danuka flapped her wings and pushed off into the starry night sky. Nagora looked over her shoulder to the glowing red spot on the receding horizon as she bent to pat Danuka's neck.

Kîyânaw kiwe, Okâwîmâw. We are going home, Mother.

In the
LAND of SKULLS

— † —

To the Maze
Âpihtâwâyihk

† NOW: *the night of the wedding.*
The Dragon Talker and her dragon
return to the maze in the Land of the Skulls.

Nagora clung to the saddle loop with all her strength. She leaned forward, pressing her cheek against the back of Danuka's neck, and closed her eyes tight, allowing the dragon the freedom to fly at the speed she desired.

Only when the dragon slowed and glided in an ever-decreasing spiral did Nagora open her eyes.

On the dark patch of land in the distance below, two miniscule circles of light, one within the other, shone like beacons. They grew as the dragon spiraled downward, her wings holding the gliding descent to a constant speed.

It's the maze, Mother! The *Mêmêkwêsiw* are waiting for us. For the first time, Nagora was seeing the maze from above. The immensity of it made her realize why it had taken her so long to rebuild it, even with the help of the Little People.

The night-shadowed paths gave the maze a look of foreboding. Though, the beacon light in its center offered hope. I can't wait to see the maze from the sky in daytime.

Danuka flapped her wings to slow the descent as she alighted to perch on a lintel of the outer hatching circle. The lights from the outer circle dimmed and moved amongst all the feeder eggs that were spread around the space outside the inner circle.

Those moving lights joined the ones around the inner circle. Together, they brightened to illuminate the hatchling eggs spread out on stone boats around the well. The gold veins of the eggs appeared brighter in the light provided by the Little People.

Nagora slipped from the saddle onto Danuka's extended wing. She walked past the large wing talon toward the tip of the wing.

Here, Mother? Yes, I will hold still.

Nagora stood with legs spread shoulder-width apart and knees flexed as her dragon lowered her to the floor next to some feeder eggs.

Two parallel strips of light appeared on the stone floor ahead of Nagora, showing her the way to the inner circle. She followed the lit path.

Just as she arrived next to the pillar where it stopped, she heard the whoosh of a single pump of Danuka's wings. The dragon glided to perch on the lintel of the inner hatching circle above the spot where Nagora stood.

Danuka instructed Nagora in her task. I am to take a feeder egg and walk around the hatchling eggs to find the warmest one. When I do, I must hold the feeder egg above it. The hatchling egg will grow hotter and hotter until the gold veins melt and the young dragon breaks through.

It will be hungry. I will lead the young one to the outer circle and give it its first egg.

Then I take another egg and go find the next warmest egg. I understand, Mother. Doing this shows the young dragons I am their Dragon Talker.

Nagora did as Danuka had instructed. She walked around the hatchling eggs twice, holding her free hand above each egg to feel its heat. Mother, it is difficult to feel the difference. I am not sure which is the warmest.

You say I am to trust what my hand feels? I will.

Trust. Here I go again. Trust my hand. I can do this. Nagora walked around a third time, focusing on the heat coming from each egg and noting the color of the stone boat it rested on.

This one—the green and black boat.

She held the feeder egg above the hatchling egg, almost touching it. Immediately, she felt the heat increase. She looked past the feeder egg to the one below it as it grew hotter and hotter. Its gold veins glistened as miniscule bubbles rose to the vein surfaces.

The heat from the egg forced Nagora to move away.

In the blink of an eye, the gold in the veins turned to liquid, flowing into the depression of the stone boat the egg sat on.

Without warning, the shell split into pieces as the hatchling burst out of the egg in a cloud of steam. Its body was wet and translucent, like Danuka in her new skin just after shedding her old skin.

The young one flapped its wings and snapped its jaws at the feeder egg Nagora held. Holding the egg low, she led the miniature dragon to the outer circle of feeder eggs.

She set the egg down, and the young dragon attacked it. Nagora laughed as the creature played with the egg, rolling it among the others as it tried to find the soft spot to gain access to its first food.

No time to waste, Mother. Okay.

Nagora picked up a feeder egg and returned to the inner circle. Already the green and black stone boat was gone, along with all the pieces of the first hatched egg. The Little People are busy too.

By sunrise, the last of the eggs had hatched.

Nagora was tired and hungry, but utterly fascinated by the young dragons, feeding and playing with each other. What she found even funnier was how the first ones to hatch, now with bellies round and distended, were curling up to fall asleep next to a feeder egg. Their skin had already changed to a moss green color.

Danuka advised Nagora that it was time for her to go to her lodge to rest.

You want me to take a feeder egg with me. For me to eat—to give me strength. While I rest, you will watch over the young.

The dragon gave Nagora final instructions she hadn't expected.

Before I return, I am to write two letters, one you will deliver to Prince Gabe and Sagora in Skull Bay and the other to Sarah and Dannor.

The letter to Gabe and Sagora is to invite them to my lodge. I am to bring it here when I return. You will deliver it to them while I guard the young.

When they come, they will bring me to Skull Bay to stand before King Godomor and his people to brand Sagora. That information took Nagora's breath away.

My turn to brand my twin! Sagora already had herself branded with the Tiwaz, like me! But this time, to the signers, those who fear twins, she is the returning twin. Again we are identical in appearance, but will not be once I brand her.

An icy chill crawled up Nagora's back, like it had eighteen years ago when she stood before the stained glass window of the dragon outside the Temple of Fire in Windhaven in the Land of the Danu—the first time her dragon had called her to duty.

Mother, have I no choice in this?

It is your will, Mother.

When Prince Gabe returns to the Land of the Danu with Sagora to claim Baerik's body, Sagora's new brand will be proof to Raynhard and his people that the warriors of the Land of Skulls no longer threaten to invade.

And I will give Prince Gabe the letter to Sarah and Dannor. He will deliver it to them in Windhaven.

Mother, what message do you want me to write in that letter?

That you and I call Sarah and Dannor to duty here at the maze at once.

Yes, I will eat and then rest before writing the letters. Yes, Mother, I trust what you tell me.

As Nagora walked the path out of the maze, she felt as if all the stones she'd set while rebuilding the maze walls were speaking to her.

Legend tells us dragons fly so high they can see the future.
Reason tells us that to know the future is a curse.
Our hearts tell us the seeds of hope are sown in the reality of
the present.

†

†

Dear Reader,

Thank you for reading *BLAMED*. For the benefit of future readers and to help me as an author, you would truly warm my heart by leaving an honest review at:
https://hnhenry.com/home/#testimonials
OR wherever you purchased this copy of *BLAMED*.

Sincerely,

H. N. Henry

P.S.: *BLINDED*, Book VI of The Dragon's Game series, is in the works. To be the first to know of its upcoming release, sign up to my newsletter at: https://hnhenry.com/home/

ABOUT THE AUTHOR

Other than writing, his passions include kayaking, baking bread, and trying to learn how to play guitar. He shares the profits of his work with a local community cause, *Point de Rue.* They help homeless people on the streets find meaning and passion in their lives. Learn more about it here: https://www.pointderue.com.

To learn more about the author and the other books in the series, please visit: https:// hnhenry.com/home/

†

Titles in **THE DRAGON'S GAME** series:

BANISHED BOOK I

BRANDED BOOK II

BETRAYED BOOK III

BRED BOOK IV

BLAMED BOOK V

ACKNOWLEDGMENTS

The Dragon's Game books wouldn't have come about without the generous and invaluable support of these people throughout the creative process.

From the beginning, Staecy-Lee, my editor, gave my manuscripts tough, honest critiques. Her hard questions made me see my stories with fresh eyes for the benefit of my readers.

Randi, my proofreader, closely read the final formatted-for-publication texts, finding inconsistencies in details, descriptions needing clarification, and grammatical errors my own eyes could no longer see.

Staecy and Randi, avid readers of this genre, also offered truly valuable and insightful comments that have made me a better writer. Learning from them has been a pleasure and a privilege.

My passionate beta readers of the first original brick, in first name a-b-c order, Ann, Daniela, Danielle, Maria, Marie-Josée, Randi, and Staecy-Lee generously delivered invaluable feedback and constructive criticism that helped spawn *BANISHED*, Book I, and from the volume they read, give birth to Books II and III of the series. I am forever in their debt for their support and encouragement.

I am grateful to the stained glass window artist, Guido Nincheri (1885-1973), who over ten years (1924-1934) created the beautiful windows in the Cathedral of the Assumption in Trois-Rivières, QC, Canada. From the photographs of those windows that I took on February 27, 2006, I was able to digitally manipulate images from two of the panels to create the unique dragons that appear on the covers of the first edition of my books, a humble homage to Nincheri's masterful work.

Though not referenced as Cree in the context of my stories, I have used Cree, in Roman orthography form, for the chapter titles and chapter numbers throughout the books in the series. More importantly, it is the " ... strange yet familiar language ... " Nagora, the main character, a.k.a. *Ka Peyakot Mahihkan*—Cree for *Lone Wolf*, hears in her mind and eventually uses to communicate with her dragon and other characters. At those times, when used, Cree is referred to as the *Language of the People*, in reference to the *First People* of *The Land* where my story is set.

The *Language of the People*, or "dragonspeak" as some readers of The Dragon's Game books call it, in a way, reflects the status of the Cree language in our land today. Though Cree is the most widely spoken Native language still spoken in Canada, it has yet to be recognized as one of this country's official languages. Similarly, in the fictional setting of *The Dragon's Game* books, the *Language of the People* is now only spoken by a few in a divided and renamed land where two different languages (those of the invading Outlanders) have become dominant in use.

To the Online Cree Dictionary Team: *Kinanâskomitin*. Thank you, I am grateful to you for making this resource available to all. It has been indispensible in helping me lend realism to that second language in my stories. I hope my readers will have as much pleasure as I do in discovering the living Cree language.

In the end, what appears on the pages of my books is mine, and I take full responsibility for any errors that show up in the final versions.

www.ingramcontent.com/pod-product-compliance
Lightning Source LLC
Chambersburg PA
CBHW030645120726
47905CB00001B/70